Flip-Flopped

Flip-Flopped

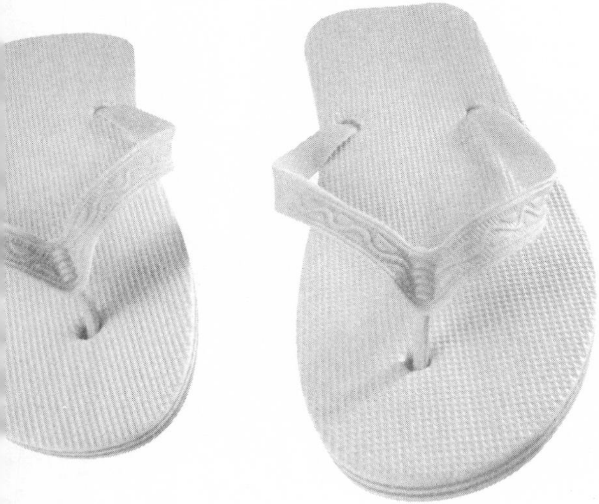

JILL SMOLINSKI

THOMAS DUNNE BOOKS
ST. MARTIN'S PRESS NEW YORK

THOMAS DUNNE BOOKS.
An imprint of St. Martin's Press.

www.stmartins.com

ISBN 0-312-28514-0

First Edition: July 2002

10 9 8 7 6 5 4 3 2 1

FOR MY PARENTS

ACKNOWLEDGMENTS

A big *mahalo* to my wonderful agent, Kirsten Manges, for finding a home for Keeley, and to my editor, Sally Kim, who then whipped her into shape as no one else could; to my trusty readers, Candy Deemer and Sandra O'Briant, and writing coach par excellence, Monique Raphel High; to Mary Jo Reutter, Heather Wakimoto, John Elder, Scott Fabbro, Monica Harley, Lisa Kemp Jones, and the Smolinski family for advice and support; to the Book Club Chicks, Hermosa Beach Kindergarten Moms, and my pals at SCAG for never failing to ask, "How's the book coming?" (thus shaming me into finishing); and to Danny, for patience above and beyond the call of a nine-year-old—and for always making me laugh.

A special thanks, too, to George Ku and Daisy Brehm, whom I hold forever close in affectionate memory. *Aloha* and *aloha*.

Flip-Flopped

1

AFTER FIVE YEARS together, I was still in love with my husband. That would probably have been a good thing, except I was serving him divorce papers. It was July Fourth.

In case anyone is missing the symbolism, that's Independence Day—as in, Okay honey, I set you free. You can go off and do all those things that you want to do. Those things like watching TV, surfing, and—oh, I don't know—scratching your balls, which is what you were doing when we were together, only with two hazel eyes (mine) boring into you, wrecking all your fun.

Maybe if my eyes were blue it would have made a difference. Maybe then you would have felt like it wasn't me, but the sky watching you with such disappointment. Just the blue sky sighing and shifting back and forth on her legs, complaining about how she expected you home two hours ago.

But no, hazel eyes have all that green and brown in them—earthy colors that say, "Get back here, you cheating bastard, and while you're at it, pick up some milk because we're out."

On that particular Fourth of July, the first holiday since Kam and I split—or more accurately, Kam split—he and I had agreed to share our son Dante for the day. I'd take him to the parade. Kam would get him for fireworks. Great effort would be put forth so I wouldn't have to stop by his house and see Her.

The Dante exchange, we'd decided, would take place at precisely 2 P.M. at the northeast corner of Peach and Flower, in front of the Kona Kofferie (now actually a Starbucks, but as if by a communal but unspoken agreement, every person on The Big Island refused to acknowledge the change).

It was there that Kam would wait, alone, watching floats and bands go by. I would bring the boy.

What Kam—named for Kamohoali'i, the shark god—did not know was that I had a plan.

Central to my plan was Regatta—leggy, slim, with a penchant for red lip color. These facts are irrelevant to my point, except that it made her look really good in Ray-Bans. Regatta was my closest friend and hair stylist; there were no secrets between us.

Here was how it was to come down: I would attend the parade with my son. I would, however, stand across the street from the agreed-upon meeting spot, allowing me to see, but not be seen. At a quarter to two, Regatta would happen to "bump into" Kam. She would chat, perhaps flirt a bit. They knew each other, after all. Then she would say, "I have something for you from Keeley," and, *bang*, hit him with an envelope containing papers from me suing him for divorce.

I'd get to see the shock on his face—especially if I brought binoculars. Dante, with the innocence and self-absorption of a four-year-old, would be clueless to the events transpiring around him. And in the end, I'd have a great story to hold up like a trophy to all those people who'd been saying, Gee, you must be so *humiliated*.

The plan was nothing short of brilliant, except for one fatal shortcoming: me, Keeley Baker-Kekuhi, big wussy.

Oh, I'd arrived at the appointed spot. I'd even managed to conceal myself and Dante quite effectively behind a billboard-size woman standing in a red, white, and blue muumuu. The parade was almost over by the time I saw Kam arrive, which was not coincidentally the moment my original plan crumbled to dust on the ground.

At the risk of sounding shallow, I do have to mention that Kam is exceedingly good looking. After weeks of avoiding him—no small task when you have a child together—I'd managed to forget that little fact. He stood—what, forty feet from me?—hands in his shorts pockets, shirtless, a flat, brown belly you could bounce a quarter off, his hair concealed in a bandana.

But, as usual, his smile was my undoing. His mother used to say he had an angel's face and the devil's grin. I'd first met Kam while collecting lava samples. It's what I do—study volcanoes. He was leading a tour group and seemed to come from out of nowhere while I was working. I remember how those lips of his turned up mischievously as he said, "What's a nice girl like you doing in a place like this?" and my knees nearly buckled beneath me.

Now I was watching him smile at Regatta, who had just walked up, as planned.

I saw them chat, as planned.

And flashing through my mind was, This is a mistake, *he still wants me, he's just confused, he's said so and I could rip off those flip-flops and suck on his toes and keep working my way on up*—and other assorted, nasty thoughts that were not part of the plan and clearly had no business being on the mind of someone about to initiate legal proceedings toward divorce.

Regatta needed to be stopped. Dignity, I'm relieved to say, prevented me from bolting across the street. That and a giant fruit basket float cruising down Flower Avenue.

I peered out from behind the lady in the muumuu long enough to holler, "Regatta!" but you can't imagine how distracting the noise of dancing bananas can be. She couldn't even hear her cell phone when I dialed it.

The situation was getting desperate. The fruit was turning the corner, as fruit sometimes does. A marching band moved in. I tried to flag Regatta down.

No luck; she'd moved on to flirting, the optional part of the plan. Apparently, she couldn't twirl hair and have a clue what was going on around her at the same time. I resorted to beeping her. Success! She glanced up at me quizzically before reaching into her purse for her phone.

Mine rang. I answered it by saying, "I'm having second thoughts." At that precise moment, the lady blocking me sat down, and the marching band parted like the Red Sea. Dante and I found ourselves staring straight at Regatta and Kam. It was so intimate we might as well have been at a cocktail party eating tiny weenies.

"What do you want me to do?" she asked. "*K-a-m* is right *h-e-r-e*."

"Reggie, he can see me. And he can spell."

"How about pig latin?"

"Never mind that. Look, just abort."

"Keeley," she said. "This is your moment. For once in your life, seize the opportunity."

I could hear Kam in the background saying, "Is that Keeley on the phone? Let me talk to her."

She did one of those exaggerated shrugs at me as she handed the phone over.

"Keel, you're looking good," he said. "I like the red hair."

"*Mahalo,*" I said, but my tone was begrudging, or at least that's what I was aiming for.

"Is that a halter top? You don't have a bra on, do you."

"Oh, for crying out loud—it's hot, I'm wearing summer garb."

"I can see your nipples."

"You can *not*. Give the phone back to Regatta." I could see his head bobbing, squinting to get a better picture of me and my breasts.

"Those are definitely nipples. A see-through halter. How come you never wore shit like that when we were together?"

"You are not seeing my . . ." But then I stopped. "It's paisley, okay? The top is paisley, and there happen to be two squiggles right where my . . . my ipples-nay are."

"I get it. Like nipple covers," he said. "That's even better." He waved, I suppose a friendly hi to my nipples. Dante waved back.

"Give the phone to Regatta."

He handed the phone back to her but wouldn't stop grinning at me. Regatta had to snap her fingers in front of his eyes to get his attention. A Brownie troop passed by, grass skirts over their uniforms, carting a boom box blasting "Rollin' with My Homies."

"Keeley," Regatta said. "Shall we?"

"Yes—wait, no—oh, I don't know."

"He is so very charming," she said dryly, her arm across her chest.

"Do you think this is too mean?"

"It's *mean*ingful, babe. If it's what you want, it's what he deserves."

I could hear his voice through the phone. "What do I deserve?"

HERE'S A STORY. Once there was a little Midwestern girl who married a Hawaiian guy because she thought they were destined to be together. But then he started fucking somebody else.

To think when I first arrived on the islands fifteen years ago, I didn't know anything about how to tell a tale. Now I was sounding like one of the elders. There are no great legends where I come from in Detroit, even though the area was ripe for them—like how the great gods stamped their feet to make the land so very flat. How they danced from town to town, building the suburbs and luring the white people out to them by playing Pat Boone songs on their flutes. How they left us then because—face it— it's cold there and not a whole lot is going on.

My sister Sandra's theory was that it wasn't the place of our birth that robbed us of our stories. It was the times. Our whole generation was so stoned on Cocoa Puffs and Saturday morning cartoons, that we didn't have the energy left to tune in to the history of our lives. Plus, I'd have to add, other peoples' lives were so much more riveting. As long as they weren't real or anything.

Sandra and I talked nearly every day while my marriage was busy falling apart. Well, actually, not *talked*. E-mailed. Come to think of it, I don't think I'd actually seen Sandra since she left for Ecuador back in '82.

ME: This being separated sucks. I'm so horny. And broke.

This note, typed on a Friday night from my work computer, was sent highlighted in red for "urgent." Not that it needed to be. Sandra—or as I had come to know her, Wanderlust@flipnet.com—must have been continuously on-line, because I'd never waited more than a few minutes for a response.

WANDERLUST: Hang in there. Buy a vibrator. Clip coupons. Collect Green Stamps. Do you remember Green Stamps?
ME: Do I! Remember how we saved forever so we could get a sewing machine?

WANDERLUST: A sewing machine?

ME: Yeah, remember? Can't you just see all the items hanging on the wall at the Green Stamp store? Can't you picture how jealous our brothers were when we got to pick a prize and they didn't?

WANDERLUST: Keel, we don't have any brothers.

ME: Hmm.

WANDERLUST: Honey, did we wind up trading in the sewing machine for a TV?

ME: Yeah, now that you mention it . . .

WANDERLUST: That wasn't us. That was a *Brady Bunch* episode. We only had enough stamps for the Fry Daddy.

ME: Oh, God, you're right.

WANDERLUST: I know I'm right.

ME: Does that mean we weren't part of a singing group called the Silver Platters?

WANDERLUST: 'Fraid not.

ME: Crud.

This happens to me more than I'd care to admit. It was Sandra who had to break it to me that our mother never wore an apron nor was she represented solely in shades of black and gray.

IT WAS AFTER two o'clock. I was running out of time and parade. "Hold on," I said to Regatta, who was still on the other end of the phone. I had a question that was about to bubble forth from me, and I wasn't going to trust it to just anyone. Not even her.

I turned to that lady in the muumuu. She would know. "Would you say a month is a long time or a short time?" I asked her.

Without apology, she gave me a lazy once-over—starting at my sandals, up my too-skinny legs, to the halter top, and then to my heart-shaped face, where my eyes were probably now so round and huge they were crowding my nose out of the way, so eager were they to take in the wisdom I needed. She asked, "Which do you want it to be?"

"I don't know. I don't know anything."

"Ah, *manawa lōihi*, little child. Time is long. It flows slowly like lava from the mountain."

"If the next few months were to go too fast," I told her, "A person's divorce could be final and her life altered irrevocably before she knew it."

"A life can change in an instant."

I put the phone to my ear. "Reggie, today had seemed so right. Now I'm not sure."

"It's your choice, but don't forget what he's done. You can't act like things are the same."

"I know, I know." I stared at my feet. I desperately needed a pedicure.

"What if I could promise you a sign that it was the right thing to do?" Regatta asked.

"Forget it. I'm not into all your jungle voodoo," I said.

"I meant a real sign."

"What? A rainstorm? A volcanic eruption? I'm a woman of science, for crying out loud."

"Every morning when the sun rises, fate takes science by the hand and goes for a stroll," Regatta said in her wisest and most annoying voice.

"What does that *mean*?" I said. "Okay, okay, suppose Kohala erupted right now, and we were all washed away in a sea of molten lava. And suppose it was truly a sign. How could I be sure that it was *my* sign?"

"Oh, this is your sign. But you must act fast."

"Is this a limited-time offer? Will my destiny coupon expire?"

"Promise me," she said, and I could see her turning away from Kam and cupping her hand around the mouthpiece so he couldn't overhear. "If I can produce a sign that speaks to you and tells you there's life after Kam, promise me you'll give me the green light on the papers."

"This is stupid."

"*Ho'ohiki.* Swear."

"Reggie—"

"*Ho'ohiki.* Now."

"All right, I swear. But you must swear you'll watch after Dante when the earthquake swallows me up."

"Mock me all you want," she said. "Just look to your right—at the end of the parade route."

And there it was, just as she'd said, the sign.

My jaw and cell phone dropped to the ground at the same time. I expected a choir of angels to sing, but instead, speakers suddenly blasted, "Julie, Do Ya Love Me?" There, atop a huge jukebox made from crepe paper and chicken wire, stood Bobby Sherman, Davy Jones, and Peter Tork, live and, as they say, in the flesh. Sure they were like a hundred years old, but Davy had held up pretty well. I could see his dimples from yards away. They were doing a Miss America wave under a banner that read, KDIG PRESENTS THE TEEN IDOL REUNION TOUR! My mouth went dry at the sight of my first true loves—well, two of them, anyway.

Dante had picked up my cell phone from the cement. "Mom," he said, yanking on my arm. "It's Aunt Regatta. She wants to know if it's a go."

"Ask her what Peter Tork is doing in my sign. Oh, you know what, baby, never mind." My hand reached for the phone.

I gave Regatta the go-ahead, and she gave me a thumbs-up from across the street.

"Baby," I said to Dante. "Let's take you over to your daddy."

And after all that, just as I saw Regatta pulling out the envelope, the Teen Idol Reunion Tour float passed between us, blocking my view.

Davy Jones waved in my direction and—I am not lying—leaned forward and blew a kiss *right to me*. I gave him my most demure smile in return, coyly playing with the diamond ring I'd been wearing as a charm on my neck.

2

KAM TOOK THE bed when he'd moved out of the house. It was one of those lumpy futon jobs laid right on the floor, with sewn-on buttons holding it together that always left me with circular creases on my arms and face in the morning. I'd been aware Kam was planning to leave. I didn't know the futon was going with him. That is, not until I came home from work to find the empty space in the bedroom and a trail of dusted linoleum where he'd apparently dragged the futon through the house and out the door. I could just picture him rolling up the thick mattress and then stuffing it like a Christmas tree into the hatchback of his car.

That night I crawled in to sleep with Dante. By the next afternoon, he and I were at Sleepland, lying flat on a bare mattress while my personal sales associate, Lionel, described the benefits of spring coils over foam. I elected to purchase the Serta Perfect Sleeper box spring and mattress set. It can be remembered as the very bed Joey Heatherton danced on in her blue Quianna nightie and perfect shag haircut. It was also the puffiest and most bedlike, and when I lay on it, I made no indentation, as though it contained the strength to push up harder on me than I could possibly weigh down. I also bought a comforter, pillows with no purpose aside from being decorative, and a bed frame that served to suspend the Serta Perfect Sleeper above the hard ground, leaving precisely nine and a half inches of air to circulate freely beneath.

"That is the bed of all beds," Lionel said, writing up the bill. "You'll sleep like a baby in that bed."

Which, to be honest, was exactly what I would have preferred to be doing on that muggy Fourth of July afternoon. Instead, I found myself standing in a line at P'aouai Park with a surprisingly large mob of other thirty-something women eager to get an autograph from a few has-been teen idols. The contents of the parade—floats, bands, and all—had spilled into the park where, overnight it seemed, the earth had also belched up an entire carnival. The scent of greasy popcorn and cotton candy filled the air. A woman next to me in line wore a T-shirt that read I'M JULIE, AND, YES, I DO LOVE YOU!

Regatta was checking herself for eye goo in her compact mirror. "Do you think he'll remember you?" she asked. When I looked at her, clearly stumped, she said, "I'm talking about Davy."

"From when I was a kid?"

"You've met him before? I was referring to when he blew you the kiss."

"Not a chance," I said, although secretly I worried that he might. I had told Regatta about the Monkee Incident, as we were now referring to it, after I dropped Dante off with his father (the same father who, according to Regatta, barely glanced at the divorce papers before stuffing them in his back pocket with a nod of his head).

Regatta insisted that, as a result of the Monkee Incident, it would be quite a lark to play groupies. It might also be noted that lark value is significantly increased with alcohol, which was why we'd already made a stop at a mai tai booth. By the time we got to the area where they'd set up the Teen Idol Reunion Tour autograph signing, the line stretched halfway across the park. This was the biggest thing to happen on The Big Island since . . . well, this was the biggest thing ever to happen here.

"Damn, I forgot I was wearing butt flossers," Regatta said, peering down the back of her skirt at her thong underwear. "I was going to have them sign my panties."

"You're planning undergarment signing? I really don't think I'm up for this."

"Come on," she said, letting her waistband go with a snap. "You can't mourn forever."

"It's been forty-five minutes."

"And it's been four months since he sprang his little surprise on you. It is time to stop acting like a widow and start behaving like the spurned lover that you are."

I crossed my arms defensively. "That's exactly what I want to be doing—being spurned. Facedown on my bed, all scooched down so my toes hang off the end. With the covers over my head." The line moved forward a few feet, and we shuffled with it. "And the shades drawn."

"You know what you need?" Regatta asked as though she hadn't heard me.

"Do not say that I need to get laid."

"You need to get drunk."

"Maybe," I said, poking the parasol aside with my nose and taking another sip of my drink.

"And then laid."

I HAVE NEVER been one to instigate trouble on my own. Which is why, I suppose, I have always sought out those who will find it for me. There was no need to pay a therapist $120 an hour for this insight. My mother has provided it to me free of charge.

It's true, Kam had a way of making me behave strangely. Perhaps it was his placid nature that brought out the opposite in me, as though I considered it my personal responsibility to restore balance to the universe. We had been that way from our first date—of course, not that I'd recognized it then. It is only the wisdom gained from the passage of time, and a desire to blame someone else for my failings, that brings me to conclude it now.

We had been heading to a party at the house of some friend of his a few towns over, an hour-long drive down Highway 1. It was one of those dank Hawaiian afternoons they never show in the brochures—so neither warm nor cold that it seemed to be lacking weather entirely.

Kam, unaware that he was supposed to have first-date jitters, was humming coolly along to some Stones tape. To create the illusion of verbal interaction, I'd taken up counting roadkill and reciting from signs that we passed, although it was hard to read most of them. These weren't the slick billboards I'd grown up with. They were tacked to telephone poles or tree trunks and blurred by rain.

Here was me: "Peter's Farms . . . free pineapples. Or maybe it says three pineapples, hard to tell . . . oh, wait, there's another dead chicken. What's that now, four?"

Now Kam's contribution to the conversation: "Hyeah."

One can see, then, how he was baiting me. How he forced me to chatter endlessly about nothing in particular. "Only four more miles to the World's Largest Man-Made Volcano," I read aloud at one point. "That's the second sign for that."

"Hard to believe."

Progress. Those were three words in a row. I pushed my advantage. "You know, where I come from, there's a rule. Four billboards and you have to stop. No matter what." I shifted so I was sitting Indian style.

"That one's new to me," he said. "I've never dated a girl from the mainland before."

"We're very strange."

"Yeah? How so?"

"Every morning when I get up," I said, as we passed another signpost, "I put on shoes. Then I wear them all day long."

That either offended or amused him back into silence, save for the humming, until we passed the sixth sign for the World's Largest Man-Made Volcano. FREE PALM FROND ART TO EVERY VISITOR! TURN HERE!

Kam turned the truck. "We'll follow your rules on this one."

"We don't have to do this. I know we're already running late," I said, although secretly I was eager to catch a look at it. I've been to the World's Largest Crucifix in northern Michigan (eight signs), the Mackinac Island Fudge Museum (four), and Ohio's Biggest Clam (only three, but the risk paid off; it was easily six feet across, that clam).

The trail off the main road was rocky and more pothole than road. The truck had to pick its way over them, and even then I was being bumped up off the seat.

"Strange how we can't see the volcano from the road," I remarked. I'd half expected to see it poking through an opening in the clouds. After all, this was the world's largest, not just the biggest in the state or even the nation. It warranted *six billboards*. I shivered.

We pulled up to the gift shop, which served as the entrance to the rest of the attraction. It was made of wood planks, dulled and rough from years of rain and heat. The day itself held a kind of dampness that had drained the color out of everything. Not only was the sky gray, but the dirt around our feet was gray, too. The foliage on the trees around the gift shop was gray. The hair on the wrinkly old woman who greeted us at the door was gray.

"Full tour or self-guided," she barked, and it took me a moment to realize we were being addressed with a question.

"Self-guided, I guess. We're in a hurry," I said, glancing toward Kam for validation. "We just wanted to see the volcano."

She frowned. "Can't. Gotta see the shrines to the gods, too."

"All of them?" She and I haggled back and forth a bit and finally settled that she'd allow us to see the volcano, for the low price of four dollars each, if we made sure to visit Our Goddess of the Highway before leaving.

"What about that free palm frond art?" Kam cut in, not caring that his insolence could cost us our chance to see the World's Largest Man-Made Volcano.

"With purchase," the old woman answered.

We entered the gift shop, which was no bigger than fifteen feet square and plagued with the same gray dust that was even starting to form a thin layer over Kam and me. I grabbed the first cheap thing I saw, a volcano-shaped pencil sharpener, but Kam carefully surveyed every item before choosing a surfing monkey figurine.

It was many minutes later that he and I stepped out the back door, clutching our purchases and palm frond "art"—and may I add, the woman didn't much care for my suggestion that it could at best be described as *craft*—hoping that the trek to the volcano wouldn't take too long.

"Look, here it is," Kam said simply, and in fact, there it was. Steps from the shop stood a mound of dirt that rose just above the height of the gift shop. On top of it was rigged a bucket on a system of pulleys and ropes. A sign was taped to a rope that dangled from the pulleys. PULL HERE.

"You can have the honors," he said.

I stepped over to give the rope a tug. The bucket tipped, which spilled a clear liquid into a hole at the top of the mound of dirt. A white froth bubbled up, which was in seconds absorbed by the dirt. Vinegar and baking soda, the World's Largest Third Grade Science Project.

"I kind of like it," I said, leaning against Kam.

We watched as the bubbles fizzled at the top of the dirt pile. Kam's shirt was scratchy against my cheek, and I breathed in his scent of fabric softener mixed with the wet dirt. His arm went around my shoulder. It was almost as though his stillness was seeping into me through osmosis, a cozy laziness that kept me standing there, not fiddling or talking or much of anything but breathing in, then out, as though it had stopped being an involuntary process.

"We probably should get going, huh?" I finally said.

We turned to head back when my eyes met those of the old woman blocking the door to the gift shop. We still had one more sight to see. Her glance directed the way to Our Goddess of the Highway, overseer of cars and trucks (but no protector of small animals, I knew, as was evidenced by the number of roadkill I'd counted before stopping).

Squeezed between the shop and a hot water heater was the shrine, an aluminum stand that held hundreds of votive candles. Above was the Our Goddess of the Highway statue, bearing a striking resemblance to the Virgin Mary. Only she was garishly painted, her feet surrounded by dozens of Matchbox cars, glued on and dripping with lacquer.

"There isn't really a Goddess of the Highway," Kam informed me.

"She's probably new," I countered. "Now that you have the highways."

He looked sideways at me, as if I were a rare and strange bug he wasn't sure he wanted to stomp on or put in a jar and keep. Then he smiled, the devil's grin again, and said, "Maybe so."

I dug through my purse and found two quarters, and I dropped them in the tin box. Kam picked up a match and tried to light a candle, but a brisk wind suddenly picked up and blew it out. He tried again, and then the third time, the candle lit, and we stood together as the night closed in and the flicker of the flame made Our Goddess seem to glow and dance.

Kam's voice seemed almost reverent as he said, "For all the speeders, may Our Goddess of the Highway guide them safely past the fuzz." Then he closed his eyes.

I can't explain why I did what I did next, but with one hand, I grabbed his head down toward me and kissed him. My other hand, as though guided by forces outside me, reached inside his khakis and without hesitation grabbed on to his unsuspecting penis. Kam's eyes flew open, which sobered me. I yanked my hand out and stepped away.

"I can't believe I did that," I stammered. I spun around and took several large steps toward the gift shop and then looked back at Kam. He was still standing there, shirt tugged from his pants, big stupid smile on his face. In my hurry, I ran smack into the old woman.

"Um, thank you, ma'am," I said.

Kam strode up to me, hugged me from behind, picking me up so my feet rested on top of his. He walked me forward a step or two.

"See this girl?" he said to the woman. "I'm going to marry her."

She walked over to the shrine with a surprising grace for someone her age and blew out the votive. "Well, of course you are," she answered.

And later that night, Our Goddess of the Highway got quite an eyeful there in the back of Kam's truck, parked aside Sleepy Palm Road, just off Old Highway 1. In fact, I'd venture a guess that she blushed all the way down to her scarlet toenails.

THAT WAS THEN, of course, before I'd decided the best way to move my life forward was to go chasing after someone I'd had a crush on as a girl. I craned my neck to see if I could get a glimpse of Davy and friends. It had been nearly a half hour since Regatta left on her mai tai mission, and I was feeling less larky by myself. The line had moved maybe ten feet.

Just past the kiddie rides, I could make out a gaming area. It had the usual stuff—Skee-Ball, mini horse races, shooting and—oh, my God!—a dunking booth where you could win a giant inflatable Gumby! Desperately, I clutched the shoulders of some woman behind me in a velour jogging suit. "Hold my place?"

"Only if you return the favor," she said, wriggling from my grasp and pulling out a lighter. She flicked it at the tip of the cigarette dangling from one side of her mouth. "I gotta piss like an English racehorse."

"I'm just going for Gumby, there. Trust me. He and I will be back in a minute." I started toward the booth. "Oh, and if you see an unusually tall Asian woman carrying two drinks—and she'd better be carrying two—let her in line, will you?"

She waved her cigarette in the air. "Anything for the sisterhood," she declared loudly. A general cheer went up from the line in support of the sisterhood.

One woman shouted, "I'm a believer!" and there was more cheering and merriment.

By the time I heard the beginnings of what would become a full Monkees greatest-hits medley performed a capella by a bunch of nostalgia-drunk women, I was halfway to the booth. A guy who was too dry to have yet been dunked sat on a plank poised above a water tank.

He was smiling cheerily, and waved from his perch. "Looks like we have a taker!" he called in a British accent. "Pity she's wasting her money!"

I set down my two dollars and picked up three balls from the counter. "How many to get the Gumby?" I asked the carnival worker.

He scratched his bristly face. "Dunk him with all those and it's yours," he said. "Think you've got it in you, there, dollface?"

I tossed a ball up and caught it. "Cake. I could've pitched professional if they'd had a women's league," I said, omitting the fact that no league would ever really take me. Truth be told—yes, I had a freak talent for throwing. But I couldn't bat or run for shit.

"Hey, pitcha, pitcha, pitcha," the man in the booth called.

I focused on the target and then leaned forward for the windup. "That's pitcher, with an *r*, Brit boy," I said, and I tossed hard. It hit the target clean in the center, sending him plummeting into the tank.

He hoisted himself back up. "Well, well, well," he began, before I dunked him again.

"Don't bother getting up," I said as I nailed the target one more time and then collected my Gumby. It was nearly as tall as I was, and I had to balance it on my hip like a surfboard to carry it.

I got back in the line, which unfortunately hadn't progressed much in my absence. "Pee away," I said to my place-holding friend.

A voice called, "Hey there! You with the arm!" and I was hit with a spray of water. The dunking booth man stood in front of me, shaking himself like a puppy.

"Watch it," I said, hopping back. "You're getting me with that."

"You're one to talk. Look at me," he said, arms spread so I could take in the thoroughness of how I'd soaked him. "You've quite a throwing arm, there."

My mind searched for a quippy comeback, but up close I found him cute in a boyish sort of way. Nothing erases my wit faster than a pretty face.

Velour Jogging Suit sidled up flirtatiously and said, "I love your accent. You sound just like Davy Jones. Say, do you know him?"

"Actually, I—," he began, but the woman in the I'M JULIE T-shirt cut him off.

"That's right! You're both English. I bet you're old friends. Are you old friends?"

"Yes, well—"

I interrupted him this time—those ladies' stupidity was too much for me to take. "Just because two people are from the same country doesn't mean they know each other."

"Of course, that's—"

"Too bad, though," I continued. "I'm getting awfully tired of waiting in this line."

He said, "Funny you should—"

But I wasn't done. "I don't even know why I'm here. My girlfriend talked me into it; then she left. I just want to get my autograph and go, too."

He blurted, "I could help you!" as though I wouldn't let him speak if he didn't get it out fast enough or something.

"Excuse me?"

"That's the amusing part," he said, hands in his soggy pockets. "I *do* know Davy Jones."

"You're kidding."

"No, no, not at all. We're old friends from—well, from London, naturally. Why do you suppose he's brought his tour to our little island? If you'll excuse me for a minute, maybe I can persuade him to allow you to—"

Velour Jogging Suit, clearly aiming to wedge herself into any deal I might strike, gave the guy such a playful nudge it nearly knocked him down. "Who are you, anyway?"

"Maybe he's the fifth Monkee," said I'M JULIE.

"Fifth Monkee?"

"There was a fifth Beatle," she said defensively. "I thought maybe . . ."

"I'm Ian," he said, and—not that I cared—my popularity in line nose-dived when he said it only to me, putting out his hand. "Ian Gardiner. And you are?"

"Keeley," I said, giving him a real handshake, not one of those limp ones women sometimes sneak on you.

Regatta walked up just then.

"He's a friend of Davy Jones's," I explained, as though she'd asked.

Regatta sized him up. "You a carnie boy?"

"Come again?" he said.

"Carnie boy," I answered on her behalf, "traveling worker with the carnival."

He smoothed down his shirt. "No, no, not at all. I must look terrible."

He kept talking to Regatta, something about how he'd been roped into volunteering in the dunking booth to raise funds for some local arts program he was involved with. I lost track because I was watching his teeth moving up and down, thinking they were darned white and straight for a Brit, and squinting to see if I could tell if they were caps. He glanced over self-consciously, and I realized that the conversation must have steered back to me. It was at that moment that I first formulated a theory that will serve me well in life, which is as follows: Even when things are going along just fine, all it takes is the smallest thing—the most seemingly innocuous incident—to remind you how truly your life sucks. Like here. I sensed he was trying to pay me a compliment, bring Regatta in as an ally to win my affection. I heard him say to her, "And up to my booth struts this goddess, and I say to myself, Ian? What's a nice girl like her doing in a place like this? And . . ."

The déjà vu hit me like a fastball to the gut. It also wasn't lost on Regatta, who knows every intimate detail of my relationship with Kam, including the first words he ever spoke to me. I saw her squeeze her eyes shut, as if to try to make the words invisible.

"I have to go," I said, my arms around Gumby, using him as a life raft, backing away.

Ian was stricken. "I've said something wrong. I've offended you. What did I do?"

"Nothing, but I need to get going," I said, well aware that the color had drained from my face, that a tear was streaming from one eye.

I heard Velour Jogging Suit say, "You all right, honey?" but she seemed hazy, her voice carried away in a cloud of cigarette smoke.

"Fine. I'm fine," I mumbled, and attempted a smile. "Nice meeting you," I said to Ian, taking another step back. His head moved from Regatta to me back to Regatta, to see if one of us was going to explain the sudden shift in climate.

"May I ring you? Would that be all right?" he asked.

Regatta answered him with a shrug of apology and then led me away from the line into the thick of the carnival.

"All right now," she said, and smoothed my hair as we walked. "It's okay. Nothing so bad that it can't be made better with a nice mai tai."

Or two for starters. One for me and one for Gumby.

That is not to imply I was so out of sorts that I forgot he was inflatable, and therefore would wind up giving his drinks to me.

3

THE FLUORESCENT LIGHTS in the office had been flickering all morning, keeping time with the throb of my head. My face rested against the edge of the computer keyboard. With one hand, I pecked in numbers from a stack of papers that littered my tiny office. The tapping of the keys echoed through the maze of mostly empty cubicles, the lone sound of a single mom who'd burned all her sick time when her son had the chicken pox and couldn't even take off the day after the Fourth of July to nurse a hangover.

My encounter with Kam that morning hadn't helped matters. I'd stopped by his house to drop off Dante's favorite doll, which, in my zeal to humiliate Kam, I'd forgotten to pack. My hopes that I could get away with a drop-and-run were dashed when I pulled into the driveway, parking behind the beat-up Chrysler Kam sometimes drove. There he was, bent over the engine.

"Hey, Keeley," he said, glancing up long enough to acknowledge me as I walked toward him. I lifted the doll in a wave by way of greeting and as an explanation for my visit. Not that it mattered—he conveniently disappeared again behind the propped hood.

"Where's Dante?"

"Her has him. He's eating breakfast."

My stomach twisted at the sound of her name. Well, okay, his girlfriend's name wasn't Her, but he knew that a pronoun was as close as I would go to admitting her existence. "I hope Her knows not to give him peanut butter."

"She does. He's having eggs or something."

I nodded, leaning against the car door, realizing only then by the warm vibration against me that the engine was running. My fingers fiddled with the doll's hair. I let myself be comforted by the familiar clang of tools against metal, and Kam's breathing, heavy as he strained to bolt bolts, or screw screws, or whatever auto wizardry it was he performed while hidden behind the curtain of the car's hood.

The noises stopped. The unexpected silence prompted me to remember where I was. I tossed the doll into the car and was about to call out a hasty good-bye when Kam said, "By the way, I got your little note yesterday."

Again, the clanging of tools. There was, after all, work to be done and a wife's response to be avoided.

"You had to have seen it coming."

Rather than responding, Kam exclaimed, "Yep, that'll do her!"

With that, the motor revved, sending a flood of gasoline fumes into the air. I hadn't been ready for it, nor had my tender stomach, which pitched like a boat on the waves. I waited for the engine to die down. When it didn't after—oh, I don't know, approximately fucking forever—I yelled to Kam, "Shut off the car! The smell—it's . . ." My head started to do a Tilt-A-Whirl spin along with my stomach. I needed to get away before . . . before . . . hmm, first, perhaps just a hand on the car to steady myself . . .

Kam hurried to where I stood. I felt him brush against me as he leaned through the window to switch the key off. "Sorry."

And there he was, inches from me—a proximity once not even worth comment. Now I couldn't so much as look at him without seeing divorce papers wedged between us. There was no reason for me to feel guilty. Yet I could only bring my gaze to rest over his shoulder, beyond him to the tree-lined road, the very road on which, if I'd been smart, I would have kept driving and simply whipped Dante's doll onto the lawn as I sped past.

"You all right?" Kam's hand rested on my waist.

I shook him off; I didn't need his charity. "What? You think this whole divorce is just tearing me apart?"

"You look like you're going to throw up."

"I'm fine."

Kam cleared his throat, the only even remotely nervous habit I'd ever noticed him have. "*Is* this whole divorce tearing you apart?"

"Excuse me?

"Because we don't have to do it yet."

"Don't have to do what exactly?"

"Anything so final. So fast."

I'd have sworn at that moment he must have jump-started the engine again, because my insides lurched, and there seemed to be a high-pitched screaming in my ears. *Anything so final? So fast?* I glared accusingly at the ignition, but the keys dangled untouched. Apparently, I was the one revved up.

"You sure you're feeling okay?" Kam pressed.

"I'm *fine*." I took a step back, gathering my composure, briskly wiping dirt from the car off my skirt. "And trust me, if I waited for a Hawaiian to decide what's not too fast, we'd be celebrating our fiftieth anniversary together. You, me, and Her."

"Forget it. Never mind," he said, turning away, his voice hard and flat.

"Oh, I don't mind."

"I'm sorry I said anything."

"Yeah, well, you *should* be apologizing."

"Sure, whatever." And he went back to fixing his car, his tools muttering and snapping at me from behind the hood as I left.

I'D FINALLY REACHED the point where I thought I might be able to choke down a piece of toast for lunch when my friend Bob from planning thundered into my cubicle.

"Hello, there, party girl," he boomed.

"Leave me to die in peace."

"So, did our little Keeley have too much Fourth of July fun? Nobody's here, take a sick day. Go home. Lick your wounds."

"Wish I could." I slid a computer printout across the desk toward him. "Check this out for me, will you? These are the seismic readings I've been doing."

He picked it up, looked at it, looked at me. I knew the expression. It was pity. "You took these measurements? By yourself?"

"They're all wrong, aren't they," I asked, and if it was possible, I slumped further. "The pattern of tremors is all off-whack. You'd think I'd never taken seismic readings before."

"You've had a lot on your mind lately. Don't sweat it." Bob patted my shoulder; then he started to rub my neck, and shamelessly I leaned back into his hands, letting them loosen muscles that hadn't anticipated such bliss that afternoon. Coworkers who felt free to hug and touch usually made me squeamish, but I'd always been a bit of a massage whore.

"This has to be a month's worth of work, wasted," I groaned.

"Forget it. No sense in worrying so much about your job. You're single now. Spend your energies on your disaster of a love life."

"You're all heart."

"I can't stand to see you like this. You know us married guys—we want the vicarious thrill of knowing somebody out there is getting some. Which reminds me," he added cagily, "Lucy knows this fellow who would be perfect for you."

"A blind date? No thanks, not ready for that."

"What's to be ready for? You'll have a nice dinner, get to know someone new."

"I don't think so. . . ."

"It'll be good for you," he said, ignoring my protests, releasing his grip on my shoulders. "Get back on the ol' horse. Yep, that's just what you need."

Bob stepped to the opening of my cubicle and added, "Don't sweat it about those readings. Everybody makes mistakes."

"But I thought that I was holding it together." I spun my chair to face him, a bit too fast perhaps, causing me to rethink that toast idea. "My personal life could fall to hell, but—damn it—I'd be a pro at work."

"Be thankful you have a cushy government job. As a matter of fact, we rely on you to screw up once in a while. Otherwise, you'll make the rest of us look bad."

Then he stepped out of my cubicle and, as he always did, slid closed an invisible door.

VOLCANOLOGY HAD NOT been my first career choice. As an undergrad at the University of Michigan, I'd studied geology. I'd been into rocks ever since first grade, when my best friend, Connie Inman, got a rock tumbler for Christmas. It was a tiny, noisy machine into which we'd put ordinary backyard stones. An endless three weeks and countless kilowatts of electricity later, they'd emerge from the rock tumbler transformed into shiny gems.

My plan was to get a bachelor's degree and then head off for a career in mineralogy. I'd gone so far as to meet with a recruiter for a job examining the small particles that make up aerosol cans. I was thinking of accepting an offer. That was, until the entrance of Professor Olmos into my life, my third lover and a more profound influence than I'd ever have expected. (My first lover, for the record, was at age eighteen—a trombone player who'd sneered at the Styx and Pablo Cruise in my album collection but helped himself to my virginity anyway. Number two was a poet who wrote nothing but haikus. On the day I broke up with him, he screamed at me, "Keeley, you are cruel. How could you leave me like this? I loved you so much." Even in his pain he was limited to five syllables, then seven, then five.)

Professor Olmos was a visiting lecturer from Chile who wore his hair in a ponytail and seemed too young to be an object of authority. He was an expert on volcanoes, an area of study not given much consideration by Midwestern students whose field trips usually involved clay and limestone. It was the fall of my senior year. I remember the fall part distinctly because the first ten minutes of class had been devoted to pushing the windows open in the hopes that the crisp air outside would drive some of the mustiness out of the aged lecture hall. That left forty minutes to cover the entire history of volcanoes.

In the middle of Professor Olmos's presentation, roughly around the Proterozoic era, a leaf blew into the room. It got caught in an air pocket, which caused it to dance in the stream of light and dust no more than a foot above the visiting professor's head. I watched from my spot in the front row as the leaf went up, then down, then up again, almost dreamily, hypnotically. He was midsentence when I found I couldn't take it any longer. I leapt from my chair and in one movement snatched the leaf from the air.

Which, of course, left me standing in front of the professor, holding a leaf. The hall of two hundred previously bored students tore into applause. I handed him the leaf as though it were something he'd asked for and then took my seat.

Professor Olmos delivered the remainder of his speech without once taking his eyes off me. "Tectonic plates," he said to me alone, his wooden pointer poised on the chart projected on the waterstained wall, "are subducted and reassimilated into the mantle," and there was no mistaking the meaning underlying his words.

After he dismissed the class, I let him restack the papers on the podium several times before heading over to talk to him. "So," I began, swallowing to calm my nerves. "Tell me, professor. What percentage of eruptions would you say migrate down into a rift zone?" I could feel the heat rising to my face.

He clicked off the podium light. "Shall we discuss that over a drink?"

It took nearly a month of drinks and dinners and visits to museums before I found myself in his bed. It was another month of drinks and dinners and having sex, which really cut into the visits to museums, before he announced he was off to lead a study in Iceland. He would be observing pyroclastic flows on volcanoes, heading up a team of volcanologists on a two-year project.

"That's where it's at, Keeley," he said, his mouth on my left breast so it sounded more like, "Wha where ih ah Weewy." We'd been lazing in his bed all day, reading the paper, drinking diet pop, messing around. He pulled himself up on his elbows and looked at me. "Science doesn't happen in some sterile lab. It's out there. It's dirty. It's explosive, and I mean that literally. You can stare at graphs on paper that show how coal settled two inches in a decade. Or you can stand with your bare feet on the edge of a mountain and watch as the earth bursts right before your eyes—how it's hot and fiery and filled with passion."

He'd talked about his work before. That night, lying naked in his apartment, I'd felt I finally understood. It was as though the words were able to seep more easily into my skin without all those clothes in the way.

For the first time, I dared to think, Well, why *not*? All it would take was a transfer to the University of Hawaii, maybe making up some credits. Somebody had to study volcanoes. Why not me?

It was just ridiculous enough a career choice that someone should have talked me out of it. I couldn't rely on my parents for such a thing. My dad passed away when I was a girl, and my mom—well, she's a psychologist.

As such, she has always considered it her professional duty and moral responsibility to refuse to tell me what to do, no matter how I might beg. When I told her I was considering switching from general geologic studies to the highly competitive field of volcanology, she'd responded, "And how does that make you *feel*?"

Even if I'd pushed it—said that while I was nude and a bit sexually keyed up a professor had planted the idea—I couldn't have hoped for much more input from her.

"What you're telling me is that you're particularly vulnerable during sex, which may impede your best judgment," she'd probably say. "Is that what I'm hearing from you?" Then she'd sit back, her eyebrows raised so that she would appear particularly open, and wait for my response.

I needed someone to treat me like a daughter, not like a client, I'd have grumbled if I hadn't feared the repercussions. ("Sounds like you're afraid of the power of your own decisions," she'd add, because she had that kind of nerve.)

It was this very behavior of hers that had forced my sister and me to create a fictional mother when we were girls, an Everymom, as it were. Turning to her for advice was a habit I'd never shaken. This was no modern mom who'd read Spock and worked full-time. She ate Spock for breakfast, sitting there in a fluffy bathrobe, a big bouffant hairdo and even bigger bosom—the compilation of all my girlfriends' horror stories about parents who pried and judged and were guilty of other intrusions I yearned for.

Everymom would never invite me to explore my feelings. Instead, she would furrow her brow and say, "For heaven's sake, if you were in the midst of an orgasm and a boy asked you to jump off a bridge, would you do it?"

If I were being honest, I couldn't really say no. I'd have had to think about it.

"Exactly what kind of orgasm are we talking about here?" I might ask her. "Am I merely holding in my breath? Maybe squeezing my eyes shut? Or would you say that the bridge-jumping in question would be preceded by rowdy bed slapping and much screaming of yes?"

Then Everymom would lean close, her coffee-scented breath hot on my face, and say, "Bed? Oh honey, there's no bed. You're smack up against the refrigerator for this one. Your arms are reaching up, grabbing on for dear life to the freezer compartment. The rocking of the ice maker as you're pushed rhythmically against the cold door, my dear, cannot even *begin* to drown out your moans."

At which point, I'd resign myself to plugging my nose and preparing for the dive, because it would be all over for our young heroine, Keeley. "Yes," I'd whisper, my eyes lowered, too ashamed to meet Everymom's. "Yes, in that case I'd do it. I'd jump."

SO I DID IT. I transferred to UH. I earned my doctorate. After a few internships abroad, just shy of my thirtieth birthday, I landed the job at Hawaiian Associated Governments, where I could, in fact, study lava. It was all as planned, with one small hitch.

There would be no explosions, no fire. Turned out I would have stood a better chance of that if I'd stayed in Michigan and banged two rocks together. My sole assignment at work was to study the history of The Big Island's oldest volcano, Kohala. The volcano stood 1,700 miles tall, three times as wide, and—as lava production goes—was completely barren. The last time Kohala saw any action was sixty thousand years ago, give or take.

I was lucky to get that job. Anyone not believing me can do the math themselves. Start by dividing the total number of volcanoes in the world by the number of people who think it sounds glamorous to study them. Then slash it all to hell because nobody's funding anything anyway. Most of the others in my class went into teaching. I swore I'd waitress first.

Professor Olmos had clearly neglected to read the volcanology disclaimer, the one that explained how certain restrictions may apply. To be fair, a counselor at the university tried his best to dissuade me. "Volcanology is a highly specialized field, Miss Baker," he'd said. "Perhaps you would find it prudent to consider a more general career path." But he said it sitting behind a desk. Entirely clothed.

Besides, maybe it was because Kohala saved me from carrying plates on my arms and shouting things like, "Two eggs and make 'em shine, hold the pig," but we eventually forged a relationship. After a time, it seemed almost crude to picture her spewing lava.

I'd work alone most times, driving my Jeep up her winding roads. When I found the right spot, one where the lava had once run thick, where layer upon layer of rock looked particularly inviting, I'd stop. Pulling out a shovel, I'd scrape away the sediment, putting samples in plastic bags. Sometimes I'd take readings of seismic activity. Then I'd take it all back to the office. There would be weeks of entering the data into a computer, transforming it into graphs and models that would help put the pieces of history together. I was a one-woman show on this project. There was no urgency. No burning need to uncover information to save lives and homes. Just a scientific curiosity in how Kohala had once been.

I'd complain to Kam on occasion, putting my feet up on the coffee table, laying out my disappointment. "This could go on for years. Digging, scraping, and for what?"

"You don't get it. Working on Kohala. It's an honor." That's the thing about the natives. They always get all Hawaiian on you when it comes to their volcanoes.

"I was hoping for something juicier, that's all. I wish I'd get to some significant discovery."

"She's not going anywhere. There's no need to rush."

"It may sound crazy, but I'll feel like I'm on the brink of getting something big out of her. Then it turns out to be nothing. Like she doesn't want to share any secrets with the likes of me."

"*E ho'omana'onui, e ha'i 'ia mai nā mo'olelo a pau,*" Kam said. "Be patient. All stories will be told."

A MORE RECENT and less lyrical quote of Kam's—"We want custody of Dante."

It was a message I'd picked up from my voice mail a couple days later at work. I'd been ignoring the ring of the phone all day. Bob had gone ahead and given my work number to that friend of his, and the more I'd thought about it, the less ready I'd felt to put myself back on the dating front. Kam's cryptic message was the last thing I'd expected.

"It's only been days since he told me he didn't want to move too fast. Now he's talking custody," I said to Regatta as I paced back and forth in my eight-foot-square cubicle. She'd stopped by after we went to lunch, and now she sat in my guest chair, her legs curled up to allow me room.

"He's bluffing. He's trying to throw you off balance."

My shin banged into the edge of a file cabinet. "It's working," I said. I sat down on the credenza so I could rub the sore spot. "That woman has him so whipped. He'd do anything."

"Forget it. No jury in the world is going to give custody of a four-year-old boy to a father and his tramp girlfriend."

"A hula dancer, no less."

Regatta looked offended. "Somebody has to hula."

"Excuse me? Since when are you on *her* side?"

"I'm only saying there's nothing wrong with the hula. It's our history."

"It's *your* history," I said. "It's Kam's history, and Her's history."

"And Dante's," Regatta added.

I sighed. "I'm sorry I wasn't born with poi in my blood. That doesn't mean I'm going to hand over my son on a platter, big apple in his mouth, just because nobody thinks I can raise him in the Hawaiian ways."

"Calm down, mother bear. No one is saying any of that."

"You know, he's half Detroiter, too."

"Now that you mention it, I thought I smelled motor oil on his breath." She gave me that half-smile of hers, where only the right corner of her mouth goes up.

"Very amusing," I said, pulling up the left corner of my mouth to complete her smile as I always did. "I suppose I'm overreacting. I need some rest."

"You need a lawyer."

The intercom buzzed. "Maybe that's one now."

It was Beula, the receptionist. "You ever planning on picking up your calls, Kekuhi? It's your kid's school on line one. They said they've been leaving you messages for an hour. He's sick."

I turned to Regatta and gave her a quick wave of dismissal. "I'll catch you later. It appears this abysmal day is about to be cut short."

Two phone lines were lit, and I hit the top one. "This is Keeley."

"Hi, Keeley. My name is Pete. Bob Green gave me your number. He thought maybe you and I might—"

Dang that Beula, she never got things right. Some fix-up of Bob and Lucy's was the last thing I wanted to deal with right now. I cut him off to say that I had to run and took his number, all the while feeling guilty because I knew I wouldn't call him. The second line—that's the second line, Beula, not the first—was blinking angrily at this point. I answered the phone with, "I'm leaving right now."

That show of motherly devotion seemed to appease the school nurse, who skipped her usual germ lecture. I grabbed my purse and headed out.

ON THE WAY home, I stopped at the market called Market on the corner of my block. It was not much more than a 7-Eleven, only dirtier, pricier, and run by Mrs. Wakimoto, who had such a knack for pushing merchandise that I'd been known to walk out with a week's groceries at five times the price of the Safeway before I knew what had hit me.

Dante was limp with fever. He clung to the front of me like a koala as I started for the sundry aisle to get children's Tylenol. Mrs. Wakimoto ran after us. "Aw, you have a sick boy. Let me see." And in his fever-induced stupor, Dante obediently leaned down to her as she reached for his head and then tugged down the fleshy area beneath his eye. She studied him closely; then she let go. "He have the flu. I have just the thing," she said. She bustled over to aisle four, then returned with a can of Campbell's chicken soup. "Work like a charm."

I grabbed the soup and headed for the cash register. I'd learned to trust Mrs. Wakimoto's intuitions. Five years ago, it was my face she'd cupped in her hand. Kam and I had stopped in for beer and snacks before heading to my place, as we had nearly every night since we'd met a month before. Mrs. Wakimoto chased me down. Then she stood on tiptoes to stare closely at me. She announced, "You going have a baby. Congratulation."

I'd laughed her off, said Good heavens don't be silly, that's not even a remote possibility, oh you nutty islanders. Nonetheless, I walked out of there with a worried look on my face and a home pregnancy kit tucked in between the six-pack of Bud Light and a can of Pringles. "That woman will do anything to make a sale," I told Kam.

The Jeep's wheels grinding on gravel had been the only sound on the short ride to my house. I lived in a two-bedroom bungalow, tucked in with eleven others just the same, all painted varying shades of beige. A sparse grove of palm trees leading into a woods disrupted the view of Kohala through my kitchen window. As Kam and I unpacked the few groceries, I gazed at the mountain past the dying house plants on the sill. Seeing Kohala didn't make me think of my job. My mind was obviously on other things. Like how I should buy a new couch and get rid of that old one that had a blanket thrown over it to hide the cat's claw marks. And whatever happened to that cat, anyway? . . . Stuff like that.

Kam was surprisingly eager to get on with the test. I'd no sooner changed out of my work clothes before he was shoving the opened box in my hand and directing me to the bathroom. "I read the directions," he said. "One dot means no. Two dots means yes."

"What?" I said. "Just like that? No foreplay?"

"Please do it."

"A boy usually buys me dinner before I'll urinate on a stick for him."

"Cut the jokes."

I disappeared into the bathroom. By the time I invited Kam in, I'd set up the test stick in its plastic holder, the test strip area facing away from us. We sat cross-legged on the carpeting, our backs against the sink cabinet, facing the shower curtain in the hopes that it might rise and we'd catch a movie.

"If you are pregnant—," he began, but I interrupted him before he could continue.

"Let's not get into all of that if we don't have to."

As it was, this was sizing up to be one of those moments in life I'd just as soon forget. It would never make it as one of the family tales I'd pass down through the generations. It would be quietly left off the roster of those occasions when I'd gather up the grandkids. Those times when I'd pull them close to my billowy skirt, the children, getting cozy right there on the stone steps because, well, I couldn't get in and out of the hammock so good anymore.

Those times when the scent of my Ben-Gay would waft through the air, tickling their noses. Then one of them would be so kind as to freshen my Scotch. The littlest boy, Timmy, I believe it was—but who could keep them all straight? He'd look up at me, eyes shining. "Grandmaw, tell us the story," he'd plead, and I'd take a nice big bite of fried pork rind while the others echoed, "Please, Grandmaw, tell us. Tell us."

I'd say, "I suppose you mean about our first date together, Kam and me," because I certainly wasn't going to carry on about waiting for the results of some home pregnancy kit, that was for sure. They'd nod, and I'd chuckle to myself at how little'ns never seem to tire of hearing the same tales over and over again.

"I'll never forget it, our first date," I'd begin, and I could see them settling in, waiting for words so familiar they could probably recite along. "Hardly knew the guy. Yet we did the nasty right there in his truck. That very night." Then I'd sigh, my expression as dreamy as theirs.

True, part of my mind was starting to slip. I could barely remember what I'd had for breakfast that morning. But I'd recall with perfect clarity how years before Kam and I'd held each other under the second night of the full moon. In vivid detail, I'd tell them everywhere his hands went, everywhere his mouth went. I'd tell them how I didn't worry about whether it seemed too slutty or too soon or if he'd love me or hurt me or call me in the morning. I'd tell them how for once in my life I let it happen.

"—Five minutes is up," Kam said.

We rose to our knees, our elbows resting on the countertop. "Here goes nothing." With that, I spun the stick around, the stick with two pink dots. Not one, but two. Pink dots. *Well, kids,* I told the youngsters assembled around me. *Looks like Grandmaw's got a bun in the oven.*

Kam cleared his throat. I blinked and stared at the dots again, but there was a fog rolling into my head, obscuring my vision.

I pulled myself to my feet. Without realizing I was going to do it, I unbuttoned my shirt, one button at a time, top to bottom. Then I pulled the shirt off and tossed it on the floor. Kam watched in confusion.

He stood to face me, and I could sense he was trying to read my expression, but I wouldn't meet his gaze. I was too busy staring over his left shoulder at a tile, oatmeal colored, with flecks of blue. There were hundreds of these tiles lining the tub, but I was concentrating hard on that particular one. I reached up, unsnapped my bra, and let it fall to the ground. Kam stepped forward, his arms out as though he was going to hug me. I stepped back, away from him.

"It's going to be all right," he said. "I'm going to be here for you."

Through the mist in my head, I thought, *He must have seen the same Wednesday After-School Special that I did*. It was almost word for word what the boy had said to the girl he'd knocked up. What he'd said because he thought it was what she wanted to hear and he was too chickenshit to say what he really meant.

I answered him by kicking off my sandals and then unzipping my shorts. Numbness and hysteria were at odds inside me. They collided in my head, creating a high-pressure system that was clouding my ability to see or speak. I yanked the shower curtain aside, twisted the hot water dial on, and then held a hand beneath the running water while I slid off my shorts and underwear.

Without a glance back to Kam, without bothering to so much as close the shower curtain, I stepped into the tub. The spray hit me with the force of a scalding waterfall, shocking the fog right out of my head. It pushed the fog down to the ground, where it rose as steam around me in the shower, leaving behind room in my mind for reality to sink in. I crossed my arms around my belly.

Then I cried. These were no delicate tears streaming down my cheeks. I'm talking here about real crying—soul crying. Wailing at the tile wall. I was making a noise somewhere between a gasp and a scream, and although I knew Kam was staring at me, I didn't care. He was wordless, his arms up, grabbing on to the shower curtain rod as though it were the rumble bar of his Jeep.

Hearing myself cry made me cry all the harder. Then I felt Kam grip my waist. Without stopping to take off his clothes, he stepped into the shower. His arms went the rest of the way around me. This time I let them. "That's good. Get it out," he said, and I buried my face in his shirt, breathing in the puddles of water gathering in the fabric, letting his chest muffle my sobs.

Eventually my tears ran out, along with the hot water. "I'm cold," is all I said. He reached past me to shut off the water. I felt suddenly naked. Well, I was naked, but suddenly I felt naked.

His chin rested on the top of my head. "If it's a girl, I hope she looks like you."

It must have been the water in my ears, but he sounded downright happy. Into his shirt, I mumbled, "I don't know if I can go through all this."

He pulled a towel off the rack, wrapped it around me. "You won't have to do it alone. I'll be there," and he pulled back so I could see the sincerity on his face, the genuine excitement in his eyes. "I'm twenty-seven. I'm ready to get married. This will be great. You'll see."

It was only later I'd marvel that he'd brought up an option that had not once occurred to me. In the short time since we'd been at the market, so many thoughts had stolen into my head. To keep a baby or not to keep baby? Could I raise it? Was I mother material? Kam's suggestion of his involvement, of marriage and all that went with it took me by such surprise, unsettled me so thoroughly, that I said, "Okay."

His lips touched my forehead while I tried to shake the vague sensation that I'd stumbled across an entirely new species. A man who said all the right things, who was eager to commit. I'd seen them on TV. Read about them in books. Here was one holding me, and I couldn't help wondering what it was that made a man five years my junior so ready to jump into marriage when I myself hadn't a clue.

DANTE HAD REFUSED Mrs. Wakimoto's soup, but by seven-thirty he'd managed to watch a Popsicle melt, which for some reason seemed to refresh him. I sat on the padded, black leather chair formerly known as Kam's Chair. Dante lay over my lap like a cat—a heated, sweaty, forty-some-pound cat in Batman underwear, barking orders on precisely how I was to be scratching his back.

"Not there. Higher," he said, and bossing me around was proving to be so successful he decided to demand a story, too.

"Sure," I said, "I'll read you one."

"No, make one up," he said. "Like Dad does."

"Make one up?"

"That's what Dad does. He makes them up. Made up stories are better."

"Wouldn't you rather look at pictures while I read?" I was stalling for time. It annoyed me so greatly to find myself thrown into a storytelling competition with Kam that not a single fairy tale was coming to mind.

"No!" Dante shouted, lifting his head from my lap and fixing on me the instantaneous fury only a four-year-old can produce. "I want a story! A Daddy story." His voice was rising. "I want *Daddy* to tell me a story!"

"Okay, okay, relax." I sped up my scratching to distract him. "I'll tell you a story," and I saw his muscles unclench as he again went limp. "Let's see now. Once there was a loving family called the Partridges, and, oh how they could joke and sing! One day—"

"Mom," he protested, and shot me a warning look that he was not fooled. "A *story*. With pretend people, not real ones."

"All right, then, a story," I said, drumming my fingers absently on his back when the idea came to me. "I'm going to tell you about Pele, goddess of fire," I said, thrilled that I was putting three credits of Hawaiian mythology to use.

"Dad already told me that."

"I'm going to tell you a different part," I said. "The part your dad doesn't know." Then I added the clincher: "The part where she gets in a fight."

Dante turned to me with interest. "For real?"

"You remember how Pele lived a long time ago. She paddled her canoe from island to island. Did your dad tell you what happened when Pele built fires to keep herself warm?"

"They turned into volcanoes," he answered.

"That's right. The first one she made was Kohala, my volcano."

"And Dad's volcano," Dante added. I flinched from the unexpected reminder of how Kam and I had met. How we had bumped into each other on Kohala—he shuttling around a group of tourists while I was setting up equipment, finding myself an unwitting tourist attraction. Why was it, I wondered, that people were forever insisting on dredging up the memory of that day for me?

"As I was saying," I said, struggling to recall what it was I was saying, "One day, Pele got in a fight with Poliahu, the goddess of snowcapped mountains. They both wanted the same man."

"Did they use guns?"

"Nah, this was a chick fight. It was more like clawing and slapping. Spreading vicious rumors about each other. Poliahu lived on Mauna Kea, and Pele made the mountain there explode."

"Cool," he said with great seriousness. I could see him registering a mental note: *When angry, blow up mountain.*

"Then Poliahu turned the lava into ice, and when she did that, she froze the volcano forever. That's why it won't ever again erupt. Like my volcano."

"And Dad's."

Enough of the dad thing, I thought, and I announced, "Time for bed." I picked him up, remembering to bend from the knees, which Kam was always nagging me to do.

"Watch this," he said, and held up his fists. "I can fight the snow goddess when I move into the refrigerator with Dad and Suzanne."

I carried him to his room, tossed him on his bed, and then handed him a T-shirt. "Put this on," I said. "Into the refrigerator? What do you mean?"

"We're going to move into the fridge. That's what Suzanne says. You can't come."

"I can't come? Into the fridge?"

"Nope. It's only for us. Me, her, and Dad."

"The refrigerator. She said that?"

"Yeah," he said, looking doubtful. "She said it like frig-ee. We're going there. But not you."

"Frig-ee?"

He was getting annoyed. "That's what I said. *Frig-ee.* It's an island. We have to take a plane." He pulled the shirt down over his head, poked his arms through.

"Frig-ee. Hon, do you mean Fiji?"

He flopped back on the pillow in disgust. "That's what I *said.*"

"You're not moving to Fiji. You live here. With me." I wrung Dante's blanket in my hands. Suzanne's family lived in Fiji. It was all starting to make sense, Kam's interest in taking Dante. They planned to move away together.

"Don't worry, Mom. I'll be okay."

"Sweetie," I said, and it took every bit of self-control I had to give the appearance of calm. "I'm sure you misunderstood her. This is your home." I was reduced to begging for validation from a child. "Wouldn't you miss me?"

His face set in concentration, and I realized then that he had no idea what it meant to miss me. Since he was born, he could count on his mom to always be there for him. His dad, however, he knew too well the pain of going without. "You can visit," he said after a moment, patting my hand.

And what flashed through my mind was a picture of my own mom. My mom who helped me with my homework, drove me to band practice, showed her love for me in a thousand ways. Doris, my mom, who in thanks I would have thrown in the Detroit River with bricks tied to her feet if I thought it would bring my dad back even for a day. Even if just for the chance to say good-bye.

"I'm afraid I wouldn't let you go that easily," I said to Dante, handing him his doll, flipping off his lamp, kissing him good night.

My body had reverted to its most primitive biological urges, and every tendon was tensed for a battle that was unlikely to take place standing alone in my son's dark room. I headed for the treadmill in my bedroom, stepped up on it. Then I ran as if for my life.

Pain shot through my bare feet as they struck the treadmill's hard surface. The rhythm of my stride calmed me, and I remembered how Kam had howled laughing the day I'd brought the treadmill home from a yard sale. I'd thought he was teasing me for being embarrassed to run in public, considering how I run like such a girl—like the girliest of girls. It's my secret shame, how I bend my arms and flick my wrists up and down while I scamper. (When I was young, my sister went so far as to duct-tape my arms down to try break me of it—an experiment that only resulted in a tragic loss of arm hair when my mom made her rip it off.) But Kam didn't care about my flailing. He was more amused at this proof that deep down I'd always be a *haole*, an outsider. When I tried to deny it, he'd asked me, "How long you live here? Ten years now? You ever once see a Hawaiian jog?"

In defiance, my legs kept pumping. I ran until my lungs felt like they'd burst. Until my muscles ached. Until every inch of me throbbed with the realization that these coming months were surely going to be hell. I'd been fooling myself to believe that Kam would roll over and let me scratch his belly while our divorce slid through the process. He was going to go out kicking, although I didn't know why. He'd dumped me.

There was a chance he'd no idea of Her's nefarious plot to take off with my life. There was even a greater chance that if he did know, he'd go along with it—that is, provided he was being led gently and frequently by the penis. No, Kam didn't understand the pain of waking up to find you'd been replaced. Although he might if I showed him.

This was nothing I could handle alone. First thing in the morning, I promised myself, I'd start asking around to find a lawyer—and not just a name plucked from the phone book, either. This case called for a lawyer with a reputation. I wanted someone as brutal as *a'a* rock on the feet, who'd make sharp stabs at Kam, so each step in his attempt to snatch Dante from me would be a dance of agony. And if I happened to be watching all this standing side-by-side with some new and improved version of a man—thumbing my nose at the one who'd placed a time limit on the forever he'd promised—all the better.

I checked my watch. It was only eight-thirty. There was plenty of time to make a phone call before I went to bed.

4

THAT NIGHT I'D only made it through to Pete's answering service. Then he and I played phone tag for a couple of weeks. By the time we actually set up a date, it was for a week later still. At first I'd worried that this was taking so long, Kam would make his move before I was ready. Then I woke up and did that exaggerated head-slap thing because I remembered where I was—as in, *Hawaii*, where one hurries to get to a crawl. Before Kam could pull paperwork together to sue for custody, he'd have to find a pen. Then some paper. He'd sit down and—Oh, hey, what's that on the tube? *Twilight Zone*? Cool. That's the one where that gorgeous babe gets plastic surgery so she can be ugly like everyone else. I love that one— and before he knew it, he'd be darned if the day wasn't gone, he was starved, and could anyone please tell him why he was holding this pen?

Yes, I've watched as visiting New Yorkers—burly ones who could hold subway doors open with their teeth—broke down and wept like babies because they couldn't handle the pace. Some say it's the heat. I blame the flip-flops. It's impossible to walk fast in those things. The rhythm of the islands had no choice but to slow so peoples' feet could catch up. That's my theory, anyway. I'm standing by it.

At this moment, however, I was sitting. On a chair so overstuffed it threatened to swallow me whole. And facing me in an identical chair— positioned close enough for the fine hairs on her knees to touch mine— was Morna Templeton, attorney-at-law.

"Tell me," she said. "What brings you to this point?"

It was not the question I'd been expecting. I lifted a mug of tea to my lips, but it was so hot I brought it down without sipping. "I'm getting a divorce. . . ."

"Yes, I know. You told me that on the phone." She brushed back her long tangle of hair and then leaned forward in her seat. "And how is it that you found yourself at such a place in life?"

How does anyone find themselves at such a place? I thought. Morna's office was a closed-in patio off the back of her farmhouse, heavily paneled and almost jungle-like, what with all the spider plants hanging from the ceiling. When Bob's sister had referred her to me, she'd warned me Morna's style was unconventional. She appeared to be one of those people who hadn't been informed that the Summer of Love was over, yet she was rumored to have a ruthless instinct for working the legal system in favor of mainlanders. Plus, Bob noted, she routinely cut her rates for clients if she took a liking to them.

So I tried to be my most likable when I answered, "I have no idea."

Morna nodded, clearly not surprised. Then she said, "Drum with me."

"Excuse me?"

She bustled over to a travel trunk in the corner and pulled out two narrow bongo drums. She hoisted her serape skirt and sat cross-legged, one of the bongos angled across her lap.

"Drum. It will lead us to what is true."

Drum? Was she joking? I stayed rooted, unsure of what to do.

Morna smiled up at me. "Well, I can hardly talk to you when you're way up there and I'm down here! Come join me. Make yourself comfortable."

Reluctantly, I pried myself from the grip of the chair and sat across from her on the floor. The carpet had the sour smell of old wool that'd been through a few floods in its day.

"Let's see what these skins can do," she effused. "Go ahead, give 'er a bang."

"I really don't think—"

"Exactly," she said, and followed it with a heavy smack on the drum. "Don't think." *Smack.* "Let yourself be one with the beat." *Smack, smack.*

I picked up my drum and gave the lightest tap I thought I could get away with. *Tap.*

Smack, smack. "How do you feel?" she asked.

"I'm okay," I replied.

"You're *what*? Let's hear it, loud and clear!" *Smack.*

I'm okay," I repeated, and, after she nodded encouragingly at me, added a hesitant tap.

"She is ohhhhhkay," Morna announced to the air, drumming out each syllable, adding extra force on the *o* and *k.*

"Well, not really okay."

"Not okay . . . *what*?"

My palm touched lightly on the drum. *Tap?*

"That's right," she said. "She's not okay!" *Smack.*

"You might say I'm more than just not okay. I'm actually quite angry." Then I remembered to add, *tap.*

"Angry, yes. Anger is good." She picked up speed on her drumming, and, what the hell—I'd been in marching band (clarinet, thanks for asking)—I knew the drill. I did my best to match my tapping to her rhythm. *Tap, smack, tap, smack.*

"That's why I'm here. I have a son." I had to raise my voice to be heard over the beat of our drumming. "His dad is trying to take him."

"Take him," Morna echoed, her voice a moan, her drumming accelerating.

"And move to Fiji."

Move to Fiji. Just thinking about it made my limbs go slack. Morna leaned over, set my hands back on the drum as though they'd merely misplaced themselves. "Get it out," she said. "Release yourself from Fiji. Drum for Fiji." She started working her drum at a furious pace, goading me on to do the same.

Drum for Fiji? I *hate* Fiji, I thought, and gave a good smack while I was at it, then another, which felt so satisfying that the next thing I knew I was banging on my drum right along with Morna. The leather stung my palms, but the pain only spurred me on.

"He's moving with his nasty girlfriend," I said.

"Girlfriend!"

"Who's too lazy to start her own family." My voice was rising.

"Family!"

"So she wants to steal mine!"

Just as I was really getting into it, Morna's drumming stopped cold. I continued for a few beats, but when I realized I was solo, I lifted my hands as though they'd been laid bare on a hot plate. The silence rang in my ears.

"Did you breastfeed?" Morna asked, her voice nearly a whisper. Softly, she swept her fingers across the drum so it made a *shh, shh* noise. *Tap, shh, shh. Tap, shh, shh.*

"Nonstop for a year," I whispered back, again mirroring her motions. I couldn't help smiling at the memory. It had taken days for Dante to latch on, but once he'd gotten the hang of it, he seemed never to want to let go. At first I'd curl up on the couch, gazing in amazement at his wrinkly pink skin, caressing his bald spot. After a time I learned to carry on about my usual business—running errands or fixing dinner—all with an infant dangling from a breast, my shirt covering his head so only two baby feet peeked out. With Kam staring jealously. Suggesting maybe it was time to switch to bottles.

"Mother's milk," was all Morna said; then she started drumming for all she was worth, and I did, too. I drummed for mother's milk, and for mothers everywhere. I drummed for women who want to take your men and your babies, and for men who are beautiful, and for men who are weak. I drummed for their stupid wives who don't even realize their husbands have been sleeping with someone else for a year although you'd think I'd have smelled her cheap perfume on him but my senses were drowned in the scent of crayons and Play-Doh and I was so used to kissing Dante that Kam's head seemed enormous when it came near me and eventually it hardly ever came near me and I was almost relieved because I was achingly tired all the time and sick of handling everything by myself and I wished I'd married a man instead of a boy and then after a while I ran out of things to drum for so I stopped.

Morna sat unmoving. I was breathing hard, and a tear of sweat trickled down the side of my face.

"I'll accept you as a client," she said, not sounding the least bit winded. "Tell me. In this divorce, what is it you want?"

"I want what's mine."

"Very well." She set her drum aside and stood up with a grunt, walking to the window to gaze out at her fields. "We'll see you get it. We go for child support at one-quarter his gross income. Alimony. Of course a split of communal property. And full custody of the child for you with supervised visits with the father."

"Supervised visits?"

"That's where we start."

"That seems so harsh."

She turned to face me. "If we're going to work together, you're going to have to trust me."

"Oh, I do," I said, not wanting that unfortunate display of doubt to impinge on my likability factor. "Completely. But about our working together." I set my drum aside. "Being a single mom has really strapped me—financially, I mean. I was hoping you might offer some sort of sliding scale arrangement. . . ." My voice trailed off in embarrassment. I hate asking for stuff. I'm the type of person who swerves her cart away from the free-samples lady at the Foodland because I don't want her to think I'm out to get something for nothing.

"I don't discount," Morna said.

"Okay, no problem, I'll find a way—"

"I am willing to barter. What skills do you have to trade?"

"Skills?" I wondered if Morna would find value in the fact that I can tie a cherry stem with my tongue. "I'm a scientist. That's mostly math, a bit of observing cause and effect."

"Interesting. Do you have any cow-milking experience?"

"I once had a cat," I offered.

Morna thought for a moment. "Tell you what. One of my iguanas has been feeling down. I think he's lonely. You take him for the next few months; make him part of your family. I'll cut your fee by half. Sixty dollars an hour."

"That sounds great. But I'm not an animals expert, you realize. My speciality is volcanoes."

"Volcanoes." She said it as a murmur. "Volcanoes. Oh, pooh—I like you. Twenty-five an hour. But you have to bring the herb tea."

"Deal," I said, and I walked over to shake on it, but instead she gave me a hug so robust it picked my feet up off the floor.

BY THE TIME we wrestled all forty-six inches of St. Ignatius into his cage, it was nearly six o'clock. "He sure is big," I said, beginning to question who was really getting the better bargain.

"He's all tail. And gentle as a bunny, aren't you, Iggy?" Morna said with a coo.

We loaded the cage into my Jeep, and I checked my watch again. I could look forward to a dirty look from Miss Beth when I picked up Dante late from the after-school program. Then Regatta was due at my house at quarter past six to baby-sit and help me get ready for my date—and I still had to get dinner. It was as though the skies had cast a spell over the entire island, rendering time irrelevant, but I was being followed by a cloud that was forever making me late.

Morna gave me a vigorous wave good-bye. Then she pumped her fist in the air and shouted, "Be strong!" as I drove away down her dirt road, wondering what on earth you were supposed to feed a giant lizard.

DANTE AND I dragged St. Ignatius in his cage into the house. I tossed the bag of take-out onto the counter, another dinner from EAT, the sandwich shop next to Market. Dante lay belly-down in front of St. Ignatius's cage in the living room. "I can catch lizards, you know, Mom," he said. He moved an index finger from side to side to see if he could get St. Ignatius's eyes to follow.

"I know. You're the best lizard catcher there is."

"I never got one this big."

"Thank God for that," I called from the kitchen, where I was rummaging through cupboards looking for something to feed the iguana. We barely had anything fit for human consumption. "Do you think St. Ignatius would like Pop-Tarts?"

"Do they have frosting?"

"No, but they do have a third less fat."

"You better ask. 'Member how you killed my rat?"

I swung the cupboard shut and walked over to lie down next to Dante. "That was not my fault. Your teacher should have told me before we

brought him home that he knew how to unlatch his cage." I kissed Dante's
ear. "Besides, nothing would have happened had your father mowed the
lawn the day *before* like I'd asked him."

ME: Know anything about iguanas?
WANDERLUST: They're mean and slimy. And those are their good
qualities.
ME: Somebody gave me one as a pet.
WANDERLUST: Did I say slimy? I meant cuddly. How are things
going with Kam?
ME: He's slimy. So what do I feed him?
WANDERLUST: I thought the hula dancer was in charge of cooking
his meals now.
ME: I meant the iguana.
WANDERLUST: Leafy greens, fruits, veggies. And don't leave it alone
with Dante until you know it better. Seriously. They're
unpredictable.

I watched from the window as Dante ran through the back yard to the
Kus' to borrow a cup of leafy greens. Daisy Ku, flanked by two of her seven
sons, answered her back door and then nodded a hello to me as she
ushered Dante inside. He would be absorbed into her household for at
least an hour—shooting toy guns that I wouldn't let him have and chasing
bad guys up and down the stairs. Eventually, one of Daisy's seven sons
would walk him home. Although I can't count the number of times I'd go
fetch him myself and Daisy would have to sort through her boys to find
him, laughing. "Blends right in with my own, don't he?" Then, with her
huge bosom resting itself on Dante's head, she'd suffocate him with a hug,
his arms straight out at his sides as he tried to reach around her girth to
squeeze her back.

At any rate, it seemed a safe time to open the cage and let the iguana
roam free. I checked to make sure the doors and windows were all closed.
"Be a nice iguana—no biting," I said as I slid the gate on the cage up and
then stepped away. For a moment, St. Ignatius did nothing. Then he darted
out of his cage and climbed up the couch, to the CD tower, and straight
to the top of the entertainment center where he crouched next to a phil-

odendron in the latter stages of dying. He seemed fine. At least I wouldn't have to worry about running over him with anything up there.

"WHATEVER YOU DO tonight, don't be yourself," Regatta said. She laid a floral skirt the size of a washcloth in my lap.

"Gosh, that's what my mom used to say," I said. I sat on the edge of the Serta Perfect Sleeper in a beige bra and nonmatching underwear, painting my toenails and trying to ignore the nervous rumblings in my stomach.

Dante was asleep by the time Regatta showed up, late but as always bearing gifts for him—this time a roll of masking tape and a Tootsie Pop. ("You don't have to give him stuff every time you see him," I'd tell her, to which she'd reply, "Yes, I do.") She'd also brought an armload of her clothes for me to borrow and Ted, her on-again, off-again boyfriend of five years. Ted was the loudest man I'd ever met, and a dead ringer for television's McGyver—although the similarity ended at looks. Ted could never, say, assemble a working firearm from spare parts found around the house; not that I've asked.

While Regatta dispensed dating advice in my bedroom, Ted was in the living room, eating my Chee-tos and waiting like a dad for my date to arrive. Every now and then he'd bellow, "That thing up there is staring at me!" which we'd ignore.

Regatta replaced the washcloth with a red slit skirt, shook her head, and tossed the skirt on the floor. "You're going to an art auction, right? I think that calls for black."

"Bad idea. Wearing black is something I might do—and we wouldn't want me to be me, would we?"

"Don't be sensitive. I only meant that you could work on your flirting skills."

"I flirt," I said, indignant.

"Jamming your hands down the front of a guy's pants is not flirting."

"Once," I snapped. "I did that once."

"And look where it got you." Regatta was perusing the mound of dresses strewn on the bed, mumbling something like, "What we need is a dress that'll make his tongue unroll and hit the floor. . . ."

My attention span for female bonding had already exhausted itself. I crawled across the bed, toes pointed up to keep my nails from smearing polish on the bedspread. I grabbed a pink shift that was so short at first glance I thought it might be a shirt, yanked it off the hanger, and pulled it over my head.

"Done," I said, bounding to the floor, wriggling the dress down over my hips. Then, in a relentless effort to preserve my pedicure, I walked out, weight on my heels, wet toes in the air, into the living room.

Ted greeted me with the requisite wolf whistle demanded of the on-again boyfriends of your best friend. "Don't you look like a big piece of candy."

Then some other voice said, "Yeah, you look tight."

To which I said to myself . . . *huh?* Is this my date standing right here? Excuse me but, do people not ring doorbells anymore? Could Ted, the loudest man ever known, possibly have tipped us off before I waddled out like a duck, and—hey, he wasn't half-bad looking in that lanky, big-nosed sort of way. He also couldn't have been much more than twenty-two. And did he just call me *tight*?

Regatta scurried up next to me, shoving a pair of stiletto-heeled sandals in my hands. "Shoes," she said under her breath, on the chance that I didn't recognize what they were.

I dropped them to the floor and slipped my feet into them. "You must be Pete. I didn't hear you come in." He was holding a rolled-up newspaper in his hands.

Ted said, "Pete and I were just getting to know each other. Did you know he's Pete Peterson, the art and movie critic for the *Bee*?"

"Bob let it spill that you're quite the fan of my column. I have to admit, I'm flattered," Pete said. He held the paper out to me. "This is for you. It's today's column—'Sugar Cane Collectibles'—in case you missed it."

I tottered over in Regatta's shoes and took the newspaper from Pete. I set it on the counter. "You shouldn't have," I said, and then grabbed Pete's arm and steered him out the door before he had a chance to ask me which of his columns I'd never seen was my particular favorite.

———————

THE AUCTION WAS at the old Kalamela Theater, a restored art-deco-style hall a few towns over in Honokaa. On the drive over, I had a chance to learn about Pete, The Early Years, but his struggles as a teen would have to wait because we'd arrived. I was already remembering why I'd rarely dated. We walked up from the parking lot through the damp night air, while he chattered excitedly about, of all things, origami, which was the type of art that would be on display that night. "As an art form, it's on fuckin' fire," he said. "Pardon the French."

It wasn't until we turned the corner that I noticed the commotion. In front of the theater, a dozen or so people marched in a circle, holding picket signs that said DOWN WITH FOLDED FILTH and PAPER NOT PORN.

"Awesome . . . Do you love it, or what?" Pete said, and the guy actually rubbed his hands together.

"What's with the protest?" Only one of us seemed taken aback by this. We elbowed through the crowd to the entrance, past a woman who spat at me, "Paper pervert!" to stand beneath the marquee. It read ORIGASMIC ORIGAMI: EROTIC PAPER FOLDING, AUCTION 10 P.M.

"It's just paper, you old bag," he shot back, nudging me to underscore his wit. He kept walking; my feet didn't move. He was clear through the doors before he peeked out to where I was standing. "You aren't bothered by this, are you? Did I not mention it was erotica?"

My discomfort at being brought to what was so clearly an inappropriate venue for a first date was exceeded only by my curiosity. To appease Regatta's wish that I be demure, I gave an Oscar-worthy performance in my role as Coy-Date-Going-Along-as-Good-Sport, a speaking part for which I could have earned a SAG card with my line, "Well, I suppose I can go in. It's not as though you're bringing me to a porno flick. It is art, isn't it?"

At the door, we were met by a two-foot-high origami sculpture of a couple in the throes of passion. "Baby!" Pete said, as he scanned the room. "What a turnout! I didn't expect so many people. And, is that Channel Seven news? I have to write a column on this. You don't mind if I do some work while we're here, do you?" I gave him a whatever shrug, and he said,

"Bitchin', I'll get us some drinks." Then he disappeared before I had a chance to say sure, thanks, I'm parched, a beer would be swell.

The place was packed. I'd have had to guess three hundred people. Smattered throughout the hall were black pedestals of varying heights and widths, each with a piece of paper art on top. I walked up to a nearby display while I waited for Pete. Auction item number fourteen, *Breast with Aureole*. One really had to appreciate the detailing the artist had derived from a square of paper. How many folds it must have taken to get the nipple to appear that round.

I stood by the breast so long, I feared perhaps Pete had left me for dead. Finally he returned with two glasses of chardonnay. As he handed one to me, he said, "Ran into friends. I tell ya, this place is jumpin'."

He led me over to a paper sculpture of an erect penis, *The Ol' Ten Inch*. "They say size doesn't matter. It's how you fold it." When I didn't respond, he looked at me and did this noise where he bit his lower lip and sucked air in, *ffffuh*. "Now don't tell me this is getting you all hot."

If Pete would've cut the innuendo—and if he weren't barely out of diapers—it might have. I hadn't had sex in months, and the last year with Kam had been just plain bad sex at that. The other night I'd dreamed I was masturbating. Things were that bad. I was arousal waiting to happen, but the only turn-on at this point was the thought of folding Bob into shapes and running him over with my Jeep for fixing me up with this guy. "Out of curiosity, how old are you?"

"Twenty-three," he said. "But don't worry. I dig the older ladies. Like a fine wine. Like good cheese, huh? You're looking damn sweet for as old as Bob said you were. You ever see that movie *Mrs. Robinson*? With that song by The Lemonheads?"

"Oh, for crying out loud, it's *The Graduate*. And Simon and Garfunkel did the song first." And fine wine that I was, I ignored when he asked, "Who?" and instead moved on.

We toured several of the displays. Pete would make crude comments and then pretend he hadn't so I'd feel like a prude if I protested. An old prude. Mrs. Robinson, only with her panties all in a bunch. He'd say, "Mmm, how do you feel about 69?" then follow it with, "As an art piece, I mean." Then he'd lick his lips, or make that air-sucking noise.

At one point—right around *Self-Gratification in Blue*—Pete pushed me aside so he could better see across the room. "I think that's Leminski over there. I'm dying to interview him. He's the master. He makes origami look easy when it's hard. Get it? *Hard?* For real, though, you ever do it?" He licked his lips. *Ffffuh.* "Fold origami, I mean."

"I can fold the crane," I said, but Pete was already halfway down the aisle.

If he'd stayed, I could have told him how I'd once folded 843 cranes. I'd folded 843 tiny gold foil cranes for my darling Kam as a wedding gift. I'd folded cranes until my fingers bled. I'd coerced my friends to help me fold cranes. I'd folded through wedding showers and bachelorette parties and through my dwindling days of singlehood, cursing Kam's mother for deliberately letting it slip she'd always hoped her son would marry a woman who'd know the traditions that meant so very much to her. But by our wedding day I'd fallen 157 short of the thousand I was supposed to have folded. When Kam opened the box from me filled with paper cranes, he said, "You didn't have to do all this. Most people these days just glue a few to a picture frame." His mother sat primly nearby in her flowered mother-of-the-groom dress, hands on her knees, looking away.

"Keeley?"

The voice came from beyond my peripheral vision. When I turned, there was a man who was no one I recognized standing in front of me. "It is Keeley, right?" The British accent tugged at my memory, as did the slight dip of a cleft in his chin.

"Yes," I said, and hesitated before I said, "I'm sorry, I don't—"

"It's Ian. Ian Gardiner." He was all spiffed up in a jacket and tie, his sandy hair slicked back. He was impeccable, as if someone had just dusted him. "We met last month. At the Fourth of July carnival. You dunked me."

"Of course. You're Davy Jones's friend."

"Yes, well, a shame you had to leave so quickly. I trust everything worked out for you."

"I'm fine, thanks."

"You look lovely. Are you here as an artist?"

"No, I'm a volcanologist. I'm here . . . with someone. You?"

"I'm an agent. I've a client here. Fellow by the name of Leminski." We sipped our beverages in sync. "So you're a woman of science," he said, as though he were saying *a supermodel*, making it sound so sexy. "And what do you think of all this?"

"I'm not an art expert," I demurred.

"But what is your opinion? I'm curious."

"I think it's . . ." I pondered how I was going to finish that sentence, and I let the din fill the space of my words in the meantime. I slid my wineglass along my lips and noticed his eyes following my movements. I was tempted to slide my tongue along the rim to see what sort of reaction that might earn. Instead, I gave him Regatta's half-smile and said, "If you must know, I think it's garbage."

He laughed. "So you *are* an expert, then."

I hadn't enjoyed the power of playing with a man's emotions for ages, and he was clearly smitten. With me. It made me almost giddy. But, as always, my reign was short-lived. An argument between two men was rising from across the room. By the time there was a crashing of glass, it proved to divert our attention.

Ian said, "Oh dear"—although he pronounced it oh *deah*. "That's my client in the middle of that. I'm going to have to handle it. I really want to talk to you more. Don't go anywhere."

"I'm not sure if—"

"Please. Stay here. I'll be right back."

He hadn't moved, although the shouting was escalating behind me. "The situation's getting ugly over there," I said.

"I won't leave until you say yes. That you'll be here."

"I'll be here."

"Terrific," he said, and hurried off.

Once again, I found myself alone, but this time feeling warm and blushy. My feet, however, ached. I took a seat on the edge of a nearby pedestal, careful not to crush the small figure sharing the space, *Vulva in Bloom*.

It was that guy Leminski's work. At first glance, it just looked like a pale blossom set in a bed of green leaves. The leaves were actually pubic hair, though, and the flower genitalia, and—the stamen in the middle there, was that supposed to be a—?

As I leaned closer to look, a large woman in a psychedelic muumuu bumped into me, causing a stream of wine to tip from my glass. Onto *Vulva in Bloom*. Which—*shit!*—must have been folded from paper towels because it absorbed the wine and collapsed within seconds into a wet pile. "Hey!" I shouted at her, but she was already gone.

This was not my fault! The lady in the muumuu did it! As if anyone would believe that. The empty glass I clutched may as well have been a smoking gun. My mind raced—was it ruined? Could I salvage it? Perhaps I could mold it back into shape, restore it to its former glory. Trying to appear as unobtrusive as possible, feigning a casual whistle—don't mind me, just browsing—I poked at the paper. It was like sticking my finger in mashed potatoes. I was doomed. *God, how much did this thing cost?*

That's when I realized I needed to do what any decent human being would in such a situation. I would flee. Escape all blame and pretend I'd never been anywhere in the vicinity of *Vulva in Bloom*, and should you attempt to claim otherwise, are you able to provide witnesses to prove it? Yes, if I moved deftly enough, I could easily make it over to *69* before anyone was any the wiser.

Just as I was readying myself to slip away, I heard footsteps coming from behind me. On this next part—in my defense—I should point out that it had been a long day. I was not at my sharpest. So, granted, I may have panicked. I snatched up the pile of what was once *Vulva in Bloom*. My eyes darted around for somewhere to stash it.

"Where is my origami?" a man shouted.

I didn't see a trash can or an ashtray for miles, or for that matter, some sucker I could plant it on. Therefore, for lack of any other ideas, I reached down the neck of my dress and tucked it in my bra.

"*You.* You there in the pink! You're sitting on it. Get up."

Leminski. It had to be him. "Excuse me?" I said, my voice dripping with innocence. Slowly, without a care in the world, without a stolen work of alleged art in my bra, I turned to face him. He was short, bloated, with greasy hair and a sweaty demeanor. "Are you by chance Leminski? *The* Leminski?" which was as close as I had to a first name for him.

He looked me up and down then gave me a smarmy grin. "In the flesh," he said, but my ability to distract lasted only seconds. "It's bad enough this crap auction tries to hide half my work where nobody sees it. Now somebody steals my art. I'm tellin' ya, it was right here."

"I'm sure it was just moved. Did you try the front?" and, I'm ashamed to say I added, "That's where it belongs."

He licked his lips at me, gave me another once-over, this time his glance stopping eye-level at my breasts. It figured. His eyes narrowed. "There it is," he growled, and I looked down to see a green stain from the paper's leaves spreading like a disease over my dress. Before I knew what was happening, his stumpy hand shot forward and reached through my sleeve into my bra. I screamed and pushed him away, but he emerged victorious with a fistful of soggy paper.

We'd by this point attracted a crowd. "Stop! Thief!" Leminski shouted, but I was merely standing there, frozen. A security guard ran up, and Leminski pointed at me as though to a witch. The guard yanked my arms behind my back, holding my wrists in one of his hands.

"There's been a mistake," I said as I was pushed roughly backward toward the door. A flashbulb went off in my face. "Go find Pete. Pete Peterson, the columnist," I said. I struggled to get free, but the guard only tightened his grasp. "I'm with him. He can straighten this out."

Just as the guard dragged me through the front door and into a waiting police car, I looked up through the blur of tears to see Pete. Across the room. Unscrewing the cap from a beer and watching without expression as they carted me away.

5

TED SHOWED UP after midnight with three hundred dollars for bail and a pack of Marlboros. "In case I couldn't spring you," he said. "Cigarettes in the slammer are as good as money." He walked out with me to his car, giving me a gentle prod to try to shake me out of my misery. It didn't work.

Jail hadn't been nearly so much fun as I'd imagined it would be. I'd always pictured it as hanging around with tough but lovable ruffians, trading stories and singing old Negro spirituals late into the night. Maybe dragging a tin mug across the bars for sport. As it turned out, the strip search lady kept referring to me as "the hooker," and I had only one cellmate, who slept the whole time. Except when she rolled over on her cot to gaze in a stupor at the green stain on my dress and mutter, "Got yourself shot, eh?"

Regatta offered to stay the night when I got home, but I wanted to be alone. Just me, my son, and my self-pity.

All Saturday morning I let the answering machine take Regatta's messages. I'd tried to ignore her call later that afternoon, but she kept saying, "I know you're there. Pick up," so I finally did. "Go outside and get your newspaper," she said. "You're not going to believe this."

I didn't have the stomach to ask why. I said, "Be right back." The *Lotus Blossom Bee*, as usual, was over on my neighbor's lawn, probably because it was their paper, but I grabbed it anyway. Then I sat down on one of my porch steps, unrolled it, and there I was. Page one, lower right-hand corner, a black and white photo of the guard dragging me off. There was no mistaking who it was. I hadn't even been granted the dignity of one of those black rectangles over my eyes, like a *Glamour* magazine "don't" fashion tip. Underneath was a caption that read, "Porno Bust in Bust—Local woman arrested for attempting to smuggle erotic art from auction in brassiere (turn to page twelve)."

So I turned to page twelve. There was columnist Pete Peterson's byline, followed by a story thankfully only about two inches in length. It never mentioned my name, but it did quote Leminski as saying the absconded art had been his most treasured work. "We had expected bids at upwards of five thousand dollars. Naturally, I don't care about the money. But my agent is insisting that I be compensated for my loss." It went on to mention that no formal charges had yet been brought against the perpetrator.

My legs somehow carried me back into the house; my arm shut the door. I couldn't take my eyes off the photo. Dante had picked up the phone and was chatting with Regatta. "Buy me the Tweety PEZ first," I heard him say. "Then I want the Garfield."

I pulled the phone from his hands. "Don't be greedy," I told him, and then into the receiver, "I'm going to have to quit my job and move to a town the *Bee* doesn't reach."

"Maybe I can change your hair. What do you think about blond?"

"Only if my friends and family won't recognize me." I picked up a felt-tip pen and drew glasses and a mustache on the photo. Added an afro. "What I can't believe is that anyone would bid five thousand dollars for a piece of paper."

"It's a bluff. They can name any price now. How can you prove they wouldn't have gotten it?"

"You know what's the worst part? Here was his agent—remember I told you it was that Ian guy from the carnival?—well, he was the first man who'd seemed interested in me since I can't remember when. And now he's trying to filch thousands of dollars from me."

"Don't let him get under your skin. He's not even worthy of your hate."

"It's not hate. It's more like disappointment."

Which for me, I didn't bother to tell her, was probably worse.

I STOPPED IN the office on Monday long enough to pick up my equipment, my sometime-assistant Ellen, and my voice mail. Morna Templeton had left a message, "We need to discuss your newfound notoriety, my dear. Call me." Bob wanted to know if I could help him sneak office supplies home in my panties. Kam, strangely, remained silent on the matter.

It was too early to be returning phone calls, and I didn't have time for it anyway. Daisy Ku had offered to take Dante to school so I could get an early start, and I was hoping to make it to the craters at the far side of the volcano before noon. I drove while Ellen rifled through her backpack.

She was a grad student at UH, specializing in chemical history, although I think there may have been a cosmetology minor in there. She was in full makeup for a day in the field, and I suspected her hair had already seen a curling iron. Not that I cared. I was grateful for the help. Nabbing an assistant was never an easy task—as a rule they flocked like groupies to the active volcanoes on the other side of the island. It was hard to sell the thrill of driving up endless narrow roads with me to walk along dried lava flows and draw maps of where volcanic ash had settled thousands of years ago. Plus the day was going to be a scorcher. The sky was still dark, but already I was sticky from the heat.

"Care if I put on some music?" Ellen asked as she produced a home-made tape from her backpack, along with two cans of V8.

"Feel free," I said, accepting the can she handed me. I'd rather have driven in silence, but if I said no to the music, I feared she might start talking.

"You'll love this," she said, popping the cassette into the player. "It's an oldies mix—totally camp, totally from your gen," which my mind finished for her, *eration.*

And as the yellow fingers of the sun followed us up the mountain road, we settled back to Nancy Sinatra's gritty voice as she sang about her boots that were made for walking, then onto an odd mix of Petula Clark, Tom Jones, Mel Tormé and, inexplicably, some Ramones. By the time we hit the end of the road where we'd have to start hiking, it was midmorning, and I was in a fine mood for the first time in days.

IT HAD TO BE 102 degrees. I pulled my shirttail from my jeans to use it as a towel to wipe the beads of sweat pooling on my forehead. "Mind if I do the same?" Ellen said as she grabbed the back of my shirt and smeared a near-perfect imprint of her face on it.

It had taken most of the morning to set seismometers at key points around the crater, one of those jobs that the planners where I worked at Hawaiian Associated Governments—HAG as it was known—asked me to do even though it defied logic. Seismometers, used to measure earthquake activity, on Kohala were only useful to measure the lack thereof. On a regular basis, part of my job was essentially to take the pulse of the volcano, look at the results, and say, "Yup, still dead."

Only the last readings I'd taken over a period of months showed a trembling—so slight it could have been caused by someone having left a vibrator running at one of the lookout points—but a scientific curiosity nevertheless.

I'd passed on the results to the planners at the office, swallowing hard and pointing out the high possibility of human error (alas, mine), without going into the particulars of why. Now I was in the process of proving I'd done my job incorrectly. While I was at it, I thought I'd get some lava samples. "Hand me that shovel, will you?" I said to Ellen. I took the shovel from her hands and then used a boot to put extra weight to dig it into the hard ground. It hit with a sharp scrape, the earth's protesting scream to my intrusion.

"What if the readings show activity up here?" Ellen asked as she knelt before me and held open a plastic bag. I dumped the contents of my shovel into it.

"Doubtful."

"But what if they do? Does that mean it's not extinct after all?"

"I suppose, but I've never heard of that happening. It would more likely mean a new volcano is forming somewhere nearby," I said, and immediately regretted it. Ellen spent the rest of the afternoon atwitter with the possibility of being part of such a discovery.

"Maybe they'd name it after you," she said as we loaded up the shovels and bags, leaving the seismometers behind to do their job. "Mount Ke-kuhi."

"Actually," I said, turning over the engine, "that's Baker-Kekuhi."

Ellen shook her head as she lifted herself into the Jeep. "Forget it. That'll never fly." As we made the long drive down Kohala, Ellen recited the names of Hawaii's volcanoes one by one to demonstrate her point that none of them were as waspy as Baker. And forget that hyphenation thing.

———————

"IT'S NOT HOW it looks," I said, tipping back and forth on a wooden rocker on Morna Templeton's front porch. I'd stopped by her farm on Thursday after work to discuss "recent developments," as she'd put it. Morna was not much of a believer in telephones.

"And how does it look?" She sat on a lawn chair across from me, tuning her guitar.

"I would guess it looks like I went to a pornographic origami auction and stole art in my bra."

She tightened a knob at the end of the guitar, and strummed a note. "One of the interesting things about appearances, Keeley, is that they are often deceiving." I continued rocking, hoping I could avoid telling the details about that night again, especially since I hadn't yet found a way to do it without my appearing ridiculous. The story had already made the rounds so many times at the office, people were starting to forget whether it'd really happened to someone they knew or it was one of those urban legends they'd read on the Internet.

"Are you familiar with the law offices of Lee, Lee, and Lee?" she asked.

"Never heard of them."

"After I contacted your husband with the terms you and I had agreed on, it was Lee who called me back. The middle one. A real dirty player, I'm afraid to say."

My feet tapped the ground, rocking me faster. "Oh." I didn't know she'd talked to Kam.

Morna put down her guitar, stood up, and came over me to give me one of those one-person-standing-the-other-person-sitting hugs that just never work, particularly when one of the persons involved is trying to rock back and forth. "It's going to be ooooookay," she said, patted my cheek, and then went back to her chair. "They'd like to get together for a chat, that's all. With both you and your husband present."

"Oh," I said again, but added a brave smile so as to discourage another hug.

"I must warn you that they've brought up the incident at the theater." She plinked a note over and over. "Sing an A-flat for me, would you?"

"Sorry," I said. "Tone deaf. Is that a huge problem?"

"No, I can do it myself."

"I meant what happened at the theater."

She attempted to sing the note, *la, la, la*, and then plinked the strings again. "I called the police station in your behalf. That artist fellow is making quite a bit of noise, but no formal charges have been filed. Of course, it would be better if the case were dismissed entirely. Is there a chance it may be?"

I shrugged, and added an "I don't know," just to underscore the depth of my unknowingness.

"I'll stall for time so we can get this settled. Lee is also giving me some hoo-ha about your being an unfit mother due to your involvement with pornography." The word *unfit* so close to *mother* hit me like a slap in the face, which Morna must have caught, because she didn't even bother dropping her guitar before squeezing in next to me on the rocker. "Now, Keeley, you'll have to learn to put your faith in me. Give me some trust. After all, I believe in you."

A throb in my head was taking on a life of its own. "So what do I do?"

"For now, nothing. Maintain the schedule of visitation you've set with your husband. He sees your son regularly, doesn't he?"

"Usually overnight on Saturdays. Once in a blue moon midweek."

"Continue that. Be cordial to him. There's enough hatred and despair in the world." She grabbed on to my hand and gave it a squeeze. "There's no mess I've come across yet I haven't been able to scrub up."

"I haven't even told you what happened last Friday."

"That's right," she said. "For all I know, you're a sexual deviant," and she went back to tuning her guitar. *Plink, plink, plink.* "Of course, you could also be a great defender of all that is decent and moral in this fine country of ours, destroying any smut that crosses your path." She looked over at me, giving her guitar one more plink. "For all I know."

SATURDAY NIGHT I had the girls over for poker. I'd dropped Dante off at Kam's, who wedged his body in the crack of the door as though I might push past him to storm inside. He said a cool thank you to my shoulder.

"I'll meet your bet, and raise you . . ." Regatta looked at the pile of chips in front of her, "two." She, Bob's wife, Lucy, and a friend of mine from college, Melissa Anne—who wasn't so lucky as me in the job market and, in fact, was working as a waitress—sat around the kitchen table. It was in the living room where I'd dragged it by myself that afternoon so we'd have elbow room.

"I'm out," Lucy announced, tossing her cards on the table.

"Me, too," I said.

"It's probably for the best," Melissa Anne remarked as she pushed chips into the kitty. "Betting is illegal. And aren't you on parole?"

I threw a chip at her head. "Bail, I've been released on bail. Besides, I—"

"Did anybody see that?" It was Melissa Anne interrupting me, leaning to the side to look past me out my picture window.

"See what?"

"Something moved out there. Like a person."

I twisted around, but a rubber tree in desperate need of a trim blocked my view. "It's just the wind," I said, but then I noticed a figure peek in from the side of the window and then disappear. It was small like a dog or a—I glanced up to the top of the entertainment center. St. Ignatius was resting peacefully. "You know, I think something *is* out there." I walked cautiously toward the window. At first, nothing. Then I saw, peeking around the edge of the sill inches in front of me through the glass, a face. A small, round face. Curly brown hair. And drawn-on brows, which were arched as she gave me a forced smile.

"It can't be," I said, running over to open the door and shout outside. "Ma? Mrs. Kekuhi? Is that you out there? Come inside."

From the bushes I heard, "You have all your friends here. I don't want to bother you."

"Please come in."

"No, thank you. I'm fine right here."

Kam's mother was back in my life for less than thirty seconds and already she'd managed to exasperate me. I headed outside, closing the door behind me after giving a brief apology to my friends. I hadn't seen her since Kam and I had split. Dante's teacher told me she'd stop by the school to volunteer once or twice a week, but she was always gone by the time I got there.

"Mrs. Kekuhi? What are you doing out here?" She stood in the dirt in front of my window, as always in a housedress and sweater.

"I wanted to talk to you. When Dante wasn't here."

I sat on a porch step. "He's at his dad's. What's wrong?"

"You are such a skinny girl."

"You came here to tell me that?"

She tiptoed her way though the dirt to take a seat next to me on the steps. Her hands were in her lap. "You should think about forgiving my son. About taking him back."

"Excuse me?" I'd have thought she'd already pulled out her sewing shears to cut me from the family photos. I'd suspected she'd done that even when Kam and I were together.

"He's a man. He belongs with his wife."

"Mrs. Kekuhi, you're forgetting. It's not as if Kam wants me."

"My son doesn't know what he wants."

My head was shaking. I had to put my fingertips on my temples to stop it. "Somehow, I'm surprised to hear you say that."

"All I know is that my son is talking crazy without you. He thinks he wants to move away. To take my grandson with him. I thought you should know that."

"I already know that."

She stood up, which made her not much taller than when she was sitting. "You go back to your friends, but think about what I said. Talk sense into my Kamohoali'i. He'll listen to you. You're his wife."

"It's more complicated than you're making it sound."

"Not for you. You're a good girl." She leaned over and gave me a peck on the cheek. It was a gesture so casual, so easy that it almost made me forget that she had never once done it before. "You've always been like a daughter to me," she said before she turned to head down the front walkway, taking precise steps like a child who doesn't want to step on a crack and break her mother's back.

"SHE HATES ME," I'd whispered to Kam the day I first met his mother at her house for Sunday dinner, after he'd told her he was going to be a father, that we were getting married.

"You're imagining things. Everything's going great. She loves you," he said, his words muffled because, as I recall, he had a mouth full of roast chicken at the time. "Ma's always shy at first."

"Don't be paranoid," he told me after I complained she'd shown up an hour late, and then barely spoken at my wedding shower. "She likes you. That's just her way."

"She'll learn to love you," he said the morning of our wedding. I sat across from him at a coffee shop where we'd met for breakfast, just him and me, to have a moment alone before the stress of the wedding that afternoon. "These things take time."

I poked at my eggs with a fork. In my fifth month of pregnancy, I was still not at full eating speed, and starting to show. "I wish she'd call me by my name. Instead of 'that girl,' or 'you, over there.' "

"Your name is too hard for her to say. It's the *l*. She gets mixed up. Besides, you're marrying me, not Ma." He leaned back, resting his head against the back of the booth. "And I have no problem with *l*s." Then he held his thumb and finger up to his mouth in an L shape, and stuck his tongue between, wagging it at me.

I tossed a piece of toast at him. "That is disgusting."

"Disgusting? I can't believe this. Where's that nasty girl I thought I was marrying?" Kam's bare foot slid under the table and up onto my chair, pushing between my legs. He was giving me that smile he did with just his eyes, the one that usually gave him a 99 percent chance of scoring. Especially since most of my queasiness had ebbed in the past month, only to be replaced with a surge of hormones so intense most nights I jumped the poor guy before he could so much as set his keys down. "How 'bout a quickie for the groom?" he asked.

My purse was already in my hand when I remembered I'd promised Regatta I'd meet her at my house so she could start on my hair. My mom was there, too, and she'd hinted there was still quite a bit left undone for a wedding that was taking place in a matter of hours. I lifted Kam's foot off my lap and let it rest in the chair next to me.

"Can't. I have a million things to do," I said as I pushed the bill toward him and stood to leave. "Besides, I happen to be saving myself for my wedding night."

WHEN I THINK about all those little girls who wrapped white towels over their heads, stepped their feet into their mothers' high heels, and practiced for the day they'd march down the aisle, I can't help wondering—where was I? Or when Barbie and Ken drove off in her pink plastic Corvette while Midge threw rice—how did I miss all that? It was as though 51 percent of the population spent their formative years rehearsing for a play, but the director remembered to hand me my lines only five minutes before showtime.

I'm convinced it all traces back to the fact that I didn't have a Ken doll. My mom never bought me one. Although it is possible that it never occurred to me to ask. My sister, Sandra, had a Ken, but I still don't recall any wedding ceremony. I do, however, remember stripping their clothes off and laying Ken on top of Barbie. Then we'd set them in a shoe box, close the lid, and put them off somewhere to do it. Whatever it was.

"This is all your fault," I told the mother who didn't buy me a Ken doll—or, while I was on the subject, an Easy-Bake oven, either. She was busy attempting to fasten the eighty buttons (we'd counted) along the back of the just-above-the-knee wedding dress I'd bought off the rack days earlier. Regatta stood in front of me, painting lipstick on my lips with a brush. We were getting ready in Kam's bedroom—the one he'd no longer be sleeping in as of today—where we could peek through the curtains and watch as the fifty or so guests started to arrive.

The ceremony was in the garden at Kam's mom's house. (There was no Kam's dad that I'd ever seen. I'd once asked if he'd died, and Kam said, "Hope so," so I'd dropped it.) The nuptials would be brief, followed by a luau in the backyard because that's what you do in Hawaii if you're not having a big church wedding, and sometimes even if you are. It seems there aren't enough excuses to bury a pig in the ground and wear flowers around your neck.

"So what exactly is all my fault?" my mother asked.

"That I'm so ill-prepared for marriage."

"Open," Regatta ordered, tapping my lip. I opened.

"I see," my mother said. "And you don't feel that the example your father and I set helped ready you for your own relationships?"

I wasn't expecting her to drag my dad into this. "That's not what I mean."

There was a rap on the door; then it pushed open and Kam's mom stepped in. "Oh, good, you're almost ready," she said. She lifted a camera to her eyes and pointed it in my direction. I turned to her and smiled, but she let the camera drop down on its strap without snapping a photo. "I only have a couple rolls of film. I'd better wait," she said, leaving me unsure what to do with the smile still on my face.

My mom said, "June, you look so pretty, that's a lovely color on you," and I wished I'd thought to compliment her.

I'd added a "Yes, pretty," but it wasn't the same. She'd turned away and was doing a slow review of the room: the dresser covered in bumper stickers (SURFERS GET IT WET), Kam's dirty clothes strewn over a chair, and that wretched poster of the bikini-clad woman/champagne bottle/sports car I told him would never go up on a wall in any house of mine.

"I didn't get a chance to pack all his things," she said to herself more than to anyone in the room; then she turned to me, giving me the consti-pated smile that would become so familiar. "Of course, that will be your job now. To take care of my Kam," she said, running a fingertip along the foot of his bed. "I just came to check on you. You finish up. I'm going to head downstairs and say hello to everyone." And she left, shutting the door so softly I didn't even hear a click.

Regatta was the one who broke the silence. "I'd say somebody has herself a case of empty nest syndrome."

"Poor Tai," I said, eager to clear the tension from the room. Then I explained for my mom's sake—"Kam's little brother. She's going to smother him to death now."

"So you never answered me," my mother said, but I no longer remem-bered the question. "You're standing before me looking positively radiant in your wedding dress. And yet you say you don't feel ready for marriage. Why is that, I wonder?"

"I meant to say wedding. I wasn't ready for a wedding, not marriage."

"Interesting that you said marriage. Well, no matter. You're all buttoned up and set to go, then."

"I need to finish her eyes," Regatta said, but she had to follow me with the eyeshadow brush as I sat down on the edge of the bed. I looked up at my mom.

"Do you think it's a mistake? My getting married?"

"It shouldn't matter what I think," she replied. "What do you feel?"

Maybe it was the dress squeezing my ribs, or the incessant ticking of the clock on the nightstand, but I wasn't going to let her wriggle away this time. "No, tell me. Should I marry Kam?"

"Do you love him?"

"I suppose. I mean, what is love?"

Regatta set down her brush. "This is headed in a bad direction. Keeley, don't—"

But she was interrupted. "I'm hearing that you may be concerned the love you feel won't be powerful enough to sustain a marriage." That was Dr. Doris Baker, not my mom, who said that one.

"Let's face it," I answered. "I've known Kam for six months, and I'm about to commit the rest of my life to him. How should I know if I love him? Did I love those guys I dated in college? I thought I did. If I'd gotten pregnant, would I have married any of them? For that matter, I thought I loved David Cassidy when I was, what? Nine? And before him Davy Jones. With all the passion my small soul could muster. What's different now?"

"You have the jitters," Regatta said. "Doris, back me up here."

Dr. Baker studied my face. "I'm wondering if it's not so much marriage, but a genuine adult relationship that you fear."

I could feel tears welling in my eyes, the ones that were glued to the good doctor's face. Regatta said softly, "Oh, no—your makeup," and she scooted behind me on the bed and held cotton balls beneath them.

"So should I marry him?" I said. It was more a challenge than a question. "You tell me."

"No, for one time in your life, I am begging you. Act like my mother. Just this once, you . . . tell . . . me."

I saw the muscles in Dr. Baker's jaw clench, but her voice was unwavering. "How is it, honey, that you expect me to know? You went away to college when you were seventeen. You live six thousand miles away. I see you a week or two in a year, and I only met Kam three days ago. I can tell you how it felt for me to love a man, or to love my children. I can tell you how it can rip your heart out when you lose that love, or when a wall goes up in front of it. But I cannot—as much as you may want me to—I cannot

tell you the choices to make with your life. I may be your mother, but"—
and her hand went up to rub her temple (Excedrin Headache Number
Forty-Six: Your daughter demands a straight response)—"the fact is, you
stopped letting me mother you a long time ago."

The effort required to suspend my tears was also holding my words in.
The strum of ukuleles from outside spilled into the room to fill the quiet.
Finally, my voice coming out hushed, I said, "So that's it, then."

"I wish I could give you what you want. That I had an answer."

I nodded, Regatta's hands and the cotton balls moving up and down
with my head. "Mom, could you go let Mrs. Kekuhi know I'm ready? That
we can get started?"

"Of course," she said, and she leaned over to kiss the top of my head.
"I love you, sweetie. I'll see you downstairs."

After she left, Regatta pulled the cotton balls from beneath my eyes.
"You are doing the right thing," she said. "You love him. You're going to
have a baby. It's a cool, sunny day, and the gods are smiling on you."

"You're just saying that so I won't smear my makeup."

"I'm saying it because it's true. And because somebody around this place
needs to."

SO HERE'S THE report on the wedding: The groom looked dashing in a
Hawaiian print shirt, white slacks, and shoes that actually covered his toes.
He said, "I do." As did I. Then we kissed, everyone went *awww*, and the
minister presented Mr. and Mrs. Kamohoali'i Kekuhi, followed by a round
of applause. Then fifty or so people went off and began the process of
getting loaded, except, of course, for me, being with child. Instead I ate
the watermelon out of the carved melon carcass and when that was gone
walked around picking it off peoples' plates and saying Hi, having a good
time?

Around six o'clock there was a mandatory hukilau dance. At seven, we
had to search for the groom so a then-sixteen-year-old Tai, who'd apparently found his way to the punch bowl a few times, could give the best
man's toast before he puked. It was seven-thirty before we found Kam,
smoking a doobie in the back shed with his four cousins from Naalehu.

He hurried as much as Kam hurries to stand with his new wife before the crowd, the only clue to his altered state being that he shoveled cake in his mouth the entire time Tai spoke, but then again, so did I. The toast was sentimental but brief, "I love you, big bro. Keeley, you take care of my big bro. I love you, man." At nine o'clock, my mother and I went back up to Kam's now-former room, where she unfastened the eighty buttons she'd fastened hours earlier. I changed into shorts and a T-shirt while she chattered on about nothing really, because those Mai Tais are stronger than most people realize.

At ten, the groom gathered Regatta in her role as maid of honor and one of his surfing buddies to serve as witnesses, as he bestowed upon the bride an honor he'd been saving for his wedding night. "You get to name my penis," he announced to his lucky lady, who without hesitation decided on Bill. "Do you mean maybe Big Bill? Or Wild Bill?" he asked, but the bride was insistent that his penis was just Bill, and so Bill it was.

At eleven o'clock, the happy couple waved good-bye to the handful of guests remaining—the four cousins from Naalehu who were now playing quarter bounce on one of the picnic tables, as well as the mother of a single remaining son. They drove off to the Hilton Waikoloa. There, the groom would be expected to deflower his bride, currently five months pregnant.

By the time the bride emerged from the bathroom in her white silk nightie, her husband was passed out on the hotel bed. The bride shook him, and when his response was a drunken grunt, she said, "Wake up. I intend to have sex on my wedding night, and I thought you might prefer it be with you." It is still not known whether the groom did in fact fully awaken. But he managed to roll over on top of his new wife, slide her white silk nightie up, and bite softly on her belly, along her breasts, her neck, and then push into her, although it was not Bill's name, but Kam's that she later cried out. He said nothing at all, not being much of a talker.

THE RINGING OF the phone in the house finally shook me back to where I sat on the porch. "You can let the machine pick it up," I yelled to the girls. I stood up, kicked the dirt off my shoes, and went back inside. St. Ignatius, who'd been watching me through the screen, toddled after me as he always did. I never dared stop abruptly in my own home for fear of an iguana crashing into my ankles.

I could hear my voice, "*Hi, this is Keeley* . . ." The cordless was sitting on the table, and Lucy grabbed it.

"This'll be Bob—he was calling me right back," she said, and then into the phone, "Hi, hon." Then she giggled. "Oh, excuse me, this is her friend Lucy. I thought you were my husband." *It's a man,* she mouthed to me, each word slow and exaggerated, then back to the phone, "May I tell Keeley who's calling? All righty, then, hold on, let me . . . see if I can . . . find her." Her hand covered the mouthpiece. "Somebody named Ian?"

I took the phone from her without ceremony and said, "Hi." Then I headed into my bedroom because, frankly, the ladies had already gotten one free show for the night.

"Keeley. This is Ian Gardiner. The one you remember as Davy Jones's friend?"

"I remember you for you."

"Sorry to bother you at home—Pete Peterson of the *Bee* gave me this number. I suppose you can imagine why I am calling you. You no doubt recall that Mr. Leminski is my client. I find myself in the position of needing to meet with you regarding the matter at hand. Of the artwork that you . . . of the artwork."

"I didn't steal it. It was an accident."

"You and I may know there was no ill intent, but Mr. Leminski is, let's say, of a different opinion. Is it possible that you and I could discuss this in person?"

No ill intent. I distinctly heard him say it. Yes! The words were music to my ears—good music, too, not that New Age crap. There was no mistaking it. Here I had Leminski's agent on the phone, and he wanted to meet with me. He was willing to work things out. There was even an implication that he believed me innocent.

It was all I could have hoped for, which was precisely why I said no, thank you very much, I believe you should contact my lawyer directly.

The whole thing sounded fishy—a ploy to get me to reveal information that could later be used against me, maybe even drive the price of the origami up into the six-figure mark. Of course, he could be on the up-

and-up. But if that were the case, I reasoned, I was better off placing this opportunity in Morna's hands than trusting it in my own, the way my luck was running.

Ignoring his urgings that we keep lawyers out of it, I gave him Morna's number. "She's the one handling my legal matters," was all I was willing to add before I clicked off the phone and carried it back in to the living room.

I announced my arrival with, "Ladies, let's play some cards."

"It's about time," Melissa Anne said, picking up the deck and starting to shuffle. "I've had a fiver burning a hole in my pocket all night."

6

IT RAINED THE first two weeks of August. Not just the daily afternoon sneeze of rain that only the tourists noticed. This was rain that pushed the air out of the sky, leaving so little oxygen you could walk only a few feet without gasping. It pooled into rivers that shorted out our only traffic light, and all was chaos until a citizen group mobilized to direct traffic. Eventually, someone had the idea to post a hand-written "four-way stop" sign over the dead light. Even though the sign smeared right away, everyone remembered what it had said and took turns accordingly.

Somewhere around day six of all this, Daisy Ku came out on her porch covering her head with a newspaper, which disintegrated into papier-mâché within seconds. "Looks like rain!" she hollered to me across the yard. Regatta took the opportunity while trimming my bangs to proclaim that the skies needed this time to weep. By day fourteen, though, I was more than ready to tell the skies to get over it. Pull themselves up by their boot straps and move on. They didn't see me whining and, believe me, I had plenty of troubles.

Ian Gardiner had ignored my advice to contact Morna and instead attempted for days to call me. I let the machine pick up every time, growing increasingly sure that I'd done the right thing. If he'd been legit, surely he'd have nothing to fear by contacting my lawyer. Each time he called, it was as if an alarm were going off, timed to remind me of my misery.

There was finally a forty-eight-hour period during which I hadn't heard from him. "Maybe he drowned," I suggested hopefully to Morna when I called her to check in. I parted my kitchen curtains and watched a couple of locals try to dig out a VW Bug that had slid into the ditch across the street.

Morna told me to try deep breathing to handle what was clearly a pent-up anger problem. Oh, and by the way, she'd added, Kam's lawyers were trying to accelerate that meeting between us. It seemed Leminski was pressing charges for the theft of his artwork after all. And did I have any use for spider-plant cuttings, because one of hers was really taking off.

We made plans to meet at my house on Tuesday so she could brief me on how to behave at the briefing with Kam and his lawyers. I was dismissed from my conversation with Morna with instructions to take Ian Gardiner's next call. "Get his number," she said. "But don't say another word to him. I want to do the talking. There's a chance he can be reasoned with. That client of his, on the other hand—that Jim Leminski—is a complete boob."

BY THE TIME Tuesday arrived, the rain still hadn't let up. (It was day sixteen—I knew because the *Bee* was keeping count as though we were all prisoners of some weather war, which wasn't far from the truth.) I'd just returned home from another day stuck in my cubicle rather than out in the field where I needed to be. It was torment to know that my seismometers at this point were undoubtedly gliding down the slopes of Kohala. I ached to get up there—if not to stop the carnage of thousands of dollars of equipment, then at least to salvage their remains. To know that, yes, they didn't make it, and as painful as it would be, at least I could get on with my life.

But until then, the uncertainty had me edgy. I'd snapped at Dante that morning over leaving the screen door ajar. I'd laid into him that St. Ignatius could have gotten out. It wasn't until I saw Dante's bottom lip quiver that I realized I'd been screaming, and I dropped to my knees to draw him close in a hug. "I'm sorry, pal. Mommy's a little tense. It's the rain," I said. "But you do have to be careful. Iggy's only ours on loan."

So it was not without irony that I was the one who left the door open and let the iguana escape. I'd just dropped Dante off at Kam's and was miffed that he'd greeted me with his shorts casually unbuttoned, which was inappropriate on a level only Kam could achieve. I was propping my back door open to shake off my umbrella, during which time St. Ignatius scampered past me, rolled down the porch like a meatball, and disappeared into the bushes.

"Iggy, no!" I shouted, pulling off my only decent pair of work shoes and leaping barefoot into the shrubbery, the nettles stabbing at my feet. I grabbed at a bush—some leafy thing that used to flower but hadn't in years.

St. Ignatius was nowhere to be seen, and Morna was due to arrive at any time. I was screwed. She'd want to see Iggy, I had no doubt about it. Check on his health. Tickle him on that spot where his chin should have been. *How could I lose a four-foot iguana?* I wondered, when at last I spotted him at the edge of the garden.

And I was forced to ask, was I really that terrible to live with? That even an iguana—sensing his chance at freedom—scurried away from me across the grass. He'd made it as far as the swing set in the Kus' backyard when I caught up with him. I snatched at his tail, and it whipped against my fingers like a knife, drawing blood. That stunned me into halting.

I needed a plan, which I attempted to formulate as I stood sucking on my throbbing fingers in the drizzle. St. Ignatius seized this opportunity to make some headway. He seemed to be deliberately aiming toward the wooded creek that separated the small grouping of bungalows where I lived from Kohala. Oh, Iggy, not there, I thought. My throat constricted in panic. Plan be damned, I ran after him so fast it made my arms flail. I was at his side by the time he reached the edge of the grove.

It was only a few acres at best, and it was fairly sparse the first fifty feet or so. But then the foliage thickened, and an iguana—especially one who, it was true, may have been a bit neglected in recent weeks—could disappear quite effectively. Probably even lead a satisfying life, if he hadn't been spoon-fed pet-store iguana food by humans all his cushy existence.

He was belly-deep in mud, and he stared defiantly up at me with those golf-ball eyes of his. I lowered myself to a crouch, slowly, no sudden movements. "That's a good iguana." I got on all fours, and the coolness of the mud seeped through the knees of my khakis. Slowly, I slid one hand halfway to him, letting it linger in the sludge. The in-and-out motion of his gills was his only sign of life. Then I saw him twitch, and before I knew it, he used my arm like a bridge to dart up and over the top of me, his claws scraping against my forehead and down my back. I jumped to throw him off, and he raced into the woods.

Much swearing ensued, all of it mine. I pulled myself to my feet and chased after my renegade housepet. He was climbing his way over fallen logs, sloshing his low-rider body with an amazing determination through the stew of twigs and mud. Oh, how I rued that I still had the tender feet of a *haole*.

St. Ignatius made his way to the edge of a creek, which ran the length of the grove until it merged into a swamp near the base of Kohala. It was overflowing from the rain, so it was more like a river, and even the ground near it was soaked to the point of quicksand. My iguana was in his element, and I was far from mine. Then, miraculously, when he had the chance to outrun me for good, he crawled along a branch to a rock in the middle of the creek, and stopped. Just like that.

I tiptoed closer, afraid to breathe but knowing I was huffing from the stress. The creek here was easily six feet across. The water was black with kicked-up mud, and I wasn't eager to step a blind toe in. Yet I thought, if I could make it over to St. Ignatius, pet him on his tender spot below his chest, he'd be lulled into coming home. Dante had put him to sleep many a night doing just that.

The water rushed at quite a clip. I poked a foot into the creek. My leg was submerged to the knee and still hadn't hit bottom. I sat on the edge of the creek and, unable to identify other options, slid both legs in. When I stood I was hip-deep, and close enough to Iggy that I could have reached over and snatched him up had I been dumb enough to repeat that mistake. The water pushed at my back. I maintained eye contact with Iggy, my arms up to keep them out of the water as if I were surrendering.

Then something struck me hard in the back. I grunted from the insult of pain, and saw the water carry past me what it was that had caused it—a two-by-four plank floating down the creek. And I was hit again. This time, I turned around just in time to watch helplessly as the edge of a home-made raft pushed me in the stomach and knocked me down into the water.

I struggled to regain my balance, grabbing onto the stick Iggy had crawled across. It collapsed from the weight of my grasp, sending me plunging down again, this time banging my head against the rock. My brain reeled, and I sucked water. The water was bleeding pink.

I dragged myself to the edge of the creek and collapsed facedown in the slime, my legs dangling in the creek. A rivulet of water wound into my nose, but I lacked the will to move my face. Water and mud were pooling, blocking my air, but a searing pain in my head commanded all my strength.

It had happened so fast. I could taste dirt against the back of my throat, and I wondered where was my survival instinct. Random images flashed before my eyes . . . my son . . . friends . . . my marriage. But—and here's the pisser—of the hundreds of people and events in my life I'd have thought significant, as it turned out, all my mind's eye would focus on at such a moment was the one, the only, the incomparable Davy Jones, yes, of the famed Monkees.

IT WAS THE fall of 1969; I was seven and in the throes of dealing with breasts. Not mine, for crying out loud—did I not mention that I was seven? They were Sandra's, and no more than bumps, really, but apparently enough for my mom to take her (without me!) to the Lemon Frog department at Sears to buy a bra, and then to the mall for a frozen Coke.

So just like that I'd lost my sister and got only breasts and attitude as a replacement, and nothing seemed like it could ever be right again until my dad came home with the tickets.

Excuse me, The Tickets.

A Tea with Teen Dream Davy Jones was the event. An employee of my dad's at GM had given him three tickets. Which meant my mom would have to stay home, a loss she seemed to be handling well, I mean, considering . . . *Davy Jones*.

My dad told us all this a week before the big day, and it was hard to do much of anything during the one hundred sixty-eight hours of waiting besides study The Tickets hanging on the refrigerator, bring in jealous tour groups of neighborhood kids to ogle at them, and listen to Sandra argue with my parents over what she should wear.

It was that word *tea*. It was throwing us all. My parents were thinking party frock. Sandra was thinking bellbottoms. Me, I was thinking about how my sister had spoken actual words to me in recent days and how much I hated tea—not that I'd ever had it, but it was obvious I wouldn't like it, and surely I was going to go thirsty.

The morning of the tea, I in fact drank glass after glass of Tang, just to be safe. Sandra, for her part, caved in and wore a dress—which she tucked into the waistband of her bellbottoms as soon as we got to the hall while my dad handed in The Tickets. I didn't know where people generally held teas, but if it was in large gymnasiums filled with cloth-covered tables, we were in business.

"Ladies, shall we?" My dad turned to face us and then held his arms curved at his sides, like a superhero standing at the ready. It was a prompt for us to tuck our arms into his and walk with him, which we did.

I may have been a kid, but I was well aware that my dad was a handsome man: tall, that Pepsodent smile, and what my mom called a snappy dresser. In fact, she'd teased him that morning because he'd put on a new sport coat—had to cut the tags off and everything. She'd said, "Who are we trying to impress?" but he'd replied that he was simply trying to attire himself in a way befitting his lovely dates.

By the time we made it into the showroom, most people were seated—nearly all girls with their moms, as far as I could make out at a glance. I did a quick count, estimating being a hobby of mine, and one of the reasons I'd skipped a grade. "There are one hundred and fifty girls and eighty adults here, plus seventeen boys," I announced. Sandra grunted in annoyance and told me to shut up, which I countered with, "No, you shut up."

My dad, as usual, caught none of it and instead pointed to a table in the room's center. "That's us," he said. Other people already filled all the seats but three. The ones that remained faced away from the stage.

As we pulled out our chairs, Sandra grumbled, "Oh, *great*, now we can't *see*." That show of sarcasm was all it took to shame a woman into organizing a great switching of seats so we could catch what was happening on stage. Which at this point was zero. No Davy Jones in sight, although there was an empty table up there I assumed was for him. Truth was, I was too busy being relieved to see pitchers of pop instead of a teapot before me to notice much else.

I poured three glasses, taking care not to spill on my dress. When I handed one to my dad, he said, "Thanks, Twiggy." That's what he'd taken to calling me for the past few days, ever since I'd gotten my shoulder-length hair chopped into a pixie. I was no longer anything but that hairdo and eyes and bony arms and legs. The same lady who'd switched chairs overheard and remarked that, my, my, I *did* look like the famous model.

Sandra said, "That's not a nickname—it's her real name, from birth." She turned to me, eyes like fried eggs, skittish from her lie.

"Nuh-*uh*, it is not," one of the girls at the table protested.

My dad said, his face wistful, "Her mother and I just loved that name, and here all these years we'd thought she was the only one."

"Well, I'll be darned," a woman remarked, sucked in by my father's ruse.

Sandra took the other pop I'd poured and said, "Thank you, *Twiggy, dear.*" A waiter to my relief set a platter of cookies and sandwiches on the table, which diverted attention from me. I smoothed my skirt as best as I could. The dress was white with lime green trim and a frog applique on the front. But what made it so—well, *groovy*—was that the skirt part was clear vinyl, completely see-through, like a picnic table cloth. Underneath were matching shorts. It was just the sort of thing a British model might wear, I thought, although how they sat in apparel so uncomfortably stiff, I couldn't have said.

More than an hour passed. Just when we began to wonder if this were in fact some elaborate hoax to torment love-struck girls, the lights dimmed. A voice on the loudspeaker shouted, "Here he is—the one, the only, the incomparable . . . Davy Jones!" And then out onto the stage he strutted. He didn't look any different from *The Monkees* show: the long hair, the dimply smile, and—taking into consideration the perspective from our distance from the stage—about four inches high, just like on TV.

IMMEDIATELY, THE CHANTING was replaced with high-pitched screams, the nearest of which was directly in my ear from Sandra.

Davy sang three songs along to taped music: "Daydream Believer," "Valleri," and some other song I didn't know that he said was off his new album, available soon. Tears were flooding down my sister's face. When I asked her if she was sad, she snuffled, "I just love him so much." I did, too, I thought, in a manner less moist, but I believed no less significant.

After his performance, Davy took a seat on stage. An announcer told us that we'd be brought up table by table to meet him and get an autographed photo. After that point, bodies blocked the view of Davy, so there wasn't much to watch, besides an occasional faint or a girl being carted away hysterical, but cartoons would have been better.

It was at least a half hour before a man came to tell us it was our turn. Sandra grabbed my hand as we walked toward the stage. "I wrote a poem for him," she said. "When I get up there, I'm going to say it. It's how he'll remember me forever."

I had nothing for Davy, nor had Sandra tipped me off before this moment that I should have. Dang. I would be unremembered. "What's your poem?"

"No way. You'll steal it."

"I will not. Just tell me." We were making our way up the steps onto the stage.

"Oh, gosh, we're here," Sandra said shakily. "I can almost see him."

I stood on tiptoes, which didn't make any difference. "It'll help if you practice the poem on me."

"Okay, but it's my poem. It's how he'll remember me. This will be the absolute most important moment of my life. You got it?" She paused for effect, and then continued. "There once was a man named Davy. Who really drove the girls crazy. He sang like a star. And could play the guitar—" Before she finished, the people in front of us left, and we found ourselves so close to Davy Jones that he was, at last, actual size. Sandra's recitation stopped cold.

"Davy and crazy don't really rhyme," I said.

My dad guided us forward, and there I was. Separated by nothing but a table from the love of my life, his head down to sign a head shot. All I could see at first was the perfect line of his part dividing his hair into two equal sides. Then he looked up to hand us our photos. And—*oh!*—he was so pink and glowy and shiny. I wanted to poke at him. I didn't know why, but to see him reminded me of blowing bubbles—how they'd shimmer in the sun, floating away as if running, while you'd chase at them, laughing, senselessly trying to burst what you find so very beautiful.

"Hello, ladies. Nice to meet you."

Sandra made a squeaking noise, but that was it. My dad filled the gap by saying, "My girls are your most devoted fans."

Sandra's hands were over her mouth and she started crying so hard she made a moaning noise. Davy seemed unaffected by this, but I was scandalized. "Sandra," I said, "Your poem." She kept crying.

I looked at Davy, then back at Sandra. I didn't know what to do. "The poem," I urged. "Say the *poem!*" Nothing from Sandra. A man asked us to please move it along.

Then it came to me. I took a deep breath and pointed my arms dramatically toward Sandra—Carol Merrill showcasing what was behind curtain number one. "This is my sister's poem!" I shouted so loudly it made both Davy and my dad jump.

"There once was a man named Davy! Who, um . . ." I'd only heard the poem once, and was uncertain. "Who always drove everybody crazy!" My voice rose louder, and I could feel Sandra pinching my elbow. I didn't know if it meant stop or go, so I kept going. "He sang like a star! And could play the guitar!—"

I stopped. Sandra hadn't told me the last line. Someone snarled, "Give the rest of us a turn."

My dad leaned down and gently said, "Honey, we need to get going. That was a nice poem."

Davy's attention had already shifted to the girls waiting behind us, and the unfinished verse dangled limply in the air. I strained to come up with one more line. That's when I felt it—the warm wetness. I was peeing. Not just a trickle, but urinating full force, so hard I couldn't stop. All that Tang and pop and I hadn't gone to the bathroom once. Pee was soaking my shorts, a gushing river down my legs, forming a puddle on the floor at my feet. I needed one more line. Something that rhymed with Davy or crazy.

My dad nudged me so I'd move and let others have their turn, but I glued my feet to the ground. Sandra must have noticed, because she grabbed my dad's face to hers and said something in his ear. A man in a suit leaned over to ask us please to move along. My dad looked panicked. Then he removed his sport coat and dropped it onto the floor. He used his foot to mop up the puddle. "No problem," he said to the man, resuming his usual calm and then leaned down to pick up his coat. "I needed to get my coat I dropped."

Sandra held our autographed photos in front of the wet spot on my shorts, visible through the vinyl skirt. I let them usher me across the stage and down the stairs to the main floor. My shoes made a wet *squish-squish*ing noise.

Davy was signing the next batch of photos. "And he loves to eat pickles with gravy!" I yelled, but he didn't hear me. I said it again, more loudly, but my voice was lost in the din of piped-in music, and girls crying, and my dad chuckling, telling me that was a good one.

"Actually," Sandra said, finally finding her voice as we hit the harsh sunlight outside the building, "It's 'And I know that we'll meet again some day.' " Which, I hadn't the heart to tell her, didn't rhyme nearly so well.

I DIDN'T WAKE up as much as come to. And I wasn't seven. I was thirty-seven, and covered in mud, but nonetheless alive, having had the sense while fighting for consciousness to shift my head to breathe. St. Ignatius was gone from the rock—the slimy bastard had clearly stalked away and left me for dead. With a groan I pulled myself up from the creek and staggered, defeated, out of the woods and back to my house.

The rain had ceased. Morna and Regatta sat on my back porch, St. Ignatius perched between them. I could only imagine the sight I must have been, emerging like a creature from the swamp, blood smeared on my face, mud caking my body and matting down my hair. Then again, maybe I didn't look all that terrible. They barely bothered to glance at me as I approached.

"I assume you two have introduced yourselves," I said.

By way of an answer, Regatta lifted a hand, although her expression remained impassive. I opened the screen door and shooed St. Ignatius inside. I'd deal with him later. I seated myself in his space. Morna finally took enough notice of me to say, "Were you mountain biking? Where's your bike?"

"I wasn't biking. I wasn't having any kind of fun," I whined. "I was . . . oh, never mind." I was distracted by Regatta's hand, which was still poised in the air. "What are you—?" Then I saw it. On the finger next to her pinky. The diamond ring. And by a quick estimate, a solid carat, yet she was holding it up as though she were showing me a dead cat.

I ignored all signals from her body language and did precisely what a best friend is supposed to do at such a moment, regardless of how crappy she may be feeling. I squealed. I squealed that girly, screamy kind of squeal that every female manual ever written or imagined instructs a friend to do when she sees a diamond upon another's hand. It doesn't matter if you hate the guy, or don't know the guy, or are terrified that you're about to lose your best friend just when you most need a single buddy. "Ted proposed! Reggie, I can't believe it! Oh, my Gaaaaaaaawd!"

My forced hysteria upturned her mouth, and I threw my arms around her in a hug mixed with rain and dirt and blood, which it took her only a moment to notice. "Ew, let go! What happened to you? You're disgusting."

"And you're engaged," I said, pulling away. "Why aren't you excited?" I turned to Morna, whom I trusted had already obtained the skinny on the situation. "Why isn't she excited?"

Morna gave me that all-knowing smile of hers, the Morna Lisa grin, but didn't answer my question. Instead, she pulled my head toward hers and examined my forehead. "It appears to be a surface wound. These head injuries look worse than they are. Nothing to be concerned about. Regatta, do you think you could get a wet cloth and some bandages?"

"They're in the hall closet," I said. "And I really am excited for you, Reg. What's with the despondency? I thought this was what you wanted."

She disappeared into the house, giving me only a sigh as an answer. Morna said, "I have just the thing this circumstance calls for." She pilfered through a canvas sack at her side.

Regatta returned with a robe. I stripped down and put it on, hesitating briefly because I felt strange getting naked in my backyard in front of my lawyer. It seemed so unprofessional. Then as Regatta set to work dabbing a washcloth at my face, Morna opened a baggie of weed and proceeded to roll a fat joint, balancing my neighbor's unopened copy of the *Bee* on her knees as a table. My nudity no longer seemed an issue.

"So," I said, "Are we celebrating or are we drowning our sorrows?"

"Both," Regatta said.

Morna lit the joint and passed it to me. I couldn't remember the last time I'd gotten high, but I suspected it was B.K., Before Kam. I'd been pregnant so soon, then nursing, then too busy chasing around a toddler while Kam got stoned to do much partying myself. I took a drag and then immediately went into the coughing fit that was a dead giveaway I was never much of a stoner chick to begin with.

"Don't suck so hard," Morna said. "Take it in gently, like the scent of a delicious incense." Too embarrassed to try again with Morna reviewing my technique, I handed it to Regatta. She handled herself more expertly and even managed to tape a bandage to my head while she took a hit off the joint.

We sat on my steps, smoking and not saying much of anything, except the occasional comment from me that I wasn't feeling the remotest bit high.

"It'll kick in," Morna said.

It wasn't until the joint had burnt itself down nearly halfway that Regatta said, "Ted's moving to Boston. That's why he proposed. He wants me to go with him."

"Oh," I said.

"Is that all you have to say? Oh?"

"I was going to say, 'Oh, shit,' but I'm trying to be supportive." I hesitated, then said, "Are you going?"

"You bet I'm going. I've been waiting for this all my life. I want the whole dream. The house, the husband, the two point five kids, and here's my chance to have it. I'm not getting any younger, you know. I'm thirty-two."

"Tick, tick," I said.

"I love Ted." It was a line I would have delivered defensively, but she said it as a simple fact.

"It's just that you don't seem excited."

"I'm scared to death." Her voice sounded stilted, as though she were beginning to have a hard time squeezing words out. "And I'm not so stupid that I don't realize the proposal probably wouldn't have come if he weren't leaving. At least not yet."

I saw Morna lick her fingers and squeeze the flame from the tip of the joint. "Ladies, I need you to be cool. I believe we have an ex-husband-to-be approaching."

"Huh?" Regatta said, but as she said it, I heard the unmistakable slapping of flip-flops against flesh. Kam. He'd come around the side of the house.

"Here you are," he said, huffing. "Dante's in the car. He's been crying for that stupid doll of his."

Luckily, Morna's pot was no good. I was sober as a judge. "I told you to take it. He's attached to it."

Kam paused and looked around as if hearing a strange sound. "Is that dope I smell?"

Morna stood and held out her hand. "You must be Kam. I'm Morna Templeton, Keeley's attorney. What a pleasure it is to have a chance to meet you."

I ran inside, tore about Dante's room searching for the doll, and thrust it into Kam's hands when I returned. He and Morna were talking surfing techniques. She was squatting down, balancing on an imaginary board. He was adjusting her arms in a T at her sides. "It's all lower balance," he explained. "People think it's strength, but it's balance."

"You shouldn't leave Dante alone," I said.

He took off, but not without giving a last curious glance back, perhaps hoping to catch me pulling a bong out from behind the bushes.

When we heard his truck drive away, Morna relit the joint. Regatta laughed in relief. "I've been less scared about getting busted by my mom."

"Is it bad that he noticed?" I asked Morna. "I'm already fighting that unfit mother thing. All I need is to be labeled a pothead, too. Do you think he'll tell?"

"Oh, he'll tell," Morna said. "He'll tell Lee, Lee, and Lee. And what good will that do him? It would be a problem—let's say—if he'd called the police right now."

"The police . . . ," I said.

"He won't. He's too . . ." Her sentence dropped off so long, I started thinking maybe Morna was finally feeling the effects of the pot.

"Too what?"

"I can't put my finger on it. It involves a certain eagerness on his part to please you. That's good. My dear Keeley, that is very, very good." She took the burning joint from Regatta's hand and gave it to me. "Now we need to work on you."

"Me? What's wrong with me?"

"That Kam, he sure is a looker, isn't he?"

"Amen to that," Regatta said.

"And I can tell right off he's a decent man." She smoothed my hair. "Don't you feel bad about a thing. You chose well. And my goodness, the skin on him. Like a bar of milk chocolate."

"I married him for more than his looks, you know," I said, unable to keep the annoyance from my voice. How shallow did she think I was?

"Yes. We'd have an easier go of it if it were only about looks, I'm afraid."

"You see, Morna," Regatta attempted, speaking slowly to the point of nearly talking backward. "My friend Keeley and I are different that way. We both like things that are pretty, but I'm willing to let it end there. Enjoy the beauty of a man's skin, let myself take in his scent of salt and sweat and shampoo. Wrap myself up in the loveliness of his soul. Keeley here has to dissect everything. Pull out her microscope and get an up-close look. When you do that, a man's nothing but ingrown hair follicles and birthmarks."

"My life partner, Gregory—he has the most wonderful birthmark," Morna said.

"I didn't mean . . . anything . . . bad . . . about them," Regatta said, clearly embarrassed, not to mention wasted.

"Cherry wine. It runs over the bridge of his nose." Morna pulled a hemostat from her fanny pack and clipped it onto the stub of the joint. She drew on it once before passing it to Regatta. "He'd always hated it. But one day—we'd been together, oh, I don't know, a few weeks? We were at a coffee shop—this is before they became so trendy like they are now—and I kissed his birthmark. I couldn't keep my mouth off it. He'd tried pushing me away, but I wouldn't let him. After a while he relaxed. He told me he felt healed. The next thing you know, Gregory and I were back in the studio apartment I had at the time. I pulled out my equipment and tattooed a Band-Aid over that birthmark of his. Then we made incredible love there on the floor."

"You do tattoos?" I said.

"That had . . . to have . . . hurt," Regatta added.

"My point," Morna stated, patting my knee, "is that there is beauty in everyone—and it's up to us to decide just how much of others' beauty we have a place for within ourselves."

I thought about her story, and frowned. "How is that possibly your point?"

She stood and put out a hand to pull Regatta up. "Let's give Keeley some time to contemplate this. I'll give you a ride home. I rode over on Burrito, my sweet old mare. You, my dear, are in no condition to drive." Regatta was indeed looking a bit glazed. Morna gave me a hug. "I'll see you at the meeting."

After they'd left, I went inside and clicked on the TV in lieu of deep thinking. I was lucky enough to find men's professional bowling. It was apparently in slow motion, or maybe that dope was finally kicking in after all. At any rate, I watched mesmerized as a black ball rolled over and over, down the narrow alley toward the pins. I'd have sworn it took hours to make its final glide into them. I may have even gotten up, run to the bathroom, and assumed my spot again on the couch while the ball was still rolling. When it did finally hit, though, it body-checked the pins dead center, sending some falling face first, and others exploding into the air. And there they were: two pins left standing on either side of the alley. A split. They may as well have been separated by miles of empty space, so tricky was it going to be to pick up the spare. The second throw would have to tap one of the pins on its outermost edge and send it sliding into the other so they'd knock each other to the ground. In all my years of bowling, I'd never been able to do it.

The camera zoomed in to get the bowler's reaction. He was shaking his head as he made the walk of shame back with the measured movements of a spaceman navigating the moon's surface. He held a hand over the air blower in the ball return rack. His fingers were spread to catch the ball as it resurfaced from the bowels of the alley, and I detected an unlikely mix of defeat and determination on his face.

In retrospect, I wished I'd stuck around to find out what happened. But I was famished and left to get the half-bag of Doritos I remembered Dante had in his backpack. By the time I returned, the station had moved on to figure skating. Which as a sport I find graceful but, face it, really lacking the drama of bowling.

The phone rang, but I was screening because Brian Boitano was doing this amazingly stupid routine in a cowboy outfit. My ears perked when I heard it was Ian on the line. As I listened to his voice rattle, I debated if I was too stoned to talk to him. I decided that perhaps I was finally stoned enough. Right before he said his good-byes—that he feared if he kept bothering me he'd be labeled a stalker—I picked up the phone. "Hello, Ian? It's me, Keeley."

And for a man who'd been talking a mile a minute only seconds before, he certainly got quiet fast.

7

"ARE YOU THERE?" I asked. He was silent so long, I began to wonder if he'd dropped the phone.

"Yes, yes, I'm sorry. It's a bit of a surprise to hear your voice—but a pleasant one, I might add." He was a fast talker, literally, which reminded me of Morna's instructions to get his phone number and get off the phone. Especially now that Leminski had pressed charges. It all felt so *Dragnet.* I didn't want to screw up.

"This will have to be brief. It's my lawyer who wants to talk to you. She told me to get your number." I hoped I didn't sound stoned. I didn't feel the dope anymore. It was as though the phone's ringer had straightened me. As a matter of fact, I was quite pleased with the perfunctory nature of my reply.

Again, there was silence on the other end of the line, then, "Please give me the chance to explain to you what—"

"No offense, but I don't think I should talk to you."

A quick sigh. "Then perhaps you could at least listen? I believe I can solve everything, but not if we involve lawyers. You see, my idea is to—"

"I shouldn't be listening to any ideas." Did he think I was born yesterday? "I just need your phone number."

"Please, then, answer me this. If your lawyer wanted to speak with me that badly, don't you think she would have looked me up herself? I'm not that difficult to find. I'm known in the art business."

Huh. Maybe I was still high. That made a strange sort of sense. Especially when I considered that my lawyer was Morna, and I never understood half the time what she was up to anyway.

My lack of reaction spurred him to continue. "You and I both know this situation has gone too far, that the police should never have been brought in, that charges should have never been filed. We don't need to complicate it further with lawyers. Give me the chance to set it right."

"Why? Why do you care?"

"I . . . I prefer not to say, other than Leminski is my client. I feel a responsibility."

"If anything, I'd think you'd feel a loyalty to him. Which again leaves me wondering why you say you want to help me." I admit, this last comment was fishing. Although I wasn't even sure what I'd hoped he'd say.

"Leminski and I go way back. And as for you and me—" He hesitated, then said, "Look, I realize you have no reason to do so, but I'm going to ask you to put your faith in me."

"I don't know. . . ."

"Just one chance. If I can't mend things, then bring on your lawyer."

"I'll have to at least tell her about this."

"Tell her. But let's start with this between the two of us. I believe I can finish it there, as well. I'll even come your way. I could stop by—say, Saturday?"

"Sunday's better." It just came out of my mouth like that. *Sunday's better,* the equivalent of *Yes, why sure, no problem, so what if you and your client have humiliated me and put my custody battle in jeopardy with accusations of unfit motherhood and may be costing me thousands of dollars for what was an innocent mistake, I trust you implicitly.* But the strange truth was, I did.

"Sunday it is. Three o'clock?"

"You'd better make it two—I have plans at three." And I did. I planned to say hello to Kam as he brought Dante back from his visitation.

As I hung up, I couldn't believe I'd agreed to his scheme. Morna was going to throttle me.

Turned out I was too occupied the next few days to give so much as a thought to lawyers or visits from art reps or much of anything else.

I had been out, as one could often find me, taking historical photos of some of the craters around Kohala, when I noticed the yellow crystals forming around the rim of some ground vents, like salt on the edge of a margarita glass. I'd nearly missed it entirely. Plants had covered most of what had once been barren lava rock. It was only because I was crawling around—trying to get a few moody close-up shots to give that Ansel Adams a run for his money—that the change in color even caught my attention.

I proceeded to shoot the entire roll, making sure to capture images of the nearby dying grass, trembling so much from excitement that I was certain I was blurring the photos. Then I scraped some of the crystal into a baggie, surprised when the earth felt cool to the touch. I'd expected it would be hot, but then again, I was getting ahead of myself.

The moment I got back to the office, I dialed Skipland Ford—who went by the name of Skipper—a volcanologist I'd briefly worked with on an internship back in the eighties. I'd heard he was posted at the Volcanoes National Park on the other side of the island, part of the team that monitored Mauna Loa and Kilauea and dealt with the throngs of tourists eager to catch a glimpse of the active volcanoes. He and I had lost touch right around the time I took the job at HAG. He claimed he was busy, but I knew that he didn't want to be seen hanging with someone studying an extinct volcano. The caste system among geologists could rival the British monarchy, and I was but a step above a scullery maid.

"Skipper? Long time no talk, eh?" I'd hoped to warm him up with a bit of reminiscing, but I couldn't remember a thing about him, other than that he had a serious Corn Nuts habit—like five packs a day. I cut to the chase, describing in glorious detail what I'd seen that morning: the yellowed crystals, the dying grass nearby.

"Yeah, it's been a hot summer, my grass looks like shit, too," he said. "I've been thinking of calling that ChemLawn, though I hear they're pretty pricey."

I proceeded as if he and I were actually talking about the same thing. "I'm assuming it must be sulfur causing all this."

"Did you actually notice a sulfur smell?"

"Well, no," I hedged. "I happen to be fighting a head cold. But the yellowed crystals. What could that possibly indicate *but* sulfur?"

"And you have pictures, you say? Of the discoloring?"

"I only had black-and-white film on me," I mumbled, growing more embarrassed by the second, and figuring it best not to mention how I'd originally been hoping to get an arty shot that would make a nice enlargement for that bare space over my dresser. Nothing had changed. He didn't want anything to do with me or my mountain. As a last-ditch effort, I mentioned the seismic activity I'd been recording. "I'm thinking we have sulfuric gases . . . movement. Something is definitely happening over here."

"It could be run-off from our volcanoes," he said in a tone that sounded suspiciously like bragging. "They've been showing quite a bit of activity lately. But, hey, go ahead and run more tests. Let me know if you find anything."

If I had any pride left, I swallowed it to say, "That's why I'm calling. I was hoping you guys might want to get involved. This has been a historic study I've been conducting. I don't have much in the line of equipment. It's just been me here"—and I attempted a breezy tone—"all by my lonesome."

"Gee, Keeley . . . I'm not sure what we can do. We've been so swamped. You know how that darned Kilauea just buried Crater Rim Drive again. It's all we can do to keep up with tracking the lava flow. And the tourists! They're worse than gnats!" Then he yelled away from the mouthpiece, "What? An urgent call for me, you say? I'll be right there!"

"That's fine," I grumbled, not fooled for an instant, "I'll let you go. I guess I'd hoped, for old times' sake—"

"Tell you what. Let me take a look around and see if I can sneak you some equipment. There must be an old tiltmeter or two around here collecting dust."

I spent the rest of the week driving around the mountain, my camera bag loaded with color film of every ASA imaginable, shooting more photos than did all the tourists at Skipper's park combined.

ON SUNDAY, it took me half the morning to come up with an outfit that didn't look like I'd spent half the morning coming up with it. I'd gotten the okay from Morna to go ahead with my tryst with Ian—in fact, she acted as if she didn't recall telling me in the first place that she wanted to do the talking. After destroying my closet in the search, I decided that a denim skirt and T-shirt said, *Yes, I'm a babe, but not on account of the likes of you,* which was the effect I was going for. Had I known the sight that would greet me when I opened the door after hearing the doorbell ring—a half hour late at that—I might not have gone to such trouble.

"Is this a joke?" I said. Standing before me was Ian, scrubbed, neat, his hands clasped behind his back. Next to him, short and oily as ever, was Leminski.

"Keeley," Ian said with the giddy grin of a boy with a surprise, like a frog in his pocket. "You're looking lovely as always. Forgive us for being late, but I was having a rough time getting Jim moving. You do remember Jim? Jim Leminski? Well, yes, of course you do."

Leminski gave me a "hey." In his arms he held what appeared to be a marble block, about a foot tall, the top of which was covered with a cloth napkin.

I turned my attention to Ian. "I was expecting only you."

"Yes, and I hope you'll bear with me. I promised to set things right. My friend Leminski here has something to say to you. Do you think we could come in?"

"Yeah, and soon," Leminski grunted. "This thing weighs a ton."

I stepped aside and allowed Leminski to waddle past me and set the block down with a thud on the kitchen table still in my living room. Ian followed, pausing to take one of my hands in his for a moment and give me the lightest of kisses on the cheek, a gesture I found incredibly nervy. And if I hadn't been distracted by the smell of his aftershave and something vaguely minty, I'd have given him a piece of my mind.

Then he whispered near my ear, "Please go along with this. Trust me. I'm on your side."

I followed him to the table where Leminski had already pulled up a chair. I propped myself against the edge of the table, arms folded, my trust factor seriously jeopardized by the presence of the man whose fist had been in my bra uninvited.

Ian cleared his throat to signal that he was ready to begin, or maybe his throat just needed clearing. "If all goes well, this won't take any time."

"You need to say you're sorry," Leminski cut in.

Ian squeezed his eyes shut in apparent frustration. "Could you allow me to handle this?" His hand massaged the back of his neck. "Keeley, quite a bit has happened of which you're not aware. Certain—how shall I say it?—certain deals have taken place which greatly unburden your case. Based on these . . . occurrences . . . Mr. Leminski has agreed to drop all charges. He has only one request of you—"

Leminski again interrupted, "You need to say you're sorry for stealing my art."

"I didn't steal it."

"For ruining it, then."

"Fine. I'm sorry."

Apparently even a sarcastic apology sufficed for Leminski, because he slapped his knees and said, "No problem."

"Excuse me?" I said. "That's it? Charges dropped?"

"We'll see to it that they're rescinded first thing in the morning," Ian said.

"And you're off scot-free," Leminski added. "So hey," and his glance crawled up me, "no hard feelings between us, eh?"

I just looked at him, not dignifying his comment with an expression of any kind. "What's the catch?" Leminski hardly struck me as the benevolent type.

"No catch. Everybody's happy. Let's just say that I had"—and Leminski stopped to lean against the chair back, cross his arms, and nod toward Ian—"a buyer for the piece on, how might we put it? an as-is basis." He added, "A very generous buyer," which made Ian lower his brows at him. "Yeah, well anyway, that's the deal. Ian here bought it. You're off the hook."

"You bought it?" I said. "For how much?"

"It doesn't matter. I was glad to do it."

"Hey," Leminski said. "He got a bargain . . . considering."

"Considering? . . ." I prodded.

"This." Leminski grunted from the effort of getting up and moving the two feet over to the marble block. "I know you're a fan of my work." He leaned conspiratorially toward me, which made me lean backward in revulsion. "Hell, you wanted it so bad you stole it. Oh, excuse me, you stole it . . . *on accident*. So Gardiner here sweetened the deal. Said you absolutely had to have this—"

Leminski lifted the napkin with a flourish. There atop the marble block sat a perfect replica of *Vulva in Bloom*. I couldn't have been more horrified if he'd brought me the head of the security guard on a platter.

Ian must have paid a fortune to get this sort of performance out of Leminski. It was pitiful to picture him plotting to deliver the perfect gift, the gift that would make it all better. Only to get it so dreadfully wrong.

"Will you look at that," I said. Ian's eyes were dancing. I almost felt bad for the guy. "Thanks. I don't know what to say."

"Yeah, yeah," Leminski said, heading for the door. "You know, I don't usually do the same art twice. I don't care how much dough Mr. Moneybags here throws at me. And believe me, he threw some dough. Of course, a guy can play the high roller when he comes from money, if you know what I mean," and he rubbed his fingers together to indicate, I guessed, the presence of cash.

"Leminski," Ian said, his voice a warning.

Leminski ignored him and continued, "But, then I say to myself, what the hell, 'cause I'm thinking you're a tasty little—"

"That's *enough*," Ian said firmly. "I suggest that you shut up—or leave."

"Whatever," he said, and hiked up his drooping slacks before giving the door a slam on his way out.

Now it was just Ian, the vulva, and me. "I'm sorry about him," Ian said. Then he tipped his head toward the origami. "Something, isn't it?"

I avoided the question by heading to the kitchen and opening the refrigerator. I grabbed a couple Diet Cokes. "It certainly is," I remarked when I returned, an answer that seemed to delight him. I set the sodas on the table.

"It was clear how much you loved the piece. It's not really my style. I prefer the more traditional origami." He picked up the so-called art and took a seat on the arm of my couch. I could tell he was searching for the right words. He absently stroked the paper. "But I knew how badly you wanted this."

It was tempting to give him a droll, gosh, you shouldn't have, but I found myself flattered by all this. There was a part of me—I guessed it to be my beaten ego—that hoped he was inspired by something more than mere professional duty.

I asked a leading, "So why did you do it?"

"Do what? Come here?"

"Everything—paying off Leminski, buying me this, um . . . this."

"Ah, yes . . ." Ian's attention seemed to shift away as his fingers absently caressed the leaves. They slid coolly along the paper as they circled inward toward the delicate folds of the blossom. "Do you perchance believe in fate?"

"I guess." That was all I said. I was watching his hands. Here was a man familiar with the feel of fine paper. A man who undoubtedly could name a fiber just by twisting it between his fingertips. A man, alas, without a clue that he was at that moment fondling a vulva in front of me. I held back a smirk. His oblivion was downright charming. "I can't say fate has always been kind to me."

"It's silly, I know. But I can't shake the feeling that meeting you was no mere accident."

"Really. Why do you say that?" I was transfixed by his fingers as he toyed with the petals, one by one. His movements were so smooth, so rhythmic, it was almost mesmerizing.

"A feeling, I suppose."

I watched as his finger probed beneath the folds of the blossom, then out, then slid in again. "If it makes you feel any better, I know exactly what you mean. Life seems to just happen to me, as if there's some big plan that I have no say in." I moved closer—near enough that my hip brushed his knee. I could feel the warmth of his body through my skirt.

"That's it precisely. How fate steps in. I nearly didn't go to the fair, and I felt positively absurd in that dunking booth. Then along you come. So determined to win that prize, and yet, there was something else. Even tossing that ball in the air, you seemed so . . . so vulnerable."

His touch slid across the small bump at the blossom's center, and I thought, *Gentle, now . . . gentle . . .*

"I was," I said.

"Then, of course," and he smiled to himself, "You dunked me."

"Girls will be girls."

"Thankfully. Naturally, I had to chase you down— to get a few pointers on the art of throwing."

"Really? I thought it was to impress me with how you hobnob with celebrities.

"Yes, well, that . . ."

"Of all people for you to know"—and it seemed that the neighborhood noises hushed along with my voice—"Davy Jones. You offering to help me out like that, take me to meet him, it meant so much. You just can't begin to know . . ."

And was I imagining it, or did his hands move more urgently? He ran a finger over the top of the bump, and over, and over again.

"I merely wanted to help you."

It went back to the petals, then to the bump, then the petals, bump, petals . . . bump . . . petals . . .

"You did help me. Today."

I fought to keep my hips from moving in rhythm with him, so lulled was I by his soft voice, by his kind intentions, by his hands moving so smoothly over those petals . . . that bump.

"Perhaps some day I can help you get what you need."

"Perhaps. Some day." It felt as though everything in the room had dissipated but his hands, and the precise spot where I could feel his body touching mine, and the sound of fingers brushing against paper that was somehow amplified in my ears.

"It was only that I saw you and wondered if—" His movements paused along with his words. I ached to reach out and place my own hand on top of his, to make him continue, to direct his touch along the flower.

"You wondered if . . . what?"

And with that the spell dissolved. Something snapped him back from wherever he'd wandered. "Oh, nothing." He set the origami on the table. "I have something else for you." He pulled a wrapped package from his shirt pocket. His enthusiasm reminded me of Dante's, when he would spend his last quarter to buy me a trinket from a gumball machine. "Open it."

I tore off the paper and then lifted the box lid. Inside was a Bic lighter, the cheap seventy-nine-cent variety.

"I'm sorry," I said. "I don't get it."

His gaze shifted from the lighter, over to *Vulva in Bloom,* and back to the lighter again. "I believe your exact words in describing this sort of art were—and I'm merely quoting here—*garbage*."

It was minutes before we were kneeling across from each other in the overgrown grass of my backyard. The origami rested on the marble block between us. I held the Bic in my hand. "Leminski would die if he knew I was destroying his art again."

"It will be our secret," he said. "Let's make a toast—quite literally, in this case. To setting free the past."

I set the Bic to the paper. "Shall I?"

"Oh, wait," he said, and he reached into his pants pocket to pull out a vial of powder. He opened it and sprinkled its contents over *Vulva in Bloom.* "Don't ask what it is. I've been told a potion to bring clarity, if you believe that sort of thing. I'm just hoping for a bit more of a blaze—for effect. As for the ingredients, well, you're the scientist."

"Whatever it is, I'm game." I touched the lighter to the paper. "Here goes nothing."

The flames slowly consumed the petals, and the paper blossom curled to ash. Until without warning it burst—straight up, a geyser of fire, rising high enough to mask Ian's face. All I saw were the purples and yellows of the flames tangling before me, like arms reaching toward the sky. It was dizzying, the heat pushing me back. Only as it started to subside was I able to again see Ian's cool gray eyes, which were fixed on me, his chest rising and falling in beat with my own. The scorching smoke caressed my thighs, licking its way up, under my T-shirt, against my skin.

In a hushed voice, Ian said, "Let me paint you."

"Excuse me?"

"Your portrait. I have a studio . . ."

He was being so intense, whereas my head felt light, a balloon tethered to my body by a string. "I thought you were an agent."

"Only by trade—what do you say?"

"I don't know anything about posing. . . ."

"Who's to say," he said, lifting a strand of my hair as if considering it, "that I know anything about painting?"

"I'm pretty busy. . . ."

"Think about it, will you? We could easily work out some sort of arrangement, I'm sure. That I could pay you back for your time in some way."

My mind flashed to Davy Jones, but I tucked the thought away, not wanting to implicate myself as the sort of person who would use someone to get what she wanted. Or for that matter, the sort of person who knew what it was that she wanted. "Maybe."

"I'll accept a maybe," he said. Then he pulled himself to his feet and extended an arm to help me up.

As we walked back into my living room, Ian turned to me. He was back to his collected self. "I'm curious. How *is* it that Leminski's art made it into your dress?"

And I swear, it was mostly to avoid having to answer that question that I reached up and pulled his face to me in a kiss. He drew back long enough to remark, "I have no idea what to make of you." Then his mouth again found mine; there were no further questions.

I for one would have been content to stay there all day. That is, if it hadn't been for the door flying open and Dante barreling in, followed by his father.

8

"HE SAID WHAT?" Morna leaned closer from one of the miniature chairs in the board room of Lee, Lee, and Lee. We were waiting for our noon meeting with Kam and his lawyers. The room was darkly paneled and filled with pricey-looking antiques. It would have been an intimidating setting, except that all the furniture appeared to be twenty percent smaller than standard scale. The mahogany table we sat at barely brushed my navel.

"I told you, I'm not sure. He sort of growled it at my shoulder, but I swear it sounded like 'I'll get you, whore.'"

"Let's not panic. For all we know, it could have been 'I'll get two more.'"

"Two more what?"

"My point," she said, examining a gavel on the table and giving it an experimental bang, "is that it's to be expected there will be a certain animosity between a man and woman in the midst of a divorce. The two of you have been polite to a fault until now. Clearly, the sight of you kissing another man caused Kam to remove the kid gloves."

"He's living with a woman. I only kissed a man."

"And how was it? The kiss."

I didn't have time to tell her that I wasn't sure. That it felt good, but kissing usually does, unless the guy slobbers, which Ian didn't. That, yes, I'd been daydreaming, remembering his lips on mine. But I could no longer even conjure up the image of his face. What came to mind more easily was the flash of pain that had run across Kam's. And the memory of *that* was as much a turn-on as any kiss.

With that, Kam walked into the room along with two men who could've been twins—except one had a comb-over, and the other had the decency to be balding.

"Lee and Lee," Morna said to me.

My stomach gave a nervous growl that was so loud I had to place my hands on top to quiet it. I hadn't seen Kam in closed-toe shoes since our wedding—and where did he get that suit? While the men shuffled the chairs about to take their seats across the table from us, I whispered in a sudden panic, "You never briefed me the other day. We only got stoned."

"It relaxed you, didn't it? Try now to recapture that feeling." She gave me the Morna Lisa grin again. "There, you've been briefed." Then she stood and reached over the table, and there were handshakes all around.

Kam glanced my way through narrowed eyes. Morna said, "Kam, I tried that wonderful tip you gave me about putting my weight on the balls of my feet, not the heels. I'm not up on the board yet, but I didn't do half bad for an old bag."

That made his expression lighten, but he corrected himself, resuming his petulant stare. Lee and Lee had clearly given him a more thorough briefing than I'd received: No fraternizing with the enemy.

Lee with the comb-over spoke first. "We'll get to the point. We received the terms on behalf of your client, Ms. Templeton."

"Oh, please, it's Morna."

"Yes, well, *Morna*, let us be clear. We cannot negotiate issues of child support to a mother for a child whom we believe should reside with the father."

Morna's face remained serene, and the same Lee continued. "Our client would, therefore, be the recipient of any support payment, not the one paying it. He deserves alimony, as well. For as your client knows, Mr. Kekuhi's career was—shall we say—put on the back burner to allow his wife to freely pursue her own."

"Mmm-hmm," was all Morna replied. She began digging through the same canvas sack she'd brought to my house. I was fearful she'd whip out a doobie and pass it around. It was worse. She dragged out a needlepoint project. It was a picture near completion of what appeared to be some Hawaiian goddess, which she began stitching on. I couldn't believe it. Twenty-five dollars an hour or no. My legal representation should have been doing something more than arts and crafts. I attempted to shoot her a look to make her put it away, but her head was dipped in concentration.

Something had to be done. I wasn't sure which would be less damaging: sitting here idly while Morna worked on a needlepoint, or snatching it from her grasp and whacking her across the head with it. So I sat—but far from idle, I busied myself gnawing on my cuticles and repeatedly crossing and uncrossing my legs.

The balding Lee said, "There is, you realize, the issue of your client's fitness as a mother. Her arrest. Her association with pornography. We've also reason to believe there may be a problem with drug use and possibly even promiscuous behavior in front of the child."

I made a noise in protest, but Morna rested her hand on the crook of my elbow in such a way there was no missing the *shh* intended. Kam stared out the window. The rat.

All was quiet, save for the gurgling of my stomach. Morna's only participation was to appear to concur, then resume her needlepointing.

One of the Lees walked over to the window, blocking Kam's view, posing dramatically with his hands clasped behind his back. "We are aware that the courts often unfairly side with the mother in cases such as this. But—and please don't regard this as a threat, but rather as a fact—our client has the stronger case. So much that we hope to limit any unnecessary counters to the terms we will be proposing. There's no sense in wasting these young peoples' money that could be better spent to benefit the child."

Morna's head was bent as she stitched some wording onto the canvas. It was requiring all her attention. I wasn't even sure she was listening.

Kam had slumped in his chair, his leg over his knee. Lee's and Lee's eyes met across the room. "Our client can give the boy a good home. You can't raise a child with a series of boyfriends coming in and out through a revolving door. What sort of upbringing is that?"

I was having trouble breathing. Morna's hand squeezed mine and then went back to her busywork.

Then Lee dealt the final blow. "Our client, Mr. Kekuhi, would provide the more suitable home, and you must realize that the court will recognize that. The boy would be with a man and his wife, which is by far a more appropriate environment than your client can provide."

My entire body was shaking. *"Wife?"*

Kam's head was turned so far away I could only see the side of it—his ear with the silver surfboard earring I'd once bought him.

"Yes," Lee said, and really, who cared which one, they were both chiseling bastards. "I'm sure you're aware that Mr. Kekuhi and his fiancée will be wed as soon as the divorce is final." He leaned his hands on the table to direct his words at me. "Mrs. Kekuhi, is it fair to deny your son the opportunity to live with a real family?"

Morna set her needlepoint on her lap and said a happy, "Well. Will you look at this? Done!"

That was it. I was firing her ass as soon as we left the room.

"Now that I think about it, Kam, I believe you'll really appreciate this work." He acknowledged her politely without actually focusing and then reverted his attention to Lee by the window. Morna continued, "It's a rendering of Our Goddess of the Highway. See? I've stitched her name right here, above the cars at her feet." Reluctantly, Kam looked again at the canvas she held up.

"Say, Kam," Morna said. "This is quite a coincidence. I'm just now remembering that your first date with Keeley was to see Our Goddess of the Highway. I must confess, Keeley couldn't resist telling me the story. It was so tender. How you knew then and there that the two of you would be married. Uh—" And she held her hand to her heart. "It was the most romantic thing I've ever heard."

Kam's eyes were brown—an odd thing for me to notice at that moment, but they just seemed so brown as they looked at the needlepoint. There's no other word for them.

One of the Lees said, "Very interesting, Ms. Templeton—"

"Morna," she corrected.

"Thank you, Morna. But let's stay focused on the—"

"Oh, focus, shmocus." She stuffed the needlepoint in her bag and pulled herself to her feet. "There are two decent people here. One of them is my client, and one is yours. What you gentlemen forget is that my client has been the primary caretaker for the boy—or to borrow the term her son Dante might use, she's Mommy. And a darned loving one." She walked to the door, and I followed at her heels like an iguana.

"We have significant reason to doubt her competence—," Lee began.

Morna interrupted, "You're being silly. Kam, honey, watch these Lee boys. You keep your balance."

And I was dying to see Kam's expression, but Morna nudged me out the door before I could.

KAM HADN'T SAID a word during the meeting—in sharp contrast to me. I'd said one. "Wife." It was echoing in my head as we left as clearly as if I'd shouted it into a cave. *Wife, wife, wife . . . ife . . . ife . . . ife.* We exited the building that contained the law offices of Lee, Lee, and Lee—come to think of it, where had the third Lee been during all this?—when Morna spotted the downtown shuttle and scurried toward it. "There's my ride!"

I ran after her. "Aren't we going to talk?"

I needed to know what it all meant. Did they really have a case against me? But Morna called out, "Sorry, dear, no time right now," and jumped onto the shuttle.

"Get back here! You hear me? Get back here!" I shouted to the shuttle as it ambled down the street, seeming to grow smaller as it carried Morna and all my answers into the distance.

"Don't sweat it," some old surfer dude said to me as he passed by, "These shuttles run every hour. You can grab the next one."

At that point, there was nothing left for me to do but go back to work, swallow my worries—and plot how I was going to replace Morna with a normal lawyer.

Even though I knew I wouldn't fire her. I pondered that as I drove back toward my office. My allegiance wasn't just due to her bargain-basement rates, either. There was something in the way that Morna got to Kam that intrigued me. I knew him well enough to be certain that he'd have dismissed the efforts of a more aggressive lawyer as easily as he'd shake water off a surfboard. Morna's brand of nice, however, seemed to slide unnoticed under his skin, making the muscles in his jaw jump without his even understanding why.

I glanced at my watch. 12:35. Nap time in Miss Mary Jo's prekindergarten class at Sea Sprite Elementary, only a few blocks away. What the heck, I thought, and steered the Jeep in the direction of the school. It was too late in the day to drive up Kohala and retrieve the seismometers anyway. Why go back to HAG to sit in a cubicle wishing I were somewhere else, when I could actually *be* somewhere else?

The pre-K students were housed in trailers separate from the main school building. I skipped signing in at the office and went straight to Dante's classroom. With great care, I opened the door and slipped in. The shades were drawn and the lights off. Mats were strewn in no particular pattern over the floor. Atop the mats lay the snoozing students of Miss Mary Jo. I was astounded at the collective noise eighteen sleeping children could create. It was like an oncoming train, all the breathing and snoring and mumbling.

Miss Mary Jo tiptoed over. "Dante didn't mention he was leaving early."

"I'm not taking him," I said. "I just stopped by."

"His grandma will be glad to hear that." When I looked at her quizzically, she pointed to a table in the corner. I was still adjusting to the darkness, but there was no doubt that was Kam's mom sitting there. She waved a pair of scissors at me by way of greeting. I'd forgotten that she volunteered once a week.

I hadn't identified Dante among the pile of sleeping bodies. I didn't want to deal with Kam's mom, but knew I had to at least say hello. I made my way over. "Hi, Mrs. Kekuhi," I said.

"Why you never call me Ma?"

I skipped the obvious response, that I'd never been invited to do so, and instead said, "It's nice of you to help out in Dante's class. He loves having you here."

She shuffled the letters she'd cut. "I like being here." I started to resume my search for Dante, when she said, "Hey, I have an idea. I'll have a special meal at my house. You'll come."

"Thank you," I said. "But I don't think Kam and I should be—"

"On Saturday. And I mean special just for us. Nobody else. I'll make your favorite dinner." She blinked at me twice. "What's your favorite dinner?"

But Saturday was when I'd invited Dante's school friends and some neighborhood kids over for a party. I was wise enough not to mention it. I had everything planned, and all I needed was Kam's mom to show and screw it up. "Saturday won't work," I said smoothly, avoiding even having to lie. She continued to look at me expectantly, so I told her I'd call her to talk about a time. I wanted to look for my son right now.

"Okay," she said, going back to her cutting. "You call me."

Dante was in the center of the pile, lying sideways across the mat so his head rested on the legs of the girl next to him. I climbed over the sea of bodies. I kneeled and gently lifted his head off the girl and onto his pillow. Then I pulled up his blanket and lay down next to him. I had to position myself on my side with my legs completely straight to avoid over-lapping onto the other mats. Dante rested his head against my neck, his leg slung over my thigh. I could feel a wet spot of drool forming in the indentation near my clavicle.

He was warm, with the dense breathing of the deeply asleep. His hair against my face smelled like sweaty dog, but not unpleasant. The girl I'd pulled Dante off sat up and looked at me through bleary eyes. "You're a mom," she said in a raspy voice.

I answered, "Uh-huh," because, yes, well, I was a mom, damn it.

"Are you supposed to be here?"

I indicated as best I could while lying down that I didn't know. Over my shoulder I saw her gather her pillow and blanket and scoot over so she was snuggled along my back. She had to have been lying as straight as I was, a toy soldier on its side, her arm slung over my waist. Her chin was sharp against me.

And it's funny how memories would haunt me at the oddest times. Kam and me, lying on the couch. I was hugely pregnant, my belly pro-truding over the edge, reading one of those parenting books that say things like "You'll recognize when your baby cries for food, and when he or she cries for attention," and I was thinking, No I won't.

In my mind, it was Kam's chin that probed into my shoulder. His arm rested on what used to be my waist, aiming the remote at the TV but not actually clicking it on. He reeked of paint. He'd gotten halfway through painting the nursery when he'd walked out, saw me waddling by and, well, wouldn't it be pleasant if we relaxed a bit?

"That paint's going to dry. You need to finish," I said.

"In a while."

"It's going to get blotchy."

"Don't worry. It'll get done." Even while arguing, he rubbed my belly. Big circles with the remote still clutched in his hand, around and around where Dante slept and hiccuped and grew inside me.

After a time, I grew weary of worrying about the paint. It was no use. I knew it was going to dry. That Kam would have to start from scratch tomorrow, buying new paint, doing extra coats to even it out. Or if not tomorrow, the next day, or the next, or between pushes while I was delivering the baby at the hospital, or while I was taking the baby out for a stroll, or for his first day of school. It would get done, or then again, maybe it wouldn't.

"I'm hungry," I said.

"Me, too. For pizza. Let's get a pizza."

The phone loomed across the room. It might as well have been across the Pacific. "Papa Ono's has a special. You should call them."

"Sure, bring me the phone."

"I'm fat. You get the phone."

And to the naked eye, we must have appeared to be utter slugs, lying there, doing nothing. Yet it was a skill I'd always envied in others, and with Kam, somehow, it came to me naturally—the ability to do nothing. I don't mean nothing with the TV on. Or while you're chatting or mentally planning the grocery list. I mean the sort of nothing that empties your head and unclenches your muscles. That lets you look at a ladybug passing by and think, *Look, a ladybug,* rather than, *Did I remember to turn off the burner?*

Kam chinned me—that is, dug his chin hard enough to propel me up. I ordered food before reclaiming my spot on the couch. Sure, a case could be made that he was a lazyass, but I knew it was more. That I'd somehow married a Zen master in surf jams. And although he was clearly not willing to teach me his secrets, he'd give them to me as a gift when he was near.

Miss Mary Jo opened the shades. In a gratingly cheerful voice, she sang a wake-up song.

"My birthday is in six days," Dante said when he woke up.

"I know."

"I'll be five."

I helped him put away his mat. He marched about to his fellow class-mates one by one and said, "This is my mom. She took a nap with me today."

One by one, they gaped at me in awe, making me realize that, by joining them on the mats, I'd gone where no mom had gone before.

A FEW NIGHTS later I was at the office, trying to squeeze in finishing three months of backlogged expense reports before heading to meet Ian for a dinner date. The flurry of form filling-out was a ruse, I knew. A shameless stall technique. *Why did I have to go and kiss him?* I scolded myself as I stapled a wad of receipts to the Employee Expense Reimbursement Form No. 2: Non-Food/Non-Travel. There'd be no turning back now. Ian wouldn't be hoping for a good-night kiss. He'd be expecting one. He was probably stopping at a liquor store buying Binaca at that very moment, and I had no one to blame but myself. There would be no coyly putting him off pretending that I was the type to move slowly at the beginning of a relationship. I'd blown my cover right around the time I shoved my tongue down his throat.

I'd managed to add up columns A through F, including the dates, funding source codes, and reasons for all expenditures, when Sandra's e-mail appeared, "What's new?"

ME: You're just in time. I need an excuse to get out of a date.
WANDERLUST: Try telling him something suddenly came up. What's the problem anyway? Wait, don't tell me. He's ugly.
ME: Actually, he's a real catch.
WANDERLUST: And you're tossing him back. Hmm. Could that mean that he's . . . too small?
ME: Wouldn't know. This will be our first official date . . . although I've already managed to kiss him. He's Kam all over again. Or if he's not, then I seem to be determined to turn him into Kam—find myself doing the same stupid things from the get-go. Mom would have a field day with this.

WANDERLUST: Take it slow and you'll be fine. Speaking of Mom, how is she doing? Haven't heard from her since her big breakup w/ Doug.

I stared at the screen with Sandra's words blinking at me. For starters, she was a bit tardy with the take it slow line. But also, there she was, half a globe away in Guam—at least I was pretty sure it was Guam—how was it that she knew about some devastating event in my mother's love life, whereas I didn't know a thing? I wasn't even aware that my mother had a love life.

Not wanting to admit my ignorance to my sister, I sent up a test balloon.

ME: They broke up?
WANDERLUST: Two weeks ago.
ME: That must have been hard on Mom.
WANDERLUST: Of course, considering . . . you know.

Well, that wasn't going to work.

ME: I can't stand it. Who is Doug?
WANDERLUST: Jesus, Keeley. How can you not know who Doug is?

Okay, that stung. Before I could defend myself, I shut down the e-mail. I could feel the presence of someone hovering behind me at my cubicle opening. It was my boss, Richard Wagner, pretending to read the Dilbert cartoon strips taped over my office nameplate. How long had he been standing there?

"Hey, Wagner." I patted the pile of forms on my workspace. "Just catching up on some paperwork."

He stepped in without saying a word and sat in my guest chair, his knees brushing the file cabinet.

"Have a seat," I said.

"You ever planning to pick up those seismometers, Kekuhi?"

"Baker-Kekuhi," I corrected him, although I couldn't keep my tone from being apologetic, as though I were sorry he could never get my name right. "I haven't been able to get them yet. They're awfully high up there. I wanted to let the mud clear."

He continued as though I hadn't said a word. "Because I'd like to get that equipment back. You know what each one of those babies cost?"

"I realize, but it would have been too risky to take the Jeep up there."

"Five thousand bucks. Each one is five thousand bucks."

"Yes, I know that, but—"

"I want those seismometers back, Kekuhi."

I groaned in frustration. It was bad enough that—not knowing what to do with the only volcanologist on staff—I'd been inexplicably placed in the finance department, but Wagner's only concern since he'd become my boss a few months back was to make sure I knew at all times what I was spending. He was the reason I went straight to Skipper when I noticed the sulfur. Wagner wouldn't approve money for so much as a three-hole punch unless I could prove it were absolutely vital to the future of the agency.

"Fine," I said, struggling to keep my voice even. "I'll get them first thing tomorrow."

"You'll get them now."

"It's almost six o'clock," I protested. Along with my words, I tried to give him my most defiant stare, but it was so hard to fix on any of his features. As seemed to happen to all the men who spent too many years in government work, he was indiscernible from the off-white wall behind him. It was as though his skin and hair and even the fabric of his shirts had faded to provide the camouflage required to sneak up on hapless employees trying to write personal e-mails before cutting out for a date.

"That gives you three hours until nightfall."

"But—"

"Kekuhi," he said, standing to leave. "I've given you plenty of time to handle this on your own. Now don't force me to put another mar on your record. You will get the seismometers tonight."

And a full minute later I was still giving him the surliest look I could summon, until Bob peered in and asked, "Don't you have better things to do than stare at the wall?"

———————

I **WALKED INTO** the Beach House Cafe thirty-five minutes late and dressed in my fieldwork clothes. The maître d' was so skilled at his job, he was able to stop me cold at the entrance simply by thinning his lips disapprovingly. "May I help you, *madam*?"

"I need to find someone here. I have a message for him."

"Oh, goody. A messenger girl. Won't it be a treat for the patrons to watch you galumph through in your work boots."

Not wanting to rely on verbal intimidation alone, he'd moved to the side of his podium to also bar me physically from the restaurant. It was one of those sparse, yuppie places without nearly enough light and overrun with flower arrangements consisting mostly of twigs.

I'd been bullied enough for one day. "You could help me find my friend," I said. "Or perhaps you'd prefer I stay here and holler for him."

He managed to snort in disgust and ask, "Your friend's name?" at the same time. He was just that good.

When I told him, he said, "Mr. Gardiner has been waiting for you." He grabbed a menu and led me to Ian by taking tiny steps and then waving me forward until he'd led me across the restaurant to the bar.

"I'm sorry I'm late," I said when I saw Ian. He pulled his jacket off the bar stool next to him and gestured for me to have a seat. If he noticed how underdressed I was, he didn't show it. I remained standing. "I'm afraid I owe you a double apology. I can't stay."

"Oh . . ."

Perhaps I flatter myself, but he looked crushed. "I have to work," I said.

When he saw I wasn't going to sit, he stood, which was so awkward that I half sat, half leaned on the stool. He did the same. "Can I talk you into a drink at least? They make an excellent martini." All he had in front of him at the moment was a glass of water. Kam would've been on his third beer if he'd been waiting for me a half hour.

"Believe me, I could use a drink right now, but I have to get to the top of Kohala to retrieve some equipment. As it is, I'm racing the sun."

"You're going by yourself?"

I answered him with a shrug.

"I would think that would be dangerous."

"It's not as if it's going to erupt any time soon."

"Or ever," he added; then an eyebrow shot up when I gave him a teasing grin, as if to indicate, *or so you think.* "It is extinct, isn't it?"

I couldn't stand it. Here I held news that would absolutely light up the island gossip line—known affectionately by locals as the Coconut Wire—yet none of the people who needed to hear it would listen to me. I'd been itching to tell *somebody.* "Actually," I intimated, leaning close as though there might be spies nearby, "I've been doing a few tests. Seismic readings and the like. I keep telling myself I'm crazy—that I must be wishing so hard for a discovery that I'm reading more into what I see than what's really there—but I swear I'm seeing signs of the beginnings of activity. Not much at this point, but they're there."

"That's astounding," he said. "I've never heard of such a thing happening."

"Well, it does—but rarely. Of course, I have to do more tests. That is, if I can get the equipment I need."

"And that's what you're doing now," he said, "Retrieving equipment?" When I nodded, he added, "But I'm surprised they'd allow you to drive those roads by yourself at night."

"I usually have an assistant on the remote trips. This was very last minute. My boss is insisting I go."

He put his jacket on and then to my surprise offered to tag along and help out. "I'll be your assistant. We'll take our date on the road."

I sized him up. He was wearing a casual work suit, but swank. All linen and crisp and a light neutral tone that would suck up the mud immediately. I shook my head. "That's sweet, but you're not exactly dressed for it."

He countered with, "I've a pair of hiking boots in my car. For emergencies." After I remained silent, he said, "You shouldn't be going alone. Your boss is a fool."

Ian was right, of course, on both counts, and I found myself taking him up on his offer.

"I'd still like to buy you that drink," he said. I saw him lean over the bar to talk to the bartender, who after a moment handed him a bottle of red wine and an opener. Ian laid a stack of bills on the bar. *Damn,* he was perfect. He was just the sort of man I should try to have a crush on, rather than the losers I usually did.

BY THE TIME Ian and I had managed to find the seismometers and stash them into the back of my Jeep, the sun had long disappeared, leaving a moonless night. By moonless, I mean without a moon, as in dark as hell. The sort of dark where you go to check your watch, and no matter how close you hold it to your face, or how wide you open your eyes, there's still nothing but black in front of them. Until you realize that it doesn't matter what time it is anyway because it's obviously past sundown, you can't see, and you've been on the islands long enough to know that sometimes that's all the information you need.

We'd actually been doing well until that last seismometer. Ian and I searched for it for twenty minutes before realizing that it had slid down a cliff. He was the one who'd spotted its yellow legs jutting obscenely from the brush near a hiking trail. It was far too steep a climb to try the direct route. Instead, I drove on until we located the trail that led down to where my equipment lay dying. I pulled the Jeep onto the path and continued.

"You realize this is marked as a hiking path," Ian said. He was standing on the passenger's side, holding onto the windshield, beating back branches of trees that swatted against us.

"I'm going slow," I answered defensively.

He didn't say anything for a while. He was trying his best to keep staving off the trees and hang on. The road was growing rockier, the trees squeezing more closely onto the path.

"Keeley?" Ian said. "How is it—and I'm sure you have a plan, you clearly know your way around this volcano—but I'm wondering how is it that you suppose to get back? I don't see that there's room any more to turn around."

The return trip. I threw the vehicle into park so fast it slammed Ian against the windshield.

"Sorry," I said.

"Nothing's broken," he grunted, and I wasn't sure whether he was referring to the windshield or his bones. I'd been so determined to move forward, I hadn't thought about how I hoped to get back. I was unable to explain why, but I felt I had to finish the job—and not because Wagner threatened me. I was driven with a tenacity even I was unable to explain. I couldn't stop when I'd come so far. It was as though I were in the final scene of *The Sound of Music* and the Mother Superior in the form of the finance director at HAG had sent me off with that "Climb Ev'ry Mountain" song and her faith in my abilities. How could I disappoint her and all those little Von Trapp children?

"You know . . . ," Ian began. He was going to tell me we'd have to give up. Those were words I didn't want to hear.

"Yes, I know," I said, in resignation.

"We'll have a better go of it if we hike."

And thus we did, a grueling mile-long trek along craggy rock that tore at our ankles—especially Ian's, who had been mistaken about those hiking boots in his car. He asked me questions about the rock formations as we walked, which calmed me. In fact, after a while I found it downright pleasant identifying rocks by their scientific names with someone who couldn't slap the Hawaiian terms back in my face.

It was an hour later that we returned to the vehicle—exhausted, seeing only by flashlight and cradling five thousands dollars' worth of mangled seismometer that we'd carried straight uphill in our arms.

"Your Jeep is at quite a peculiar angle there," Ian said. It looked as if the driver's side were dipped in a hole.

I stored the equipment while Ian sized up the problem. "You're not going to want to hear this," he said. "But your front wheel has a flat. There appears to be a rock wedged in it."

I answered with a groan and went over to him. The tire was, in fact, speared with a chunk of dried lava. "Pyroclastic rock," I said.

"Well, then," was Ian's only response. He set about jacking up the Jeep and pulling out the spare tire. My job apparently was to sit on a nearby tree stump, hold the flashlight, and hand him tools. His hair flopped in his eyes while he worked.

To feel more useful, I dug out the bottle of wine and opened it. We took turns swigging from the bottle, although—being less busy—I managed more turns. Ian loosened the lug bolts and yanked off the tire. He pulled out the rock that had cut through it. "Look at this. It's shaped just like a shark's fin."

"That figures," I said, not attempting to disguise my sarcasm. "My ex is named after the shark god, Kamohoali'i. Perhaps this is all his doing."

Ian hoisted the spare tire onto the axle, wriggling it into place. "Do you mind if I ask you a personal question?"

"You're changing my tire. I'm hardly in a position to be uppity."

"How long have you been divorced?" I took another swig of the wine. I hesitated long enough that he said, "You don't have to answer."

"It's all right. We're not technically divorced. Yet. We're in the middle of all that mess."

He set his tools down and turned to me, which gave him a flashlight directly in the face. "That explains a quite a bit," he said, holding up his hand as a visor.

I shifted the light. "It does?"

"That day when he walked in while we were . . . that day in your living room. Your ex looked as if he'd have liked to eat me alive."

"Really? He looked that mad?"

Ian fixed me with an expression I couldn't read. "It gets easier," he said. "The first few months are the worst. You feel as though you're falling headfirst off a cliff. But it gets easier."

"I sure hope so." I held the wine bottle toward him, but he shook his head, so I kept drinking it myself. "It sounds like you're speaking from experience."

"Unfortunately, yes."

"Kids?"

"Two, Jonathan and Megan. They're at university."

"*University?* Jeez, how old are you?"

He laughed again. I clearly amused him, and I suppose it was a rude question, but the man had a knack for removing what limited social graces I possess. "I suppose I'd have to be around the same age as your man Mr. Jones," he said. "You're a bright girl; you can do the math."

I was polite enough to calculate in my head that he had to be fiftyish—surprising when I thought about it, he didn't seem much older than me—but I was more embarrassed that he'd bring up Davy Jones. As if I were some teenybopper who pined every moment for him. But as long as he'd broached the topic . . .

"So where is Davy Jones these days?" I asked innocently.

Or, not so convincingly benign as I'd hoped. His smile drooped a bit. I guessed he thought I wouldn't take the bait. Or would reply, Davy *who*?—oh, Ian, it's only *you* I want. And who knew? Maybe I would want him, maybe I wouldn't, but in the meantime, was it my fault that he kept dangling my past in front of me like a shiny coin? It seemed a lifetime before he answered, "L.A., I believe. I'm not certain. I've been a bit out of touch."

"I know what you must be thinking. That I'm some kind of a nut for wanting to see him at my age."

"Not a nut. But I'll admit, I am curious."

"I wish I knew myself. A feeling of unfinished business, I suppose. I had sort of a thing for him when I was a girl. All the girls did."

"And you still do?"

"No! Well, yes. Maybe. I don't know." I peeled at the edges of the wine bottle's label. "Oh, who knows anymore. Isn't this why people get nostalgic? Trying to relive a time before their lives got really shitty?"

Even though the light was no longer in his eyes, he was squinting at me. "We'll be ready to leave in a few minutes. I'm almost finished here." He turned back to the wheel.

As it turned out, the Jeep was at such a downward angle, Ian had to push on it from the front while I kicked it into reverse to inch it back up the hill. When we reached the main trail, he was splattered with dirt.

I went to take a drink from the wine bottle nestled between my legs, but I realized it was empty. Ian noticed, too.

"You've done all the driving this entire night," he said. "Allow me to take it from here."

He opened my door, and in resignation I scooted over to the passenger side. He hopped in and then let the engine idle while he leaned toward me. *Here it comes,* I thought, *here's the kiss.* Luckily, I was drunk and therefore horny—plus he'd been so nice. I didn't mind the idea nearly so much as I'd thought I would.

But instead of kissing me, his arm went around my shoulder in a fatherly hug. "Sometimes we all need to chase shadows," he said in a tone that smacked of Regatta's when she was dispensing island wisdom. "I'm going out of town for a couple weeks on business. I would very much like to see you when I return. And if there is anything I can do to help you with your—how did you put it? Unfinished business? I'm glad to do it."

With that, he turned the Jeep around and started down the mountain trail.

9

DARNED IF SKIPPER didn't actually cough up some tiltmeters—even threw in a couple seismometers as my free bonus gift. I'd had Ellen set up the seismometers. Then I spent days dragging the tiltmeters around, taking precise "before" measurements of Kohala's craters, rocks, and other points of key interest. If lava was forming inside my mountain, sending rock swelling upward, this would tell me.

It was well over a week later when I came back from lunch to find a stack of computer printouts on my desk along with a note: "K—Ran these numbers. Looks interesting. Bob."

There was my old seismic data and—*where did he find this?* Some tilt-meter readings I'd taken when I first started at HAG. Height, depth, width—real sexy stuff if I did say so myself. I thumbed through the papers, sitting before I realized I'd even sat, pushing my Styrofoam container of leftover moo shu out of my way.

Bob—have I mentioned yet how much I love and admire Bob?—he'd run the old data against the stuff we'd been collecting in the past few weeks. I studied the numbers page by page, swallowing nervously as I went on. There was no mistaking it this time. I looked at the numbers again, then again. Even though I'd been suspecting it for weeks, the last time that simple evidence before my eyes was so hard to fathom I'd been staring at two pink dots.

Could it be that my sixty-thousand-year-old heap of rock was having a baby? I'd heard about new volcanoes forming inside dormant ones, but never inside a volcano so long extinct as Kohala.

Back when I'd mentioned the possibility to Ellen, I didn't really believe it myself. If it were really happening—and what else could it be?—then this was going to be huge. This was going to be huger than huge.

I gathered up the papers and headed for Wagner's cubicle, which, by HAG standards, was one square foot larger than mine with an opening toward a window to reflect his status as management. He was sharpening pencils. They were lined up in a row on his desk, the points even as though he were making a number-two picket fence.

"Have a minute? I have news."

He finished sharpening a pencil without looking up. He blew on it; then, only when it had been set next to the others did he say, "Have a seat."

I set the computer printout on his desk, even though I knew he wouldn't know what it meant. It sent one of the pencils rolling onto the floor. "Kohala is showing definite signs of activity. It's all here."

He remained expressionless. "When someone knocks something off another person's desk, don't you think she should retrieve it?"

"Did you—?" I hesitated, and then I stooped down to pick up the pencil. I didn't want him distracted. He was a finance guy, not a volcanologist. I'd have to spell it out as if I were talking to Dante. "This could mean a new volcano is forming."

He realigned the pencils but said nothing.

"To the best of my knowledge, this has never happened before."

Another pencil went into the sharpener. *Whrrrrrrr.* He blew on it, then set it down. "That's very good. You should add that to that little report you're working on. Which reminds me, when do you think you'll be done with that? I have some projects I'd like to start you on."

"The little report I'm working on," I repeated, stunned.

"Of course, I realize that's important information you've been collecting. But surely you're tired of just working on volcanoes all the time, every day. I have something that will challenge you, Kekuhi. Let you show us what you can do." He gave a supportive punch to the air.

My left eye twitched. I smiled to calm it. "My position here is to study Kohala. The report is ongoing. It's my job."

"But you work for me, and I head the finance department, don't I?"

I remembered the deep breathing Morna always told me to do. I drew a breath in, then let it out. In, then out. *Don't play his game,* I told myself.

My smile grew to a grimace. "If there is activity on Kohala—and I believe there is—it will affect every person who lives here," I said, trying so hard to keep my composure that I was speaking in a monotone. "It could mean earthquake, or even eruption."

I paused for effect, but his face was impassive.

"We'll need more information, of course," I continued. "That will take more equipment. More staff. This is nothing we can ignore."

"Now, Keeley, you know that this department doesn't have money sitting in a jar waiting for you to help yourself."

I was smiling nearly hysterically at this point, like one of those awful clowns used to frighten children in movies. "I realize my budget specifies that I study the volcano for historical purposes, but that's because it was never anticipated Kohala would ever be anything but extinct. Circumstances have changed. Surely there's a way to obtain funds from somewhere. Lives are literally at stake."

"If it means that much to you, I'll allow you to issue a proposal for funds, but I expect you to draft it on your own time. Scrounging for dollars is not in your work agreement."

"And this proposal would go to—"

"To me. If you impress me—and I'm sure you will—I'll put it in next year's work plan."

"*Next year?* That's too late!"

"There are procedures, Keeley. We can't go flying off and changing everything just because you have a whim."

There was no talking to this idiot. Clearly, I'd have to go around him to get what I needed. I picked up one of his pencils, one he'd already sharpened, and put it back into the sharpener. *Whrrrrrr.* There was only the sound of wood being electronically whittled. I pushed on the eraser until it peeked from the sharpener. Then I pulled the stub out and set it next to the other pencils.

"There you go, extra sharp," I said, and I saw him pluck it off the desk frantically as I grabbed my papers and left his cubicle.

I wound through the maze of cubicles to Bob's office. Although he expected me to be raving about the papers in my hand, I was carrying on about my boss. It was only when he pointed out the skew in my priorities—how I clutched evidence of a natural phenomenon in my hand while I was blathering about office politics—that I realized I needed to make a change.

Bob and I worked on a letter on and off for a day. He coached me on the art of playing the game, starting by crossing out my first line—"My current boss is a complete twit."—and replacing it with, "I feel the finance department is not as ideal a fit as others in the organization might be for my unique talents." We added a few more vague lines about my desire to focus on challenging tasks. Then I set it in the head of personnel's in-box.

I had a hunch about this. I could almost smell the freedom.

THAT WEEKEND, STANDING in a bridal shop, trying to peer over a mountain of ruffle to see in the mirror how stupid I looked, I had to give Regatta credit. At least she wasn't trying to convince me that it was a dress I'd be able to wear again and again.

Dante was hiding beneath the skirt. I could feel his breath on my legs near where I'd rolled my jeans up. When I'd tried to kick him away, I tripped on the hem, and both Regatta and the saleslady *tsk*ed me in unison. So he'd stayed under there. He must have been playing cops and robbers, because I could hear the muffled noises of guns shooting and men dying against my shins. "*Pkow, pkow . . . arrrrrrrrgh.*"

"I like this one," I said, which is what I'd said to each of the dresses I'd tried on, especially since I'd noticed they were getting progressively fluffier.

"I'm not sure about the color."

"It's lavender. You wanted lavender," I said.

"Lavender is in," the saleslady assured us.

Testimony to how strangely Regatta was behaving, she took fashion advice from me and a saleslady who was wearing a sweats ensemble with pumps. I was just relieved I didn't have to suffer whatever monstrosity was next in line.

As it was, I was already running late. "Could someone unzip me? I've got to get going."

"Going? Already? You haven't even had a chance to see my gown yet." Regatta clutched the binder to her chest she'd brought filled with magazine clippings of gowns even more frightening than what I was wearing.

"I know, I'm sorry." My arms reached back to try to undo the zipper myself. Dante sat on my feet. This whole dress-trying-on event had come as quite a shock when I saw it penned-in on my Day At-A-Glance, at 10 A.M. Right next to "Pick up Dante's cake," also at ten and . . . Hmm, come to think of it, I'd never remembered to order the cake. And here it was half past eleven, I had nine children and their parents arriving at my house at three, and I still needed to stop by the library for a party games book. "You know how things always go slower than you expect with a kid along."

"Yeah, about that—I thought it was just going to be you and me today."

The saleslady chirped in agreement. "Little boys and bridal dresses don't mix."

"You know that I couldn't help it," I said defensively. "I didn't have a baby-sitter." I couldn't believe it. Since when did Regatta find Dante an annoyance?

It certainly explained how when I'd arrived with him that morning, he'd asked as usual what she had for him, and she'd said, "Nothing today, I didn't know you were coming." The real Regatta, the Regatta who was my best friend and not this binder-clutching impostor, would have rummaged through her purse for something—a stick of gum, a tube of Chap Stick, a receipt, *something*. She'd have pulled off her socks, stuck them on his hands, and told him they were puppets. She wouldn't have said, as she had, that we'd have to make the best of it.

"My cousin had to come with me to pick out my wedding dress, and she's only a bridesmaid. You're my matron of honor." Regatta whined the word *honor*, dragging it out—as in hon-*noooor*—to emphasize how I'd been bastardizing the title.

"It's just not a good time now."

She mumbled something in the direction of a rack of veils.

"Excuse me?"

Big mistake. "I said, you always seem to have plenty of time when it comes to discussing your problems, but never any to help me when I need it."

The saleslady *tsk-tsked* me again.

"I've done a lot for this wedding," I retorted.

"Like what?" We were mirror images of each other: arms crossed, feathers ruffled, only I was losing ground. I hadn't done a thing, truth be told. It was mere months away, which in real wedding time, not in condensed pregnant-bride time like I'd had, was close.

I went back to tugging on my zipper. "I don't know what you expected. I didn't even plan my own wedding. You did it for me."

Normally, Regatta would have laughed and agreed I was hopeless. Instead, she went in for the kill. "All I've heard from you in the past week is, 'Why didn't he kiss me? Why didn't he call?' over some guy you don't even like. I ask you for one thing—to help me out with my wedding—and you can't do it."

I yanked the zipper down the rest of the way and pulled the dress off my shoulders. It stood limp around me.

"I don't see what the big deal is," I said. "It's not like you're marrying the Prince of Wales. It's Ted, for crying out loud. Ted! The guy who six months ago you weren't even sure you were going to keep seeing, let alone marry."

"Ooh, my," the saleslady said. She seemed to discover an urgent need to fold scarves and set busily about it.

"Thanks for that reminder," Regatta said in a quavery whisper. "You're a real friend."

My dress sank into a heap on the floor. It exposed Dante, who rose like Venus from the layers of taffeta. He cocked his finger and thumb into a gun and poked it into my belly. *"Pkow, pkow."*

WHEN REGATTA LATER bailed on her promise to help with Dante's party, I was neither surprised nor worried. I'd planned a low-key event anyway. There'd be six of Dante's schoolmates and three neighborhood kids. They'd dine on chips and hot dogs. Then we'd play the simple party games of my youth, like drop the clothespins in the milk bottle—although I'd had to hunt for days to find a store that sold clothespins, and the closest I came to a milk bottle was a sand-weighted two-liter of Diet Coke.

I was ready for the guests' arrival with minutes to spare. There was even a moment to unwind while Dante chased balloons around the house.

I sank into the couch and watched him. It was hard to believe that my baby was already five. It seemed like only . . . well, not yesterday, but certainly not a half-a-decade ago that he came into my life. The doctor had held him up—slippery and startled—his head bobbing like one of those dashboard dolls with the springcoil necks. I couldn't believe that I'd been carting around inside me this fully formed human already so clearly stuffed with a personality and a will.

The story of his birth was one Dante couldn't hear often enough. Time and time again, knowing well the answer, he'd ask me—as I tucked him into bed or pulled off his shirt for the bath—"Mom, what did you say when I was born?" I'd always give the same answer: "Ouch!" Then he'd snort a laugh, finding it terribly amusing he could bring me pain on his entrance into the world, and I wasn't even angry with him.

While he waged war against the party balloons, I pondered whether he'd remember this day. Years from now, would this be one of the scattered images that would rise like baking bread to his consciousness? After all, out of—what?—the literally thousands of days of my youth, I've retained only a handful memories. Playing Mousetrap in Grant Smith's basement. Climbing the narrow stairs on our visit to the Washington Monument. Clasping my sister's hand to defend against Tommy Bellon charging at us in a neighborhood game of Red Rover. Pieces of assorted days, not much more.

I'd once asked my mother if I were repressing some horrid incident, but she said, no—not that she knew. Childhood recollections are rare for most people.

So imagine, then, how special it would be if this were to be one of the precious thoughts he'd hold dear for all time. The memory of how his mother had brought together his friends to celebrate his fifth birthday. How she made the extra effort to be there for him. Not that I'd want him to add, "as opposed to my dad." This was not about a lack of Kam, but rather, a tremendous presence of me.

The doorbell rang. "Our first guest!" I shouted to Dante.

It was Trevor from his class. His father dropped him off, asking, "His little brother is in the car; would it be an imposition—?" I assured him it was fine, siblings were welcome.

The next guest was one of the three girls I'd invited, Emily, who had the same overbite as her mother—the mother who told her to be sure to mind her manners before leaving.

The rest, it must be admitted, seems a blur. Before I was even aware of what was happening, I had a dozen children in my charge and no other adult in sight. I had assumed that the grown-ups would stay and that brothers and sisters would not. Although this was the first party I'd thrown, I'd been to enough to know that's how it worked—at least it did at four-year-olds' parties.

I'd wised up by the time Maxwell arrived. He was he last child I'd remembered inviting, and I wasn't letting go of my final chance for adult help so easily. "I hope you'll be staying for the festivities," I said nonchalantly to his mother. "It'll be great fun."

Her shoulder was cocked toward the door. "I had been planning to use this time to get a manicure. It's been booked forever. But if you need me to stay . . ." Her voice trailed off as she peered longingly outside, where she knew the parents clever enough to arrive earlier had escaped to freedom.

"Don't worry about it. I have help coming," I lied, allowing her to flee. The door slammed behind her just as the back door opened. Four of the seven Ku boys ran in, presents in their hands. And now there were sixteen, plus Dante.

There was a cry from the vicinity of the bedroom.

"Go get your mom," I said urgently to one of the Ku boys. I dashed into Dante's room, only to find a girl, Phoebe, gaping at St. Ignatius in his locked cage. She was backed up against the wall as though he were attacking. I sighed with relief.

"It's locked," I assured her, taking her hand. "Come on, everyone. The party's outside." And I moved children and gifts to the backyard. I soon noticed I was shy a couple of children. Great. Fifteen minutes into the party and I'd already lost some of the guests. It felt like there were bees in my stomach. I grabbed that Ku boy again.

"Didn't I ask you to go get your mom?"

"No."

Well, okay, it might have been his brother, but I didn't have time to argue. This was not going according to plan. Only three of the children were at the table of art supplies I'd set out. The rest of them seemed to be whirring around the yard, as though they were loud, colorful pieces of trash caught up in a wind tunnel.

I had to find the others. "Stay . . . in . . . the . . . yard!" I shouted. Only the ones at the art table looked at me and nodded obediently as a single unit.

Once inside the house, I grabbed the cordless and dialed Daisy Ku's number while I looked in closets and under tables. Three boys were in the kitchen, pulling cans from the pantry.

A boy with no front teeth explained, "We're gonna feed the lithard."

"He's already eaten." I shooed them out the door and started to put the food back, still trying Daisy Ku. No answer.

Again, I heard the shrieks of a child. I let cans clamor to the floor as I darted outside. It was Dante. (*And, see,* I silently scolded all those child-rearing books, *I told you I wouldn't recognize my baby's cry.*) Oh why, I asked myself, did I ever leave them unattended? Dante sat on the lawn, tears leaping from his eyes. Trash and bodies seemed to dance all about him.

"Those . . . are . . . my . . . presents!" he howled.

Then I saw it. The toys. The torn wrapping paper. A group of boys making tracks with Dante's brand-new laser gun toward the woods. Girls at the art table incorporating the bows and ribbons into their projects. Dante's indignant howls at having had his gifts opened. And me, standing impotently with a ringing phone pasted to my ear.

"They're miiiiine!" he wailed.

"Everybody get back here!" I screamed to the air in general as I ran over to Dante. "It's okay, baby, we'll collect your presents," I told him, but forgot to lower my voice, which propelled his hysteria to the next level.

I found myself joining the commotion—trying to corral children, collect presents, and dial my phone to reach someone, anyone to help. But clearly the gods of screening were cursing me for all the times I hadn't picked up my phone. I was leaving messages all over town, but no one was home. Not Regatta, or Melissa Anne, or Bob, or . . . and the list was growing more desperate . . . Ellen, or Kam's mom, or Ian. I tried Morna, grumbling when I didn't reach anyone over how I had the only lawyer in town without an answering machine.

I dialed the phone again. "You!" I shouted at a girl who was stripping off her clothes to put on what appeared to be a firefighter costume. "Yes, you, the nudist. We're not trying that on right now. Put on your clothes!"

"I'll have you know I'm fully dressed." That came from the phone.

"Kam . . . ," I said.

"What's going on? It sounds like Vietnam."

Although it shattered any shred of pride I had left, I did what I had to do. I asked him to come over. It is possible I even begged. Though I hadn't invited him the first place—though he was the last person I'd want to see me failing—I had no choice. Begrudgingly, I asked for his help and, as begrudgingly, he gave it.

By the time he skateboarded up the side driveway, his backpack and hair blowing in the breeze, I was putting an ice pack on a boy's knee, saying, "Now, how did you hurt yourself?" Kam did an ollie off the board, then shuffled across the grass to me.

"This party rocks."

Phoebe skipped happily by. She looked like a porcupine, her skin pinched all over with the clothespins I'd bought for the milk-bottle game.

"Shut up," I said before Kam could say anything else.

He held his lips together.

"Here's the deal," I said, fighting the urge to cry. "I need to start lunch and locate kids. Not necessarily in that order." I did a quick count. Fourteen were outside. Then I went inside and pulled two of the little reprobates from Dante's room and one from beneath my bed.

When I walked back outside, the children were sitting on the lawn, legs folded, hands in their laps. Kam faced them, ukulele in hand. The three I'd rescued against their wills ran to join the others.

"Itsy Bitsy Spider!" a girl shouted.

Kam shook his head, then crooked a finger at Dante, who crawled over to say something in his dad's ear.

"It's Dante's birthday," Kam said. "This is his request."

I walked defeated to the barbecue and lit the gas. This was utterly not fair. I tossed hot dogs on the cold grill. Kam began strumming.

"Here we go," he said, his voice getting that musical quality in it, although he was talking. "You know what to do."

He used his best islander voice as he sang:

The sky is leaky.
They say wikiwiki!
You crazy hupo you gotta get outta da rain real queeky!
But I say no, mun!
And den I show dem
I shake my cheeky, cheeky, cheeky, cheeky, cheeky!

As I turned dogs on the grill, the children leapt to their feet, and shook their bottoms toward Kam. A Kodak picture-perfect moment, and me without my camera.

He stopped strumming. A boy stole toward the house.

Aha, I snickered to myself, even though it could be my undoing. Now Kam would understand how impossible it was to maintain control over these savages.

"Where you going, pal?" Kam said.

"Gotta pee."

"Nope. Nobody allowed inside."

"I gotta peeee!"

"Nobody inside." Kam nodded toward the garden. "You can go over there."

The boy's eyes widened as he looked at the square of dirt where Dante and I had tried in vain to grow a few experimental plants. "For real? Right here?"

"Kam," I said from my post at the barbecue. "You have got to be kidding."

"Lighten up, girl. Let him have some fun."

As I heard urine hit dirt, another boy shouted, "I gotta go, too!"

Before I knew it, I had a lineup of boys at my garden as though it were a urinal. One of the girls—I recognized her from the art table that had been neglected by everyone else—marched over to me, indignant. "I am not going to pee in that garden."

"Nor do you have to," I said.

"Because it's gross."

"No one's going to make you."

"Good," she said. Then she grabbed the hands of the other two girls and led them to the side of the house, where I saw them pull down their underwear and squat.

One by one, they returned to their spots in the grass. Kam sang "I Got Sand in My Pants," "Hula Hands," "Hukilau," and a few other tunes in Hawaiian that I didn't recognize.

He entertained the troops. I pushed the two picnic tables together and set seventeen hot dogs on as many plates. When Kam took a break, I called everyone over for food. The music had served as a drug, transforming them into Stepford children. They walked in a neat row to the table, sitting calmly and saying things like "Emily, dear, could you please pass me a juice box?" and "Why certainly, it would be my greatest pleasure."

Kam grabbed a hot dog off the serving plate and blew on it to cool it.

"Thank you," I said. "For coming over."

"Not a problem."

"Really. I don't know what I would have done if you hadn't shown up."

"It's cool. I wanted to get out of the house anyway. Suzanne was on my ass to clean the garage. You know how it is."

And, no, truth be told, I didn't know how it was, but I was dying to find out. Could it be that there was trouble in paradise?

"The garage, huh?" I said, cleverly keeping the hated cleaning task before him.

"Yeah, I tell you, sometimes I . . ."

He paused. It took all the self-control I had not to speak. Not to ask, *You what? You wish she wasn't such a shrew? You wish I'd take you back, but of course I won't, but thanks for asking?*

My train of thought was derailed by Dante, who dived into my arms. "Can we do the piñata?"

At the birthday boy's request, I hung the piñata—a hula girl. There was much satisfaction to be had in watching the children pummel her with a baseball bat. The piñata was so tough to break, though, that I eventually had to drag it down and stomp on it to open a hole. Kam lifted it high and let the candy spill to the ground.

The children were drunk on sugar and violence by the time their parents arrived to retrieve them.

Phoebe tugged on my shirt, I assumed to say a polite thank-you. "Don't you have goodie bags?"

Her mother said, "Phoebe! That's rude," but the damage was done. A fun party where they got to pee outside and beat up a hula dancer would be remembered as the time no one got a goodie bag.

"Be right back." I went to the kitchen where the carnage from the kids' search for iguana food covered the floor. I hunted around for anything of which I had seventeen. A few minutes later, I returned with a grocery bag stuffed with goodies.

"Here you go!" I said to Phoebe, using my chirpiest voice. I handed her the M. C. Hammer CD I never listened to anymore and a can of Dole peaches in light syrup. She looked at them, perplexed, but after a prompting from her mother said thank you.

And as each child filed out, I handed over a CD and a canned good. Some towheaded kid almost caused trouble, claiming that he already had The Go-Go's *Greatest*. His dad shushed him and apologized, but I winked at the boy and made a quick switch, giving him Lou Rawls. I was sending every child home happy if it killed me.

The last child (Meatloaf's *Bat Out of Hell*, Dinty Moore stew) finally left. I was about to collapse when Kam asked, "Isn't that your doorbell?"

I surveyed the yard, panicked. Were these the final parents come to claim their offspring? Had I lost one? I had none left to offer, save my own firstborn.

With a groan, I headed through the house and opened the front door.

"Hey beh-beh."

It was Elvis, as in Presley. What could I say but, "May I help you?"

"I'm here for the party."

"Excuse me?"

"A birthday party for—" Elvis pushed his cape aside so he could reach into his pants pocket for a piece of paper. "Dante."

I couldn't stand it anymore. It was as though he didn't even know. "You're Elvis," I informed him.

He spread his arms. "That's raiiiight, beh-beh."

"I'm afraid there's been a mistake."

"There's no party?"

"There was, but it's over. And—no offense—but I didn't ask for an Elvis."

He studied his paper again. "This was a last-minute order. Somebody by the name of Gardiner. Called from New York, looks like. Said to send over anything we could get here fast, except a stripper. That's me. This costume stays on, beh-beh."

Ian. He must have picked up his messages, heard my desperate plea and sent entertainment to help.

Dante bounded to the door. "Mom! We forgot the cake!" He stopped short. A man in shades and rhinestone-studded bellbottoms in his front foyer was odd enough to earn an, "Oh, hi," before he turned back to me. "You didn't do the cake. Nobody sang me happy birthday."

"Baby, I'm sor—"

Elvis brightened. "I'll sing it!"

I shook my head, but he was already heading into the house with the same strides Elvis must have used to command the stage in Vegas. "Live it up, lady. I'm paid for."

"Who are you?" Dante asked him, eyeing his cape, smelling potential superhero.

Kam, who was in the living room setting the birthday cake on the table that I still hadn't pushed back into the kitchen, answered, "Elvis."

Acting like it was the most natural thing in the world, I gathered around the cake with my son, my soon-to-be-ex, and the King of Rock and Roll. I pulled out the Bic I'd gotten from Ian and lit five candles. Elvis led us in a very Elvisy rendition of "Happy Birthday."

Dante's face was serious as he blew out the candles.

"What did you wish for?" I asked.

Smoke wafted before him. He looked at Kam, then at me. He hesitated, suddenly seeming so grown-up as he said, "I wished . . . that you and Daddy . . ."

Oh, God, no. I shifted uncomfortably on the floor. Kam was oblivious. My heart tore.

"That you and Daddy . . . that you would buy me a Game Boy," he finished, his face innocent and hopeful.

"Yes, well," I said, flushing hot, "That costs a lot of money. We'll see."

"Have any other requests?" Elvis asked.

I said no, but Kam said he'd love to hear "I Can't Help Falling in Love With You." I couldn't believe it. The song from our wedding. Dante had crawled into Kam's lap. I set a slice of cake in front of him.

Elvis began singing, those familiar words about fools rushing in.

Kam leaned back, content. I couldn't figure out what to do. Hawaiians can gather for days and sing songs in intimate groups. Me, I never could do it. My eyes looked at the floor, at the refrigerator, at Dante eating cake, which was where they stayed, watching as the ring of chocolate grew around his mouth. He'd somehow gotten icing on his forehead and in his hair. I kept watching as he chased a piece of cake that refused to submit to his fork around his plate. But I wouldn't look up at Kam, even though his chin rested just above Dante's head. It wasn't until I heard the last line of the song that I lifted my glance to meet Kam's, who as it turned out wasn't paying any attention to me at all.

He'd turned to the hall clock. "Man, six-thirty. I didn't know I'd been here so long. I told Suzanne I'd be back by five."

"You want a note?" I said dryly.

"I wish. She's going to chew my butt off for this one." He offered to walk Elvis out, then lingered at the door. "Keel, this was all right." It seemed as if he might kiss me.

"You'd better get going."

I handed him a can of clam chowder and the Billy Vera & the Beaters CD we'd fought over so bitterly when we first split and I hadn't listened to once since. Then I watched as he climbed onto his skateboard and rode away.

KAM HAD BEEN surfing the day I went into labor with Dante. I was awoken by the first cramps of pain at dawn, two weeks before my due date. So I was cheated of my Lucy and Ricky moment—that scene where I'd say, "This is it," and in his panic Kam would rush out of the house, forgetting me, only to return, slapping his forehead and saying, "Lucy," or in my case, "Keeley." I rolled over to find his side of the bed empty. My only thought was that I wished I'd known. I could have been sleeping diagonally all that time.

I drove myself to the hospital. My contractions were close, but they weren't hard. Kam's mom was sent to search his favorite surfing spots.

Meanwhile, I sat in the emergency room while the registration nurse attempted to shame me into going back home. "If you're not hollerin', you're not dilated."

"Can't you check?"

She gave me a quick up-and-down. "There you go. Now you been checked. You got a couple hours still."

"I feel pressure. What if it's the baby's head? My contractions are less than five minutes apart."

"Honey, I seen folks in more pain trying to open a bag of Lay's. You're dilated to a two at best."

"You don't know that for sure. I may have an unusually high threshold for pain." I'd heard the horror stories of women who'd unknowingly passed the point where they could get an epidural. I was not taking any chances.

I'd worn her down. "Wait here," she finally said. "I'll see if I can get you some help."

I fumbled nervously with the zipper on my overnight bag while I waited. This would be so much easier if Kam were here. I wanted someone to clear a path for me. That was to be his job. That, and making sure I wasn't writhing around nude like those women in the movies they terrorized us with in Lamaze.

"Keeley . . . is that you?"

I twisted in my chair as best I could, swollen as I was. It was Marv Bergman, the head of the ride-share department at HAG. Here was a man whose job was to force everyone to carpool, which he aimed to achieve by hugging a lot—the reason I drove alone.

"The baby! You're having the baby!"

"I guess so."

He sat next to me, placing a hand on my belly. "How far are we dilated?" I'd thought Marv was gay. How did he know about dilating?

"Been through this many a time myself," he carried on. "I have five at home, all under eight." He held up a bandaged hand. "That's how I got this. Shut it in the crib."

I tried to readjust my thinking to a newly heterosexual Marv. He prambled on. "Children are such miracles, aren't they? Your husband must be beside himself."

"Yes. He's very excited."

He glanced around the emergency room. "Where is he?"

I had to admit to him that Kam wasn't here yet, that he was surfing. Marv chucked my chin and called me a brave soldier. He told me many a gal went through this without a husband, especially these days.

"Really," I said. "He'll be here any minute."

"Of course he will."

"He couldn't be more thrilled."

"I don't doubt it," Marv said. "In the meantime, why don't I help you get a room? I'm sure your *husband* would want someone to help you with that."

I told him, yeah, well, good luck. I pointed out the admissions nurse, who'd never gone to get help. She'd only moved a few chairs over, the bitch.

The same pattern of hugging that convinced people to get together in a car to share a ride to the office also worked on the nurse to get me a room. He scored one of those cushy birthing rooms that are supposed to look like your bedroom at home, complete with floral wallpaper and oil paintings of ladies in repose. Not bad given that, as it turned out, I was only dilated to two.

Marv insisted on staying with me until Kam arrived. At first, I was embarrassed. I barely knew Marv, had only spoken to him a few times at the office.

But clearly he knew the drill. He brought ice and mopped my brow. He promised to beat away any stray doctors who wandered in to stuff their fingers up and check me just for sport, and not to allow me to tear off my clothes in the passion of labor. And, yes, he hugged the life out of me, but he also did that stupid *ha-ha* breathing so I could concentrate for once on how lame he looked, instead of wondering if Kam were making fun of me.

Around the time I dilated to four, Marv hunted down an anesthesiologist for my epidural, who said call him when I was a six.

A few minutes later—I knew I was a six, I just needed proof—Marv stopped me as I hollered, "You! You there with the mop! Drop it and get over here! I need to be checked!"

Then he found a doctor who said I was an eight and moving fast, crying shame that I hadn't gotten that epidural, now it was too late.

I was easily a nine by the time Kam's mom called, saying she'd found him in the waves at Keaukaha Beach. He was on his way. Hang in there. And lucky for her I was not then, nor was I ever, much of a screamer. I bore my pain in controlled *ha-ha* breaths.

After that, Marv treated me with a brand of pity I hadn't anticipated. It was one thing to be the single mother he'd thought I was. It was another altogether to be abandoned in the labor room.

"If your husband doesn't make it—but I'm sure he will—you pretend I'm him. Call me by his name."

"What? 'You loser?' 'You waste of a surfer boy?' You want me to call you *that*?" I was propped belly-up on my elbows, legs akimbo, buried beneath a pile of blankets a foot high to weigh down the shakes I'd gotten—as though I were a pea and a tiny princess were going to settle herself on top of this whole sweaty, grunting mess.

Big hug. "You don't mean that. It's the pain talking. What's his name?"

"There's a head there. I know there's a head."

"His name . . ."

"Kam. His fucking name is Kam, and my doctor's name is Yvonne, and she'd better get her ass in here soon or . . ."

Marv ran to get a nurse, who peeked between my legs and announced, "I'm gonna go find me a doctor and a catcher's mitt."

When the doctor hustled in, Marv introduced himself as Kam.

This was going to have to be set straight. "He's not . . . Kam, he's . . ." to be continued after more *ha-ha* breathing.

The doctor gave Marv a nudge toward the head of the bed. "She needs you near her face, Dad. She's ready to push."

And I say to hell with those movies where the hero comes dashing in at the last moment, flushed from hurrying, pulling seaweed from his hair. It doesn't happen in real life, believe me. In real life, you don't even care anyway. You're in so much pain, your focus is entirely on pushing and wishing you were dying—so much that you practically tune out the guy's voice at your ear, whispering *"I'm Kam, this is Kam here for you."* You reach up to grab his long, black hair to give it a yank so he'll hurt, too, but his hair is short, and the doctor is saying nice job, Keeley, one more big push . . .

"It's a boy! Ten fingers, ten toes."

Marv released his grip on my neck. He scurried to see the baby. I'd like to say I was weepy and sentimental, but I was simply glad it was over.

Marv sobbed like a woman. "Oh, Keeley, he's so beautiful. He's perfect."

The doctor handed Marv a scissors. "Here you go, Dad. You can cut the cord."

"Oh, no, I couldn't . . ." Marv looked up at me hopefully.

"Go ahead, Dad," I said.

I saw his bandaged hand tremble, and perhaps it's only in memory that I recall hearing the distinct snip of the umbilical cord being severed.

That's when the doctor lifted Dante to me. I thought, Hmm, a baby, how interesting. *If only I weren't so tired.* I heard Marv snuffling, and I felt somewhat embarrassed that I couldn't work up enough emotion to equal his.

Then I looked at Dante, and I would have sworn once again the child-rearing books were wrong—that this boy with only inches of vision was zeroing in on me. For a moment, it didn't bother me that I seemed un-moved. Here was a purple boy in front of me, bearing the light and the cold with a confused dignity. Somehow I knew then and there we were going to get along fine.

Dante was washed, bundled, and laid on my chest by the time Kam stepped through the door, jarred by the weeping man who greeted him with a hug before announcing his job here was done.

Kam walked hesitantly over to me, smelling of salt and regret. Sand clung to the damp folds of his arms and neck. "I'm so sorry," he said. "I would never have gone surfing if I had any idea . . ."

I answered him by peeling back a corner of the blanket, showing him the wild mess of the baby's hair. Kam bent over to kiss my head, then Dante's.

"I'll always come through for you, I promise," he said, softly. "But some-times I need more time."

He was serious—I laughed at the absurdity of it, his naive sincerity. "I'm afraid that things were a bit out of my hands on this one."

The nurse came in to take Dante for his Apgar test just as I was placing him in Kam's nervous arms. For a moment there, we must have made the picture of a perfect family—and again, me without my camera.

"SO," MORNA SAID a few days after Dante's birthday as she and I turned the corner, "That sounds like some party you had. How many children were actually injured, would you say?"

"Excuse me?"

We'd met at my office and left for a walk because as long as we had to discuss all this divorce business, Morna said, we might as well stretch our legs. HAG's building was on Sleepy Girl Street, a tree-lined boulevard filled with shops, dry cleaners, eateries, and the bland office building that housed the cubicles that contained me and my sixty-seven coworkers.

Morna pulled me by the elbow out of the way of an old woman coming up the street pushing her groceries in a cart as though it were a weapon. She snarled at me in Hawaiian, while Morna asked, "Was it just the one child? Were there stitches involved?"

"Nobody was hurt," I said defensively. "One boy got a scrape. I fixed it with a kiss and a Band-Aid." I couldn't remember what I'd said to Morna when I'd left her a voice mail during the party, but it must have been desperate. It must have . . .

I stopped cold. "You don't have an answering machine. I wasn't able to leave you a message."

She gave me her patient look, the one that indicates she has faith any moment I'll begin making sense.

"If you don't have an answering machine, then you didn't get my cry for help."

"That's quite true, dear."

"Then how do you know about the party?"

She took my hand in hers and started walking again toward a small park where people from HAG often lunched. "I find this park to be such a lovely and relaxing place for a stroll," she said. "It's the *alaihi* trees. A person positively cannot feel anything but peace in the shade of an *alaihi* tree."

As I moved one foot in front of the other, I realized she didn't need to answer. I knew how she knew. I couldn't believe he'd do it. I picked up speed, wanting to get to those damned soothing *alaihi* trees as quickly as possible.

10

WHEN I DROPPED off Dante a few days later at his dad's, Kam acted as if Elvis had just left the building and everything was fine. I stood in my designated spot on his porch when he opened the door, wiping his hands on a dish towel.

"Man—five o'clock already? You want to come in?"

I'd never been invited in before, but I couldn't take him up on it now. I was busy being the ice queen. "No thanks, I need to get going."

Dante scooted through the open door into the house. Kam grabbed the backpack from me, leaning close as he did. "Your hair smells nice."

"Dante has a field trip tomorrow," I responded. "They're going to a petting zoo. He'll need two dollars and a sack lunch."

"All right." He looked at me, confused. One day we were sitting around a table singing, and the next I was smelling nice and not saying thank you to his compliments, as though no betrayal had occurred between these two events.

"Make sure he's at school on time."

"Okay."

It wasn't until an hour after I'd left that I remembered Dante needed to wear his school T-shirt for the field trip. I dug it out of the laundry basket. It was damp but clean enough for a five-year-old. I tried calling Kam but hung up without leaving a message when I got his machine. I could just picture Her listening and making faces, which was what I would've done if she'd called.

Kam lived less than a mile away. I grabbed the shirt and headed over. I'd leave it outside where he'd be sure to see it when he and Dante returned from wherever they were.

From the porch, I could hear the television blasting cartoons in the living room. Dang, they were home. Not that they could see me. The curtains were drawn on the picture window near where I stood. I debated whether to leave the shirt and run. With a sigh, I rang the doorbell.

Dante's head appeared in the window between the folds of the curtain. When he saw it was me standing there, he pressed his mouth to the glass and blew so his face puffed like a blowfish. Then his head disappeared, leaving a wet smudge mark behind.

"Hold on!" he shouted through the door. I heard the turning of locks. Then he pulled on the door, but it didn't open. More turning of locks. Again, he tried the door. Still stuck. He kept locking the deadbolt and opening the other, then switching it around, never quite getting the two in the open position at the same time.

"Honey, try lining up the locks so they're both up and down," I shouted.

"Huh?"

I heard more jiggling of the door, then his foot kicked the bottom. "Man it!" he said, his version of swearing.

"It's all right. Get your dad. He can do it."

More kicking of the door, more loudly this time. He was getting frustrated. "I can't!"

"Just get him, sweetie. It's okay."

"He's not home."

Oh, God. Suzanne was baby-sitting. I was glad he couldn't see through the door the dread on my face. There was no way I wanted to deal with that woman, especially on her turf. I was intimidated enough without giving her home team advantage. She was probably watching right now, uncaring that my son was on the brink of a breakdown, just so she could get a chuckle at my expense.

"I'm bringing you your shirt for tomorrow. I'll leave it here. You can get it later."

Locks kept turning. He kept pulling on the doorknob.

"Dante?"

Then he pulled it open. "Got it!" He stood in the foyer, beaming with the success of his door-opening venture. Behind him was a needlepoint of a sunflower with the words, KAM AND SUZANNE WISH YOU A SUNNY DAY! My stomach turned like the locks.

As I bent down to give him a kiss, my eyes may have strayed toward the living room. Kam's body usually blocked the door. I'd never seen their home. He had real furniture now, like grown-ups do. It all matched, as though he'd pointed to a display in the showroom and said, "We'll take that," and she'd leaned her head on his shoulder and sighed, "Won't it be homey, dear?" Kam had once told me Suzanne's parents' owned the house. They must've sprung for the furnishings, too. There was no way they could pay for this on a tour guide's and hula dancer's salaries.

Dante grabbed my hand. "I got a Rainbow Warriors poster for my birthday. I'll show it to you."

"I can't, sweetie, I . . ."

"Come on, Mom. You never seen my room."

"Not today. I don't want to bother Suzanne."

"You won't. She's not here."

I let him pull me into the foyer. "What do you mean, she's not here? Who's watching you?"

He peeked at me through bangs that desperately needed trimming. "Me! I'm a big boy now."

"You're alone? Where are your dad and Suzanne?"

He shrugged, tugging on my arm to lead me toward the stairs. The locks in my stomach were spinning. Who would be stupid enough to leave a child barely five years old on his own?

"How long have they been gone?" The blare of the television suddenly seemed unbearable. I shut it off.

"Dad said he had to do some stuff."

"Would you say it has been five minutes? Or ten?"

"I dunno." He was growing wary, sensing his dad was in trouble but not sure why.

"What was on TV when he left?"

He relaxed. Clearly I'd moved on to other subjects. *"Underdog."*

The channel 13 lineup. *Fractured Fairy Tales* had been on when I turned off the TV. Kam must have left soon after I did. That meant Dante had been unsupervised for at least a half hour already. I may have known nothing of how five-year-olds' birthday parties were supposed to go, but I was well aware that a boy that age was too young to stay home alone. No one I knew did that. Except, of course, the father of my child, who had plenty of time to go blabbing to his lawyers about my incompetence, but couldn't manage to find the time to actually watch his child.

Morna would tell me to take deep breaths, but I was finding it hard to get air at all. Dante was pushing on my butt, trying to move me toward the stairs. "Pleeeease!" he begged.

"Okay, but don't push." He skipped ahead of me, leading me up the stairs. It was almost as if I could feel molecules parting like water to make way for me. The room moved; I stood still. I touched a silk vine wrapped around the banister. Photos dotted the wall up the stairs. Pictures of Kam and Her, Kam as a baby, and some people I didn't recognize, probably her side of the family.

Dante was playing tour guide; like father, like . . . He pointed out the bathroom, the guest room, then his Dad and Suzanne's room. The same impulse that makes me rubberneck at traffic accidents made me peer in their room. It was decorated in the same florals as the rest of the house. She had a bedspread nearly identical to the one I'd bought at Sleepland when Kam and I first separated, but, unlike me, she'd carried the color theme throughout the room, giving it those feminine touches that have always eluded me.

"Close your eyes!" Dante said. I let him lead me the rest of the way to his room. "Now look!"

When I opened my eyes, I finally saw Kam. Not literally Kam but, I realized for the first time, the only vestiges of the man with whom I'd once shared a home. His surfboard leaned against a wall, next to his collection of vintage skateboards. I saw the fishing poles he'd always kept in our living room because, he said, he liked looking at them. Dante's poster was pinned next to his father's old framed picture of the woman/liquor bottle/ sports car. And in the middle of the floor: the futon my husband had dragged from our home when he left me for another woman.

"It's a great room, baby."

I leaned against a sticker-covered dresser I recognized from Ma's house. Dante proceeded to give me a show-and-tell of his possessions. His Matchbox cars. A broken kite. A Happy Meal toy.

Then I noticed on the futon a snapshot from Kam's and my wedding. He was feeding me cake, carefully because, as I recalled, he was too stoned to try anything like shoving it in my face. I'd never seen the photo before.

"What's that picture?"

"Dad gave me that."

"Really . . ."

"I sleep with it when I miss you." Then he squeezed his arms around me with the instincts of a child smart enough to know when to act sentimental.

I couldn't wait to get out of that room. "Time to go downstairs," I said and, over the sounds of Dante's protests—"I haven't even got to show you the good stuff yet!"—I ran down the stairs like Cinderella, only without losing a shoe because I wearing some ninety-dollar loafers Regatta had talked me into buying and darned if I was going to leave one of those behind for Suzanne to try to stuff her nasty foot into.

Once I reached the front foyer—safe again, except for that needlepoint screaming at me—I was unsure what to do. I could wait for Kam to arrive, and then shout, *aha*! But what if Suzanne came home first? There'd be no satisfaction in *aha*-ing her. She'd probably have the gall to berate me for being in her house.

It was going on seven o'clock. Dante reached for the remote and clicked the TV back on, the image of his father.

"Get your stuff," I said suddenly. "You're coming home with me."

I grabbed his backpack and his shirt. I should leave Kam a note, I thought. There was probably a pen and a notepad on some decorative holder in the kitchen, right next to the phone where it belonged. It would only take a minute.

Yet I didn't. I just followed my son out the door and—I wouldn't have thought myself the type of person who would do this, although no one could say Kam didn't have it coming—I left the television on and the front door a few inches ajar.

THE FIRST THING I did when I got home was call Morna. Two could play this running-to-your-lawyer game. There was no answer, and, as always, no answering machine. I debated calling the police, but for what? I should have done that while I was still at his house, I scolded myself. I couldn't wait to get out of there, but I'd blown my best piece of evidence. Morna would know what to do, if I could get hold of her.

Kam hadn't called by eight o'clock. I read Dante a bedtime story through gritted teeth. At eight-thirty, I put him in my bed, knowing he'd fall asleep immediately there. That left me free to sit at the table and drum my fingers, get up, glare at the phone, walk over to the window and stare at the emptiness outside.

My mind was running over the scenarios. Either Kam still hadn't returned, or he had and wasn't telling me he'd lost our son.

A voice somewhere in the back of my head suggested that perhaps Kam had only meant to step out for a minute or two, but then something had happened to him. I swatted the thought away. Kam had blown it this time. I didn't want any stray thoughts of pity diluting my ire.

By nine-fifteen when the doorbell rang, I'd nearly convinced myself that Kam had lost Dante, forgetting he was sleeping safely in my room. I could picture it—Kam runs to pick up some weed. He decides he'll go ahead and sample the merchandise. By the time he returns, he's too stoned to even notice his son missing. No, even better, he returns home and sees the door open. Dante's gone, but Kam notices the television playing and sits down, forgetting what had concerned him earlier.

I almost expected *Munsters*-like creaking, so slowly did I open the door. There stood Kam, looking worse than I'd ever seen him. The color had drained from his face to leave him taupe.

"What brings you here?" I was going for a tone of bemusement, which was wasted on Kam at the moment.

"Keeley, I . . ." His words fell. He ran his hands down his face as if he'd stepped from the ocean and was wiping off water.

"Gosh, Kam, whatever could be the matter? Come on in."

"These last two hours have been hell. I don't know how to tell you this, but I've . . . I've . . ."

"Lost something?" I was standing before him, hands on my hips, ice queen smile on my face.

And it was as though I could hear a ping go off in Kam's head. He rushed past me to Dante's room. It was empty. But across the hallway it was possible to see into my room, see the lump of boy on the bed, lost only in his dreams, but not lost. Definitely not lost.

"You bitch," he said in a low voice.

"Excuse me, I didn't quite catch that."

His head was shaking, the ping of understanding rattling around in it as he came toward me. "What is this? You come over to my house and steal my son?"

Kam angry, it was a rare sight, at least from the front. Kam Angry was usually grabbing his keys or his skateboard and hauling ass out of the house without saying a word. This was new. Maybe Suzanne had taught it to him. It was interesting enough that I wanted to poke at his anger, make it fester. "You probably would have noticed if you'd been home."

Something flickered across his face. "I was gone for a minute."

"Try an hour."

"That is such bullshit." His voice trembled. "You have no right to come into my home and kidnap my son."

"Oh, please. And you, of all people, have no right to accuse anyone of kidnapping."

"I never came in here and stole Dante."

"No, you're leaving that up to your lawyers."

His hands reached up and pulled his hair back. "I knew you were bitter. I never thought you'd sink this low."

I was no longer so interested in seeing Kam Angry From the Front. I hated being yelled at—and I was not bitter. I was pissed. There was a difference, which I pointed out to him. "You want custody of our son so you can leave him home alone? Is that it?"

"Jesus, it was a minute!"

"You are such a liar." I nearly spit the words. "Are you out of your mind? Leaving Dante alone? I'll have you know I called Morna. So you can go ahead and make a case out of me throwing a bad party. I think they'll be much more interested in hearing how you abandoned your son."

"I'm so glad I got out of here. I don't know what happened to you, what turned you into such a bitch."

"Gosh, I don't know. Perhaps it was following my husband's dick all over town, wondering where it might be on any given night."

That was a good one, I told myself. It shut Kam right up; I could see his mind racing for a retort. I'd hoped it was something better than calling me bitch again. That was really hard to come back at. "As far as I'm concerned," he said, "This is war. Don't bother trying to talk to me. Don't call me for favors. Don't wear tight clothes and think I'm going to give a shit—"

My hand reached out and gave him a shove in the chest. I'd never done anything like it before, and I was as shocked as I'm sure he was. I didn't push him hard. Just enough to make him take a stumble back. Just enough to move him out of the way so I could see that Dante was standing in the hallway, holding the stuffed iguana I'd gotten him for his birthday and sucking his thumb.

"Dante . . . ," I said.

With his surfer's balance, Kam stayed on his feet and headed over to our son. He picked him up. "We're going home," he said.

The sight of Dante leveled my emotions. In a calm voice I said, "It's late. Let him go back to bed."

But Kam pulled his keys from his pocket and headed out the door, the only difference between this and when we were married being that now in his arms he held his son.

MORNA NEVER ANSWERED her phone that night. I'd tried until midnight. She did, however, happen to stop by my cubicle the next morning to bring me breakfast.

"I was in deep meditation, but I had a sense you were trying to reach me," she said, pulling a scone out of a paper sack and handing it to me. "And I said to myself: I'll bet she's hungry. So here I am!"

I couldn't help scowling. If she'd had some weird hippie vibe it was me ringing her, would it have killed her to pick up the phone? I grabbed a scone and broke off a piece. I was starving, not to mention sleep deprived. I'd been up most of the night fretting over whether I'd blown my chance to really stick it to Kam. I should have never left his house. I should have called the cops right then.

"Have a seat," I told Morna.

"Oh, no thanks, I prefer—"

"I'm not being polite. I actually mean sit down. And you'd better hold this." I picked up a notebook, a stack of paper, and a stapler and handed them to her. Delilah from personnel was hovering near my cubicle. I didn't want to give the appearance that I was conducting personal business on company time.

Morna sat agreeably and then began stapling the papers I'd handed her, stapling all four corners, then a line along the top. She looked busy enough, I decided, although her Birkenstocked foot swinging as she worked might raise a suspicion or two. My voice low, I told her what had happened the night before. Her head was down to concentrate on her stapling, so I was unable gauge her reaction.

"Be honest with me," I said. "I could have nailed Kam on neglect, am I right?"

"Most likely."

"Is it still possible? Or did I miss my chance?"

She'd made a row completely around the outside edges of a piece of paper, attaching it to nothing. "Hmm, your chance . . ."

"You don't have to keep doing that," I said, snatching the stapler from her. Her head lifted along with her brows.

"Sorry." Contrite, I handed it back. "I guess I'm miffed at you."

Her hands rested on the notebook, her face open. "Because—?"

"You weren't there for me last night. You didn't answer my call. I realize how stupid that sounds. You're my lawyer, not my mother. I know you have a right to a personal life, but—"

"My dear Keeley." She set the office supplies I'd given her aside and leaned forward to give me a firm kiss on the forehead before sitting back down. My gaze shifted up, as if I could see the stamp of her lips left behind. "Divorce law can be such a cruel game. You must feel like you're a marker on a playing board. Someone is moving you around, and who could blame you if once in a while you'd like to roll the dice yourself. Choose your own course. It's only natural that you would."

I wanted to ask her to answer my question, but Delilah stood at the door of the empty cubicle across from me. What was she doing here? Was it not obvious I was in the middle of a very important meeting? Morna must have caught my attention wandering, because she turned around in her chair.

"Hello, there!" Morna said to Delilah, startling her into spilling some of her coffee. "Keeley and I were finishing up some business. Am I interrupting a meeting that the two of you had scheduled?"

"Nothing urgent," Delilah said. "I had some news for Keeley. It can wait."

"Scone?" Morna held out the bag and then added, "News for Keeley! That certainly sounds intriguing. Positive news, too, I'll bet."

"Um . . . Keeley?" I'd never seen her so flustered. Long-hair types weren't supposed to meander into sacred government offices and then dare to be friendly.

My desire to see Delilah squirm under the intimidation of Morna's charm was exceeded only by the fact that I was dying to know if she was there with a response to my letter. I came clean. "Morna is a friend," I said. "You can tell me."

She stepped into my cubicle, occupying the two-foot square of space not otherwise filled with desks, equipment, or people. Her bottom teetered on the edge of the two-drawer file cabinet. After giving one last unsure glance toward Morna, she said, "I believe we may be able to honor your request to change departments."

I nearly leapt and kissed Delilah on the forehead myself. I settled for the more restrained, "That is good news."

"Personally, I'd hoped to put you in with the planning department . . ."

"That'd be great!" I said, a moment before it sank in that she said she had *hoped*. Anything was better than where I was, however, so I added, "I mean, wherever you move me I'm sure will be fine."

I could see relief wash over her face. "I'm glad to hear that. I agree that finance is certainly no place for you. I can't give you all the particulars until we run everything by management, but I'd wanted to stop by and find out how flexible you are."

"Very." I was already rehearsing my good-bye speech to Wagner. Thank you for the fine opportunities you've provided me, but duty calls elsewhere, you penny-pinching, micromanaging . . .

"Wonderful. You'll probably be notified next week when it's official." She nodded to Morna. "Pleasure meeting you."

Morna stood up. "You can walk me out. I've taken enough of Keeley's time."

I wasn't about to let her squirm away that easily. "About that issue we were discussing," I said, attempting to be vague in front of Delilah. The personnel department at HAG wasn't exactly known for discretion. "Will I be able to . . . I mean, do you think Kam and I—?"

Alas, Morna was not one to mince words. "I'll be frank—it would have been better if you hadn't left with the boy. You absconded with the evidence, and perhaps even opened yourself to kidnapping charges. But still," Morna continued, "If Kam is the type of person I believe him to be, you may be able to use this incident to your advantage. That is, if that's what you want."

"It's what I want."

"I'll take care of it, then."

As she left, I felt an unexpected chill through my arms.

OVER THE NEXT few days, not much happened, however—except that Dante seemed to have taken up biting. I discovered this when I pulled a note from Miss Mary Jo out of his backpack: "Dante bit a classmate today. Please discuss at home."

But as Dante was already asleep in bed by the time I found the note, I felt it best not to wake him to have our little heart-to-heart.

The notes that followed grew increasingly snippy. "Dante again bit a child. You NEED TO discuss this with him."

And—note clutched in my hand—I kissed his sleeping cheek. "Keep your teeth to yourself, little man."

Problem was, I'd been at the office till nine-thirty every night. Daisy Ku was picking up Dante after school. It was temporary, I told myself. Until I could officially move to a new department, I was doing two jobs: Wagner's annoying finance tasks, and the studies on the volcano that were growing increasingly necessary. Without a budget, everything was taking so much longer—and my Skipper connection had fizzled. He'd shrugged off my data, claiming it was inconclusive, and did I have any temperature readings? I was forced to drive around the mountain alone, sniffing for sulfur and taking water temperature readings with ancient equipment the professional equivalent of a drugstore thermometer. Then I'd clock countless hours in front of my monitor entering the data.

I knew Ma would be glad to take Dante, but I didn't want the hours I'd been working to get back to Kam.

On a night I managed to get out of work by eight, Dante was still awake when I picked him up at the Kus'. I'd expected him to be happy to see me after being apart for so long, but he refused to come home. I had to carry him kicking across the lawn. Daisy tried to help me by saying, "You gotta go, Dante. I'm handin' out the spankins now, and you don't wanna be here for that! Okay, boys, you all line up for the spankins!"

Two messages were lit on the answering machine when I walked in the door. One was from Ian, wanting to know what time to pick me up for the date we'd set up for Saturday night. The other was from Miss Mary Jo—and if I'd thought her notes were curt, they were nothing compared to the condescending tone of her voice. "I'm *uncertain* whether Dante re-alizes his *behavior* is *inappropriate*. Have you made that *clear*?"

It was time for Dante and me to have a long-overdue chat.

"I hear you bit some kids at school," I said. I was sorting through his backpack, pulling out squashed bananas and an uneaten baggie of rice cakes.

He'd already forgotten he hadn't wanted to come home. He slapped a flyswatter against the refrigerator door. Magnets and papers flew to the ground. "I guess so."

Which put me at a critical juncture. I couldn't condone the behavior. If I told him it was wrong to bite, he'd shut me out for being preachy. Yet worst of all, if I talked to him heart-to-heart—really drew him out and helped him understand his motivations—I'd risk sounding like my mother. It was a chance I had to take. "How come?"

I handed him some broken cookie crumbs from the bottom of his lunch sack, which he stuffed into his mouth without question.

He answered by chewing.

"You didn't use to bite your friends."

More chewing.

"Biting hurts, you know."

He looked up at me, moving his eyeballs only, not lifting his head, which gave the impression that he was rolling his eyes. His chewing slowed, as if I were the most insipid human on earth, and he a miniature teenager put here to defy me. I wanted to smack him one.

He had it coming, and I was going to give it to him good.

"I'm wondering, Dante," I said, "if the fact that you're suddenly biting children is an expression of your frustration over seeing your father and me fighting."

Chewing.

"And if by biting the other children, you're seeking an outlet for that anxiety, as well as a chance to draw attention—however negative it may be—so that you can sort out your confusion over what you witnessed." Gently, I removed the flyswatter from his hands. "Do you think that might be why you're biting?"

He swallowed and tipped his head up to me so he no longer appeared defiant. He just looked like a little guy dealing with stuff even grown-ups prefer to avoid.

"It feels good when I bite," he said matter-of-factly.

I hadn't expected to get to what was real so fast.

"Well, knock it off," I said, handing him another piece of cookie. "It's not okay."

THAT PSYCHOLOGY CRAP never worked on me, and apparently it didn't much affect my son. The school called me the next day to report that he'd sunk his teeth into a girl. This one was spunkier than the others and had returned the favor. When I went to get Dante from Daisy Ku's, he had a mouth-shaped welt on his arm. I felt a twinge of guilt mixed with embarrassment. How many parents had found Dante's teeth prints on their children?

Daisy saw me check him and motioned me into her kitchen. "He said a girl did it."

"I know. The school called. Dante started it. He's been biting kids all week."

"Auwe!" She opened the refrigerator door and disappeared behind it. Now I could only hear the sound of containers being shuffled around, and Daisy's humming.

I glanced into the living room. A pile of assorted boys were sprawled in front of the television. Dante was in borrowed pajamas, digging his fist into a bowl of popcorn. He opened his mouth wide to cram a handful in. Most fell around him in an avalanche.

"I'm thinking I should cancel my date tomorrow," I said to the refrigerator. "I'm supposed to go to an art opening with that guy, Ian. But maybe I should spend the time with Dante instead."

The door shut, and Daisy shoved a cube of butter in my hand. "Butter. Not oleo. That'll stop the biting."

I examined the stick. "What? Does he eat it?"

"Rub it on his teeth. It's better if you do it in the morning right before school."

"Thanks, but I don't think—"

"Believe me. It's what I did with Chuckie. That boy chewed more than a dog with a bone. Just put a dab on your finger, then smooth it over his teeth. It's gotta be butter, too. That oleo doesn't do a darn thing."

I tucked the butter in my purse to appease her. As if strong-arming Dante into clothes in the morning and getting him breakfast weren't hard enough. I'd seen what teeth on skin could do. I wasn't getting my finger near his mouth.

"I'll give it a try," I lied, "But I'm still not sure about the date."

The second part was true. I was seriously waffling. Ian seemed a bit too good to be real. Like Groucho Marx, perhaps I was suspicious of a club that would have me as a member. Sure, I knew I deserved a kind, smart, and—for that matter—really *pretty* guy. I simply found it suspicious that such a man would realize it, too. Besides, I'd had someone declare his affections for me immediately before, and I still stung from the memory of where that landed me.

Better that I devote my limited time to Dante, I decided. The poor kid was obviously having a tough time with everything that was happening.

Daisy pulled a broom from the closet and started sweeping. "So you're going to an art opening. Sounds fancy."

"It should be. It's in the Healoha House."

She gave me a stern look. "You're not going to look at more of that terrible paper, are you?" Daisy Ku was a devout Catholic. Although I knew the origami incident must have bothered her, she'd never said a word.

"It's paintings, and I don't think I'm going to go, anyway. I think Dante's

biting has to do with me working so much." I didn't mention the fight
with Kam.

"All this crazy talk! This guilt! You *haole* worry too much!"

"It's the timing of it all. Dante didn't start acting up until—"

"*Auwe!* He's a boy. Boys bite. They kick and hit and punch. He's at that
age. Use the butter. It'll do the job, I tell you. Then go on your date."

I thanked her and then went to the living room to collect my son. To
look at him—watching TV, facedown on the floor, bottom in the air,
surrounded by the pile of popcorn that hadn't made it into his mouth—
he seemed so sweet.

I knelt to scoop him up. His body rolled away from my hands. His hair
was lit from behind by a halo of television light.

"I don't wanna go."

"It's late," I said, my voice soft.

"I don't wanna go with you, Mumma. I hate you." He said it with the
same gentleness I'd just used. Then he rolled back to the TV.

Daisy ran water in the kitchen. The Blues Brothers headed a police
chase through a mall. My son was despising me with such ease he didn't
even bother to yell it. All I could do was hide in the crowd of Ku boys,
wishing they were watching something sappy so I'd have an excuse to cry.

AFTER I'D CARRIED Dante home and put him to bed, I called Ian. I sat
on the edge of the Perfect Sleeper, pulling off my socks.

"Keeley! It is a delight to hear from you. I'm looking forward to our—"

"Yes, about that," I interrupted, not wanting him to get too far into the
pleasantries—although I had to say he was, as always, pleasant. "I can't
make it tomorrow. I'm sorry this is such late notice. Something came up."
Realizing how lame that sounded, I added, "My son . . . is not . . . feeling
well."

Ian was silent for a moment. I tried to determine if it was anger, but
when he spoke I decided it was more in the manner of finding the right
words. "That is disappointing news."

"I was looking forward to it, too," I offered, remembering that I had
been before my son had pulled a Linda Blair on me.

"Well, I understand that you're busy."

"You're not kidding. I've been crazed." A bath. I needed a bath. I was so tired, my follicles ached. I headed into the bathroom. "I'd love a rain check."

"You'll be missing quite an opening. I was really hoping you could make it. Particularly since, I must confess, I did a bit of boasting that my date was going to be the loveliest girl in the room."

I twisted the bath water on. Okay, I felt cheap, but I loved being called lovely.

"We'll have to do it again some time," I hinted.

My mind raced to come up with some way to prolong the conversation. What with the other men in my life lately sharing their disdain for me, it was nice to hear a kind word from someone representing that gender.

But he said, "I hear the bath running. I'll leave you to it."

And that was that. There were the usual polities. The standard good-byes. But at no point, I noted, did he say, "Yes, let's set another date."

What was up with that? I wondered as I finished pulling off my clothes. I sank into the tub, even though it had only a few inches of water. It wasn't the steamy Calgon-take-me-away sensation I'd been hoping for—but then again, I hadn't been willing to wait.

I ENDED UP going into work on Saturday, sorting through stacks of computer printouts. If I could get enough evidence, I thought, I could go over Skipper's head. As it stood, if I couldn't sway an old friend into believing, what chance did I have of getting total strangers to part with tens of thousands of dollars?

I needed bodies to handle the workload. Not to mention my desperate need for equipment that dated later than the pieces I managed to dig up at HAG—stuff I was convinced they'd bought back when Kohala erupted the first time around, thousands of years ago. I found myself drooling with the desires of a child at Christmas pouring over a Sears catalog at the thought of being able to send divers to look for lava leaks underground. For that matter, even possessing the most basic tools to measure gases and soil pH levels or—dare I dream?—access to helicopters so I could set up equipment beyond where my Jeep could take me. For all I knew, the mountain was a literal hotbed of fumaroles and palagonite, and I wouldn't know it until it was too late.

Dante spent the day running up and down the deserted corridors. Not exactly the bonding experience I'd had in mind, but I was starting to relax about him. He seemed to be back to his usual sweet self. Besides, we would still have the entire night to engage in tender mother-son moments.

Back at the house, I was setting up the Hi Ho! Cherry-O game board when the doorbell rang.

It was Kam, coming to get his son for his visitation. Just as he did every Saturday night at six, or thereabouts. Dante ran past me out the door with his backpack. He shouted a cheery, "Bye, Mom!"

Kam said not a word. He turned and followed Dante out. The strange thing was, I'd known he was going to his dad's, yet I'd made plans with him anyway. It was as though I'd thought I could experience Saturday night in some parallel universe—one in which two parents could share time with their child.

"Bye," I said limply to the two similar figures making their way down my front walk. One tall, one small. Both in surf jams, hair too shaggy, walking loosely. Kam knew I was watching. The least he could have done was appear self-conscious. Get those hands out of his pockets, and skip that part where he turned to Dante, easy smile on his face, saying something that made my boy crinkle his nose in return.

And to quote Gilbert O'Sullivan and the most depressing song ever recorded, there I was, alone again, naturally.

Morna had made some noise earlier in the week about filing a complaint against Kam for negligence. "You may get what you want, my dear," she had told me. Which I found to be an interesting comment, as it implied I knew what it was I wanted. It occurred to me that this could be the last time I'd watch Kam saunter down my walkway.

The Hi Ho! Cherry-O game still sat on my table, ready to be played when Dante returned. The computer clock said 6:37. Just to feel a connection to a human, I e-mailed Sandra.

ME: I gave up a date for my son, then he left me for another man.

I went to the kitchen and opened a Diet Coke. 6:42.

When I returned, Sandra still hadn't responded. It had been more than two minutes. Was nothing right in the world?

I went to my closet, the room lit only by the flicker of the computer screen. I pulled out a skirt and some shimmery top I'd once bought when in a mood. As I put them on, I thought about Kam, how he'd promised no longer to respond when seeing me in anything tight. By pondering while dressing, I'd managed to kill seven more minutes.

In the meantime, Sandra had replied, from where she was in Tanzania, I believe. What time was it there, 4 A.M.?

WANDERLUST: Sons are not lovers. When are you going to find yourself a grown-up man?

I shut off the computer. When, indeed.

I picked up my keys, climbed into my Jeep, and drove to Healoha House.

11

WHEN I'D REHEARSED the scene in my mind, it was in slow motion: Ian watching from the doorway as I arrived. The way he shyly pushed back his hair as he ambled over to open my car door. And his face revealing his elation at my unanticipated arrival. Then we'd do that air kiss thing, which no one does in Hawaii, but no one goes to art openings either. I'd blush, thinking how refreshing it was to feel so adored.

The sting I felt at arriving without reception was irrational. He wasn't expecting me.

Still, it took all my nerve to bluff my way past the sign-in desk. The lady there grilled me to such a degree, I was surprised she didn't ask for a blood sample. Perhaps she read the *Bee* and recognized me as an art thief. Or maybe it was the grease stain on my shirt—seemed I'd forgotten to take Daisy's butter out of my purse, which I'd discovered when emerging with a fistful of it instead of my identification. I was waved away in disgust, which I chose to interpret as being invited in.

I meandered the narrow hallways. One led to another but to nowhere in particular. I paused to check out the paintings, which I took to be those squares of canvas to which someone had applied paint.

A handful of people were on the same hallway circuit. All wore black and therefore possessed the courage—if not the right—to say things like, "Bold, really, the use of symmetry."

I resisted the temptation to join in, to add a "What do you think of the angle of that squiggly thing? Ninety degrees, wouldn't you say?"—less out of respect for art than fear they'd jeer, "What was that, *Butter Girl*?" (Then one would look down his glasses and declare, "Good Lord, I believe it's *margarine*.") I nabbed a martini off a passing tray.

It was going be harder than I'd thought to find Ian. He was definitely here somewhere, however; his name was checked off the guest list.

I wandered into what must have been the main room. More paintings on—thankfully—less claustrophobic walls. Chamber music. Candlelight. People engaging in social discourse; clusters of them about the room, paying no attention to the art or to me. Thus giving me an opportunity to fish that tempting little olive from my martini, my finger chasing it about in my glass which, frankly, proved to be the most entertainment I'd had since arriving.

When I looked up, triumphant from my olive hunt, my eyes met Ian's.

He was standing at the edge of a group of people across the room. We must have noticed each other at the same time. I gave him a wave hello, but the expression of delight I'd been expecting didn't cross his face. I used my waving hand that was now dangling stupidly in the air to brush back my bangs, as though that was all I'd meant to do in the first place. It was the butter stain. I was sure of it. He was going to pretend not to know me.

I found myself in the slow motion footage I'd imagined earlier, only a really shitty version of it. There was no use bolting from the room, either. I would just run endlessly through those hallways—one leading into another only to wind up back here, that much lower on the dignity scale for my efforts.

Ian said something to the people he was with, then headed over to me. "Keeley, this is a surprise." And I noted, not necessarily a welcome one.

"My son was feeling better, so I could join you after all," I said, attempting to sound casual.

He glanced back the at the group he'd been with, and that's when I noticed. The woman who'd been standing next to him. Although I can't imagine I'd managed to miss her before. She was gorgeous, and not in the usual way, but in that billowy, bored way that made her seem like a photograph of herself. Posed and airbrushed and without a doubt, as Ian had hoped, the prettiest girl in the room.

"Oh, dear," he said to me, as always pronouncing it *deah*, which was suddenly more adorable than I'd remembered. "This is quite—"

"Embarrassing," I finished. "You're here with someone."

He jingled pocket change nervously. "I'd thought you weren't coming."

"It's all right," I assured him. "I've been having a great time. Saw some nice paintings. I'm thinking of tucking one into my dress on my way out."

And if he hadn't at the moment been throwing me over for some supermodel, I'd swear—as he flashed those crow's feet at me (and *dang* they were cute)—that he was glad to see me.

"I'd love to show you about," he said, "But I fear it wouldn't be . . . um . . ."

"No problem." I set the still-full martini down on a nearby cocktail table.

"It is nice to see you."

"Like I said, it's been fun. Don't worry. I'll be getting going. I didn't mean to horn in on your date."

Which was, of course, his cue to correct me, to tell me that it wasn't a real date. That she was his sister or a professional colleague or just some lady who happened to be standing there, for heaven's sake. A goddess such as myself was not so easily replaced.

He only nodded. "Promise me you'll drive carefully."

"BASTARD," I GRUMBLED a few days later beneath my breath.

He'd foiled me. Wagner, the dirty cheat.

Delilah had stopped me in the coffee room while I grabbed a Diet Coke from the staff refrigerator. My stomach was still reeling from encountering things long dead in there when she dropped the bomb.

"Good news!" she said.

"It's official?"

"Official. You are now a member of the public relations department. It's not a perfect fit for you but—"

"But much better than where I am now," I assured her. "Public relations. Thank you." I'd met the head of the PR department before. She seemed normal enough.

"The best part is, you'll still be reporting to Wagner. He's taking over the department."

"Huh?" That was the entirety of my reaction. I had, I'm sure, that look on my face where one corner of the lip goes up and both eyes cross—that same sort of expression I'd get from Wagner every time I used words that employ more than two syllables.

"He was excited about bringing you with him. Insistent, in fact. Said he had big plans for you. So you see how ideally everything worked out?"

The deed was announced at the all-staff meeting. At least I'd been given a warning. My coworkers shifted around in their seats to get a glimpse at me. (Was this a surprise? Will we get to see her cry?) But I put on my Brave Girl Face and appeared serene with that Lamaze trick of focusing on an object in the room. Which in this case was Bob, who was mouthing, "I'm sorry," in my direction.

Throughout the day, people stopped by my cubicle to offer their condolences, except Beula. All four feet seven inches and eighty pounds of her snarled at me, "Well, congratulations, Miss Everything PR Girl. Looks like you won. God forbid they give a plum job like that to a lowly receptionist. This is the millionth promotion I've been passed over for. I'll be answering these damn phones till I croak from old age."

I'd have taken Beula's wrath personally if it weren't for the fact that she talked that way to everyone. An understandable bitterness at what once may have been an unfair lack of respect had turned her mean and dry as a dog bone. Even the executive director was afraid of her.

I didn't tell Delilah what was wrong—she'd seemed so proud. Instead I went crawling behind her back to the personnel director. He dismissed me with undisguised annoyance, saying HAG couldn't fiddle in every minor personality conflict. He'd been under the impression this was an issue of function, which was now solved, wasn't it?

Wagner had orchestrated this to torment me; I was sure of it. I'd have confronted him on it, if I hadn't been so busy avoiding him all day—and successfully at that, I snickered to myself. That was, until I stepped in the elevator to go home, my arms loaded with stacks of data that I hoped to review that night.

"Well, well. If it isn't the newest member of HAG's PR department. Welcome aboard." It was Wagner.

I backed up like a trapped animal, ready to fight with my mightiest weapon: sarcasm. "So is this part of your duties now—riding up and down greeting people?"

"If that's what the job takes."

"Good use of our taxpayer dollars." I hoisted the papers in my arms, which were slipping from the weight.

"We all need to pitch in. We're a team!" This was underscored with a left hook punch to the air. "There's lots of work to be done. No room for egos."

I resorted to watching the floor numbers change. His stupidity was a shield against the sarcasm.

My arms ached. Floor four, three . . . Each number as it lit up was more fascinating than the one before. The elevator stopped at the second floor. The doors opened, and people shuffled in. I had to hunch my shoulders to avoid physical contact with Wagner. The doors stayed open as if holding out for the entire population of the floor. The man in front of me pecked the CLOSE DOORS button.

"By the way," Wagner said as though delivering welcome news, "I have an assignment for you."

"I don't see how I can handle anything else. I'm swamped. This whole Kohala thing is ready to explo—"

"This is top priority," he broke in. "Urgent."

I said nothing, so he continued. "The big guy wanted to give this to somebody else with more experience. But I told him, 'No way; I got just the gal for the job. It's a primo deal, a chance for you to show me what you can do."

"I'm already doing all I can do."

He gave an exaggerated sigh. "I probably shouldn't tell you this, but I want to help you out. I've had grounds to fire you for some time. See, I've been documenting the assignments I've given you that have not been completed. Real work that's essential to the agency."

This was not happening, I told myself. I was not crammed in an elevator while my insipid boss threatened my job in front of strangers who were suddenly coughing and shifting their feet to mask the sound of our conversation. The doors closed.

"Do you get it, Kekuhi? If you want to stick around to work on that volcano you love so much, maybe you want to take what I say more seriously."

"But, I—"

"But nothing. You seem to forget—you're a subordinate. You can't go rushing off deciding what you want to do any time you please."

"Fine," I said. I'd buckled, but I wasn't about to give him the pleasure of hearing me ask what the assignment was. The elevator descended under the weight of my humiliation. Floor one . . . lobby exit.

Wagner finally cracked. "You get to rename the agency."

"Excuse me?"

"That's right—a new name for Hawaiian Associated Governments. We've taken hits in the media for the acronym. People seem to find it amusing," he huffed. "You will deliver your ideas at the next advisory board meeting. New name. New slogan. They'd better blow me out of the water."

"This isn't my area of expertise," I said weakly. He answered with a you-can-do-it fist in the air.

Besides, I didn't want to admit it, but I was already busy working on a better name than HAG. *Drag,* I thought. *Snag, fag, lag, brag.*

WAGNER WAS TRUE to his word. He was going to incorporate me into the public relations department if it sucked the life from us both. It was as though he'd planted a tracking device on me. He'd stop me on the way to the bathroom, at the copier; he'd sneak up on me at my desk, always with a task he said would take but a minute.

I hardly slept the entire week. *Sag, tag, bag.* Rhymes for the agency raced through my mind like a mantra while I lay in the dark. They went with the rhythm of the fan that I ran every night for the sound it made. The soothing hum that drowned out the stifling quiet of a Hawaiian night.

Kam used to complain about the fan. He said he felt as if he were sleeping on a runway. Maybe that's why I liked it. That sensation of jetting away, as far as possible from the shame spiral my life had become. The empty space on bed next to me had never loomed so vast. My son, Kam, Regatta, my boss—they all hated me. Even Ian, who I'd hoped would at least be an ego boost, had tossed me aside for some anemic starlet.

Then the last straw, a power outage. That alone was no tragedy. We had them weekly. Some worker on the night shift at Iwalani Water & Power would tire of being unable to see the stars and say to his buddy,

"Hey, bro, how 'bout we pull a switch and get rid of some of dis extra light, hah? It's blockin' da stars." Off would go the porch lamps, the night-lights, the alarm clocks, but . . . dang it . . . then my fan quit, too. It whirred to a stop in an agonizing death scene, making me want to throw myself atop it, crying, "Spin, just once more, I'm beggin' ya, take me away from all this nothing."

I suspect it was the demise of white noise that led me to what I did next. My hands acted of their own volition—feeling for my purse on the floor, digging out my cell phone, dialing. Somebody out there had to want me, damn it. I was going to thrust my life forward, no matter how far back I had to go to do it.

Ian's machine picked up. At the beep, I said, "I know this is late to be calling, but—"

There was the fumble of a phone on the other end and then a groggy voice. "Keeley?"

"Yeah, it's me, sorry I'm—"

"What time—? It's half of two. Are you all right?" He sounded more confused than concerned.

"You said you could take me to see Davy Jones." I pulled the sheets up so they nestled against my chin.

"Pardon?"

"Davy Jones," I repeated. Perhaps I'd shocked him by getting to the point so quickly, but the time didn't seem right for small talk. "I don't know if you mean flying to the mainland or what, but I really want to go. As soon as possible. I don't even know how I'll pay, but I'll find a way. I desperately need to—"

"I said I'd take you to see Davy Jones?"

My heart sank. "Didn't you?"

"Hold on, please . . . wait . . ." There was more fumbling on the other line; then he was back and, to my dismay, asking the one question I didn't want to answer. "Why is it you're calling at this hour for this?"

"I just . . . need to get out of here."

He hesitated. "Are you in some sort of trouble? Because I know people who could—"

"I'm not in trouble."

"Okay, well, then . . ." And in the pause that followed, I realized how foolish I must sound, what a huge request I was making of someone I hardly knew. The last time I so much as saw the guy was at the art show, which, of course, had been cut short. What with him being on a date. *Oh, God*—I knocked the phone against my forehead—*what had I been thinking? A date.* With the supermodel/starlet/overly tall famine victim. She was probably there right now, in fact, snuggled next to him on the bed, giving him little kisses down his chest, unfastening the buttons on his pajama bottoms. Whispering, Baby, who is that lunatic calling in the middle of the night?

"I'm sorry, this was a dumb idea," I stammered, eager to get off the phone, to pretend I'd never called in the first place. "I can't believe I even—"

"Give me a day or two to pull it together."

As he said it, the fan kicked on, making me shiver even though the night was warm. The alarm clock blinked midnight.

"You don't have to do this. Really."

"I realize that, and, to be frank, I'm not even certain where Davy Jones is these days. But you sound desperate, and if I can make it happen—" His voice perked up, "Well, why not? I have more air miles than I know what to do with. It could be great fun. Quite an adventurous second date, wouldn't you say?"

"Third, if you want to get technical. The second was the art show." I'd meant it to be amusing, as in Ha, ha, remember that time I walked in on you with that other woman? Remember how you could dig up a gorgeous date at a moment's notice, whereas I'm more the type who prefers begging men for favors at all hours of the night? You know, amusing in that way.

"Yes, well, all righty then," was all he said. "Why don't I plan to call you after I've had a chance to work out some of the details."

THE NEXT MORNING, I woke at dawn with a stabbing pain in my side. Dante had crawled into bed with me and was lying sideways, digging his feet into my waist.

I shifted his body around so we were cuddling, careful not to wake him. He needed the sleep, and frankly, I needed the affection. These days, once he was conscious, there was no guarantee I'd get it. When I pressed my lips to his forehead, even in his slumber he wiped it away.

Three stolen kisses and as many forehead wipes later, I sat bolt upright, sending Dante tumbling to the mattress. Had I actually committed in the middle of the night to an exodus with a near-stranger to see a former teen idol?

Oh, hell, yes, I thought as I leapt from the bed. It was sinking in, what I'd put into action while my fan faltered. I stood in my Hawaii U sleep shirt, my feet cool on the floor. "I'm going to go to Wallyworld," I whispered gleefully to the lump of covers that was my son, "and I'm going to have fun."

The timing, of course, couldn't have been worse. Or better, depending on one's perspective. My job hung in the balance. Dante needed me. I didn't want to imagine what Kam would do if he got hold of my plans. And I was willing to risk it—all to get face-to-face with a man who, to be honest, I should have gotten over thirty years ago.

It was about the stupidest thing I remember doing, at least on purpose. Yet my mind raced: When would we leave? What would I do with Dante? (The Kus had the chicken pox; Kam was off-limits. But forget that.) What would I wear? When I'd been a girl, the see-through vinyl skirt had been so perfect. If only I'd kept it.

It wasn't yet 6 A.M. I was itching to tell someone. Who could I possibly call at this hour who would care?

ME: I'm going to meet Davy Jones.
WANDERLUST: And I'm off to see the Wizard, the wonderful Wizard of Oz.
ME: Seriously. Some old school chum of his is taking me to meet him in the next couple days.
WANDERLUST: Why would you want to endure that humiliation again?

I clicked off the computer without answering. Sandra was sounding more like Mom every day. I played hard-to-get for the time it took to brush my teeth; then I got back on line.

ME: Hoping you would know. My excitement over this is downright embarrassing.

WANDERLUST: That's okay. Why, any girl would sell her left breast, not to mention her puka shells, to meet a hunk like him.

ME: You're mixing your teen idols. David Cassidy wore puka shells.

WANDERLUST: Can't believe I loved Davy Jones so much at one point it drove me to poetry. Now I can't even remember how he accessorized. Had no idea you were still a fan.

Me, neither, I thought. Truth was, I hadn't given much thought to Davy Jones for thirty years—that was, until the Ian connection.

Sandra had been the one keeping *Tiger Beat* in business. She had the bigger allowance and no problem pissing it away for the latest foldout. Then the summer before I entered sixth grade—those were the Donny days—I'd ambled into Sandra's room, scandalized to see actual wall. She'd stacked her posters on the floor. "You can have them," she'd said without emotion.

"You're throwing them away?" I picked up a headshot of Donny from the floor. It had torn on the fold when she'd pulled it down, so now it looked as if he had a gap between his front teeth. I desperately wanted it. I wanted to grab the entire pile of them in my arms and cart them to the safety of my room.

It was obvious. Sandra had jumped camp. She'd been talking about some boy named Scott for weeks now. I'd combed her *16* magazines to find him, only to discover this Scott fellow was *in her class.* Hard to fathom being able to conjure up interest in a boy in your grade—to find one of interest who could—oh, I don't know—*sing*, for example. Or know that the correct answer to the question, "What do you like best in a girl?" is *"Her sense of humor."* Or, for that matter, a boy who could look at you unblinkingly and really see you. I seriously doubted Scott could do any of those things. So far all Sandra could say to recommend him was that he'd shot a spitball, hitting the librarian.

I crumpled the poster and let it drop to the floor. "No thanks," I said, matching her lack of emotion, "I'm not into that stuff anymore."

So, lo these many years later, I made sure I had the last word with Sandra before logging off.

ME: You could have warned me you were going to grow up so fast.

LEAVE IT TO Regatta to ask the question that I would have preferred to keep buried in the back of my mind where it had been harming no one.

"So I know why you want to meet Davy Jones, it being your destiny. But why do you think Ian is willing to take you there?"

I had stopped by the salon where she worked to get a trim on my lunch hour. We spoke to each other in the mirror, where I tossed out the answer I'd been telling myself: "He's just being nice."

"Yes, because he has a crush on you," she said. "Sit still, will you? You're squirmer than a child. My question is, why would he then take you to see another man?"

I stalled by taking a mouthful of the tuna melt I'd brought with me and then making those motions people make when trying to show that they're far too polite to talk with their mouths full. Regatta took the opportunity to spritz me with water, letting it drip down my neck and soak my collar. She was never one of those people who'd ask a question and then move on because they really didn't care about your answer. She'd wait silently until we'd both grown old if that's what it took. I continued pretending to chew.

Life was on its way back to normal. All seemed forgiven in an instant between Regatta and me when I'd told her about my trip. I would like to say it was on the strength of my charm, but in fact, I had something Regatta wanted in the upcoming Davy Jones visit. Like a male friend of mine who used to stock *People* and *Glamour* on his coffee table as Girl Bait (*"You all go for them,"* he'd sneered, *"like mice to cheese"*), I finally had some decent Regatta Bait. The whole thing was practically dripping in lark value. She couldn't stay away, no matter how annoyed she was with me for my poor showing thus far as a matron of honor.

Before I could sneak another bite of my sandwich, she said, "Well?"

"What are you saying? That you think Ian's up to something?"

"Not at all. He seems to be jumping through hoops to get to you. *Tres* romantic. So considering that, it's going to be difficult to sneak off and sleep with Davy Jones."

"*The* Davy Jones?" That was Lawrence piping in, the fabulous guy who had the chair next to Regatta's. I'd never seen him with a customer. He seemed to be there for atmosphere.

When I nodded, he said, "Don't bother, honey. Picked him up on the gaydar. Won't be interested."

"Davy Jones is not gay." I believe Regatta and I said that in harmony.

"Gay," he said in a superior snip.

"Not."

"Then why do you think your man there feels so safe taking you to see him?"

A woman with perm solution on her head two chairs down said, "The ladies are right. He's as straight as the day is long. Saw it on TV. I think he was an *E! True Hollywood Story*."

The matter settled, Lawrence leaned over excitedly. "So, then, are you going to *do* him?"

I turned to tell him I had no idea what—much less who—I was going to do, but Regatta chided me, "I'm holding a scissors here. Do you want me to put your eye out?"

So I told them about the plan Ian had outlined when he'd called me at work earlier. Davy Jones regularly performed Friday nights at a small Hollywood club. Ian said that the two of them had been playing phone tag—hadn't had a chance to actually connect, and if I wanted to postpone . . . When I'd been unable to contain a disappointed sigh, Ian said, "But, of course, let's do it! Nothing ventured . . ." He and I would fly out of the Hilo airport tomorrow morning, and with the time change, arrive in time to check into our hotel and head over.

"It's all most appropriate," I assured everyone. "Separate rooms. The Marquis."

"*Money*," Lawrence cooed. "Forget Davy—is your delivery boy available?"

"That's the problem," Regatta piped in, facing me as she snipped a straight line along my bangs. "You'll have to be very sensitive to Ian's feelings, Keeley. Don't flaunt Davy Jones in his face."

From the Perm—"What's the big deal about Davy Jones? Isn't he kind of a has-been?"

"Unfinished business," Regatta said, with such finality even I felt it was an answer.

Hair tickled me as it fell to the floor. Regatta looked at me with seriousness, her face inches from mine as she worked. "Remember—Ian came into your life to bring you to Davy. We know that, but he doesn't. Be kind."

Before I left the salon, Regatta agreed to watch Dante for the night. Lawrence stuffed a multipack of condoms he happened to have handy in my fist. When I balked, he snapped, "It's not as if I'm lending you my worn panties. They're unopened. Better safe than sorry."

AS I HAD once been sorry for want of birth control, I tucked the condoms in my suitcase when I packed the next morning. It was silly, I told myself. What was I going to do—throw Davy Jones up against a jukebox and have my way with him?

When the phone rang, I assumed it was Ian checking in, given the early hour. I was wrong. It was apparently Lauren Bacall, or maybe Barry White, judging by the throaty voice. "Keel, it's me, Reg. I'm . . . sick . . . as a . . . dog."

I'd like to say my first thought was, *Oh, my poor friend*, but, as usual, it was poor me. "You sound awful," I said, taking the high road. "Need anything?"

"Been . . . throwing up . . . all night. Can't . . . take Dante."

I assured her it was no problem; I'd come up with something (a lie). My heart sank as I cradled the phone. My escapade was over before it had begun. There would be no trip to Wallyworld for me, I thought, as I started pulling clothes out of the suitcase. No madcap fun. Just a pitiful, unending march of fights with my son, with my boss, with my ex, with his mother . . .

His mother, I repeated. The mother who was on my side. The one who didn't want her son to leave with her grandson. Who, face it, had nothing better to do than watch Dante while I went jetting off on my . . . uh . . . business trip.

The clothes were piled back in the suitcase and Ma confirmed to pick up Dante after school. I was on my way to the airport my usual ten minutes late. Life was sweet.

There were those initial awkward moments when I met Ian at luggage check. He was leaning against a pop machine talking on his cell phone. He jumped when I tapped him, nearly dropping his phone.

After he'd said a hurried good-bye to whoever he was talking to, he reached over—I thought to hug me hello—so I hugged him back. Except that he was only taking my bag. I pulled away as though I'd been unmasked as a masher.

With that, I began my mental travelogue, moments of note and/or humiliation to gift-wrap for Regatta for her later amusement: *10 A.M.. Boarded, traveling first class; flight attendants better-looking up here than in coach.*

Seats in the full upright and locked position. Tray tables stowed. I was prepared to use my seat cushion as a flotation device should the need arise. And I couldn't think of a thing to say to the man sitting next to me.

All I wanted to talk about was Davy Jones. I wanted to giggle like girlfriends over the fact that we were going to come face-to-face with one of the Monkees, then scream while holding each other jumping up and down, hysterical and teary-eyed. Somehow I couldn't picture myself doing that with Ian. As a result, it was feeling so serious. I had no idea the etiquette for having a man I'd once kissed introduce me to one I'd once loved. Regatta was right about this being a delicate situation, I thought, glancing over at Ian's profile as he motioned to the flight attendant.

"Let's make a party of this, shall we?" he said. "What are the chances I can talk you into a Bloody Mary?" as though that were going to take some real arm twisting.

When the drinks arrived, he tapped his glass to mine.

"A toast . . . ," he said, "To getting you good and sauced so you'll finally confess to me why we're on this odyssey."

10:20 A.M. Things suddenly become interesting.

"I'll have you know I'm quite the lush," I said, meeting his eyes, sipping with bravado. "I can drink you under the tray table."

Noonish . . . mid-Pacific, so not sure exact time zone. Killed time regaling each other with "I was soooo drunk" stories, strangely encouraging current alcohol consumption rather than serving as impediment.

Besides tales of getting falling-down pissed, to quote Ian, we talked art, politics, history, science. I'd forgotten how sexy intelligence can be—mine, I'm referring to. No one had challenged my wits on social turf in a long time. It was as though with each question Ian asked, each topic he raised, he was undressing me. We were in a game of strip conversation, and I was barely hanging on to my undies. Frankly, the entire time I explained the difference between pyroclastic and monoclastic volcanic flows, I could've sworn I saw his breathing deepen. I felt so cheap.

Reset my watch to L.A. time. 1:15 P.M. Would have thought first class would rate a more current movie than Dirty Dancing.

I may have let it slip that I hadn't had sex in a year. What was I thinking, letting Ian give me that *Cosmo* quiz?

Demanding that he 'fess up to his last lay as a show of solidarity proved fruitless. Admittedly, I was fishing to see if he'd wink and say, "Ah, yes, last week—you remember my billowy acquaintance, Chantal, don't you?" But he'd only talk about the last time he was in love. Which would have been dull except that it had been twenty years . . . *twenty!* While I tossed my high school graduation cap in the air, the woman who would become his ex-wife was tearing his heart to ribbons. Since then, it had been nothing but loveless, empty sex.

Actually, as I recall, the conversation went something like, "So you haven't been a relationship for two decades, then?"

To which he replied, "I believe what I said is that I haven't been in love"—a remark he then punctuated by poking me in the side of the head with his stirrer.

The flight continued. A secret uncovered—Ian has never flown coach.

Ever. I would have thought it not possible, but apparently there is an entire fleet of wealthy British schoolboys who've never known a moment's discomfort. He told me this with a certain guilt, as though excesses of money from Mum and Daddy plagued him.

"Didn't you grow up with Davy Jones? I don't recall his being rich," I said.

"He wasn't—but then, you'd know that, wouldn't you? You no doubt quite fancied the fellow. Know every detail of his life. That he was born in Manchester. That he loves horses. Am I right?"

But I was not keeper of the knowledge. That was more my sister's department. I just remember those eyebrows of his—and that on July Fourth, one of the most difficult days of my life, he'd blown me and only me a kiss.

Robin Hood alive and well on flight 222, service from Hilo to Los Angeles International Airport. Unclear on time, but Patrick Swayze just mouthed, "Nobody puts Baby in a corner." Love that line.

My duty was to distract the flight attendants while Ian raided the liquor cart.

It would have been easier the other way around—they'd already exhibited, let's say, a certain willingness to flirt with him. Yet he needed to be the one to actually give the free booze to poor masses in coach. How else would he be freed from the chains of opulence that bound him?

I feigned an interest in having pancakes rewarmed, which my servers were surprisingly eager to comply with. "Something bready is just the thing, hon," one of them said. From the corner of my eye I saw Ian hovering near the cart. When he slipped through the curtains dividing the sections, I purred, "Oh, never mind, not hungry after all."

Ian returned moments later, flushed with success. "Handed out eleven bottles to thirsty passengers," he whispered. "Quite a challenge. They refused to believe it could be free."

Attempted to recreate Vulva in Bloom *using cocktail napkins. A visit from a flight attendant.*

"You two are having too much fun here!" she drawled. "Let me guess. Honeymooners?"

"Us? No way," which didn't come out the way I'd meant it to. "Nothing against him . . . just marriage."

Ian appeared uninjured. In fact, for no reason I could fathom he piped in, "We're business partners, actually."

"Really! What business y'all in?"

After only a moment's hesitation—I could almost see the wheels in his brain turning, little gerbils making them go round and round—he said, "Monkeys. Yes . . . *yes* indeed, she and I are in the business of monkeys."

"Very amusing," I deadpanned, jabbing him with my elbow.

"No kiddin'!" the flight attendant exclaimed, and then shouted to a coworker "Hey! We got a couple here into some real monkey business!"

She laughed heartily at her own joke, sitting on the arm of an empty seat across the aisle. "So, what—you run a zoo or something?"

The liquor theft had clearly emboldened Ian, and he leaned forward as if being so kind as to include her in our intimate circle. "They're performing monkeys, actually." He had the same punch-drunk look on his face that I'm sure my sister had held when she tried to pass me off as Twiggy years ago. "Some skill at singing, pretending to play instruments, that sort of thing."

He prodded me to go along with him, which merely forced me to fiddle with my seat buckle. I hate tricking people for the sport of it. I find it all so pointless. I remember once meeting a guy at a bar who told me his name was Mike, and at the end of the evening said, "Ha! I fooled you! My name is really Steve!" to which what could I say but, *So?*

"Well, isn't that cute! I never met monkey trainers before."

"Keeley, why don't you tell—what does your badge say there? Isobel? What a lovely name. Why don't you tell Isobel the sort of music our monkeys perform?" Ian said leadingly.

All right, I thought. I can play this game. I can be spontaneous. I can make a mockery of the working class for no other reason than my own amusement. I looked directly at Isobel the flight attendant and proclaimed, "Guitars! They are guitar-playing monkeys, if you must know!"

My discomfort and, sure, maybe that fourth Bloody Mary, may have caused my voice to come out a tad louder than I'd intended. Isobel's hand brushed over the plastic wings pinned to her collar as she gasped, "Oh!" then recovered with an, "Isn't that interesting."

Before I had to invent any more details about our faux business, Ian sent our friend Isobel off with a request to fetch us extra blankets.

As soon as she left, he smirked at me, "You're a dreadful liar."

"As if you're any better? *Monkeys?* Please."

"You didn't find it convincing?"

"Let's just say I'd be more likely to believe my son when he's telling me, why yes, he ate all his green beans, and yum, they were great, and no, there's nothing hiding there underneath his napkin. . . ."

Ian stirred the ice in his drink, giving me an opportunity to notice, for the first time really, how handsome his profile was. "I believe I had her going there."

"Don't worry about it," I assured him. "Being a bad liar is a good thing."

"Meaning . . ."

"Being a *good* liar is a *bad* thing?" I leaned back, pushing my chair so far that I was nearly resting in the woman's lap behind me. "Let's just say I've had my fair share of dishonesty in the past year or so." I tipped my face lazily to Ian and—have I yet mentioned that fourth Bloody Mary?—intimated, "Men who have affairs. They tend to lie to you."

"I'm sorry," he said, softly.

"Don't be. You're one of the decent ones. I can tell." My hand reached out and clasped his, his fingers tangling warm with mine. "Liars suck. I can bet you've never cheated on anyone you loved."

"You're right. I never have . . . never would. But when it comes to the truth, there's so much gray area. There are times when a lie is the decent thing to do." For a moment, all I noticed was the clinking of glass coming from the front of the plane, flight attendants busy at work. "Say, for example," he continued, "a woman is wearing an extraordinarily ugly dress. Naturally, at that point, complete honesty would be unkind. What harm is there, really, in saying to her, 'My, what a pretty dress.' "

"Hey, isn't what you said to *me* this morning?" I protested, but sleepily, hardly able to keep my eyes open.

Ian was reaching past me saying a thank-you. I felt a blanket warm over me. "Sometimes people do the wrong things, but for the right reasons."

I released his hand, cuddled up with my airline blanket "As far as I can determine, you do all the right things."

There was the distinct batting of my pillow being fluffed, of my tray table being restored to its stowed and locked position. Then I passed out dead asleep.

At some point, I felt Ian shake me awake. I barely noticed the ride to the hotel, or him showing me to my room.

"We should leave for the club by ten," he said. "Get some more sleep." He opened my hotel room door and directed me in. "I need to get a bit of work done. I'll wake you."

12

IAN ROUSED ME as promised with a knock on my hotel door at nine. "Wake up, sleepy Jean."

Oh, *har har*. By the time I showered and met him in the lobby, I was pleased to find that the imprint from the Tylenol cap I'd fallen asleep on had pretty much faded from my face. I was squeezed in, shoved up, and balancing on heels that were less fuck-me-pumps than what-the-fuck-pumps—i.e., I'd tower over Mr. Jones, but what the fuck.

Ian had clearly not availed himself of beauty rest as I had. He clicked off his cell phone and tucked it in his pocket as I tottered up. There were craters beneath his eyes.

"You didn't get any sleep?"

"I had some business to handle. Plus I wanted to give one last try to catching Davy Jones to let him know we were coming."

"Funny how you always call him Davy Jones. Like it's all one name."

"Yes, I suppose that is an odd habit," he concurred, leading me by the arm through the hotel entrance. He fumbled in his pocket for a ticket before handing it to the valet. I was bouncing on my toes. "Nervous?"

"A bit," I admitted.

"So am I. I'd feel better if he were expecting us."

Our rental car pulled up—I recognized it because it was something sporty, not the cheap compact I would've rented.

The valet opened my door, and as I tugged my skirt as low as I could to avoid giving a free peepshow while climbing in, Ian said, "I fear there may be a hitch—that after coming all this way, you might not get your chance to meet Davy Jones."

"To be truthful," I said, just as the door slammed shut, "I fear that I might."

I'D NEVER TOLD Ian about meeting Davy Jones when I was a girl. The flight had been such a funfest, I saw no need to spoil it. Oh, sure, everyone loves a good pants-wetting story. And had it ended there, I might have even called the flight attendant over to listen in as I recounted it. We could've swapped tales about innocent childhood embarrassments. Pants wetting. Knee skinning. Test flunking. Parents dying.

See, that was the rub. A perfectly good anecdote about meeting Davy Jones just gets all the joy sucked out of it when I get to the part about how unknown to me—or anyone—that was my last day with my dad.

Who would have ever suspected? As my father's foot dragged his new sport coat back and forth over the floor, a blood vessel within his head was rupturing. An aneurysm. Cutting off the circulation to his brain so surreptitiously that by the time he collapsed while mowing the lawn the next day, it was too late.

I'd been at Connie Inman's house when my dad was rushed to the hospital. That's where I stayed for the next several days while he finished the process of dying. Sandra went to my grandma's. Neither of us were allowed into the intensive care unit, so there was no point, really, in our visiting, it was explained.

That was fine with me. Hospitals were boring. I was having more fun picking out get-well rocks to polish for my dad in Connie's rock tumbler. No one actually told me he was dying until he was dead. So I spent his final days riding bikes and drawing with chalk on the sidewalk and sitting so close to the rock tumbler that the noise of it gave me a headache. Mrs. Inman had to give me two St. Joseph's Aspirin for Children because I still couldn't swallow Bayer.

She was actually the one who took me aside, and said, "Sweetie, your daddy has gone on to heaven. I'm so sorry."

I'd refused to believe her because I hadn't had a chance to give him his get-well rocks yet. I'd picked out a quartz, an agate and a genuine petoskey, matching the stones against a chart that came with the tumbler. My mom came to pick me up in the station wagon with Sandra already in it and drove us to the funeral home. I had the rocks in the pockets of a dress I'd borrowed from Connie. My fingers rubbed their rough surface—I'd had to pull them from the tumbler early. A full polish took weeks. There just hadn't been enough time.

Sandra was sent off so my mom could talk to me alone in the chapel. Lipstick smudged her teeth. "I can imagine that this is difficult for you," she said, and she paused to hold a Kleenex tissue to her nose, but didn't blow. "I know how close you were to your father."

"It's okay," I said.

"Then I wasn't here for you because I was at the hospital."

"I'm all right."

She sat forward on her chair, straightening the collar on the dress I wore. "Your father was the one who always held you on his lap, who cuddled with you girls. Do you want to talk about it?"

"Not really, I'm kind of hungry. And my leg itches. I got a bug bite."

"Of course, honey. It's understandable that you'd deny your emotions. That's normal."

She was wrong. Nothing was normal, even I could see that.

There was a brief tussle during which my mom wanted to take me to see my dad, I'd refused, aunts and grandmas were called in for counsel, much whispering and staring at me took place, and in the end my desires prevailed because, for crying out loud, I had this bug bite and a rock tumbler headache and I just wanted to go home because I'd done my homework so why should I get gypped out of watching TV?

I pulled the rocks from my pocket and handed them to my mother. I was scratching my leg furiously. "Give these to Dad, okay?"

She said, yes, that it would have to suffice as closure. But a few nights days later, while Grandma was helping out with the laundry, she pulled the quartz, the agate and the genuine petoskey out of my mom's dress. "Oh, aren't these pretty. Perhaps you can add them to that little collection you're starting."

I threw them in the trash. "They're ugly. Just backyard stones. Nothing worth keeping."

I went upstairs to where Sandra was sleeping. She was always sleeping. I crawled into bed with her. "I miss Dad."

"Me, too." A light pulsed from her lava lamp.

I turned over, and nudged my bottom up against her, two spoons tucked together in a drawer. In the dim light, I could make out the Monkees posters that filled every available space on Sandra's walls. Posters of the Monkees together, each of them alone, and a few assorted other magazine tear-outs, like Bobby Sherman. I'd counted once: 134 eyes stared at me from the room from sixty-four pieces of paper.

I could feel Sandra's tears against my neck. Her hand rubbed my tummy, then it slipped down beneath the waistband of my underwear. "Boys have weenies. And to make babies, they stick them in here. In your 'gina," she said.

"I know," I said, and I did. But I hadn't known how tingly it would feel to have her fingers down there—almost itchy, but not unpleasantly so, not like that bug bite. I lay still, with her hand nestled in my underwear, listening as she breathed back her snot until it formed the rhythm of a snore and I knew she was asleep again.

I reached my hand down my undies and twisted my fingers in with hers. Davy Jones stared at me from the wall, his dimpled smile innocent of how drastically my life had changed since I'd seen him last. I met his gaze, but eventually he won the stare-down contest. He didn't need to rest, whereas I was so very tired, I didn't even have time to finish counting the petals on the flower he held out to me.

IT TURNED OUT the nightclub was in an industrial section of downtown, seedy and deserted. As we walked from where we'd parked the car, my heels kept stabbing trash so it trailed behind me like toilet paper until Ian would point and say, "Uh, there on your shoe . . ."

He reached for a weather-worn door marked only by the number fifty-two. "Are you sure this is it?" I asked. I couldn't imagine *the* Davy Jones performing in what appeared to be a crack den.

But he compared the address to one scrawled on a slip of paper he held. "I believe so." He didn't seem to trust his own words. He shot me a you-sure-you-want-to-go-through-with-this? look. I nodded valiantly and pulled on the door.

Three girls of the nineteen-going-on-fifty variety stood in the entryway chugging on clove cigarettes. One in low-slung pants that displayed hipbones you could hang a purse from said, "That'll be ten bucks cover. Each."

Ian thumbed through his wallet. I confirmed this was, in fact, the place where Davy Jones—formerly of the famed Monkees—would be performing.

Hipbones rolled her eyes as she collected money from Ian. "Just love it when the thirty-somethings stop by," she cracked to her friend with the bellyring. She didn't even bother to lower her voice, as though old age had surely deafened me.

Like I was going to take that from someone who probably sipped beer through a straw for the speed buzz.

"I'll have you know that my friend here is a close personal friend of Davy's," I said, haughtily, crooking my arm in Ian's.

"I'm sure he is."

"They grew up together in Britain. Go ahead, Ian." I tugged on his arm. "Say something British."

"Oh, yes, please!" Bellyring mocked me, "Chip, chip, cheerio, we doooo so adore hearing from our foreign friends!"

Then they collapsed in a heap of hysterics and cigarette smoke.

"If we're going to do this, let's get it over with," Ian said. He dragged me by the arm through the second set of doors.

The door shut behind me. I could hear one of the girls howling, "Weren't they just too, too shag-a-riffic!" while another added, "Pip, pip, righteo, ol' chap!"

Well, Regatta, we're not in Hawaii anymore.

Taped music boomed so loud it vibrated through the floor and made my teeth hum. It was unidentifiable as a genre: elevator music on steroids.

There was no stage. Just a riser beyond a bank of pool tables, at which— my stomach churned—male and female versions of those evil girls in the entryway bumped bottoms as they shot billiards in the tight quarters.

"Let's get you settled with a drink," Ian shouted. The whites of his eyes glowed in the black light.

He located a chunk of prime real estate along the bar where I could lean—far enough from the speakers so at least I could hear myself think. What I thought was that I must be getting old if I needed quiet to hear myself think.

In one ear—"Excuse me, ma'am," from some kid with chin fuzz who bumped into me while turning around with his handful of Beck's. In the other—Ian, telling me to stay put, that he was going to find Davy Jones and let him know we'd arrived.

"Don't leave me," I said urgently, clutching his jacket. But he wriggled away, handing me a Stoli in the manner one might hand a fussy baby a pacifier.

"I want to catch him before he goes on stage."

He pulled out his wallet—I feared he was going to abandon me so long he felt compelled to leave cash for another round—but then tucked it absently into his pocket. "I'll be back in a spot."

Which left me alone with my thoughts, trying not to look like a barfly and wondering what I'd say to Davy Jones when I finally met him.

I was on my second drink and no sign of Ian. At some point, the music stopped. I craned my neck at the riser, but no one appeared. *I was your biggest fan*, I mentally rehearsed. *Always thought you should have done lead vocals on "I'm a Believer," that Micky Dolenz was such a glory hog, don't you agree?*

"We need to leave."

It was Ian, taking my arm, huffing like he'd just run a ten K.

HE'D MANAGED TO tug me far enough along that I lost my perch at the bar. As we passed the pool tables, a cue jabbed me in the back.

I turned to glare at the perpetrator, a pink-faced young thing who nodded to me, still bent over his shot, "Sorry 'bout that. Nice tits." It was not a moment of relevance enough to add to the story I'd tell Regatta later, but it did erase the sting of the earlier ma'am and, therefore, served the purpose of halting me in my tracks.

"Let's go," Ian said, his voice agitated. "I'll explain why when we get to the car."

"You can tell me here."

He sighed, and—gently this time—directed me to a jukebox, away from the boy at the pool table who'd just neatly sunk the eight ball, followed by the white one. Before Ian could say a word, I heard the strum of a guitar.

"Finally," I said. I could see Davy Jones across the club. He sat on a stool, alone with his guitar. Without introduction, he began playing some bluesy tune I didn't recognize—but, oh, that voice, all gravelly yet pure. I'd know it anywhere.

No one paid him any attention. They didn't cease their gaming or their chatting to watch the act. It was as though he were just an ordinary lounge singer. My heart ached for his dignity. I wanted to leap on a pool table, turning slowly like Norma Rae, holding up a sign that said, *PAY ATTENTION, BABIES, THIS GUY ONCE AFFECTED ME.*

I COULD FEEL Ian standing behind me, close enough that I'm sure the fibers of our clothes were mingling. He insisted on whispering little annoyances in my ear. Could we please, please leave? Did I not understand? There was no point in sticking around. Davy and he, they'd had a row—oh, they never did get along very well. He'd been afraid something like this was going to happen.

"You had a fight?" I asked, still watching Davy.

"Quite an ugly one at that."

"What about?" Davy's song featured a *la-la* chorus, as though he'd decided to sing backup to our conversation.

A sigh from Ian, then, "Nothing, but I think we ought to—"

Davy was on his second round of *la-las* when I finally turned around. I was nearly pleading. "We've come so far. We're so close."

I could see him swallow. "You're right. You stay here. I'll wait outside. You can say your hellos, but don't bother claiming to know me. It won't do you any favors."

"Never mind. It wouldn't be the same," I said, my voice trembling. "Then I'd just be another pathetic groupie who doesn't know when it's time to let go. I can't do this without you." I could sense Ian waffling, so I added, "Isn't there any way you can patch things up with him? Just for tonight?"

Ian massaged the back of his neck. "Oh, sod it," he groaned. Then he leaned down and—knock me over with a feather—kissed me. Full on the lips. Brief, but plenty warm and wet, and, come to think of it, quite pleasant.

"That was unexpected," I remarked.

He absently brushed my bangs off my face. "I've nothing to lose."

DAVY DIDN'T SING any Monkees tunes. Maybe he was saving the good stuff for the second set. He thanked the crowd and said he was taking a quick break. Then he set his guitar on the podium and strode in our direction.

"Here he comes," I said, my heart racing.

Ian had somehow backed us up so we were flush against the jukebox. "Keeley . . . I . . ."

"It will be okay," I assured him, more because I wanted it to be true, rather than of course having an idea if that were the case. "When friends go back as far as you two do, one disagreement isn't enough to end it all. It'll work out. Really, it will."

Davy paused to sign an autograph, another thirty-something having obviously made it through the gauntlet in the entryway. He handed her back a pen and some magazine she'd toted especially for the occasion.

Just as Davy sauntered by the closest pool table, Ian urged, "Don't say anything yet. Let him pass."

Which was apparently not an option, because Davy was walking straight toward us. I debated whether to try to say something myself, or let Ian handle things—Ian, who had moved so he was using me as a shield. And before I knew it, there he stood. Right in front of me. The one, the only . . . I opened my mouth to at least say hello, but then it occurred to me, *ohmyGodDavyJones*, and nothing came out.

Although I didn't exactly tower over him, I found myself crouching slightly until we were eye to eye. Oh, those eyes—I hadn't had much of a chance to see them as a girl, they'd shifted so quickly to the girls behind me in line. But after all these years here they were before me, milky brown and calm. No anger there at all. In fact, they were rather welcoming. I felt as if I could curl up in them. Pull down the lids like a shade. Go to sleep.

"Pardon me, will you?" he said, and his hand brushed my arm as he reached past me. He plunked two quarters in the jukebox's coin slot.

Then he motioned to Ian, who seemed to be studying the ceiling. "You there—you in the black shirt. Mind hitting E-12 for me?"

I found myself blinking, a reflex to clear my head. *You in the black shirt?*

Ian muttered a dull, "Sure, no problem," and fumbled for the buttons. Reality didn't so much sink in as plow through my very insides.

"You . . . you don't know him," I stammered, as much to myself as to Ian.

His head was down, stroking his chin in concentration as he hunted for the letter E, only to move on to his desperate search for the number 12. He said nothing.

It didn't matter. I didn't need his answer to know. I was on my own. What had I been thinking? I *knew* it was too good to be true. I'd concocted this fantasy in which opportunity was limitless. My time with Davy Jones would be rolled out before me like an endless red carpet, letting me leisurely stroll along it until I knew exactly where it was I was going. Now the carpet been pulled from beneath my feet, and I was nowhere.

Ian managed to press the E and the 12, and Davy nodded a thanks, then said to me, "Stones. Always end my set with 'em." And given my profession and my turmoil at the moment, pardon me if my first thought was, *Rocks? Davy Jones loves rocks just like I do?* until I heard the unmistakable opening rift of "Satisfaction."

He turned to leave, accidentally stepping on the edge of my shoe. No big deal; he missed my toes. I wasn't even sure he'd noticed he did it.

That was, until he gave me a offhand, "Sorry, doll," before continuing on his way.

"No need to apologize," I said, my voice thick. I watched as he left to a back room. Curtains wafted closed behind him. "It was nobody's fault, really."

I ESCAPED TO the ladies' room before I had to endure listening to Ian's weak excuses. Just my luck, Hipbones and Bellyring were there, leaning against the sink, primping.

I tried to slip past them into a stall, but there was only one and it was filled.

"Blimey! If it isn't our British friend! Our little Spicette!"

"Old Girl Power!"

I could hear the sounds of puking in the stall, no doubt the third girl from the entryway. I leaned exhausted against the wall.

"Señorita, jou wanna towel? Jou dunt look so good." I gazed through slits to see a woman in a maid's uniform, sitting next to a countertop of sundry items.

I pulled a fistful of change from the bottom of my purse and set it in a basket marked TIPS. Then I took the premoistened towelette from her hands.

"Look," she announced to the others, "Some people—they tip."

"That's because she's probably *royalty*," Hipbones said. "A close, personal friend of the *queen's*."

The towel against my neck was as lemony fresh as I'd hoped it would be. "Ladies," I said, too weary to fight. "I have a tip for you, as well. Don't trust men. They're all the same. Liars. Every one of them."

"Halle*fuckin*lujah to that," Hipbones said, "Chip, chip." She'd moved on to applying lotion full-body, as if she'd just stepped from the shower.

"I hear ya," Bellyring interjected. "Some guy out there tries telling me he's a rap star, and he's wearing fuckin' *boat shoes*."

Hipbones was looking for a place to put the lotion left over on her hands; she was eyeing me. "Your Britty chap break your heart, did he?"

"Shaah! Hardly!" I said, taking a step away from her. "But he dragged me halfway across the ocean claiming he knew Davy Jones. Turned out to be a big, fat lie."

She nodded knowingly. "Been there a hundred times, girlfriend. Sonofabitch gets you to fuck him. Tells you, oh, yeah, Eddie Veder and I are, like, seriously tight. So you waste a whole night sucking off him and all his buddies . . . and for *nothing*. They don't even know anybody in a damn *house band*."

"Lying pricks," Bellyring agreed. "All of 'em."

"Tallyho," I said, accepting another of those refreshing towelettes from the restroom lady.

And for someone who hadn't gotten what she'd wanted that night, I had to marvel, awash in fake lemon scent, how I wasn't feeling nearly so dissatisfied as I would have thought.

13

"SO YOU ASSUMED that I wouldn't notice? Is that it?"

Those were the first words I could make myself speak to Ian. That was, besides, "Let's get the hell out of here." Oh, and "Please don't talk, I have a splitting headache."

"I thought I could it pull it off," Ian answered, shifting gears as we cruised through the empty streets of downtown. I'd asked him to put the top down—I needed air. My hair was flying like Medusa's, stinging as it slapped me repeatedly across the face.

"How did you figure?" I said, each word a dagger, yanking hair strands from my mouth.

He gave me a sideways glance, as if afraid no matter what he said, I was going to pounce on him—which may have been true. But he would've had it coming, so I crossed my arms and said, *"Well?,"* because he owed me some answers or, at a minimum, needed to take his lumps like a man.

"Truth is," he said hesitantly, "I'd figured that if Davy Jones were playing at such a small club, he couldn't be doing all that well—financially, I mean. Naturally, he could be there for creative purposes. You know, testing the waters with a new style where no one will see him. But nonetheless, I make a fair amount of money, and it seemed simple enough to . . . well . . ."

"Bribe him?"

"I was considering it more of a hiring situation. He is, after all, an actor. How hard would it be to act as if he knew me?"

I shook my head, digging through the glove compartment—I thought I'd seen Ian stash some Altoids there earlier. I pried open the box, popped a mint into my mouth, letting it burn on my tongue as if I'd set a searing hot iron there. My mouth was in agony. "Mint?" I offered.

"No, thank you," Ian answered, wary.

I put them away. "It obviously didn't work. The bribe."

"Obviously." He absently switched the radio station, which had been on so low a volume I hadn't even realized it was playing. His fingers drummed on the steering wheel, stalling for time before continuing. "You have no idea how hard I'd tried to set it up beforehand—make an offer to Davy Jones for an evening's work, essentially. His manager thought it was a prank. Wouldn't give me the time of day. And once we got to the club, I searched everywhere for him, but . . ." His words trailed off.

We idled at a red light, and I watched a couple of boys cross the street who couldn't have been more than nine years old. It was well past midnight. Where were their mothers? They moved on, swaggering in their baggy pants, little boys in men's clothes.

Ian shifted back into drive, and we passed through a couple more lights before he finally said, "It was never my intention to deceive you."

"Actually, it seems to me that it was exactly your intention," I said. Blunt. No mercy. "What I can't figure out is *why*."

"Do you really want to know?"

"Sure, what the hell."

"Quite simply," he said, "it was a way to get your attention when I first met you at the park. Just an impulse. I'd been joking a bit—sort of like with the stewardess—and when it seemed to interest you, I went with it. Then I ran into you at the auction. I'd hoped you would have forgotten, but then Davy Jones is the first thing you mentioned. It seemed to spiral out of control from there. I knew I had to come clean eventually, but I kept telling myself, 'Right after I do this, then I'll tell her.' Once you met him and got this thing—whatever it is—out of your system, I hoped you'd find it funny when I told you the truth."

"Hilarious. I'm laughing my ass off."

"Look, it was an impossible ruse to carry on, I knew that. Too many details that didn't add up. Even tonight, I panicked when I pulled out my wallet, realizing you might spot my ID—that if you saw my age, you'd realize that Davy Jones and I couldn't have been childhood friends."

"Wha—? Why? How old are you?"

"Forty-two?" he said, as if it were a question.

Unbelievable . . . it just kept getting better and better. "And those kids of yours in college? Are they actually at home with the nanny, waddling around in diapers and slurping on pacifiers?"

"No, I promise everything else I've ever said to you is true. I was going to tell you about this. Really. I was. There was no way I could sustain such a lie and ever hope to carry on a relationship with you. I was well aware of that, but—"

"Why did you even start with it?" I snapped, exasperated. "I mean, give me some credit. It's not as if I wouldn't have given you the time of day if you *hadn't* said you knew Davy Jones!"

He gave a smooth spin of the steering wheel, and we turned onto a boulevard lit so unexpectedly bright that it made me wince.

"You sure about that?" he asked.

Instead of dignifying that comment with a response, I cranked up the stereo, filling the 'hood with some song I'd never heard before but, damn it, we were all going to hear it now.

It seemed forever before Ian deposited me at my hotel room and said a weary good night. There was not a chance that I was going to be able to fall asleep any time soon, not with my brain on overdrive as it was.

May as well hit the honor bar for a nightcap, I decided. Or two, three. Bag of peanuts. Caught a little porn on the TV. Didn't even care if Ian would see it on the bill. It was the lullaby I needed. I found myself mesmerized by its music; enchanted by its tender lesson that, if his penis is large enough, even a man with a bad haircut can get the girl.

I WOKE TO a knocking sound. The door. I pulled the phone from my ear.

The phone? I gave a tentative "Hello?" into the receiver. There was a rustling noise in the background. I raised my voice. "Hellllooooo?"

"Good morning," Ian called from the hallway.

God . . . Ian. I was so confused. "Hold on!" I called.

"Sure, dear," said the voice in the phone. It was Mom. "Surprised to hear you up and about so early. Bet your head feels like a wrung mop. Do you need to go throw up? Should I call back?"

"No, wait here," I said, though she was right about the mop thing.

I got an eyeful of myself in the mirrored closet. Naked. Eyes nearly glued shut from mascara and sleep. Serious bed hair. I tossed on a hotel robe and rinsed my mouth with a lukewarm Diet Coke before cracking the door enough so Ian could let himself in.

Then I went back to the phone to worm details from my mother without divulging that I had no idea I'd called her. Seems her phone had rung at 5 A.M. Michigan time, scaring the wits out of her. Just her drunk daughter, ha ha. I chuckled along while I watched Ian pick up the honor bar carnage, casting looks of alarm my way.

As my mom reminisced about the night before, it did come back to me more or less. She'd talked about the breakup with her boyfriend Doug. As I was starting to recall, it was because I'd inquired. Share with me your feelings about Doug, I'd asked, throwing back at her the sort of language she might use on me. Perhaps it was the liquor talking, but I'd said it without a sarcastic bent. I was sincerely curious to know. And, as it turned out, that bastard Doug had broken my mother's heart.

"Honey," she said. "I wish you hadn't insisted I stay on the line. You don't have that kind of money. Still . . ." She sighed, sounding like . . . good heavens, sounding like a *mom*. "I haven't held you sleeping like that since you were a baby."

As I said my good-byes, I was already obsessing about the phone bill. Direct dial from a hotel had to cost a fortune.

"Looks like I missed the party," Ian said.

"I couldn't sleep." I smoothed my hair, which I knew must look as if it were about to take off in flight. "I made a few phone calls. I'll pay you back."

"Don't worry about it."

"No, really, I want to."

"Please. It's not a problem. This trip didn't work out as I'd hoped, that's for sure. But looking at the bright side, I suppose that the turn of events has saved me a bundle. Do you have any idea"—and he paused to unscrew the cap from a bottle of water and take a swig—"the amount of money it would have taken to get Davy Jones to play along?"

"Glad I turned out to be such a bargain," I grumbled.

"Not judging by the looks of this mini bar bill." When I tightened my robe around me, scowling, he added, gently, "I'm joking. I'm well aware that I've blown it with you. If you don't mind, at this point, I'm simply trying to get out of this town with a shred of my pride intact."

THEN BACK TO real life, via Hawaiian Air flight 433, where Ian and I both slept or pretended to the entire way.

When I got home, I found out that Ma Kekuhi—in a move reminiscent of when she was my mother-in-law—had taken Dante to Kam's house after all. Seemed there was a last-minute Mah Jong game at the Elks' lodge, and she was feeling lucky. Tried to call me at the number I'd left, she told me, but the hotel desk said my line kept ringing busy. And, by the way, this biting of Dante's was becoming a real problem. Had I tried butter?

Kam and Suzanne were sunning on the front lawn when I pulled up. Crud. It would take me forever to extract Dante from the inflatable pool. So I cajoled. Made promises of ice cream and endless knock hockey. All the while, I could feel Suzanne giving me the once-over, more than once.

"You're looking freshly tossed," she purred. "Romantic getaway?" As if she thought being able to detect the postcoitus scent on the enemy was part of her evil superpowers. My scoffing only egged her on.

"Come, come now, don't be coy—who is your mystery man?" She was having herself a lovely time taunting me about having jetted away with some secret lover, relishing in my discomfort.

That was, until Kam snapped, "She's not seeing anyone; leave her alone," so suddenly that it startled her quiet and made the corner of my mouth involuntarily twist up.

THE REST OF the weekend was spent knocking about in a bit of a stupor—like posttraumatic stress.

Among the messages blinking on my machine when I got home were two from Morna (just checking in!) and Regatta gasping from her deathbed, "So . . . tell me . . . Was I right? Are you . . . a . . . believer?" Thankfully, Ian was respecting my request to leave me be. Now if Wagner would only get off my back.

There I was, returned from a well-deserved sick day (cough, cough, I'll be all right, honestly, merely a touch of the flu, well, Dante, he had the flu, I had . . . um . . . a leg cramp). There were eleven voice mails from Wagner. Action Items. (As in, "Kekuhi, Action Item for you.") To be followed by something pulled off his to-do list and selected especially for me like a *Newlywed Game* prize. "Remind me that we need to collect for a staff gift for Beula—important in-house PR." Implying that I hadn't cashed in the one sick day I'd worked so hard to accumulate, but rather that he'd caught me spending the day leaning on the water cooler.

"The problem," Bob explained as he leaned on the water cooler, "Is that letter you wrote to personnel."

"*I* wrote?"

"It put you on his radar scope. Made him realize you were trying to escape. Now he's going to bar the castle gates to keep it from happening again. Deep down he loves you."

"You know I hate you."

Bob would not be invited to help me draft my next letter—less for his attitude at the water cooler than for the abysmal advice he'd given me the first time around.

I waited until lunchtime when I knew the place would be deserted, glancing over my shoulder as I typed. This was a piece of correspondence I didn't want anyone sneaking up on me to see. It was to a one Mr. Hoffman, a name I'd gotten after much bouncing around from office to office in Washington. I couldn't wait forever for Skipper.

Hoffman served as director of something or other volcanically-related at the American Geologic Society. Most important, he was the man who could approve a team of volcanologists, complete with equipment, to rush to my aid. I pictured them running in, stampeding Wagner with their work boots, flattening him into a pancake who could only moan, "But . . . I . . . never . . . okayed . . . the . . . funding. . . ."

I now had weeks' worth of fact-finding under my belt. Seismic activity. Rising temperatures. There was data in there so sexy it would give the average volcanologist quite the woody.

"Mr. Hoffman," I typed furtively. "Greetings from The Big Island. I am being held captive on an island by incompetents who are making me do busywork while a possibly active volcano sits unwatched."

Which I then deleted, starting over. It took me four drafts before my fingers on the keyboard would do more than complain, before they'd type a reasonably professional letter outlining what I'd found and requesting help. To be on the safe side, I did a search and delete to rid it of all the exclamation points and any references to the word *asshole*. I was just that thorough.

THEN CAME AN urgent call from Ted. Regatta had been admitted Mahani Hou General. Her flu was worse than we'd thought. She'd apparently started going into convulsions from fever. Ted's voice—besides being loud as usual—was ragged, as if he'd run her there in his arms himself.

All I could think was, You can't ever tell her. Regatta would be mortified to know she'd done something so vulgar as to convulse.

The next few days and nights were spent in a vigil by her bedside. I had to tell personnel it was a family crisis, that my sister was ill. I'd squandered my only sick day. Dante bounced between school, the Kus', and Ma Kekuhi's. The latter of whom was issued a stern warning from me that she was to call if there were any sudden Mah Jong crises.

"If you don't want Kam to move away with Dante, listen to me. I have to be strict about visitation."

She said, "*Whhhaaat?*" that habit she had of pretending to not understand the language when I said something she didn't want to hear.

"Tough love," I told her.

Ted, Regatta's mom, Lawrence from her salon, and I squeezed into our half of the hospital room. Behind the curtain was a nearly transparent woman who would shout *Ah!* in terror every time Ted spoke, as though his pitch were a dog whistle to her ears.

Regatta mostly moaned and sweated fever. She was out of danger, the doctor said. If there were to be mental retardation, it had already happened. He seemed hurt when we didn't all high-five over that news.

Lawrence read aloud continuously from *Chicken Soup for the Soul*. "Stories of strength and courage. It will inspire her to get better," he sniffed.

"Just so she won't have to hear it anymore," Ted attempted to whisper.

A sneer from Lawrence. *Ah!* from behind the curtain. Regatta's mom sighed. I ran to fetch her a beverage. It was what I could do. Provide juice and pop to the thirsty.

On day three, Kam called my cell phone. "What's this with you telling Ma I can't have my own son?"

"Your visitation is Saturday," I said, my voice hushed. "You can have him then."

I was sitting near the foot of Regatta's bed. Lawrence had painted her toenails to give her a motivational boost. ("Nothing says 'I have full command of my faculties like fuchsia!'" he'd chirped.) I was blowing on her toes before she'd shift and they'd smudge—which was sure to send Lawrence sniffing and Regatta's mom sighing again.

"This is bullshit, Keel. I'm taking him."

"Don't do this, now. Please. It's not the time."

I could hear him breathing through the phone, collecting himself. "Look, Ma told me what's happening. I feel bad for Regatta. I do. But we wouldn't have a problem if you weren't being so stubborn. He's my kid. I'm taking him home."

"Please do," I said as frostily as I could. "But you don't have my permission. This time I'll be smart enough to call the cops. What was that you accused *me* of? Kidnapping?"

He hung up. Nothing but silence in my ear.

I realized I'd been devouring my fingernails. Three people were attempting with limited success not to stare at me.

Regatta's mom finally spoke. "She appreciates all you're going through to be here. I know she does."

Lawrence began leafing madly through *Chicken Soup*, mumbling something about remembering a story on a woman able to triumph over the pain of ending her marriage.

Ted, hoping to offer comfort, said, "She'd been talking about firing you as the matron of honor—you know, because you weren't doing anything. I'm sure this will change her mind."

Ah! from behind the curtain.

I couldn't have agreed more.

Then on day four, as suddenly as it had begun, the crisis was over.

Without warning, Regatta propped herself up on her elbows to take in her surroundings, saying simply, "You guys look like shit."

I'd intended to guffaw—to deliver a smart comment I was formulating in my brain in which I abused her for how silly she must have looked convulsing. But instead all that came out was incoherent blubbering. I was reduced to nothing but tears, snot, and relief.

"Well," huffed Lawrence, standing as if to leave immediately. "I suppose then we can untie those yellow ribbons from around your salon chair."

I WAS PLAYING back messages, including one from Ian—apparently he wound up with my sunglasses, and would I like him to mail them back?—when the phone rang. It was Regatta.

"Well, Grasshopper, you made it all the way home without once mentioning your trip to Los Angeles. You have learned well."

"It's the new and improved me," I said. "I can actually think of others when they're near death." I didn't add that I'd ached to tell her constantly. That I was annoyed she'd had the audacity to be unavailable when I needed her. I wanted to shake her to consciousness and say, All right, I've marched boldly forth—now what?

"Weelll?"

"I didn't do the monkey."

"Oh, no," she said, as though I'd said the lottery pulled my numbers and I'd forgotten to buy my ticket. "Strange. I had such a strong feeling."

I told her about what had happened that weekend. How Ian had fabricated his relationship with Davy Jones, about my chance run-in with him at the jukebox.

"He *spoke* to you?" Regatta squealed.

"Yep, said to me, 'Sorry doll,' " I boasted, feeling a thrill of accomplishment. "Stepped on my foot!' "

"That is *way* better than to get an autograph from him at P'aouai Park."

"I know."

"Keel? Can I ask you to think about something?" She waited, and when I didn't respond, she said, "You had a guy take you all the way to L.A., for no other reason I can see than that he didn't want to let you down. Don't you think that's sort of amazing?"

"Forget about Ian. My entire relationship with him was based on a lie."

"Granted . . . but how are you feeling about things? I mean, do you feel like you still need to meet Davy Jones?"

"Does anyone really *need* to meet Davy Jones?" I quipped.

"Hell yes—you did," she said firmly. "And now you don't."

THAT NIGHT I had a dream, a thing I hesitate to mention. I hate it when people tell me their dreams. I instantly glaze over. You're helpless even to stop them with an *"Oh yeah, I heard that one."* Same thing happens to me when books shift to italics just after the heroine falls asleep or, heaven forbid, when the TV or movie screen goes murky for a moment. Dreams are only interesting to the people who have them, and then not for long. Look how quickly they're forgotten.

It's enough to say that Kam and I were kissing. In the dream, not in real life. What was creepy was that Ian stood nearby, directing. As in, "That's right, give the girl a bit of tongue. You know, Kam ol' chap, she right enjoys it if you reach under the blouse and play a bit with the funbags. Give 'er a go, eh?"

Instead of waking in a cold sweat, as I should have, I closed my eyes and tried to fall back asleep. Pick up where I'd left off. I was just that demented.

PERHAPS IF I'D shared my dream with Kam, he'd have been titillated enough to get off my case.

Turned out he hadn't taken Dante home from Ma's that day while I was in the hospital. Yet he wasn't letting up. He wanted more time with his son. That was Dante's name now. My Son or, for variety, My Boy.

He called to nag me about it hourly, it seemed. I'd never seen him so determined. About anything. Not even that time I saw him struggling to open the last bottle of beer without an opener—even then he set it down, forgot about it, had a Mountain Dew instead.

Wouldn't you know, I complained to Morna, the guy finally sets a goal and it involves opposing me.

She told me to keep up the good work. Don't allow him extra visitation. We were this close, she said—and since we were on the telephone, I had to use my imagination—*this close* to nailing him on negligence.

Seemed while I was in L.A., Morna had kept herself amused with learning that Kam had gone to the police before coming to me that fateful night I'd taken Dante.

This is good, Morna told me. Helpful for us. Very bad for Kam. It was all the proof we needed that he'd left Dante unsupervised.

Which raised the question, What were we waiting for?

"There are complications, dear. Give it time. They'll iron themselves out." But that was all she'd say.

Then a few nights later, me with my complications apparently wrinkled and unsightly, Kam showed up at my house. He announced in a loud voice he wanted to take Dante for ice cream, who then nearly mowed me down running to his dad's car.

I was hardly going to pry my son out peacefully with the news of my original plans for the evening, which involved grilled cheese sandwiches and baths all around.

Pausing for a moment—away from little pitchers and their big ears— I informed Kam that he was a manipulative bastard. Then I walked past him to tell My Son, My Boy, that it wasn't his daddy's turn. It was my turn. *Sigh.* To take him for ice cream. (And it was going to have to be real ice cream, too—from a parlor—not a frozen treat pulled covered in ice dust from the chest at Market. There went my evening.)

"I wouldn't have thought Kam so clever," I told Morna when I stopped by her house on the way home with a pint of butter pecan. We sat at her kitchen table, the ice cream between us on the table. The lights were off so we could see Dante outside playing one-man tetherball by porch lamp.

"Sounds like the work of Lee, Lee, and Lee. They must be advising him. Divide and conquer, that's their specialty," she said, digging her spoon into the container. "They have no grasp of the big picture."

"So now what?"

She'd picked up the carton, was hunting for a nut while my life hung in the balance. Again, the "get what you pay for" adage sprang to mind. Then she waved the spoon at me so as to say, *worry not,* before putting it in her mouth.

I continued, "If he shows up tomorrow and says he wants to take him to the park, or fly him to Disneyland, I'm screwed."

"Not at all," she said. "You go with him."

"Excuse me?"

"If he wants to see Dante, let him. But only if you go along."

"Me . . ."

"Beat the Lees at their own game. You can't lose. If you accompany them, you're demonstrating your willingness to cooperate for the greater benefit of the child, even if, for the child's safety, you certainly can't extend unsupervised privileges. If Kam won't have you along, seeing his son must not mean much to him after all."

I looked outside, as though I might find words buzzing around the light that could express how Kam and I couldn't be in the vicinity of each another for minutes without messing it up somehow.

Dante had wound the ball on its string around the pole, and was hanging from it, letting it drag him along as it unraveled.

"In fact," Morna continued, back on her nut hunt with a vengeance, "This is just what we need to set those pesky complications straight before your hearing next week."

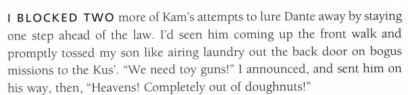

14

I **BLOCKED TWO** more of Kam's attempts to lure Dante away by staying one step ahead of the law. I'd seen him coming up the front walk and promptly tossed my son like airing laundry out the back door on bogus missions to the Kus'. "We need toy guns!" I announced, and sent him on his way, then, "Heavens! Completely out of doughnuts!"

I met Kam on the porch, both of us with such innocent looks on our faces we could have been cast on the spot for *The Waltons*.

"He's at a friend's. I'll be sure to tell him you stopped by."

Kam shouted, in case I'd merely stashed Dante in the back. "All right! Just checking if Dante wants to do some night fishing!" The Lees had trained him well.

"He's not here."

"Too bad! Because the fish are jumping!"

"Stop yelling. I'm telling you. He's gone."

Only a wife would notice the subtleties of how he held in his frustration. The way the side of his nose twitched. How he pushed back his hair, clutching it there in his hand for a moment before letting it free, like a shampoo commercial because he's worth it.

"You can't keep me from him forever."

"I can try."

His eyes were on my breasts. It wasn't a sexual thing for him, at least not entirely. It helped him think. I'd once read how when people are collecting their thoughts, their eyes shift up to the left. Kam's dropped, as if the swell of flesh on a woman was his own Magic 8 Ball. *Oh, Magic Breasts, will my bitch of a wife give me access to my son?*

I crossed my arms. *It is uncertain.*

"Keel, I don't get this. There was a time you were begging me to spend more time with Dante."

"There was a time I wanted a lot of things I didn't get."

FOR THE FIRST two years of his life, Dante slept between Kam and me at night. My reasoning for allowing this was that I was already sleep-deprived enough without having to get up to deal with a crying child. I could just roll over.

It was when Dante was about six months old that I remember waking with a start. He was missing from the bed. Frantically, I felt around for him with one hand before realizing that I in fact held him with the other, pinned like a football flat against the side of the mattress. I scooped him back up, confused.

It took me a while to piece together that Dante must have scooted up and over me. He'd started to roll off when I reached out—dead asleep—and nabbed him.

Kam had been astounded. I heard him sitting in the backyard with a group of friends later, telling them the story. Saying how Dante would be nothing but baby goo if he'd decided to travel the other way. He'd have never had the instincts to grab him the way I had.

One of the guys cracked, "You'da caught him if he was a six-pack."

"Or that new CD player of yours."

That night without consulting Kam I traded our beast of a bed for his brother Tai's futon mattress. Told Tai I wouldn't be requiring the frame. I'd be laying it flat on the floor. That was where it stayed until Kam dragged it out the day he left.

It was insanity that now I'd have to fear Kam's being able to move away with Dante to Fiji. But it could happen. I'd heard the stories. I saw *Not without My Daughter*—well, the previews at any rate. That was enough to get the gist that Sally Fields's child was nearly taken by her ex and that it was *based on a true story*.

I, like Sally, would do what I had to do.

So bring on Morna's hearing, I told myself, and make it in a square room with windows leading only to other square rooms just the same.

Dusty linoleum floors. Walls blank except for a crack bleeding its way up. Then, in the center, a bare bulb dangling. A lamp of truth that I could use to blind Kam while I barked questions—probing ones he couldn't answer honestly without making the lawyers murmur and the judge shake his wigged head in disgust.

Where were you the night of—? Oh, pick almost any night. The answer would be the same. He'd be right home . . . in a minute . . . as soon as my bud here finishes this story . . . promise, hon . . . right there . . . give the Dantser a kiss for me.

I gave Dante plenty of kisses, thank you. All from me. I would announce them like incoming missles. A kiss from Mommy to the head. A kiss from Mommy to the tummy. A kiss from Mommy to those tiny fingers even though, ew, we can use a bath now, can't we?

Kam would come home and, dang it, catch me perfectly content without him. Sharing a jar of peaches with Dante or reading a book while he played with the Tupperware.

It changed the content of the air, Kam's being in it. I was no longer running through the backyard sprinkler with Dante. I was running through the backyard sprinkler with Dante *while Kam took a shower*. I was strolling Dante around the neighborhood *while Kam helped Roger install that new engine*. I was watching Dante play in the sandbox at the park *while Kam finally got around to doing those dishes just like he promised—eh, hon?*

Then at some point, freshly showered or slack from a day of surfing, he'd say, *"Where's that boy of mine?"* Then he'd toss Dante in the air with such vigor it made my son nearly choke on joy and made my heart twist into a mean lump.

Believe me, if I got the chance, I was going to turn that lamp on Kam— maybe slap him around a bit. I was going to ask him why he was suddenly so ready to be a dad when all he could manage to be with me was a man with a baby.

NOVEMBER 4. FOUR months since I'd served Kam the divorce papers. Nothing seemed close to settled. It seemed there would be at least a couple months before I could hope to claim to be done with all this.

Dante had been Mr. Potato Head for Halloween. He was not the adorable plastic potato from my youth, but the one from the *Toy Story* movie. That was for him a critical distinction. He also insisted on carrying a gun. Mr. Potato Head going on a violent rampage. Candy wrappers everywhere. Film at eleven.

And other big news—I spoke with one Mr. Hoffman today. I was not to get my hopes up, he warned me, but he and the others at the AGS were intrigued by my proposal.

I was on the phone with him for an hour, explaining how I'd come by the data. He kept asking, "It's just you? There's no one else working with you?" I tried to walk the line between appearing appropriately needy yet still competent enough that—should they decide to put resources behind the project—I wouldn't be left behind.

"I'll call you," he'd said finally, and I had to appreciate that even in my businesses life, I seemed to attract men who liked to keep their options open.

TED AND REGATTA were planning to have 225 people at their wedding. I suggested it was possibly more than the island's population; that they might have to go to Honolulu and hire people to fill seats like they do at the Grammys.

Regatta held up the guest list, frowning. I saw her eyes shift sideways to me. I tried to appear useful. She still needed to cut thirty-two people.

It was Saturday night, date night. And where was I? Sitting cross-legged on the floor in front of Regatta's coffee table, using a silver pen to write out the names and addresses of the A-list guests, which I did with more commitment than the bride herself could have mustered. Even when my hand started to cramp, I dotted my *i*s, crossed my *t*s, looped my *j*s invitingly.

I'd been scared straight when she was in the hospital. Being a matron of honor was more than an entitlement in Regatta's world. It was a duty. I vowed to take it as such.

She and Ted weren't making it easy. Since Regatta's near-death experience, they'd become so gushy. I'd spent enough time with them as a couple to know that they used to be normal. Now she'd say, Hand me the tape, will you? And he'd croon, For a kiss first! And she'd giggle and give him a peck while reaching around his back for the dispenser.

Then she asked him to grab the extra silver pens from her room. An ordinary request. Before he made the long journey there, he felt compelled to growl in her ear, say he'd be counting the minutes until he returned.

"Get a room," I grumbled when Ted left, only partially kidding. "Since when are you guys all over each other? It's sickening."

Regatta yelled for Ted to make the bed while he was in there, then turned to me, grabbed my pen-writing hand to get my attention. "I'm going to tell you something I'm not telling anyone else. Not even Ted," she said. "When I was in the hospital, I was visited by a messenger of the gods."

Sounded good. I stopped writing for this one, even when she let go of my hand.

"While I had the flu, I had plenty of time to lie around alone and think. I know this sounds terrible, but I was wondering if I could go through with the wedding. If I could spend the rest of my life with Ted. He's not who I pictured myself with. He's so clunky and loud, I know that. People tell me that the things that bother you now will become magnified when you're married. So I'm picturing Ted lumbering around, bellowing at me through a megaphone each morning, and I panicked."

She gave a glance toward the bedroom, checking for Ted. "Then while I was in the hospital bed, I heard a voice say my name. I felt a breeze that froze me to the bone and warmed me at the same time. It wasn't a dream. It was as real as you and I are sitting here. An angel. And he said, 'I have a story for you, Regatta, a story you need to hear.' "

Her lip trembled, and she held up a hand, as in please-I-need-a-moment-here, then continued. "Right before we're born, we're shown our soul mate, the person we're going to spend the rest of our lives with. Well, one day a soul stood before the gods, and he saw that in his life he would be a brilliant and handsome man. Then the gods said, 'You are lucky, for your wife will be kind and loving to you, but, alas, she will be a hunchback.' And the man said, 'Oh, but she is my one true love! I beg of you, spare her! Give the hunchback to me so that she may be beautiful!'

"So you see, I understood what the angel was telling me. Ted is my match. He may be flawed, but that means that I'm better with him than I would have been by myself. Don't you see? He took my hunchback."

As she told the story, I could feel my mouth go dry. It wasn't an angel dispensing wisdom. She was paraphrasing one of the stories Lawrence had read from *Chicken Soup for the Soul*.

Hadn't she noticed how her angel kept snuffling because, Oh, God, this is sooo moving, to such a degree that another angel who was far more embittered about soul-mates and marriage had to come in and finish reading the damn thing?

"You think it's stupid, don't you?" she said, tipping her head up, fanning her eyes to dry tears before they spilled.

Which put me at a crossroads. Making a decision as pivotal as whether to get married based on a story you think is from an angel but is really from a hair stylist in Armani slacks, loafers, no socks, could send her life spiraling in a direction it was never meant to go.

Then again . . .

"It's so romantic it makes me want to gag," I said, putting pen again to paper. "It's no fair that you get all these signs, while I'm stuck barreling through life without a clue of what's to come."

And if that didn't put me in the matron of honor hall of fame, I don't know what would.

THE NEXT MORNING, I was busy Windexing the stovetop when the doorbell rang. I neglected to peek out the window before recklessly opening the door.

"Hi!" Kam shouted. "I'm stopping by to see if Dante—"

"Oh, knock it off," I said dryly.

Dante could be heard from his bedroom. "Daddy? Is that Daddy?"

Even the way Kam leaned against the doorjamb and tucked his hands in his pockets seemed smug. Dante ran over to him, stepping on my foot on the way. Kam picked him up, jostling him in the air the same way he had when he'd been an eight-pound baby, not forty-seven pounds of waggling arms and legs.

"Hey, bud. Want to go snorkeling? That is"—and he paused to look at me meaningfully, balancing Dante against his stomach—"if it's okay with your mom."

"*Pleeeeeeease*, Mom, can I?" That was from my son, who was quivering with hope like an upended Jell-O mold.

I smiled in mock sweetness at Kam, crossing my arms so I could give him the finger without Dante noticing. In return, he flashed me his eye-smile. He'd won—or so he thought. He could afford to be generous.

Morna's advice ran through my mind. Now that I was actually face-to-face with Kam, however, I wasn't sure if I could pull off demanding to accompany them. It smacked of tagging along with my big sister while she complained what an irritant I was.

Dante interpreted my hesitation as permission. He dropped to the floor, making those yay noises learned from watching too many commercials.

It was when Kam said, "I've got your snorkel and mask in the car, pal," that I got annoyed enough at his presumption to do what I had to do.

"Sounds great," I said. "I'll just need a minute to change into my swimsuit. How long do you think we'll be? Shall I pack snacks?"

Kam's features rearranged themselves into something resembling disbelief. He gave an uneasy chortle as he tried to gauge whether I was serious.

I carried on as though I hadn't noticed a thing. "You know, Kam, my time with Dante is so precious to me, I couldn't bear to miss out on it. That's why I find it so sweet of you to invite us both."

"Keel—"

"I can't think of the last time I went snorkeling. This will be such fun. Won't it be fun, Dante?" and he bounced his head in agreement.

Kam looked back toward the car.

Even though I was trying to play cool, I followed his gaze. There was Suzanne in the front seat of his pickup. It occurred to me like a black cloud entering my brain that if I was going through with this, she was coming along.

My voice revealed the dull anxiety that was washing over me. "I'll make PBJs. Do you think Suzanne would care for one?"

"You're serious . . ."

"Why? You prefer tuna salad?"

DANTE AND I piled ourselves and a load of towels, snorkeling equipment, and cooler into the back of Kam's truck. He cranked the radio, the local stoner rock station. Between the noise and the wind and the bumpy road, it was fairly easy to pretend I wasn't sharing a ride with Suzanne.

Except I kept stealing glances her way, hoping to see some flaw. A blemish. A wrinkle. She was the sort of woman to whom men would say *"You're beautiful when you're angry,"* and mean it. I would know. She was clearly furious. Still beautiful. Ugh.

Mental note—fire Morna. This was a disaster. It was one thing to hang out with Kam. Even though I expected it to be uncomfortable, he and I had plenty of experience being in close proximity despising each other.

After all, there were all those months after Dante's birth as the passion slowly dimmed between Kam and me. Even from the day I discovered he was cheating, weeks passed before bags were packed and futons removed— weeks in which I waffled over whether to forgive him. All that time during which I'd stupidly assumed he'd want to fix things if only I'd let him. Until the day I realized he was still seeing her. That this wasn't just a little boy's mistake that could be punished with a smack on the bottom.

Eventually he'd let it slip he'd taken her to Kapakihi Pond. Having sex with her was bad enough—this was the final blow.

He and I had met there, at the small, secluded waterfall on the east side of Kohala. That was where he'd delivered the famous first line while I was setting up equipment. Where he motioned toward me and said, "Everybody, we're in luck. We have a volcanologist here. Maybe she can tell us how this pond was formed," and I'd launched into a brief but I believe fascinating diatribe on tectonic plates and water flow patterns.

He gave me that devil's grin and knees (mine) proceeded to buckle. He said, "And all this time I thought it was a goddess's tears."

One of the ladies on the tour said from the side of her mouth, "You better get this boy's number, 'cause if you don't, I will."

Five years, one baby boy, and enough of my own tears later to fill a bathtub, Kam had shared our spot with Suzanne. I mean, it was one thing to trot it out for a bunch of tourists . . . but for her? They'd been sitting on a rock, apparently, toes in the water, sun on their faces, when he told her that he loved her.

He didn't actually give me those details. I didn't need them to know that this was no fling. That my life as I had imagined it was over.

I WOULDN'T USUALLY be the type to stick Kam with unloading the truck himself. But when Suzanne headed to the sunny side of the lagoon carrying nothing but a beach bag, I was hardly about to be her personal cabana girl. I grabbed only the armload equivalent of what she had along with my towel, and that was all I needed. Plus my snorkel, but that was it, besides my swim fins, and sunscreen, and Dante. It was hopeless. I was a lugger. We were not the women men craved. The luggers were the ones they married and left.

The laying of the towels was nothing less than a political maneuver. Suzanne fluttered a blanket to the ground. She perched on the edge of it as if to sit as far as possible from where I might settle. For a moment, I was tempted to butt my towel up against hers, plunk down and say, "Lovely day, isn't it?" But sanity prevailed, and I first set Dante's towel a reasonable distance from the blanket, then mine farther.

Then I said, "Lovely day, isn't it?"

"Mmm-hmm." This was delivered in the style of, *And you are in my air because—?*

And since she was putting sunscreen on an endless leg as she said it, I was dutifully intimidated.

I surmised she was to be lounging on this outing. Kam set up camp, unfolded her beach chair, and would have fluffed her pillow if she'd had one. I geared up Dante and myself. If she was out here, I was going to be in the water. To survive this day was all I wanted—to live long enough to fire Morna for this terrible idea.

"That's a darling suit," Suzanne said to me, our clearly being on speaking on terms now that Kam was present. "It's so wonderfully practical."

He beamed at her, his little trooper.

I lowered my goggles over my eyes and adjusted the snorkel. Then I grasped Dante's hand, and he and I walked backward on flippered feet into the water, this being easier to manage than forward.

"Daddy!" he shouted through his snorkel. "You coming?"

"In a minute, bud." Suzanne knelt behind him, rubbing lotion on his back. Cripes, there were *families* here—there was no excuse for the way they were carrying on.

Most of the lagoon was shaded by trees from the non-sunny side, making the water cool on my legs. I kept stepping back. I couldn't drag my eyes from the scene before me—until Dante glugged and I realized the water had reached nose-level for him.

Kam trudged his way in as I started to explain to Dante how to breathe through his snorkel. "Never go in water over your head," I told him. "That way, if some gets in your tube, you can always pull it off and stand up, okay?"

He nodded and submerged. I followed, facing him beneath the surface. I waved. He stuck his tongue out at me, his face shadowy and distorted behind the mask.

I gave him a watery undersea hellooooo. He answered me with a squeal, pointing past the mostly drab fish in our midst to a vivid yellow one darting by.

I started to follow it but collided with Kam's swim trunks.

When I came up out of the water, Kam bypassed a perfectly good opportunity to tease me about crotch diving. Instead, he nodded to where Dante floated. "He's a natural, heh?"

And I wouldn't have thought it possible, but from there we passed the rest of the morning quite pleasantly.

We'd take turns—one of us floating with Dante while the other swam off alone. I spent the better part of a half hour chasing what I thought was a baby shark, crashing into swimmers and coral in my pursuit. Until all at once it turned to charge right at me, startling me so much I swam frantically away to escape.

A quick break for lunch (to be remembered as the time when Dante chose my sandwich over Suzanne's fried chicken), and it was back in the water without the requisite thirty-minute wait period.

Suzanne pouted to Kam. "I thought we were going to leave soon." He dived neatly into the shallows, not answering.

I went back to snorkeling until I felt a tap on my back. When I pulled up from the water, there was Kam, dangling a bag of frozen peas in front of me.

"You ever use these?"

"Dante's more a corn man, I find."

"No, like this," Kam said, and lowered himself into the water. Dante did the same, then me. If we'd joined hands, we'd have been the image of floating skydivers.

Kam gave an underwater thumbs-up toward Dante; then he tore at the plastic bag. Peas released into the water.

The fish that had been gliding by suddenly came stormtrooping in our direction in a frenzy to get at the peas. They crashed into each other and me, slapping against my goggles, getting tangled in my hair. Hundreds of them. It was a writhing, frantic wall of fish, and it both frightened and thrilled me. I shooed them away with my hands, squealing so hard into my snorkel that I inhaled water into it.

I pulled up, standing in the thigh-high water, blinded by the water trapped in my goggles, still laughing and trying to gasp air but getting only water. A near-drowning experience again, this time mere feet from Suzanne.

Hands pulled the mask and snorkel off me.

"You okay?" Kam was grinning. "I thought you were going to let yourself die standing here."

"Mom!" Dante yelled. "You forgot to pull your mask off!"

I was still sputtering when I noticed Suzanne stride out up to her perfect ankles.

"Kam, it's time to go."

We straightened, scolded children that we were, fish knocking against us like confused ballet dancers.

KAM HELPED ME carry my belongings back into the house when he dropped me off.

"That wasn't so bad," he said.

"Suzanne in particular seemed delighted to spend the day with me. I quite enjoyed the way she glowered at me at every opportunity."

"Give her a break. She's younger."

"Thanks, I appreciate the reminder."

"I'm only saying that she's not a mean person. She just acts that way when she's intimidated. She's not like you."

This brinked on fascinating in that way those pseudo-Myers-Briggs tests on the Internet are. "And how am I exactly?"

"You know," he blinked at me. "Yourself, I guess. Self-contained. Like people are all very well and good, but if we fell off the island tomorrow, you'd be fine. You don't need anybody."

"I'm not like that," I said, feeling prickly. "I love people. I'm a real people person."

"Okay," he said.

"Well, I love Dante anyway. I need Dante."

He hoisted the cooler from my grasp and stacked it on the countertop, adding almost apologetically, "So do I, Keeleygirl."

IT WASN'T UNTIL the next day at work that I finally thought of the perfect comeback. I should have told Kam, "Ha! Good thing I didn't need you. I'd have been awfully disappointed since you've never once come through for me."

Now it was too late. I could only hope that he'd tell me again I didn't need anybody. Then I could nail him with the line as though I were just that clever.

I tossed my backpack on the floor, hastily unlacing my boots before Wagner could wander by and reprimand me for doing my job. I'd spent the morning on Kohala, updating the temperature readings I'd collected days before from a few of the ponds. That's why I should have had those flapping wings in my stomach, because of work, I reminded myself. Not because of Kam.

My computer hummed to life. I couldn't wait to type in the data, as if by committing it to megabytes, it would validate the fact that the water was getting warmer by the day. That it would make sense then, how somewhere at the base of the mountain, rock—just that, rock, for thousands of years—had in recent months gone molten. That it was simmering, expanding, a slow, growing burn pushing upward.

I logged on and started entering the temperature readings by geographic grid. Yes, there was no doubt about it, I thought, as I pecked in "A:3— Temp:89 degrees," there was something else about yesterday's events that had bothered me far more than Kam's remark. Try as I might to sort it out by myself, I couldn't. *"D:7,"* I typed, *"Temp: 92.2 degrees."* This was when I'd usually call Regatta, but I'd have to endure twenty minutes of wedding plans before I could get to my concerns. Talk of weddings invariably turned to talk of moving to Boston, and I wasn't in the mood. I've heard insanity described as doing the same thing again and again and expecting a different result. So God help me—right after I recorded *"E:7—Temp:93.6 degrees"* (then doublechecking; could that be right? but it appeared to be so)—I dialed my mom.

"I've been having a problem," I said. "Mind if I run it by you?"

She gave me her usual *"sure, dear."* There wasn't a couch to lie down on as I succumbed to what I'd fought all these years. I put my feet up on the edge of a trash can. This wouldn't be so bad. Some people would love free therapy.

I moved straight to the point. "I'm afraid I'm not as over Kam as I'd hoped."

I readied myself for a *"tell me about it."* Instead, she said, "Well, *duh.*"

"Excuse me?"

"Duh. It's a teenage colloquialism, meant to indicate that the other person has stated the obvious, which—as I'm sure you've realized—you have. One of the neighbors says it all the time. It's horribly rude, I know, but useful. Concise in its meaning."

"You find it obvious I'm still stuck on Kam? How could you possibly know?"

She exhaled a quick breath as if bracing herself. "All right then, tell me about it."

That was better. I went briefly into what had happened the day before.

"I can't get it out of my mind, the image of us swimming together. Kam, Dante, and me. It was as if I'd been visited by an apparition taunting me with the marriage-that-could-have-been. I'm reeling with regret."

There was nothing but the sound of my mom's aquarium gurgling on the other end.

"Well?" I asked. Where was her usual soul-probing follow-up question? Or at the very least her Freudian *mmm-hmm.*

"What do you want, dear?"

"Ah, a good question. What do I want from a relationship?"

She gave me another of those exhaled breaths. It was sounding vaguely impatient and very unlike my mother. "No, what do you want from me?"

"From you . . ."

"You need to make up your mind. Either you want me to say the things I'm used to saying, or we make a real try at change. I'm willing to respect the breakthrough we had while you were in L.A., but only if you do." I could hear her take a gulp of coffee. Her voice wavered as she continued. "I can't handle you flip-flopping back and forth. Wanting to be my daughter one minute, and my patient the next. That's not fair to me."

Curse that demon liquor, I thought. My mother and I'd had a breakthrough and I couldn't remember it.

I wanted to bluff my way through this, but something (maturity? decency?) made me admit the truth. "I don't remember our conversation," I said. "I blacked out a lot of that night."

Silence. Then, "Oh. I see."

"I swear it doesn't happen all the time. Never, in fact. I can always recount every drunken moment in glorious detail."

There was a group of people hovering outside my cubicle. The lunch crowd, which meant—yes, precisely 11:45. I could set my watch by them.

I lowered my voice. "Tell me. Did you by chance make a promise to stop using psychology talk on me?"

"I believe the term was psycho-babble."

"And what did I tell you? What was it I promised in return?"

"It doesn't matter, hon. You were drunk."

"I do some of my best thinking that way. Please. Tell me. What did I promise?" The silence may have been longer than the phone call from the hotel—but what the heck, HAG was graciously footing the bill.

Then, finally, she said, "To let me in."

I couldn't help but wonder at that moment—picturing my mom, seeming so small, as though my indifference had squeezed her into the phone receiver itself—what bargains I'd have to strike with Dante some day to hold on to him.

"Deal. But I must warn you. It's not pretty in there," I said, noticing Wagner's unmistakable corduroy jacket with the group that was arguing whether to drift en masse for Italian or burgers. There was no point in lowering my voice further. If he was spying, he'd had an earful already.

I continued, willing myself not to worry. "But you can't just stop talking. You have to fill in the empty conversational spaces. Many mothers use this time to give opinions. Now, I know that's an advanced move, and you might not—"

"Try me," she said.

"All right, then. Here goes. There's this other guy—"

"The one you were with in L.A."

"How did—? Oh, never mind. It's only . . . well, I was actually starting to like him. Then he messed up big time. Now I don't know what to think."

"Ah, yes. I know how you feel," she said experimentally. My mother in my life has never known how I felt, or said so at any rate. "Here's how I see it, honey. I love the opera. I consider it the finest music in the world. Yet I can't listen to it all the time. There are times when it's more satisfying to sing Wayne Newton songs in the shower, and you know I can't carry a tune. But sometimes that's exactly what I need."

It wasn't normal parental advice. I hadn't the vaguest notion what she was trying to say. Still, it was a start.

Wagner's jacket disappeared with the lunch crowd. I found myself humming "Danke Schoen" the rest of the day—at first because it was the only Wayne Newton song I could think of, and then because it's one of those tunes that gets stuck in your head. I was going to have to call Regatta later and sing it to her so I wouldn't have to suffer alone.

If I were lucky, she wouldn't answer in that Boston accent she'd been trying out lately. I was starting to worry that her vows would include that they promised to love, cherish, and paak the caah in Haavaad Yaad.

15

THERE WAS NO point in doing away with Morna for her poor advice. When I'd told her how I'd ignored the horror on Suzanne's face as I'd approached the car, I may as well have been telling her I won the all-town spelling bee, she looked so proud.

It's hard to resist that sort of devotion in a lawyer, especially one kind enough to lend you her karaoke player. I'd had a brainstorm—right around the time Lawrence hijacked the honor of throwing Regatta her shower, and for the flimsy reason that he happened to be the one to think of buying invitations and sending them to prospective guests. Then it hit me: What Regatta really needed was a bachelorette party. And since she was probably of the opinion that she would abhor such a thing, then clearly she needed a surprise bachelorette party. Hence the karaoke on loan.

"He's going to try it again," Morna warned me to the tune of "Me and Mrs. Jones" as we tested the machine in my living room. "Your husband needs to clock as much time with Dante as possible before the hearing. I can assure you the Lees have already told him that."

"Why don't we move the hearing up then?" I said, only I sang it along with "We've got a thing going on." *Why don't we mooooove the hearing uuuuuuup.*

"It isn't that simple." She fiddled with dials. "There are certain . . . character issues . . . regarding you that we need to disprove. Or at least give time to go away."

"Character issues . . ."

"I personally doubt that the reason Dante's been spending so much time at the sitter's is because you're moonlighting as a stripper. I wouldn't think you any less a mother if you were. But judges are funny about those things."

"They're claiming I'm a stripper?"

She pressed a button, and the song changed. "Ah, The Dead. Now that's what I call music." She didn't skip a beat before adding, "You keep doing what you're doing. That includes refusing Kam extra solitary visitation and—if you're so inspired—removing your clothes to music in front of strangers."

"You think I'm a stripper?"

"It doesn't matter what people think. What matters is what is."

And there was no talking to her after that point because she was clearly overtaken by the spirit of Jerry Garcia—singing such a soulful version of "Truckin' " that even Dante came out from my room where he'd been watching TV to join her spinning joyously around the living room.

I waited until the song was finished, growing more furious by the second. When she stopped, glowy with sweat, she was met by the sight of me, arms crossed, ready for a fight.

"It does matter what people think," I challenged, "If those people are unscrupulous enough to"—and I remembered Dante, "Go get a Kool-Aid, honey, you look flushed." Then I continued,—"build some sort of twisted case against me. It matters quite a bit, and I'm starting to wonder if you realize that." My voice was rising in that Laura Petrie way when she used to say, *"Oh, Rob!"* But I was unstoppable, especially since Morna was doing that thing my mom always did—demeanor open, *listening.* Nothing could have taunted me more. "I don't need my lawyer to patronize me. I need her to defend me. Against the Lees. Against Kam. This is"—and I had to take a calming breath because I had the projectile tears going—"this is my *child* we're talking about here. I'm not screwing around."

"I would think not," Morna said, dropping to sit cross-legged at my feet. Under her skirts, I felt her grip firm on my ankles, as if she were weighting me down. "The Lees are building a case of lies," she said, her voice matter-of-fact. "They are ruthless, but unpopular. I was able to learn about their plans to accuse you of being a stripper through the simple act of giving their assistant some much-needed reflexology. Poor woman— prone to terrible stress backaches. Amazing how massaging the feet can cure so much—"

"So we don't stand here and take it. We get in there and fight," I interrupted.

Her arms hugged my shins, her chin resting just above my knees. "If you want me to keep you more informed, I certainly will. I've been insensitive. What you've understood to be condescending on my part is, in fact, confidence. I know things will work out but, of course, I mustn't expect you to believe that without the facts."

Towering so high above Morna, she seemed to me too harmless to manipulate my life. "I'm scared, that's all."

"Of course you are, but you needn't be. The Lees may have deceit on their side, but I have something that will surely thwart their plans."

"The truth . . . ," I said, nodding with understanding.

"Even better, my dear. I have you."

JUDGING BY THE clothes I'd seen him wear, I'd have to have guessed that Ian Gardiner was a man of impeccable taste. Probably special-ordered everything from Barneys New York; not a flowered shirt even in the farthest reaches of his closet. That was the reason I felt confident his concern over returning my sunglasses wasn't entirely philanthropic but more an excuse to see me. With a fashion savvy such as his, he had to have been able to tell that they'd cost me about five bucks at *Longs Drugs*.

When I finally returned his call, he did seem surprised when I said, "I don't think I should risk having you mail them. They're quite delicate. Is there anyway we could meet so you could hand them over in person?"

"By all means." Then—perhaps encouraged by the fact that I wasn't snarling at him as I'd been the last time he'd seen me—he ventured, "Although . . . returning eyewear is thirsty work. Perhaps a drink might be required?"

"Yes," I said, somber, "I see your point."

I had been inspired to call Ian by Bob's wife, Lucy, when I joined the two of them for lunch. There I was, regaling them with the story of my trip to L.A. and giving it all I had to give when describing Ian's deceit. But I found that with each retelling, it was seeming increasingly charming that Ian went through so much to impress me. After the part where I mentioned I hadn't returned his phone call, Lucy gaped at me.

"Wait, I must be missing something here," she said, tapping her head with a pen as if to clear it, "He is single, right?"

"He *lied*."

"But," she said in confirmation, "He is single?"

Of course, this from the woman who set me up on that disastrous blind date. But still, she had a point.

So Ian and I met for drinks and had a swell time, once we got over the initial bump of discomfort. But darned if he didn't forget those sunglasses so we had to meet for lunch a couple days later. Still, forgetful boy that he was, he neglected to bring the glasses. We had to grab a quick dinner before I picked up Dante from after-school care. By the time we got around to a Saturday night date—as far as I was concerned, just a cheap excuse to get to the part afterwards where we strolled down the beach and made out against the lifeguard station—I had to beg him to bring the glasses because I was getting tired of squinting all the time.

There may have been a wall in front of me—and, Lord knows, I was all too aware that I was the one standing there, bricks and mortar in my trembling hand. But it seemed safe enough to let Ian mill around, standing guard to my heart so I wouldn't get any crazy ideas about letting people in.

AS MORNA HAD predicted, Kam stepped up the visits—thank God, just him. Suzanne had apparently decided she'd had enough family fun for a while.

He dropped in on a Tuesday at Dante's bedtime. I let him tell our son a story and tuck him in—frankly, it was nice to have someone else get him into his PJs for once. Kam was back again on Wednesday, this time after bedtime.

"You're going to have to start calling first," I said coolly before letting him in. "He's already asleep. Besides, what if I had a man over?" And, damn it, he scoffed.

If I did not have a grasp of the bigger picture—that is, I had to endure this for only a couple weeks before appearing saintlike before a judge—I'd have produced a man just to wipe that look off his face.

Truth was, though, I wasn't ready to have Ian over with Dante home. Some people might find that interesting in light of the fact that I certainly was ready—if not eagerly anticipating the opportunity—to sleep with him, but one cannot overvalue a mother's instincts. It was too early to risk Dante's waking and wandering out for a drink, only to find a strange man with his mommy. That left only Saturday nights or begging for baby-sitting favors, but so be it.

Regatta had supported me on this one when I'd brought it up to her the other night. "No need to invite Ian over to hang out yet," she'd said. "Not if he's willing to go places and pay for dates. Enjoy it. Once you get a man settled on your couch, you have to use a shoehorn to get him off." Then she wrinkled her nose adoringly at Ted, who gave her a peck and suggested, hey, let's the four of us do a couples thing.

I let Kam talk me into allowing him to wake Dante up, tell him a story, and then retuck him in. Then he and I had a couple beers on the porch. I told him about what was going on at HAG with Wagner. He told me about a thrill ride he'd started at the tour agency where he worked.

"I haul ass around the mountain—backwards, sideways, doesn't matter. The more people crash their heads on the rollbar, the more line up for the tour. Crazy *haole*," he said, adding, "no offense."

I took a swig of beer, shifting. Tiny stones from the cement steps were embedded in the back of my legs. When I brushed them away, they left indentations behind.

"You're going to miss your tour business when you move to Fiji," I said. "Without Dante."

A muscle twitched in his jaw. He drained his beer and then stood as if to go. "I haven't told Suzanne I've been coming here. She doesn't get it. Thinks I'm with the guys—said she'd kill me if I didn't make it home by nine tonight."

"You're two hours late."

He looked at his empty wrist; then he picked up my arm to check my watch as if taking my pulse. "Well, then. Looks I'm already dead. Can't be more dead than dead, can you?"

I said I supposed not.

"Might as well have another beer."

The conversation from there remained civil. I'd even gone so soft as to volunteer that I thought it would be a shame for him to leave his house. It was decorated so nicely.

He'd tossed an empty bottle into my bushes when I'd said it. It landed with a thud.

"So I'm told," he said, his eyes on the sky, apparently trying to pick out the Southern Crown from the stars, as I knew he often liked to do on this clear a night.

WHICH WAS WHY the next morning, a bit rattled from experiencing an entire evening with Kam without once fighting, the last thing I wanted to see when I set my purse on my desk was a faxed printout of a HAG phone bill. My call to Michigan had been highlighted, the total ($8.32) circled, followed by three exclamation points.

Wagner showed up a few minutes later, straightening his tie. "I left that for you. I'm assuming the call to your mother wasn't official business. You'll need to reimburse the company."

I tried to raise one eyebrow at him the way Ian can do, but mine are connected. They shot up together. "Fine," I said.

He kept standing there. "Well?" he said.

"I don't have the cash on me." I was going to have to run to the bank on my lunch and get $8.32 in pennies and unroll them on Wagner's desk.

"No, I meant your ideas. We're supposed to meet this morning so you can show them to me before the board meeting. Three o'clock sharp. You're wearing that?" He grimaced at my T-shirt and khakis.

The board meeting. Today. Me. With nothing. I could have sworn it was next week. I'd been so skilled at pushing it from my mind so I wouldn't stress out, I must have overachieved. "My ideas . . . ," I said, stalling.

"You've been very secretive, Kekuhi—but as you can see I've shown my faith in your abilities by letting you run free with it!" followed by his usual supportive air-punch. "I can't wait to see your new names for HAG. I'll bet you've got some doozies in there."

"Yes, I do!" I shouted (overcompensation, my mom at one point in her life would have explained, before she dispensed with that sort of language).

"They're at home. I'm going there to change. I'll get them then."

I escaped to the ladies' room where he couldn't follow and keep asking me to at least tell him what I'd be proposing—not, mind you, that he didn't trust me.

I hid in a stall, gnawing on my cuticles and wishing I could be as cool as Kam about being deader than dead.

"HOW ABOUT CUNT?" I asked Bob. He and I were sequestered in the mapping area trying to throw together some last-minute presentation boards.

"What does it stand for?"

"It's supposed to stand for something?"

He stared at the blank computer screen. "Stay focused. This has to look like you mean it."

I tried to stay focused. When I'd gone crawling to Bob for help, he'd had one of those 120-watt ideas. He'd pointed out—better late than never—that I was in a no-win situation. It hadn't occurred to me until he'd said it, but he was right. If I presented a usable agency name, I'd be a permanent, card-carrying member of the PR department. If I walked in empty-handed, I'd be fired.

"What you have to do is paste a big grin on your face and do the worst job ever," he'd said. "That way they'll just pity you."

But sincerely bad ideas were as elusive as good ones. So far all we had was a symbol made by photocopying a coffee spill, standing for The Agency Formerly Known as HAG, or The Agency for short.

I heard my name being shouted down the hall. It was Beula the receptionist. Wagner must have sent her for me. "Has anybody seen Kekuhi? It's a madhouse in my lobby!"

She poked a head into the cubicle, and for a woman of such diminuative stature, she nonetheless managed to fill the place with a frown.

"Please, don't tell Wagner where I am," I pleaded. "I need a few more minutes to . . . um . . . finalize . . . these agency names."

"I don't give a rat's ass what you need to do. I got a bunch of filthy people claiming to be geologists messing up my lobby. They're asking for you." She looked at the symbol we'd mounted on foam core. "That the best you can do? What the heck is it supposed to be?"

"Geologists? For me?" I hardly dared to hope. Surely they'd have called first. It got Bob's attention, too. He turned around, raised an eyebrow at me. Dang, how did people *do* that? I tried it again. Nope—both together—making me look surprised, which in this case was appropriate.

Beulah was jeering at the board. "They shoulda given me that job. I came up with better stuff than that while I was taking a crap."

"Where did the scientists say they were from? Are they from the AGS?"

She didn't answer. I was about to run see for myself when Bob touched my arm, stopping me. "Bueles," he said, "I, for one, would be quite curious to see these ideas of yours."

"I'll bet you would—and you can forget it. They don't get this," she said, tapping the side of her head with a finger, "Till they show me the money."

Bob leaned back in his chair, hands clasped behind his head. "I don't blame you. It's infuriating how they've overlooked your obvious talents. But Keeley here—she may be in a spot to help you out. Those scientists in the lobby? Big public relations coup. HAG will be known worldwide. It's a sure-fire step up for our girl Keeley. She'll be looking for somebody to take her place. Somebody who's proved what she can do."

She looked suspiciously back and forth between Bob and me.

I was nearly drooling, but trying not to show it. Nobody could have a bad idea like Beula. It was thanks to her that the conference rooms were named after types of shoes: the Espadrille Room, the Slingback.

"All right, I'll tell you my best one," she said reluctantly. "But if they use it and I get passed over for the next promotion, I'm blowing the whistle."

She spread her fingers, moved her hands apart—a gesture of magic and wonderment of what was to come.

"HUG," she said. "Stands for Hawaiian Unified Governments. We only gotta replace one letter. And the best part is the slogan: We put our arms around the islands."

"Perfect," Bob said, sniggering as he turned to the keyboard. "Exactly what we were looking for."

It occurred to me as I ran to the lobby that Beula's slogan must have been even worse than Bob thought by merit of the fact that I kind of liked it.

WAGNER NABBED ME just shy of the lobby.

"Kekuhi, you've gone too far this time. I've had no choice but to write you up."

I peered past him to the canvas knapsacks that were strewn on the floor. Three people sat on them pretending to thumb through HAG literature.

"For what exactly?" I asked.

"Don't play your games with me. I know everything. How you went over my head and wrote to Washington. Got outside help without my permission."

"So they are from Washington!" There was no keeping the glee from my voice. I reflected back to my last conversation with Hoffman. It had ended with his sounding ambivalent, but I suppose my pleading could have been construed as an official HAG authorization.

I skirted past Wagner to greet them. Turned out, they'd come over from the west side where they'd been assisting on Kilauea with Skipper. "He says hi, by the way," one of them said, "Told us that if you say there's activity here, then it must be true. You know your stuff."

I had to turn my face so they wouldn't see me go pink. Skipper didn't even need to have meant it, I was astounded enough he said it.

They would stay a few days to check things out. If the situation was as interesting as I'd indicated, they planned to stay on.

"How many times do I have to tell you?" Wagner said when I briefed him on the situation. "There are procedures."

"We could be looking at a crisis if the—"

"Now let's not go losing our heads. It's very simple. Fill out the proper paperwork. If all goes well, you should have your little scientist friends back by spring."

My spirits went flaccid.

"Tell you what," he said, holding a manila folder out toward me. "Go tell them they can't stay. Then impress the heck out of me at today's board meeting, and I might forget to turn in this write-up. It'll be our secret."

It was a free country, I grumbled under my breath as I left. A few geologists could camp out on the mountain over the weekend if they wanted to, should they happen upon a permit—and surely I knew somebody over in the parks department where I could get one.

I looked at them sitting there in their dusty jeans and work boots. To my shame, I wanted them to like me—desperately, pitifully—in that *You Like Me! You Really Like Me!* sort of way, clutching my statuette and basking in the acceptance of my peers.

Wagner would make them jump through hoops to stay. My only hope was that they'd be impressed enough with Kohala to be willing to endure his trials.

"How would you guys like a tour of the volcano?" I asked.

When they excitedly agreed, I added, "Anyone have a bad back?"

I pilfered money from petty cash to treat my volcanologist friends to Kam's Jeep tour of the volcano. I rode shotgun, nearly falling out at the first fast turn Kam took. He'd reached out with one hand, grabbing my shirt to pull me back in. "Told you to buckle up, girl," he laughed, never even slowing. "Everybody back there okay?" he shouted, gunning it over a bump. They were too busy squealing to answer.

Kam's thrill ride was the hit he'd said it would be—and he'd barely made me grovel for him to squeeze us in last-minute. He and I were like a sportscasting team. I pointed out scientific areas of interest while he provided color.

With the board meeting hanging over my head, taking off to play tour guide with my new pals Todd, John, and Dawn was a risk. It was one that was paying off, I thought, as I turned to look at them flopping about in the back of the Jeep. I wasn't sure if they had an opinion one way or another about me yet. But they'd clearly formed a connection to Kohala, as real as if they'd met her at a party and discovered by chance that they'd gone to the same elementary school.

Kam let the engine falter at the top of an embankment. "Looks like I'm having a bit of car trouble," he said dramatically. He released the brake to let the Jeep slip back. Then he floored it in reverse, looking over his shoulder as he drove. My stomach leapt to somewhere in my throat. I knew him too well to be as unterrified as my companions.

By the time I was dropped back at the office (fifteen minutes to spare, thank you), we'd bonded in that way that even contrived near-death experiences can bring.

In fact, the rest of them were going with Kam for a beer before heading to their hotel for the night. As he pulled away, I heard Kam ask one of the guys not to let him stay for more than one or the little woman was going to pitch a fit.

THE BOARD LOVED the name HUG. "Warm yet professional!" the official minutes would later read when distributed to staff. The board president himself assured me that I had quite a future in public relations.

Wagner slapped me on the back as I skulked out. "Well done, Kekuhi. I knew you'd rise to the occasion. There are plenty more plum projects in the queue for you after this one. You can count on that."

There were a million and a half things I needed to do when I got home. They would have to wait for the next day. After I put Dante to bed, I sat on the back porch, hollering back and forth with Daisy Ku about how it was looking like rain.

Kam didn't show. Ian was out of town again. I rested my head against siding in dire need of a coat of paint. I thought I might have identified part of the Big Dipper, but it was hard to tell, what with the clouds moving in.

EVEN WITH SPENDING the next two days getting the geologists settled, I was ready for Regatta's surprise party by the time the guests arrived.

"Nice spread," Lawrence said, the token male. "May I remove the Saran Wrap from the goodies or are you holding out for that last burst of freshness?"

I offered up a tray of Jell-O shooters. "Bachelorette parties are supposed to be tacky."

"Well, then . . . success!" He picked up a store-bought rumaki and spun it around with the same sort of interest my geologist friends might have looked at a lava sample.

I'd put Regatta's cousins, the bridesmaids, to work mixing mai tais. Lucy and Melissa Anne had "Don't Go Breaking My Heart" cranking on the karaoke but were arguing over who had to be Kiki Dee.

Regatta was supposed to show at nine. I'd asked her to come over to "trim my bangs" so I'd look my best for her bridal shower, which just happened to be the next morning—a fact that Lawrence had the nerve to point out may have been more than mere coincidence.

By nine-thirty, however, the party had reduced itself to someone keeping watch while the rest of the guests grilled me, "Are you sure she remembers she's supposed to come here?"

"Regatta doesn't forget," I frowned, putting the phone on speaker and dialing her number.

"Oh," she said when I asked where she was. "I forgot."

"Well, hurry." I giggled conspiratorially to the others gathered around me. "My bangs are out of control."

"I'll do it in the morning. I'm exhausted."

"Come on, don't be a fuddy dud. We'll have a party. You and me."

"I'm already dressed for bed. I want to get a good night's sleep so I'll look halfway decent for my brunch tomorrow."

Lawrence beamed.

"But you have to come . . ."

"No, actually, I don't," she said, her voice clipped.

"Okay, forget about cutting my bangs. We'll just talk. Wedding stuff. It'll be fun."

"Fun," she sighed as if it were a four-letter word. "You know, it's bad enough I'm trying to plan this wedding by myself. But I'm up to my knees in moving boxes, too, and nobody's helping. Not Ted, not you, nobody. Forgive me if *fun* sounds like the last thing I want right now."

"But—"

"I'll call you in the morning, babe."

The line went dead. Lucy pushed down the receiver button. I bit my bottom lip to keep it from quivering.

The phone immediately rang. Lawrence picked it up. "I hope you plan to apologize to our little friend Keeley. . . . Oh, wait, hold on." He handed the phone to me. "It's a *boy*."

Hmm, Ian? It would be nice timing to restore the tattered shreds of my ego.

Turned out it was the stripper confirming. "You may as well not come," I started to say, but Lawrence grabbed the phone and gave him Regatta's address.

"Never say no when a perfectly good man is willing to remove his clothing," he said, picking up a food tray. "If Princess Regatta won't come to us, we'll simply have to take the party to her."

FOR A WHILE I was afraid she wasn't going to lower the drawbridge and let us in. I knocked while Lawrence waved his platter temptingly at the peephole and said, "Doll, it's worth your while to invite us in. We have lunch meats!"

"Shhh . . . all right, please, the neighbors," she said, opening the door. "I can't believe you're here. The place is a mess. I'm a mess."

All true—her eyes were puffy, like she might be getting a cold. The apartment was filled with boxes in varying stages of being packed. I knew that Ted was in Boston apartment hunting, but I hadn't allowed myself to realize she was leaving until I walked in.

I heard a bad Brooklyn accent say, "Dis da party? Where's da bride to be?" It was Tony Manero of *Saturday Night Fever* fame who'd walked in with us.

Regatta looked at me with horror. "Tell me he's not a stripper."

"Surprise," I said.

"Yo, mind if I dance on dis?" He scooched the coffee table away from the rest of the furniture.

We took places on the couch and on tipped-over boxes for the show. I had to hold a leg over Regatta to keep her sitting, assuring her that any minute now she was going to be enjoying this.

The stripper put "Stayin' Alive" on the boom box. He started to gyrate to the music. He looked familiar, I thought, although it certainly wasn't

John Travolta he resembled (except for the white disco suit he was squeezed into). Couldn't quite place him, though.

Lucy and the cousins whooped, "Take it off, baby!"

He tore his jacket and shirt off in one motion, swinging it above his head. His belly flopped over the top of his pants like an airbag released.

"Put it on, put it all on . . . ," Lawrence groaned. Regatta giggled. Ha! I knew she'd get into the spirit of things.

Lucy somehow tucked a dollar beneath his writhing stomach.

"Thank ya, beh-beh."

"Elvis!" I cried. I knew he'd looked familiar. "You're Elvis!" He'd just torn off his breakaway pants as I'd said it.

Lawrence whispered, "Perhaps in The King's later years."

"I'm Tony Manero, disco dancer extraordinaire," he said weakly. He stopped dancing, holding his hands to hide a gold lamé G-string. "You must have me confused. . . ."

"I'd know you anywhere! You came to my son's party."

"Oh . . ." And he burst into tears, sitting down on the table. "I'm such an insult to the name of Elvis Presley . . . stripping!"

"Nice job, Keel," Regatta said.

I'd like to say one of us made a comforting gesture, but we all sort of sat there, shrugging and making wide eyes at each other.

Elvis blew his nose on his jacket sleeve, blubbering as he reminisced about the old Vegas days, where an Elvis impersonator was allowed some respect. He'd sometimes marry twenty couples in a single day at the chapel where he worked, he said, then looked at Regatta through bloodshot eyes. "Do you have your wedding dress yet?"

She gave him a supportive nod, as if she hoped her answer might cheer him. It reduced him to sobs again.

"Maybe you could do a favor for a pitiful old man. Maybe . . . you could put it on?"

"I don't think . . ."

"Yes!" Lucy said. "What a perfect idea!"

With much egging on, Regatta agreed, only after the bridesmaids and myself promised to try on our dresses in an act of solidarity. They'd been delivered to Regatta, but not altered yet, as was made clear by the fact that all of us could have fit in my gown alone.

Lawrence fashioned groom-wear from Regatta's closet, creating an ascot from a scarf and suspenders from a couple belts.

When we came out, the stripper had changed into Elvis garb. Regatta had been fretting so much that he might put back on the disco jacket he'd blown his nose into that I—quite understandably—had to feed her mai tais to push the image from her mind.

We wound up doing several run-throughs of the ceremony, with Elvis officiating. Lawrence stood in as groom until I got jealous of that cool ascot and made him switch outfits.

Besides, I was more inspired in the role of groom, clomping up the aisle and bellowing my lines.

At one point, Elvis asked Regatta, "Is practicing helping you with your second thoughts, beh-beh?"

Since I was Ted, I boomed, "Don't be silly! My wifey-to-be isn't having second thoughts!"

She clutched her cat Tipsy, who she'd been holding as a bouquet. "Yes, Teddy, actually I am."

I was about to yell, "Why?" but I remembered I was me, not Ted. A tear rolled down her face. "Oh, Reggie," I said.

I led her away to her bedroom, gesturing importantly to the others to wait. Through sniffles and tears, Regatta told me how Ted had e-mailed her pictures of Boston apartments—horrid beige boxes surrounded by snow and suburbia. She'd been hit with a jolt of what it would mean to leave her friends and family when I'd called.

"Just when I'd had my vision that Ted was the one, I wondered if I could go through with it after all. I want the man, but not the choice that seems to be coming along with him."

"Have you talked to him?"

"No, and I can't now. I'm snockered."

I suppose the lessons learned by a better woman would have included that one shouldn't use alcohol as an excuse to reveal one's feelings, but it had actually proved fairly fruitful for me in recent months.

"You have to talk to him," I insisted, determined to find the words that would serve if not as an inspiration, at least as a horrible warning. "What's your choice? Letting him go, figuring another Ted will come along soon? Because, trust me, you might get your next Ted. And you know what?

The poor guy won't stand a chance. You won't give him a chance. Because the . . . Ted . . . who lives in your memory isn't the one you had"—and I barely paused when shifting to a more comfortable position on the bed, I was on such a roll—"he's the one who could have been. If only you'd tried harder. If only you had more time. And all the Teds who follow, the ones with charm and money who press you against the lifeguard station while you're kissing until—"

"Uh, Keel," Regatta interrupted. "Are we still talking about *me* here?"

Sheepish, I handed her the phone. "Call."

Ted was waking up when Regatta reached him at his hotel room in Boston. She talked to him; then we passed the phone around while we unpacked boxes and then repacked them. I suggested we pack by color. It was working fine until Lawrence nearly had a breakdown because he needed another ecru item and he swore people kept trying to pass off wheat. (As if I don't know the difference! he huffed.)

At one point, Regatta stumbled up to me. "I'm going to meet Teddy in Boshton sho I can shee for myshelf. Shank you for my bashelorette party. Ish very nishe. You wan me cut your bangies now?"

The next day's brunch remains a bit of a blur. I do recall Regatta having to open the shower gifts lying down on several restaurant chairs pushed together. I received many startled compliments on my haircut. Mostly, though, Regatta's mom and her aunties *tsk*ed us. "These young kids today can't party like we used to, eh?" an auntie boasted, inspiring the ladies to exchange drink recipes, arguing at length how to concoct a Harvey Wallbanger.

Lawrence had to beg them to stop before he tossed his tea cookies.

"AMAZING," IAN SAID, holding up a handful of the delicate lava ribbons known as Pele's Hair. "You say this grows wild on the volcano?"

"It doesn't grow—it formed when the volcano erupted," Dawn corrected him.

"Hard to imagine in all that time that it hasn't been snatched up by collectors," he remarked, turning a chunk of it the way Lawrence had studied the rumaki.

"Taking it would bring bad luck. It's believed to be part of the goddess.

The tourists aren't really allowed up here, and the locals respect that sort of thing," I said. "You know, now that I think about it, my cleaning lady never removes the hair from my shower drain. You don't suppose she believes that I'm—"

"You *are* a goddess," Ian interjected. He said it with such conviction no one even teased me. Excellent. Positive reinforcement—even shameless—was much needed and appreciated.

I'd been putting in fourteen-hour days on the volcano for the past week. Equipment had arrived by truck from AGS, so I could finally run some of the tests that HAG . . . HUG . . . whatever . . . had been too cheap to finance. The findings were alarming—rocks shifting, the heat of its insides continuing to rise.

And me, of all people, the resident expert. No one seemed able to so much as set up a seismometer without my advice. That's why I had to tell Ian when he called that if he wanted to see me, he'd have to scale a mountain to do it.

Astoundingly, he interpreted what I said as an invitation rather than an excuse. He rented a pickup and—following the directions I'd learned to give after years of living on the island ("Turn left at the twin palms, then go straight to the warrior's bush"), managed to find his way to the camping spot.

I watched Ian climb out of the truck. John stroked his beard thoughtfully in that way bearded men always do. "Those are some shiny boots your fellow's got."

"Shut *up*." I had the total junior high flashback—the one where you think your date for the dance is groovy as heck in his powder blue suit and then your sister walks up and says nice *cummerbund*, and ruins everything.

Ian's outfit had obviously been purchased for the occasion. I was surprised he didn't still have the tags on his work shirt. When he walked over to where we were sitting by the campfire, his jeans made that new-denim scuffing noise. John laughed, "We'll have to put you to work—break in those spiffy duds."

Ian held up a bag, unaffected. "Could I interest anyone in some ribs?"

He'd brought take-out food and a jug of Gatorade—"For emergencies," he quipped, "I was a Boy Scout. Therefore, you'll find I'm not without resources to survive in the wild."

Between his good-natured response and Dawn—a slip of a girl fresh from grad school, more freckles than face—pinching my arm, whispering, "Shoot, girl, first that tour guide, now him . . . Do you know any *ugly* guys?" I remembered, Oh, *yeah*. Emotional angst aside, Ian's cute and I'm horny. This is a good thing.

It wasn't much of a leap, therefore, to my resentment of John and Todd's showing him around the grounds. The opportunity for outdoor sex was so fleeting in a relationship. Once boys figure out you're willing to put out and they don't have to get sand up their asses, it's nothing but the four-poster from that day forth. If only he and I were alone.

"Don't let me interrupt your work," Ian said. That was when he found the Pele's Hair. He set it on a rock, then pulled a pad of paper from the truck. He set about doing a charcoal sketch while I resigned myself to sifting through the day's findings with the others.

After a couple of hours huddled over graph paper, charting the measurements we'd taken that morning, I had the distinct sensation of being watched.

It was Ian, taking me in as his hand stroked the paper.

"Hey . . . I thought you were drawing flowers—not me," I protested.

"Can I help it if I recognize beauty when I see it?"

"Ooookay," John said, pushing himself to his feet. "You don't have to run over us with a truck." (Hmm, hadn't thought of that.) "We'll leave you lovebirds alone for a while. C'mon, guys. I'm sure we have some gaseous fumaroles we could measure."

Todd pulled a pen from his pocket protector. "Huh?"

"That's right," said Dawn gamely, "And some ground deformations that need observing."

"Don't be silly," I said, handing them their jackets and a bag of gorp Ian had brought, shooing them like stray goats. "You're welcome to stay."

This is where I should be saying that we soon lay arm in arm in the warm afterglow of our lovemaking but—*grrr*—Ian kept drawing me after they left.

"I'll only be a few minutes more," he said, shielding the sketchpad from my view. "Please . . . the light's so perfect on you there."

His hair flopped over as he worked. I pouted. If I'd known I was going to be sitting there doing nothing, I wouldn't have given away all the gorp.

He chatted absently about how he hoped to be able to paint me soon, talked a bit about his recent business trip.

"So where's your son while you're putting in these long hours?" he asked after a while. "With his father?"

"My neighbor takes him, or his grandma."

"His dad doesn't see him much, then?"

"I can't let him. I have a hearing coming up. I need to show he's a neglectful parent."

Ian lifted his head. "Is he?"

I shifted on the rock I was sitting on, kicked aside a leaf. "Aren't you done yet?" I said instead of answering. "I was hoping we could squeeze in a little mashing."

He closed the sketchpad, set it down, a glimmer of interest creeping to his face. "Define mashing. . . ."

"You know, *mashing*. Making out. It's the best we can do given that the others could return at any time." I crawled over, brushed my lips along his ear and said, "For you British types, that'd be more than snogging, but not quite shagging."

He made this noise in his throat and—yes!—still at the who-cares-if-I'm-lying-on-pine-needles-stage, pulled me to the ground.

We needn't have bothered remaining clothed. John, Todd, and Dawn made so much noise upon returning—"Yup! Here we are! Three geologists returning to the campgrounds!"—we'd have had time enough to escape from straitjackets.

Ian shot a mortified look in my direction as they walked up. "Well, I'd best be off," he said, his face coloring.

The others were snickering. "Have a nice visit?" John asked, checking me out. I soon realized why. Charcoal handprints covered my shirt and pants. I brushed myself off, a pointless exercise. No use. The charcoal stuck to me like a scarlet *A*.

Ian picked up the Pele's Hair he'd found, eager to make his escape. "Think I'll keep this. I may be able to work it into one of my pieces." No fear at all of repercussions from the gods. Clearly he'd never seen *The Brady Bunch* in Hawaii episode where the boys find that cursed tiki statue.

"I'll ring you," he said, giving one last embarrassed glance at my shirt before getting in his truck and driving off.

I could still hear tires scraping on dirt when Todd let out a whistle. He was holding the sketch pad Ian had left behind. There, following several pages of rocks and plants, was the sketch of me.

It was not the me dejected on the rock. My arms were up, my face in rapture. I floated from the mouth of the volcano like a wisp of air—nude, of course, to the amusement of the others.

"I'll give him that—," John remarked, "The man is certainly a hands-on artist."

WHEN I PICKED up Dante at Ma Kekuhi's a few nights later, Kam was there. He'd been calling me on and off all week with what we'd begun to label Dantecdotes: adorable stories of our son that we couldn't get enough of but would bore anyone else to tears. As in, Kam had been at Ma's when she'd served Dante sausages, explaining they were made of pig. He'd stabbed one with his fork, examined it. "Must be a baby pig," he'd said, and then without concern took a bite. How darling is that? I chuckled for minutes afterward when Kam called me at work to tell me—but when I tried passing the story on to Bob, he just said, *"Heh, cute, hand me that map, will you?"*

I didn't know why the disembodied voice on the phone could be so comfortable but when seeing him in person, Kam still felt like Kam. Maybe because he smelled like Kam, vaguely warm, a spice not quite identifiable. Not that I walked up and sniffed him, but it was a scent you knew was there if you got close enough.

"Stay. Have some ribs," Ma said, pulling a platter-size plate from the row of shelves that she called cupboards.

"Thanks, but I had ribs the other day."

"Not my ribs," she said.

Ma was so offended—and I so indebted for all the baby-sitting she'd been doing—that I sat down and gnawed on a slab, even though I'd already eaten.

Kam grabbed a seat at the table across from me, regaling me with more stories. He'd moved his visits with Dante to Ma's since I'd started working more. It would be a lot easier if he could just take Dante, he hinted, but without malice. The other night he'd stayed so late, Suzanne deadbolted him out. He'd had to sleep in the hammock. While I was trying to digest that piece of information, he moved on to another story.

I could barely swallow. The hearing was days away. He didn't exhibit the slightest unease.

I had to clutch desperately on to my hatred like a worn but comfortable stuffed bear. "Thanks for dinner," I said, readying to leave. I steadied a now-sleeping Dante on my hip, "I'm off to my stripping job. Ma, do you happen to have any pasties handy?"

"Beef pies? Whatdya want beef pies for? Take some ribs home. I'll go pack some for you."

Kam brought Dante's backpack over, balanced it on the shoulder where my son's head wasn't resting. "I didn't tell them that. I swear."

And as a matter of fact, he did smell like Kam, which I noticed when he leaned close to adjust the backpack strap.

"You could have set them straight." I'd meant it to come out searing, but even to me it just sounded sad.

"It's not that easy. The Lees are friends of Suzanne's family. They're practically working for free. I don't feel like I can just—"

"Never mind," I spat. I hoisted Dante's weight up; he lifted his head, glanced blearily around, and then dropped it to my shoulder again. "You know, we wouldn't even *have* to hire lawyers if you weren't letting the wifey-to-be run your life."

"What's the problem? You jealous *you* don't get to do it anymore?"

Ma bustled in and handed me a foil-covered platter. "Enough there for at least two meals," she announced.

Must've been a mother's instincts—my hands were now too full to strangle her son. "I could care less who's in charge of running your life," I said, pushing the screen door open with my back. "I'm just tired of that bitch thinking she can run mine."

Ma's brows shot up defensively. "What *I* do?"

16

LEE, LEE, AND Lee postponed the hearing again. Morna insisted we at least meet with them, this time on her turf.

"This could be significant. We've agreed to get our stories straight before we go in front of a judge," she told me. "If we're successful, it will save everyone involved a great deal of stress."

She and I were going to get together first to go over the terms. I dropped Dante at school and rushed to her farmhouse. I thought I was on time, but Kam and the three Lees were already on her porch sipping lemonade when I arrived. Kam was again in close-toed shoes. It couldn't have been more unnerving if he'd been wearing a clown suit.

"Keeley!" Morna said, greeting me with a hug. "My fault—told you the wrong time. Let's not dawdle and keep these good gentlemen waiting any longer."

We followed her bustling through the house, past the rooms I was familiar with. "Quite a trek, I know. I keep meaning to choose a more convenient spot for the conference room," she said gaily, opening a door at the end of a long hallway.

It was like entering a carnival funhouse. The room was crammed with mirrors. They lined the walls; they balanced on stands, bouncing off one another at odd angles, bending light filtering in through the curtained windows. Pieces of my reflection repeated dozens of times, splitting with Morna's, with Kam's, with hundreds of the Lees, it seemed.

"What is this?" one of the Lees—or, actually, about fifty of the Lees—said.

"Bitchin'," the many Kams said appreciatively, spinning slowly around with their hands in their pockets.

"I'm so glad you like it!" Morna declared. "I've collected mirrors for years. Quite a hobby of mine. This one here"—and she gestured to a standing mirror in a shell-covered frame—"is said to have been owned by King Kamehameha himself. Which is, of course, hogwash, but nice to imagine, don't you think? Please, everyone, make yourselves comfortable."

There was a glass dining table in the center of the room. I could see Kam's shoes propped on the empty chair across from him. I had a sudden flashback of his bare foot between my legs when we'd had breakfast the morning of our wedding, pushing my legs apart, probing upward.

I averted my glance, only to see his face—the one looking away from me at the table—staring straight at me from a mirror.

Shit. I silently cursed Morna, who'd taken a seat next to me. I studied my fingernails. When was I going to learn to cut her loose before she could do further damage?

She leaned forward, her elbows on the table. "Gentlemen, let me get straight to the point. Before we can address the issue of child support, we must come to an agreement on custody of the boy, Dante."

They murmured agreement.

She continued, "Sole custody should be that of my client. She has been his primary caretaker for five years, and I can determine no reason that should not continue."

All right, now she was cookin'.

I peered up in a gesture of support, but all I could see was Kam again, and again, like that fucking shampoo commercial, where he'd told two friends, and they'd told two friends, and so on, and so on.

"To the contrary, Ms. Templeton—," a Lee said.

"Morna."

"Yes, well, *Morna*, we have abundant evidence of Mrs. Kekuhi as an unfit mother. We are prepared to bring before the judge issues of kidnapping, theft, and gross sexual misconduct on her part."

"Evidence," Morna said. "Interesting. Such as . . ."

"Police reports regarding art theft."

"Those charges were dropped," I protested. Morna held my wrist, rubbing my pulse point with her thumb, a silent *shhh*.

Lee, annoyed at my brief outburst, straightened papers in front of him before continuing. "There are also police reports supporting that the child was removed from the residence of Mr. Kekuhi during his regularly scheduled visitation."

"Is that it?" Morna asked.

"Hardly, I'm afraid. There is also the matter of Mrs. Kekuhi's unusual work habits. We have sufficient reason to suspect she is engaging in inappropriate activities. The boy's grandmother is prepared to take the witness stand regarding the hours the boy has been in her care while his mother is off doing Lord knows what."

I tipped my head upward, willing tears not to drop. I would not cry in front of him. The room and its mirrors spun. I reminded myself that the Lees had nothing on me, yet that was small comfort. Truth was, I'd hoped Kam would have set them straight—his silence was pummeling my emotions. That night sitting on my porch . . . the Jeep ride with the geologists . . . telling stories at Ma's house. How was it possible Kam could seem so genuine then, yet be a part of this now?

Morna said nothing as Lee opened an envelope. "We regret that we felt the welfare of the child was in such danger, we were forced to contract the services of a private investigator. We'd hoped our fears would be proved wrong but, unfortunately, quite the opposite was revealed."

He pulled several photos from the envelope and laid them on the table. There I was, opening the door in my robe at the Marquis hotel letting Ian in. Then me again, crawling up to him at the mountains. Another with his hands up my shirt, then reaching down the back of my jeans.

"You had me followed?" My voice came out as a squeak. The tears dropped, landing inches from the photos. "He had me followed!" I squeaked to Morna, then back to Kam. "You had me followed!"

Kam's fingertips grazed the photos. "I swear, I had nothing to do with this," he said quietly.

"Blatant and public fornication. With evidence such as this," a Lee said, "you can understand why we feel confident any judge would support our case that the boy would be at risk to remain with the mother."

While Lee spoke, Kam picked up the photos one by one. "This is bullshit," he said, and tossed them to the floor.

"Ah, a wife's infidelity. We know this must be difficult for you to confront," another Lee said to Kam.

"You have to believe me, Keel. I would never do this."

"I no longer know what you'll do!" I couldn't get my voice octave to lower, but my rage forced the words out, like someone stepping hard on a squeaky toy.

"Not this."

"Mr. Kekuhi," a Lee said, a paternal hand on his shoulder that was promptly shrugged away. "Let us not forget what is important: Your son belongs with you. Your wife is not fit to parent him."

Kam sat back in his chair and kicked off his shoes. He was regarding Lee as one might a cockroach. "Don't treat her like a whore."

"Mr. Kekuhi . . . Kam. Perhaps it's best we leave, and reconvene when you've regained control of your emotions. When you're able to face the peril your son would be in if left in the custody of your wife."

"Damn it, Lee, leave her alone. She hasn't done anything wrong. She's a good mom. A great mom. She loves the hell out of that kid. This bullshit about her being some kind of a slut stops. And it stops now."

Well, halle-*fuckin*-luja, to quote my girlfriend from the L.A. bar; it was about time that boy spoke the truth. I felt awash in gratitude, much in the way prisoners of war must when their torturers remove lit cigarettes from their skin.

One Lee gathered up the photos from the floor. Another said, "We'd best be going."

I'd nearly forgotten Morna was in the room until she spoke. "There is still an issue we must cover. May as well get it over with now." She released the grip on my hand I hadn't even realized had remained. "Kam, sweetie, I'm afraid we need to discuss the night you left Dante unsupervised."

To my surprise, he nodded, his face grave.

"You went to the police. They have on record he was left alone for at least a half hour, by your admission."

"Now, Morna . . . ," a Lee said.

She shushed him. "Surely, you can understand why Keeley is terrified to leave the boy alone with you. Isn't that right, Keeley?"

And, damn it, there he was again, looking pitiful from every angle. "I don't know if I'd say *terrified*," I said.

"All right then, frightened?"

I hemmed and hawed, and finally we settled on *pissed*. I was more like pissed, if a word really had to be assigned to the situation.

"All I can tell you," he said, "Is that it's not how it looks. I'd never leave Dante alone on purpose."

"But he was alone," Morna pressed. "Correct?"

"Yeah. He was alone."

"Then you understand why Keeley must be granted full custody."

And all those Kams looked at me with their sad eyes and their warm skin—those Kams who'd just been generous enough to come to my defense.

I intimated to Morna from the side of my mouth, "I'm willing to share custody, you know."

"What, dear?"

Crud. She wasn't going to make this easy. It was to the real Kam that I said, "We should share him. That's what he'd want. Both of us. You and me. Although I don't know how that's going to happen with you moving to Fiji."

"This is most distressful," a Lee said, grabbing Kam's arm. "We are no further now than before we met. Come, Kam."

Kam slid his feet back into his shoes. "Thanks, Keel. This is such a mess."

"Yes, it is."

"I'm sorry about those photos."

"No big deal." Not wanting to let him off too easily, I added, "Your photographer missed all the good stuff anyway."

"I don't know about that," Kam said, lifting himself from his chair. "The one with that bastard's hand on your ass was pretty nice."

Morna threw back her head and laughed, and the light glinted off her fillings as the sound ricocheted around the room.

MORNA'S HEARTY GUFFAW was one of many scenes that I played in my head that night as I stared at the ceiling above my bed, as I often did when slumber was too stingy to come. I saw no need to get up and accomplish things around the house. Not when I could relive the image of Kam throwing the photos to the floor—then, in rewind, the photos would magically float back up to the table—and, again, Kam, throwing the photos to the floor.

These nights alone and awake in my bed were when I missed Kam most. If he'd been there, I could've nudged him to say, "I can't sleep." It would give me something to do at least. Not that he'd wake up.

Except the one night. It had been so sticky hot it was a miracle either of us had nodded off in the first place and . . .

I pulled a pillow over my head, trying to bar the memory from edging its way into my brain. Too late. There it was . . . Dante—not the boy sleeping in the next room—but a baby then, maybe six months. Sleeping between Kam and me.

I nudged Kam, as usual. That night, the night I clearly wasn't going to let myself forget quite so easily—not spectacular for any reason I could determine other than the stifling lack of air—Kam woke up.

"It's fucking hot," he groused.

"I can't sleep."

In the light filtering through the blinds, I could see him sit up, stretching and feeling around the bed until he found his T-shirt. "Tide ought to be awesome about now." He hoisted himself up from the futon. "Let's go," he said, impatient, as though we'd made some sort of plans and I'd been dallying long enough. Actually, I thought, as I searched the dark floor for whatever clothes I'd peeled off before bed, I had been contemplating rolling over soon.

Kam had heard it was supposed to be a good night to find phosphorous tide, a green glow that would occasionally show up in the surf. The fact that I'd never seen it, Kam said, was plain wrong. Tonight we were going to take care of that.

It was nearly an hour before we dragged the kayak in the water, the boat borrowed from his buddy Roger's rental shack up the coast. Kam wore Dante in a sling over his back.

"Are you sure he's safe?" I asked, fretfully.

"You're going to love this. I know the perfect spot," he said, as if answering.

We pushed off, and Kam's paddle dipped into the black water. I matched my stride to his, staying along the shoreline, hugging a cliff as we headed north. The breeze was pure relief. I practically gulped the salt air.

I don't know how long it was before Kam laid his paddle across his lap, letting the kayak glide along by momentum alone. It was right around the time I was losing all feeling in my arms—so I'd put it at about forty-five minutes, give or take.

"Is this the spot?" I asked. I didn't see anything unusual.

"I'd thought so. I must've been wrong. It's not here."

"I'm sorry."

He pushed his paddle again into the water. "Don't be. It's a beautiful night." I'd expected we'd turn around, but Kam continued on, not stopping until we rounded an edge of the cliff. He pointed up with his paddle, and I realized what it was he wanted me to see: a waterfall—a thin stream, really but, hey, *waterfall*—spilling down the mountain and into the ocean just ahead of us. "This is even better," he said.

Kam started to untie the bundle around him that was Dante.

"What are you doing?" I said, alarmed—did I need to remind Kam that our son was still a bit weak with his backstroke?

Kam pretended not to hear me, and adjusted the sling around until he held Dante on his lap. I nearly tipped us trying to assist, telling him to be careful. "It's okay. I've got him," he said, and he shifted so I could see my son, awake now that he'd been pulled from the warmth of his cocoon, making those baby hiccup noises as he decided how he felt about all this.

Kam gave Dante a jostle. "See that waterfall up there, bud?" he said to him. "That's holy water. A blessing from the gods."

I'd heard of that before, I boasted to myself—probably that Hawaiian mythology class coming in handy again. Water that fell directly from the mountains into the ocean was considered sacred by ancient Hawaiians. On a practical level, they could hold their paddles to the stream, letting fresh drinking water flow down to them, to a bucket or right into their open mouths.

Kam thrust Dante into my hands, then picked up his paddle. "All right, lucky boy," he said.

"Kam . . . What are you doing? . . ."

He shouted something in Hawaiian—*maka laka waka whatever*—and gave a war whoop. He dug in, and on his strength we charged forward.

I squealed, laughing and holding Dante close to me. He started crying.

"It's okay, baby," I said, comfortingly. "Your father's a lunatic, that's all."

The water doused Kam first. He'd held his paddle skyward between his hands, his face up to receive the stream. I hunched over, instinctively protecting Dante as we passed through. The trickle of water missed him, but slapped me cold on the shoulder.

Kam brought the kayak to an easy stop past the fall, dipping his paddle to resist the forward motion. "Come on, hon," he said to me, shaking his head. "We've got to do this right." He crawled around on the kayak until he was kneeling, facing me.

Hands in the ocean, he was backing us up toward the falling water in the manner he'd paddle his surfboard out to sea.

"Kaaaaaaam . . . ," I giggled, wearing the same maniacal grin I get on roller coasters. Not knowing when the boat would reach the water. Not daring to look behind me.

A mischievous smile on his face, Kam said, "You have to do it."

"I can't," I whined. "He's so tiny . . . it's so cold . . ."

"You have to . . . it's a blessing . . . it's lucky . . ."

Muttering *sorrybabysorrybaby* through teeth clenched in anticipation, I gripped Dante in my hands and held him high. Kam inched us on. The water hit me in the back first, an icy wet finger climbing my spine.

Then we all met the water together. I shrieked a laugh, Dante wailed, and Kam gently spun our boat until we were so thoroughly soaked that— though we never did get around to finding any glowing tide—we had to have been about as blessed on that night as three people could hope to be.

TODD, JOHN, AND Dawn moved camp to my house. The more data we collected, the more it seemed stupid to let them stay at risk. Not that we expected Kohala to blow anytime soon. But it was one thing to be tromping around on a volcano all day with your wits about you. It was something else altogether to be woken in the night by lava in your sleeping bag.

They'd talked about going back to the hotel, but AGS—in a move smacking of what my company might do—gave them grief over whether the expense was necessary. When John called Hoffman in Washington, he was told, "Lava flow on Hawaiian volcanoes is typically slow. Don't you think you could outrun it?"

"Can you believe that? Outrun it?" John later griped. "I hope they'd be willing at least to buy me a pair of Nikes."

I worried Dante might be upset by the intrusion to his routine, maybe regress to biting. It was going to be close quarters. Todd and John would bunk with St. Ignatius in Dante's room, he was moving to mine, and Dawn was on the couch. My worries were over the first night, when I had to peel Dante from John, who'd been giving him rides around the house on his foot. I put my boy to bed as he begged me, "Please, Mom, can we keep them?"

Then we lingered in the living room, going over the next day's plans. I was going to have to stop in the office before doing anything else. Apparently, I'd been written up again. This time the offense was refusing to stay properly chained to my cubicle.

"I will not tolerate renegade employees," Wagner said on the voice mail that I played on my speakerphone while we gathered around and made fun of him.

"What exactly happens when you're written up?" John asked.

I stared at him, flummoxed. "What happens?"

"Yes. Are you put on probation? Fired?"

Truth was, I had no idea. I'd never even heard of writing someone up until Wagner started in on me. It sounded so ominous. *Written up*. But as far as what actually happened as a result? "I don't know if anything happens."

"Then what are you worried about?"

A fine question, I thought. Huh.

I let the machine pick up a call from Ian and then grew panicked halfway through. What if he said something racy while everyone was listening? He didn't—just asked if I'd consider posing for that portrait he'd asked about so long ago.

The shocker of the evening, however, was the next call: Pete Peterson, the blind date who'd left me to rot in jail.

"Had a great time at the art auction," he said, making me wonder if we'd been on the same date. "Give me a call soon. I'm up late. You can call me tonight, or tomorrow, love to hear from you. Soon, I hope."

"Man-o-live," Dawn said. She shooed us off the couch so she could unroll her sleeping bag. "Wish I had whatever it is you've got."

WHAT I HAD, apparently, was information, which I learned when picking up voice mails the next day at work. Right after Regatta's message ("Oh my gosh, Keel, Boston is *awful*—you are *not* going to believe how cold snow is") was another from Pete.

After some drivel about how much fun he'd had on our date—as though we'd gone out yesterday and not months ago—he got to the point. He'd heard inklings about possible volcanic activity on Kohala. Could I confirm or deny? You know, give him an exclusive. For old times' sake. And, hey, let's get together soon. There's a show opening . . . Hawaiian dancing . . . *topless* . . . eh?

I had debated whether it was time to let the public know about what had been found. I'd hoped to be farther in the research before making any announcements, but it looked as if Pete was making the decision for me. There was no way I was letting him break this story.

I nearly skipped on the way to Wagner's office. "I need your help," I said.

"You . . . need . . . me?" He had a what's-the-catch look.

"I have a public relations idea. I'd like to write a press release."

That delighted him so much, his usual supportive air-punch accidentally socked me in the arm. "Good for you, Kekuhi. I knew you'd come around."

The story exploded on the island the next day. Every television and radio station and newspaper made it their headline story—alas, except the *Bee*, which was inadvertently left off the press release's distribution list.

Pete's furious phone message was the first media call I returned. I couldn't resist the chance to say, "Oh, did we miss you? You'll have to forgive me. My memory hasn't been the same since the trauma of my incarceration."

By that night, it had hit the wires and was getting coverage nationally.

Of course, nobody got it right. We'd said that there was a possibility of a future eruption, and all the calls asked about evacuations, death tolls, and the like.

I started answering the phone with, "No, we don't believe it poses an immediate threat," rather than hello.

My mom called to say she read about it in the *Detroit Free Press.* "Honey, my advice for you is to be careful."

I played the message six times. *Duh,* I said to myself, of course I'll be careful. What an inane thing to say. Then I played it again. "Honey, my advice for you . . ."

It didn't make the Bolivian papers, or at any rate the news in whatever country my sister resided in these days. She e-mailed me, but all she said was, "What on earth have you done to Mom?"

AFTER KAM'S AND my meeting with the lawyers, I agreed he could take Dante Wednesday nights. Quite a gesture, I thought, yet he only gave me a "Yeah, okay." I didn't understand his lukewarm response until, when pressed, he admitted he wasn't eager to give me a free night to go off with that dude.

"That's quite a double standard," I said.

"Yeah—you didn't have to look at pictures. Trust me, it sucks."

I stifled the urge to one-up him—to remind him that photos were nothing compared to having the real thing slapped in your face. I preferred to let his jealousy linger. And since he was so kind as to mention it, yes, it would be most delightful to see that dude.

Ian talked me into using my newly found spare time to pose for that portrait he wanted to paint of me. I wasn't sure what posing entailed, but I hoped sex. After our makeout session on the mountain, I was more than ready. I imagined myself luxuriating on a velvet couch, reclining with nothing but a scarf draped seductively over me. Ian would try to be professional, but against his will, his passion would seethe as he stared at my nearly naked curves. He'd take me in with every stroke of his brush until he couldn't contain himself any longer. It would be so very *Titanic.*

His studio was the mother-in-law quarters behind his house. Paintings were propped against every surface—all landscapes, I noticed as he gave me a quick tour, and not half bad. He led me to an airy room where he'd set up a canvas facing a recliner chair. "Sit however you like," he said.

"I'm not sure what you want me to wear," I said, silently adding, or *not*.

He arranged tubes of paint on a table. "Oh, what you have on is fine."

"This?" I was in the gray jumper-dress I'd worn to work.

"Sure. I only expect to lay down basic strokes today."

I sat, adjusting the chair into recline mode, lamenting how I'd waxed for nothing. Ian started right in at painting.

My attention span held for roughly two minutes. He wasn't talking to me. There was no TV. And he was playing Enya on the stereo. There's only so much a girl is willing to do for the sake of art.

"Are you finished yet?"

He peeked around the canvas, annoyed I'd disrupted his concentration. "You do realize this isn't a photograph."

I sat for three hours, managing to squeeze in a nap, so the evening wasn't entirely a waste. When I woke up, Ian was rinsing brushes at the kitchenette. I headed over to grab the mules I'd flipped off earlier. "I need to get going."

"All right. You did a great job," he said, giving me a chaste kiss on the cheek. Then a peck on the lips. A brush of his lips against my forehead.

"I believe I have quite a future as a model," I remarked.

"I'm afraid I'll have to disagree," he said, nuzzling my neck. "Models . . . they have a fashion sense. And this dress of yours—you remember I promised to be truthful—it's hideous. I'm afraid it has to go." In one motion, he pulled it up and over my head. Tossed it to the floor, leaving me standing there in my bra and underwear.

I took a step back. "How dare you . . . ," I said, indignant. "How *dare* you insult my dress when you are wearing a shirt this ugly." I undid his buttons one by one and then yanked it off his shoulders. "And don't try to fool me with that designer label. It's clearly a knockoff."

It turned out, my bra was an atrocity. His slacks—what? a cotton/poly blend?—unacceptable. As far as my panties, he murmured, lifting me onto the kitchenette counter and tugging them downward, they were patently misleading. Today wasn't Friday. Whom exactly did I think I was deceiving?

At least, I believe that's what he said, because he was kissing along my belly, and excuse me if my mind wandered. Things turned decidedly more friendly between Ian and me from there, anyway—that is, once I used my feet to push down those insufferable boxers of his.

I wound up inventing excuses the following week so I could squeeze in a couple of hours here or there to stop by Ian's.

"I see. *Posing for a portrait.* Is that what you kids are calling it these days?" John said when I'd asked him to cover for me while I sneaked out of work early.

Of course, I'd refused to sit for Ian again until he met my list of demands. Chee-tos. Diet Coke. Soundtrack from *Footloose* playing on the CD.

"You're really good," I told him one day, trying to divert him from his work. I'd now moved on to being draped in the silky scarf I'd first imagined, tied toga-style. Ian painted in bold color, broad strokes. The portrait that was taking shape had a life and energy I'd never seen, as if in paint he'd managed to capture the feeling of a strong wind hitting me, pushing and lifting my very being up. "You ever think of doing this full time?"

"Often," he said.

"Why don't you?"

"The usual. Fear, I suppose, that I couldn't keep up the work."

I looked at the dozens of paintings around me. "You seem to have plenty of inspiration."

"Sure, in the presence of my muse"—and he paused long enough for me to ponder the word *muse*—"anything seems possible."

"So you have a few blank days, a few blank years," I said flippantly. "Don't take this the wrong way, but I get the impression that even if your income stopped entirely, you'd hardly be clipping coupons tomorrow. You must pull down some serious bucks as an artist's rep. Your studio alone is bigger than my entire house." His hand kept sweeping across the canvas, but we seemed to be back to silence again. I pressed—"What? Was that tacky? You can't possibly imagine I'm the gold-digging type, if that's why you went quiet on me."

"Far from it. It's simply"—and he wiped his forehead with the side of his hand—"actually, the repping business pays quite poorly. It's merely my way to stay close to the art world without . . . well, actually being an artist."

"You lost me. You don't want to be an artist?"

"I don't want to be poor."

"Still confused . . ."

He exhaled a breath. "My parents would prefer that I find work other than that of an artist."

"But what does that have to do with—?"

"Your son, does he get an allowance?"

"Yes. A dollar a week. He has to take out the garbage and brush his teeth."

"I pull in a bit more than that, and I don't have to do either of those things if I don't want. But there are other strings attached. I know I must seem much too old for this sort of nonsense."

"So you're basically a spoiled playboy, is that right?" I teased.

He frowned. "Now you understand why I rarely talk when I paint."

"Still . . . you are amazingly talented. I mean it. You don't need their money. You could make it on your own."

He dipped his brush into the palette and swirled the colors absently. "Perhaps, but I have this notion that my inspiration may be fleeting. It seems as if at any time, you could float away. Like a bubble. Taking it all with you."

And although I was wearing the toga, I felt exposed—as though he might be cheeky enough to put on canvas for the world to see aspects of me that I didn't even want to confront.

17

THERE WAS A FOR SALE sign in front of Kam's house. I saw it when I went to pick up Dante Sunday afternoon. I stared at it with as much amazement as if it had sprung up overnight from the lawn. He'd never said anything about selling.

The front door was open. I stepped into the house, shouting a hello.

"Welcome!" A big-eared man, mid-fifties, pumped my arm in greeting. "I was just about to close up. We've already pulled in a couple offers on this beauty, but I'm glad to show you around. Cookie?"

"No tha—Those wouldn't happen to be double-stuff, would they?"

So I took one and then let him lead me into the kitchen. I felt the need to play along, pretending to be a buyer, having accepted his offer of nourishment. Plus my last visit, I'd stormed out with Dante before I got to see all the rooms.

"Real veneer!" he said, knocking on a cabinet. One of Dante's drawings hung on the refrigerator. "Nice, huh? A perfect family home. Let me know if I can answer any questions for you."

I thought, *Sure, you can answer a few questions.* Like why were they selling when Kam had implied he wasn't moving to Fiji anytime soon? And how could he pick up and leave like that? Didn't he think I had some say in all this?

His beeper went off. He checked it and then excused himself to go make a call, encouraging me to take a look at the backyard. Apparently the patio featured *genuine cement*!

I was reading the wall calendar (big news: Suzanne has a Tupperware party next week) when I heard the front door slam, then voices. It was them. I had one of those *Three's Company* moments where I thought, *Arrrgh! They'll catch me!* and frantically scanned the room for a cupboard to hide in until such time as I could crawl on hands and knees unseen past Mr. Roper.

Then I remembered they were having an open house. There was nothing wrong with my being here. So why did my legs feel cemented?

"I didn't say you had to come home." That was Kam.

"And what was I supposed to do?" Suzanne. "Walk the ten miles here?"

"Why not fly your broom?"

"Don't start."

"It's a joke, Suzanne. You know, a joke? Some people actually know how to laugh."

"Keep it down, will you? That Realtor guy is probably here."

A fight! I'd hit pay dirt. Although now I *was* looking for a cupboard big enough to hide me.

There was mumbling, general setting things down, picking things up noises. More mumbling, then Kam said, "I went to your picnic. What do you want?"

Suzanne's voice, low but furious and, alas, unintelligible.

Then Kam again, "Jesus . . . when did you become such a fucking wife?" The sound of feet stomping up the stairs. Kam's voice again, gentle now. "Hey, pal, didn't see you come in. You want a cookie?"

He'd be mortified to know I'd overheard. I could sneak out the sliding back door, I thought, and circle around the house to the front. *Or . . .*

I walked into the living room. "Hey, guys."

"Keel . . . where—?"

"Your Realtor let me in. I was checking out the amenities in the kitchen. You know," I said, and realized it was important to me that what I say not come out like nagging. "I was interested to find the house for sale." There. Simple. Friendly. Very unwife-like, if I did say so myself.

"Yeah, that . . ." He started to explain how since Suzanne's parents owned the house, they needed to sell it if moving were even an option.

It was hard for me to get everything he was saying, because Dante was hanging off him, yanking on his arms, saying "Daaaaad, let's go! You promised!"

Kam picked him up, hung him upside down by his feet. I patted myself on the back that I could notice his biceps in the detached manner with which I was now doing—an appreciation for the way they flexed with, really, hardly any desire at all to touch them.

"Do you mind," Kam asked, guiding Dante as he walked on his hands, "If I keep him a couple of hours longer? I did make him a promise that I'd take him to the batting cages if he went the week without biting. We were so long at this picnic—"

"I'm sorry . . . I feel like I hardly get to see him as it is." I bent down to Dante's head level. "No biting? Good for you! Mommy will take you to the batting cages."

"I want Dad. He's going to teach me how to hit."

Not this again, I thought. "I'm a better hitter than your dad. I was a professional baseball player," I said, "Back when he was a ballerina."

"I want Dad."

"Your mom's right," Kam said. "She played for the Tigers. Only she had to quit because of her chewing tobacco problem."

"Dad, you promised. I didn't bite anybody."

Kam released Dante's legs, let him tumble to the ground. "If you're going to take him, would you mind if I came along?"

We walked out with the Realtor. Kam shouted up the stairs that he was going to hit a few balls with Dante.

"Gee, you forgot to mention me," I teased.

"No *way* is the leash long enough for that."

Let it be said, if I felt anything at all during the time or two that Kam helped adjust my stance at bat, it was just the comfort of the familiar— the way my body fit so neatly into his behind me. "Choke up, girl . . . like this."

What I wasn't ready for was the warmth that washed over me watching him as he knelt behind Dante, adjusting his tiny hands on the bat, the two of them together swinging at the ball.

Could I have that? I dared to wonder, the hard metal fence bending against my weight as I leaned against it. *Is that perhaps for me? Finally?*

I'D KNOWN ABOUT Suzanne for months before I realized she and Kam were having an affair. They worked for the same tour company. At times they went to lunch or for drinks after work. At times she might say something amusing that bore repeating to me. I lacked a suspicious enough nature to think much of it.

The day he helped her move was my first sense of trouble.

"You're helping this girl move?"

"It'll only take a couple hours."

"Doesn't she have anybody else who can help her?"

"I'll be back by five . . . promise."

In retrospect, it seems obvious. At the time, however, I would have needed a clue more in line with finding panties in the glove box or florist charges on the Visa. I was that naive.

After discovering the miserable truth, I'd grilled Regatta, "Had he been saying he was spending more nights at Roger's? Or claiming to surf more often?" Neither of us could remember—but Regatta was loyal enough to say, Yes, that big cheat, come to think of it he was! with the same conviction that a day earlier she'd have remarked that Kam sure was a cutie.

There was, of course, the *aha* moment. We'd been on our way home from brunch at Ma's. He made me pull over at a yard sale.

I'd assumed he'd spotted fishing poles or surfboards, but he beelined it to a desk. I watched him squat down, opening and shutting the drawers. Dante jumped on a big-wheel and started test-driving it on the sidewalk.

"What are you doing? We don't have room for a desk."

"It's not for us. Suzanne needs one."

"Suzanne?"

The lady running the garage sale hovered. "Twenty dollars . . . or best offer."

He knocked on it. "She asked me to keep on the lookout in case I saw one. This is solid wood."

The lady slid a desk chair between us. "I'll throw this in for a couple bucks more."

"You're shopping for Suzanne," I said in disbelief.

"I'm just helping out a friend. Mellow out."

"Oh, my God! You're sleeping with her!"

"Keel . . . not here . . ."

"He's sleeping with her!" I clutched the garage sale lady's shoulder for support.

She swallowed nervously. "How 'bout I go down to ten on the desk?"

In the days that followed, I'd assumed that the fact Kam came clean as soon as we got home was a sign that I wasn't entirely his fool, that my bruised pride, if not my marriage, might be salvageable. At least he thought enough of me not to insult me with more lies.

What I didn't realize until weeks later was that his honesty was merely because he had no further need for deception. He'd already made up his mind to leave.

OTHER THAN THE fact somebody kept picking the marshmallows out of the Lucky Charms, I rather enjoyed having a houseful of geologists. I could get Dante from after-school care at a reasonable hour. He'd eat dinner while I chewed on my fingernails—there being quite a lot on my mind—as I'm sure was happening at dinner tables throughout America.

Then he'd play while we grown-ups got work done, although John was incapable of saying no to a child, I'd discovered. There I'd be, my head buried in a chart saying, "What do you think of this shift in pH levels here?" only to find him on the floor with Dante destroying LEGO villages with a plastic dinosaur.

I told Regatta about how helpful John was when she called from Boston to inform me about coats and boots, which she'd discovered as a defense against the cold. ("You'd think they'd tell you this sort of thing when you get off the plane," she griped.)

Still, she sounded pleased to hear about Dante doing so well with my new roommates. "He needs a male influence." Then, after avoiding several of my attempts to pry about the status of her wedding, asked, "How is Ian with Dante?"

"They haven't met."

"After all this time?"

"It seems too early," I said, trying to keep the defensive edge from my voice.

"I don't get it. You let some guy you work with hang out with your son, but won't introduce him to your boyfriend. What if you two get married? Will you at least let them say hello before Ian becomes his father?"

"He has a father," I snapped.

"Ooookay," Regatta said. "Change of subject. I bought you a souvenir today. It's called a scraper. You'll never guess what it's designed to scrape. *Snow!* Can you believe it?"

Later that week, not based on anything Regatta might have said, I asked Ian to pick me up at the house before we went out to dinner that night.

You had to feel for the guy. First, he had to face John and Todd, who lectured him in mock sternness to keep his hands to himself. Ah, the big brothers I'm glad I never had. Then, Dante was apparently playing hard to get.

"Honey, say hi to Ian."

"Hi." He didn't look up from *Rugrats*. He was in that TV trance. I went to turn it off, but he screamed, "Mom! I haven't seen this one!"

"I hear you have an iguana," Ian tried.

No answer.

"Dante, why don't you take Ian to see St. Ignatius?"

He merely pointed the way to his bedroom door.

"I'm sorry," I said to Ian, "I'm turning the TV off. It's not okay for him to be so rude to—"

Ian stopped me, "It's fine. No need to push things."

I was still grimacing at Dante.

"He'll come around when he's ready," Ian said, reaching to push the furrows from my brow. "He and I have plenty of time to get to know each other."

Dinner itself was rewarding in the sense that we got to wear bibs and hammer crab shells. It wasn't until we were leaving that Ian bumped into a business associate—an unremarkable incident, except that he introduced me as his girlfriend. I had nothing to add to their brief conversation. I just gave him a serene, girlfriendlike smile, one that implied I knew all Ian's little secrets, our being so intimate. My being his girlfriend. That making him, naturally, my boyfriend.

Later in the car as Ian dropped me at home, he said, "I hope that was all right when I called you my girlfriend." He cut off the engine but didn't climb out of the car. "I didn't know how else to refer to you."

"There's no good word," I agreed. "Woman-friend? *Lover?* You see the problem."

"I'm glad, then, that it didn't bother you."

"No problem." Truth was, the G-word had scared the life out of me, but I couldn't have said why. Perhaps I feared (irrationally, I knew) that the man might quiz me on Ian's likes and dislikes. I couldn't have answered a thing—not even "fave color," and that's the first one they always ask.

"Of course," he began, and he shifted in his seat so he was leaning casually against the armrest. "Given that, it is rather strange that we've never slept together."

"What?" and I gave him a playful nudge. "Am I that bad a lay—you don't even remember?"

"I mean actually *slept*. In all this time, you've never been able to spend the night."

I felt as if he'd shouted it at me, thumping me in the chest with his finger.

"It's not a good time now. You know that. Dante's right inside, and—"

"I know. It's simply that . . ." And he straightened a wrinkle on his otherwise perfectly pressed pants. "I'd like to feel you next to me in bed in the night, that's all. Kiss you while you sleep. Wake up with you still there in the morning. Not have to say good-bye so fast."

"Yeah, well, sure. Some night when I don't have Dante. Of course, you know, I usually have Dante. And with these hours I've been working and all . . ."

"I don't even know if you snore."

"All the time. Loudly. Like a grizzly bear."

He laughed. "I swear, you are so *odd*. Not like anyone else I've met. You're so . . . Oh, what's the word I'm looking for here? I'd have to say . . . so"—he resmoothed the wrinkle that he'd already banished from his pants—"lovable. Yes, that's the word for you. *Lovable*."

"Is it me or is this car stifling hot?" I said by way of response. "I can hardly breathe." I grabbed for the door handle, suddenly desperate to get away. Ian was reaching over, wiggling his fingers maniacally at me, yanking at me, pulling at my clothes, my insides, grabbing away big, nasty fistfuls of me while I gasped, helpless—only he wasn't, of course. He was nowhere near. He remained on his side of the car, leaning easily where he'd been.

"It's stuffy? Here," he said, switching the key on, "I'll put the top—"

I swung my door open before he could finish. "It's hopeless. There is just no air anywhere at *all*."

He hurried around to help me out of the car, but I'd stepped out before he reached my side.

"Thanks for dinner," I mumbled hastily, remembering my manners before escaping inside.

THANKSGIVING. I WAS at Ma Kekuhi's house for an hour before realizing Suzanne was there, too. She'd been in the kitchen helping Ma cook. It is therefore understandable why I wouldn't have encountered her. I was on horseshoe-tossing duty in the backyard, filling in on Jarts when needed.

It was Kam's turn to have Dante for the holiday. He'd invited me to join them at his mother's, promising Suzanne wouldn't be there. He even said I could bring my roomies, who'd only recently learned that my tour guide friend was Dante's dad.

I'd still hesitated. Dinner at Ma's? Wasn't this the woman who was willing to testify that I was a stripper?

"The Lees were bluffing," he assured me. "She doesn't even know what a stripper is. C'mon, Tai hasn't seen you in forever. And you know the Dantster would love to have you there."

I'd noticed Suzanne bending over the oven to baste the turkey on my way to the bathroom. That's how I learned she was there. I passed Kam in the hallway, which gave me a chance to mumble that he was a filthy liar.

"I swear, she was supposed to go see her family," he said, not bothering to disguise his bemusement. "She changed her mind last minute—decided to go next week instead."

"Great. Another day of being glared at."

"Don't sweat it. She'll spend all day in the kitchen anyway." He reached down to retie the string on my board shorts, which had come loose. He did this as nonchalantly as he might tie Dante's shoe. "There you go. A sailor knot. That baby won't come untied for days."

"Kam, think about it. I'm on my way to the bathroom."

He leaned back against the wall, hands in his pockets. "I'd be glad to undo any clothing if you need help."

"Ha ha," I believe was my razor-sharp retort.

I did manage to avoid Suzanne most of the afternoon, although it occurred to me that it may have been the other way around. Whatever. The upshot was that I got to play the quarter-bounce with the cousins from Naalehu that I'd missed on my wedding day.

There was also much basking in the glow of people telling me how great it was that I could be here for Dante's sake. I felt very grown-up, thank you.

Around five, Suzanne walked out with a dish of potatoes just as Kam and I clinked beer bottles.

"Kam, honey, could you help carry the food?"

At least she didn't have the nerve to make up Dante's plate. I busied myself spoon-feeding my son, which I had to do to get him to eat at parties.

Dinner went without incident, except for Ma saying, "You baby that boy! Don't baby him so much!" in the most compelling example of the pot calling the kettle black in modern history.

I was ready to get going as soon as the plates were tossed in the trash, but Dawn asked if I wouldn't mind staying a bit longer. Apparently she and Tai had hit it off. She was about to go take a look at the motorcycle he was rebuilding.

"I see—*rebuilding the motorcycle.* Is that what you kids are calling it these days?" I said. She giggled and said that I ought to leave at least one man for the single girls in the crowd.

The rest of us went back to the task of sitting and drinking. It wasn't as much fun because now Suzanne was superglued to Kam's side, although no one seemed keyed in to the lack of fun but me. They were laughing and telling stories because, well, that's what Hawaiians do, if that hasn't been made obvious by now.

After a while, Suzanne crooked Kam's arm in hers. "Kam, are we going to the Luos' tomorrow?"

"Huh?"

"The Luos'. I think we're supposed to go there for dinner."

He looked irritated. "I don't know. Can we talk about it later?"

"Keeley, you remember—oh, wait, you didn't know them, did you? That's right. They're friends of Kam's and mine. From our Hawaiian culture classes. Nice couple. You'd love them."

Even in the dusky light, I could see the look of hope flicker across the faces of all the men but Kam. Yeah, *chick fight.*

I wasn't playing. I shrugged as to indicate, that's correct, never met them . . . so?

"You probably know how much Kam loves singing the old songs of the islands—," she started. Then I saw him tap her for attention and clearly mouth *shut up.*

She blinked repeatedly.

He looked at me apologetically. Okay, now I was ready to play. She'd sunk low enough and I—with the instincts of a vulture—sensed weakness in the opponent.

"They sound like lovely people," I said. "Say—Kam," and I gave him the most devilish look of which I was capable, "How is our old friend, Bill?"

"Bill . . . ," he said, giving me a curious look.

"Yes, you remember Bill. From the wedding?"

"I don't remember a Bill," said one of the cousins.

"You were trashed," said another.

"I'm trashed now, too, so you'd think I'd remember."

Suzanne sat upright. I could tell her discomfort stemmed from hearing about the wedding. She had no clue who we were talking about—other than she didn't know who we were talking about, and that was annoying enough. She remained silenced by the shut up, however, which intrigued me. I'd have kicked his ass if he'd said that to me.

"Funny you should mention Bill," Kam said. "He misses you."

"Really."

"Thinks about you all the time. He told me to tell you that."

"Well, tell you what—you give Bill a big kiss hello from me next time you run into him. Let him know I'd love to see him sometime soon."

Kam gave a quick nervous glance toward Suzanne. "*Shit*, girl," he said, his eyes twinkling in my direction, "Don't do that to me."

IT WASN'T AS though I would be committing adultery, I told myself. We were still married. If anything, I'd be fulfilling my wifely duty.

I told the whole story to Regatta, only she wasn't as impressed by my cleverness as I'd been. "He said his penis missed you? That is *sick*."

"You're taking it out of context. I'm saying that I think it might be over between Kam and Suzanne. They do nothing but argue."

"So it's over. You're going to take him back? Why on earth would you do that?"

I found myself wishing that Ian were there to unfurrow my brow. Then again, this was a conversation that he might not much enjoy. That brought a twinge of guilt, but I pushed it away. He and I had never talked about being exclusive. I was beginning to see the road I had been seeking winding open before me. This was my moment, my carpe diem and—decent a man as Ian was—frankly, he was blocking the way.

"You haven't seen Kam with Dante," I told Regatta, wondering why I was bothering to try and sway her. "He's a whole new man."

"Hon, people don't change."

My talk with my mom was no more satisfying. She'd asked me to let her in, but it was as if she'd refused to wipe her feet before entering.

"That Ian sounds like such a nice boy. Don't do anything to blow it. Marry him. Have babies."

"Mom, I think I'm pretty much done in the baby department."

"What! No granddaughter?"

I e-mailed Sandra. "It's all my fault. I wanted a mom. I've created a monster."

John was on the couch reading Dante's *Ranger Rick* the night Ian called to ask if I could sit again. He was almost done with the portrait—he could probably finish it without me, but . . . it had been so long since we'd seen each other. Couldn't I fit him in?

I lied that I was going to be out of town all week doing research. "I'll call you when I get back," I said, and then hung up, concentrating fiercely on picking a loose string from my shirt.

John set down the magazine. He stroked his beard. "Keeley, are you considering what you're doing here?"

That did it.

I was going to dig out the phone book and find the nearest Baptist church. I was going to march in during the middle of service and announce to the congregation, "I am contemplating getting back with my husband—the father of my child. I'm thinking that, within the sanctity of these bonds of holy matrimony, the two of us may finally have a chance to finish what it is we started. Then, while we're at it, we'll have us some sex," and if that didn't get a hallelujah, I'd add, "In the missionary position."

My so-called friends were refusing to be supportive. Regatta had called me back, saying, "Ted and I are coming home next week. Don't do anything until I get there!" as though I were standing on a ledge threatening to leap.

If anything, I was knocking on the window and asking to be let back in. Was that so terrible? It wasn't even my old life back I sought. It was the new and improved version that I was realizing I could have—the one I couldn't entirely grasp because the image of two parents and a child together would always get fuzzy in my mind, like the photo that comes in the frame when you buy it. As far as I was concerned, I'd been sitting at the slot machine, pumping in quarters—and there was no way I was going to get up now and leave my big investment for someone else to come along with one crappy coin and cash in on my jackpot. That was my take on the situation.

Kam called Wednesday night to let me know he'd picked up Dante from school without incident. I was at the dining table, going over some charts with my roommates.

"Suzanne's out of town. It's just us guys here, doing manly things," Kam made a point of saying.

"Sorry I'm missing out."

"You should come over. Hang out."

I took a breath, and then said, "Maybe I will . . . come over. You know, to say good night to Dante, tuck him in."

After I hung up and resumed my work, John said, "*Tucking him in.* Is that what you kids are calling it—?"

"Shut up, John," I said without a trace of humor. "This is not your business."

I WENT OVER at eight o'clock, Dante's bedtime. The FOR SALE sign had been replaced with one marked SOLD.

There was nothing resembling tucking in happening. They were in the back—on the *genuine cement patio*—working on Dante's bike.

"Isn't it past your bedtime?" I asked Dante.

Kam looked up. "That late already? Okay bud, off to bed."

I offered to get Dante dressed, brushed, and tucked in while Kam cleaned up the bike parts. Then I came back downstairs and sat on the couch. Kam eventually showed up, wiping his hands on a towel. "That gear oil gets everywhere," he said, and sat carefully next to me. "Glad you could come over."

"Yeah, me, too."

"It's such a nice night. Not too hot."

"Yeah, I hate it when it gets too hot."

"Me, too. God, I hate that."

"Yeah."

The ease that we'd felt around each other was gone. There was no doubt why I'd come over, yet neither of us seemed willing to make the first move. Maybe this was a mistake. Maybe I—

Kam interrupted my thoughts. "How about we watch some TV."

It seemed to happen in slow motion, Kam going for the remote, a cowboy reaching for his gun in a draw. His fingers splayed, he made that guy grunting noise *aoof* as he stretched far forward to grasp it. This was the moment. If the TV went on, it was over—it being whatever might have been.

"How about we get shitfaced and fuck," I said.

He used the momentum he'd gathered to stand. Then he walked into the other room. Not a word otherwise, although the remote sat untouched on the coffee table.

Was I supposed to be following? Was he coming back? I mean, I realized I hadn't exactly spoken tender words of romance, but still, I'd expected a bit more enthusiasm.

Kam returned, holding a bottle of whiskey and shot glasses. He set them on the coffee table and poured two shots. We clinked shot glasses and then drank them down. Before I realized it, his mouth was on mine, tongue in my throat. I burst out a laugh, shoving him away.

"What's so funny?"

"Sorry . . . nothing," I shifted, swallowing a giggle. "Never mind, I'm ready. Go ahead."

He kissed me again, but he came in so fast—like he was dive-bombing at my face—that another laugh sort of leaked out.

"Now what?" He sat back, flustered.

"Sorry, sorry . . ." I held up a hand to indicate I needed a moment to compose myself. "Nervous, I guess." I stretched my arms behind me as if preparing to go for a jog. "Whew, all righty, I got it all out. Go ahead."

"You're ready?"

"Yes."

"You sure now?"

This time when he kissed me, I willed myself not to laugh. I have to do the same thing when I get a foot massage. Kam wound up pulling away, saying what my masseuse always does. "Forget it. This isn't working."

"Really, I don't know what's wrong with me."

He poured another two shots, then got up to go sit alone in an armchair. "At least we can do the getting shitfaced part," he said, good-naturedly.

So this was it, I thought—I was going out with a giggle rather than a whimper or, more accurately, a bang. "Hold on," I said.

I walked over, pulled his T-shirt off over his head then went back to the couch, my feet up on the coffee table. "Much better." If I squinted, that choker he was wearing almost looked like puka shells.

"So I get to do the same to you, right?"

"Nope."

I didn't say anything else. I found myself feeling surprised that he hadn't changed at all, as though I'd expected in the few months that had passed he'd have grown a paunch, or sprouted hairs in nasty places. But his abs were hard and smooth, and the only hair I saw was that trail that led from his navel down. . . .

"Okay, now I'm ready," I said. I went over and straddled his lap. He had my shirt off before I could even lean in to him, run my lips along his ear, trace my fingers down his chest.

And—damn it—we had rollicking, happy, really, *really* good sex. My life would have been much less complicated it we hadn't. If I'd been too nervous or too drunk. If when he pulled me down on him, I hadn't been staring sober into his eyes . . . but I was.

Of course, then we got shitfaced. An excess of liquor resulted in further sex of a far sloppier nature than the first go-round, but it didn't matter. The damage, or whatever one might choose to call it, had already been done.

I WOKE THE next morning to a beeping sound.

"What the fuck is that noise?" Kam groaned—the Kam who was tangled with me naked on the couch. My head felt as if there were another larger head inside of it trying to bust free.

"Beeper," I managed to say, reaching a hand down to fish on the floor for my purse. I grabbed it out—it was my work calling. I shut it off, dropped it to the floor.

That was when I noticed the sound of the television. I pushed the mess of hair from my eyes and scanned the room.

Dante sat on the chair, eating Smacks from a cereal box and watching cartoons. He was in the TV trance, not paying any attention to us—as though he got up every morning to the sight of his almost-divorced mother and father lying together in the buff.

"Shit," I whispered, grabbing up our clothes. "Dante's right here."

I got an elbow in my eye and a knee in my back—I'll assume Kam's—while we attempted to get dressed lying down so Dante wouldn't notice.

My legs were sliding into my shorts when he finally looked our way. I froze.

"Morning," I said.

"Hi."

"Did you have a good sleep?"

"Yeah." Then he stuffed another handful of cereal in his mouth and turned back to the TV.

"Coffee," Kam said, feeling his way toward the kitchen as if blinded by hangover, "I need coffee."

It had been John who'd beeped me. When I called him, he apologized for disrupting my . . . well, for bothering me. If it hadn't been a real emergency . . .

"What's up?" I said.

"The three of us went up to collect some early-morning readings. Keel, they shot through the roof overnight."

"No kidding . . ."

"There's a meeting in a half hour with the mayor. We may be talking evacuation. Of course, you're lead on this."

"I'll be right there."

I gave Dante a head scritch, then went to find Kam in the kitchen. He was fumbling through cupboards, mumbling about where she keeps the fucking coffee.

"Work emergency," I said. "I have to run."

"Yeah, okay," he said. He walked over to me in halting steps, as if his engine stalled several times; then we gave each other a peck on the lips. "I'll take Dante to school. No problem."

"Yeah, sure . . . thanks."

"Well, I'll see you later, then."

"Yeah," he said, heading back to the task of digging for caffeine. "See ya."

18

"DON'T YOU THINK evacuation is going overboard?" The mayor raised and lowered himself on the balls of his feet. I hadn't voted for him—too triangular-shaped. He reminded me of a Weeble, although, come to think of it, that gave him a certain sturdiness that could be a benefit in an elected official.

"We're not saying evacuation," I repeated for roughly the fifth time. "We're saying that we need to put people on alert."

"Let them get their ducks in a row," John added.

"So if we find that it is necessary to evacuate, they can move quickly." I went back to the overheads that we'd whipped up on the computer in the few minutes I'd had before the meeting. Besides Todd, John, Dawn, and myself, there was the mayor, Wagner, and HUG's executive director, whom I'd never even seen up close before.

"The problem is here"—and I pointed to a graph showing seismic readings—"the tectonic plates are shifting at an accelerated pace. And here"—I switched overheads—"we're seeing a marked rise in temperature. Hot enough to melt rock at this point. All of this is not adding up to the pattern that we're used to seeing. We don't think this will be the slow-moving lava that's typical."

"This could be a major eruption," John said. When that didn't get a reaction, he added, "Sky high. You know, *kablooey*."

The mayor put his hands on his hips—his elbows sticking out so now he was shaped like a star. "I don't like it. You saw what happened when we told the press something might be happening on the volcano. Headlines everywhere! If we come out crying 'Alert! Alert!' we'll create a full-scale panic."

"Don't worry, sir," said HUG's executive director, jumping to his feet. He was shorter than I'd thought. "We'll keep it on the q.t."

The mayor shook his hand. "Good. No need to worry people."

Wagner piped in, "We can send out a press release telling people everything is okay with the volcano . . . no changes at all." That earned an enthusiastic "*I like it!*" from the mayor.

They gathered up papers, readying to go. John hissed, "Can't you do something?"

"Fellows!" I said. No one paid any attention to me. I saw the mayor's hand reach for the doorknob. He was saying something to the executive director. I gave the rhythmic clap Miss Mary Jo used to get the kids' attention—clap clap clap clap clap . . . clap clap. Apparently it worked on adults, too. Three heads turned in my direction.

"Please sit down. I'm not finished."

"Now, Kekuhi—," Wagner began.

"I said sit." And, sure, I saw the mayor clear as day mouth *P-M-S* to the executive director, but they sat. I stayed on my feet, imitating the mayor's earlier stance. I'd heard people liked that—plus, I needed a stall while I thought of what I was going to say.

"Wagner," I began, "I can't believe you're being so modest, that you didn't tell them what you said to me this morning."

"What I said—"

"I came in to work, obviously flustered by events," I said, directing my words to the mayor. "I went straight to my boss, Wagner here, for guidance. Being a scientist, I don't really understand how this public relations business works. I told him, 'What a predicament! It looks like the volcano may pose a threat. What if we have to let people know?' And you know what this man—this genius—said?"

"What?" Wagner started to say, and then coughed instead.

"He said, 'We can only hope!' " I raised and lowered myself on the balls of my feet to give my words time to sink in before continuing. "He explained to me how this was an election year. A mayor who helped guide a town to safety would be viewed as a take-charge leader who put the concerns of the people first. He said it would be an honor, *an honor*, sir, to give this sort of support to our mayor."

"Well, yes—," Wagner began.

"Good point, Wagner," the mayor said. "Yes, I can see how a visionary such as myself would need to alert the people as soon as possible. Without causing a panic, of course."

"My thoughts exactly," Wagner said, "Kekuhi, you stick around and we'll talk further about that strategy we discussed earlier."

The words "I can't" refused to come out of my mouth. I was finished making excuses. Instead, I said, "I have to get back to the mountain. I'm needed there."

Before he could protest, I added, "That's why I'm so glad you've promoted Beula." I turned to the executive director. "She was the mastermind behind the change of the agency to HUG. She's already worked up some great emergency strategies, which she's ready to roll out—just as soon as her raise is approved and a temp is hired to handle her current responsibilities. Has that paperwork gone through yet?"

"I'll have to check on it," Wagner answered, appearing as if he believed we'd actually been having these conversations.

"Well, check on it, Wagner!" the mayor said. "Get this Beula on board. Sounds like my type—a real go-getter!"

IN THE MEANTIME, there was none of that waiting and hoping the boy might call. I saw Kam that night when I went to get Dante from Ma's house.

"I got hungry. I already ate all the food Suz"—He stopped himself. "That was left for me."

"There are these places called grocery stores," I informed him, "At which you can buy food."

"*Auwe*, I couldn't get cooking anywhere else like Ma's."

"You got that right," she agreed. She was chopping chicken at the counter with the vigor of someone trying to break a brick with a karate chop. *Hayah!*

"Besides, we're trying not to buy more food. Emptying the cupboards since Suzanne's folks sold the house. They want to close escrow fast."

Ma shook the cleaver at him. "You're not moving to that Fiji. You come live here." She gave the chicken a whack, the cleaver making a sickening crunching noise as it broke bone.

"Thanks, Ma," he said, "I don't think that's such a hot idea."

He motioned me to the living room. When we were alone, he said, "You all right?"

"What do you mean? About the move?"

"About everything."

"I'm fine," I said. "Well, not with the move. You know that I don't want you to move away."

"Yeah. Me, neither."

Ma called from the other room, "Hey, you . . . Keeley! You hungry? I got egg foo yung I can warm up. Just take a minute."

I yelled a "*No thanks.*" I wanted to get back to what Kam had said about not wanting to move. It wasn't like I could eat near the sound of all that dismemberment anyway.

"I'm still hanging around the house by myself," Kam said, hooking his finger in my belt loop, pulling me closer. "Maybe you could come keep me company."

Until he'd said that, I hadn't been certain of my feelings. I'd been back and forth all day—berating myself one minute, then flushing hopeful the next. Yet my answer was so sure it nearly spoke itself. "Last night was fun," I said, removing his hand and taking a step back, "But I'm not willing to be the other woman. You are going to have to make a choice."

"Sure."

"Sure? What do you mean, sure?"

Ma marched up to us, cleaver in hand. "If you're not going to have the egg foo yung, at least come eat some chicken."

"I mean sure," he said. He tugged me toward the kitchen by my belt loop.

"I wasn't talking to you," Ma scolded. "You already had chicken. Leave some for her."

THE ISLAND WAS put on official alert. As expected, all media hell broke loose. I didn't even have to care because I was busy doing what I was supposed to—looking like one of the Village People in my jeans and hard hat, supervising the volcano's round-the-clock monitoring that was now a necessity.

That didn't mean, however, that I didn't have time to pause and reflect upon the strangeness of life. How one minute, it seems, you're spiraling toward divorce. The next, your house is filled with surfboards and somebody's drinking your beer and accidentally trapping your iguana in the garage overnight. Just like that.

It had come about rather unremarkably, Kam's moving home. In fact, I'd nearly forgotten he'd be there that first night when I'd crept past Dawn on the couch, Dante slung over me. I understood immediately how those poor bears must have felt. The realization of who was sleeping in my bed hit just before the scream left my throat.

Kam had called me a couple of days after I'd seen him at Ma's. Suzanne was due back, he told me. If we were going to do anything about, uh, what we'd talked about, we might want to do it before she got home.

"She's going to start shipping her stuff to Fiji," he explained. "It'd be best if I had mine out of the way first."

I couldn't resist asking. "What did she say when you told her?"

He cleared his throat. "I haven't yet . . . some things shouldn't be said over the phone."

I thought, if he'd been selling tickets to see the look on her face when she walked into that house with his things gone, I'd have paid anything.

Of course, the first words out of Regatta's mouth when I stopped by her salon to welcome her home from Boston were, "It's lucky for you I'm back. Now I can talk you out of doing anything rash."

Sure, now she was ready to concentrate on me. A far cry from earlier, when I'd had to employ all my skills as a professional to assure her that we at HUG were doing what we could to meet the needs of the people— especially those getting married in two weeks in a botanical garden near the foot of the mountain.

Lawrence lounged in the chair next to Regatta. He was as always without a customer and therefore possessed all the time in the world to abuse me. "Yes, I hear you were considering taking a dip in the ex-husband pool."

Regatta pointed a scissors in my direction, making the woman whose hair she was cutting flinch. "Don't be fooled into thinking Kam has changed. Once a cheat, always a cheat."

"He's moved back in with me."

She dropped her hand and scissors to her side. "Oh."

"We're going to give it another try."

She must have been reviewing the best-friend handbook the night before, because her response was flawless. "That's great news. I mean it. I hope it works out for you guys."

"Thanks."

"What did Ian say when you told him?"

"I've been too busy to get together with him, what with the volcano and all. I've barely seen Dante," I replied, running my fingers over the teeth of a comb so it buzzed. "Besides, some things shouldn't be said over the phone."

IT WAS WHEN Ian asked if he could drop something by the house that I realized I could no longer postpone the inevitable. I suggested a coffee shop near work where we could meet. Neutral territory. Not that I thought he'd become violent or anything. Part of me was perhaps afraid he might cry.

I'd arrived early and grabbed a booth. The bell jangling on the door seemed to have a direct line to my nerves. I jumped every time it opened. A person with the appropriate mix of cruelty and observational skills could have played me like a lab rat. At one point, when someone bounced the door and sent the bells clanging, I nearly had to be peeled from the ceiling.

The waitress sidled up. "Decaf, I hope?"

Just then, Ian arrived with an "Am I late?" dressed for work and smelling of Irish Spring soap. I knew it was Irish Spring because the scent has always tickled my nose, making me sneeze. Over the years it has grown to be a familiar problem, as I must be attracted to a manly sort of man, or at least one who fancies himself as such and therefore is susceptible to the Irish Spring advertisements. This must have been the first time I'd encountered him so fresh from his shower at home. I sneezed my hello to him.

"Coming down with a cold?" he asked.

"My stupid allergies," I said, which I don't have, but I was determined to establish up front his complete lack of culpability. It was my fault—all of it. It was not his soap. It was my nose to blame.

We'd managed a conversation, although it was challenging to dodge references to future events, which seemed to come up constantly. Sneezing at least was a diversion.

I pushed pancakes around on my plate while I rehearsed the speech I'd worked out in my head. How he was as kind and funny and—I might have to add, watching him pour enough cream in his coffee to turn it beige—still as boyishly cute as the day I'd met him. It had been poor timing, that was all. Plus I suck.

I needed air, but I had to deliver that speech. I slapped bills on the table while he fiddled with the blinds, uncomfortable at my insistence to pay. There was no putting off what I had to say any longer.

"I have a surprise for you," he said.

I sneezed a response.

"I'll assume that means you're terribly excited. Can't wait to see it. Come on—it's outside."

Ah, outside, where fresh breezes abounded. That's where I'd tell him. I couldn't tolerate the airless coffee shop a moment longer. Although the notion of a surprise was sounding ominous, I thought, as I followed him to where his convertible was parked at the curb.

I could see it right away propped in the backseat, covered in a blanket, but obviously the painting. He was going to show me the finished painting. Crud . . . I couldn't tell him now—not at the moment of the unveiling. I'd have to stall him off a few more days, break it to him next week. Kam would simply have to understand.

"Gee, whatever can that be? Is it a pony?" I said.

He reached in to untie the rope that held the blanket in place. "I hope you like it." The blanket dropped and there it was.

He'd put in significant work since I'd seen it last. It seemed to leap from the canvas. I was painted sharper-edged, bolder than before, but with the same floating quality. He'd filled in ghost images behind me of a mountain and what appeared to be a woman holding us both in her arms.

"It's beautiful," I said, leaning on the car door.

"Naturally. You're beautiful."

"I'm serious—I love what you've added. What does it mean?"

"I'm not sure myself. I've learned that, sometimes, you simply have to let art flow over you. So . . . ," he said, "now you can see why I'd suggested I stop by your house. I can transfer it to your Jeep, but you're going to have to cart it from there."

"You're giving it to me? I thought you were showing me."

"It's for you to keep. A gift."

He started to reach for it, when I said, "I can't accept it."

I couldn't haul off this labor of love in my arms and then glance back a few days later and say, Oh, by the way, thanks for the painting and good-bye forever. He didn't deserve that. "I don't deserve it," I said.

"Of course you do. You're my muse."

"I have nothing to do with your talent. It's all you. I can't take this." The painting seemed to be urging me on, looming larger from the backseat of his car. I was fiddling with the door handle—anything to avoid meeting my own eyes on canvas. "God, Ian, you say all these nice things about me, but I'm not the person you think I am. I'm—"

"Lovely. Smart. You even have a cute sneeze." He took my hand in his, "I knew from the moment you walked up to my booth that I'd never be the same again. You are truly lovable. In fact . . ." and he paused before continuing, "I can't deny that I am in lo—"

I yanked my hand from his grasp. "Kam moved back in," I blurted. "Dante's dad. My husband. We got back together."

He said nothing, just exhaled a breath.

"I'm sorry," I said.

He pulled off his jacket and rolled up his shirt sleeves, the way gentle-men do in old movies when they're preparing to fight. Then he leaned into his car and pulled out the painting, propping it against a signpost. "I couldn't have expected it to last," he said, his voice wooden.

I was reduced to an abbreviated form of my speech: "It's not you. This is all my fault."

"No, what we had—you and I—it had been built on a lie from the start. And that, I fear, was entirely my doing."

Against my protests that I couldn't accept the painting, he left it there.

Then he drove away without so much as a glance in the rearview mirror that I could determine.

He didn't cry. I didn't cry. In fact, I was about as far from crying as it was possible to be, as if a dust storm were brewing in my insides.

I had to wrestle the portrait in its roughly one-hundred-pound frame into my Jeep. I couldn't exactly leave it sitting there all day. I swung by the house on my way to the office and unloaded it into the garage.

While I was there, I stopped inside. Kam and Dante sat on top of the clean laundry I'd piled on the couch, eating bread slices straight from the bag.

"Why isn't he at school? Is he sick?" I asked, walking over to put my hand on Dante's forehead.

"He's great. We're getting ready. Aren't we almost ready, pal?" he said to Dante.

"It's ten o'clock."

"Holy shit. Hey, bud, shake a tail feather. Let's get some clothes on you." Kam dressed him in a shirt and shorts pulled off the couch, wrinkled now because they'd been sat on. I grabbed the lunch I'd packed him from the refrigerator. Kam must have sensed my annoyance because he said, "Don't worry about it. I'll get him there."

"I can drop him on my way to work," I said. It came out with an old-woman's sigh. "I'm going that way anyway."

When I finally got to work, my roommates told me they'd moved that morning to a hotel. I hadn't even noticed anything missing. So much junk was lying around, it was easy to miss a sleeping bag or two. They tried to claim it was the money pouring in now that we'd put the island on alert.

John stroked his beard in that way he had. "Besides, you'll need time alone to start anew, you and Kam. You don't need a bunch of geologists hanging out, stacking all their gear and papers on your dining room table. You need the space free so you can *do* it there, you crazy kids."

That night I carried Dante past an empty dining room table and deposited him in my empty bed. I don't know what time it was when Kam crawled in next to us. I was pretending to be asleep.

REGATTA HAD BEEN calling me every hour all morning as she debated whether to cancel her wedding. She wanted numbers. Odds. Exactly what, she'd asked me, were the chances that the guests would be throwing volcanic ash instead of rice? She should've known better. She was a *kama 'a ina*, a local. There was no way to predict these things.

"If I could tell you, I'd be in Vegas right now laying a bet on it," I said.

She called again. "Let's say it blows as the minister is saying 'Will you take this woman?' Will there be time to get to the *I do's*?"

"I don't know."

Another call. "Do you think this is a sign from the gods that I shouldn't be getting married?"

"No. I think it's a sign that magma is heating, pushing tectonic plates upward and creating an internal pressure that may need to release itself in the form of an eruption."

The phone rang again. I answered it, "I don't know."

"Well, hello, bitch." I knew that voice. It was Suzanne. "Thought I'd give you a call—let you know that if you think I'm going to sit here while you steal my fiancé away, you've got another thing coming. May as well give up. You don't stand a chance . . . whore."

She hung up before I could say, Well, hello, bitch to you, too.

19

"YOU GOTTA WEAR the hard hat. It makes you look official." Beula handed one to me, which I took reluctantly.

"It looks stupid with the lipstick."

"Hey—," she groused, "Who's the public relations professional here? Trust me, the camera is going to love you, baby." She stood on tiptoes to examine my face. "Nothing we can do about those bags, though."

She'd set up a press conference to explain the latest developments on Kohala and to answer questions about the alert that had been issued. A temporary stage had been erected at the base of the mountain—"Photo op," Beula said with authority. Power ran off generators, which were humming loudly enough to at least cover the sound of my stomach's nervous gurgling.

I'd never been on television before. I was a wreck, even though there was a possibility I might not have to say much. The mayor was going to do most of the talking and defer only technical questions to me. The local cable station was running live coverage. I could see news cameras from several networks setting up. Pete Peterson took a seat on a foldout chair.

"See that guy?" I said to Beula, pointing Pete out. "If you can possibly help it, don't call on him."

"He's with the *Bee*. That's an important paper to us. It'd need to be a good reason."

"He was mean to me."

"Well, then, looks like Mr. Mean *Bee* Reporter is going to have a lonely day. Nobody messes with my favorite volcanologist."

Beula had to reapply the lipstick I'd bitten off three times before we were ready to get started. The mayor came over to say hello.

"I want a hard hat, too," he whined.

There was quite a fuss while we tried to locate a hat for the mayor. Finally I gave him mine, and we walked on stage to meet the press. Beula introduced us; then she pointed to a reporter for *Channel 7 News*. "You!" she barked, startling the wits out of me, but the reporter didn't flinch.

"Mr. Mayor, what is the level of threat?"

He gestured to me as though I were one of the prizes he was showcasing on *The Price Is Right*. I stepped to the microphone and started to answer. Beula was waving frantically, and I could see Pete Peterson sniggering. The mayor leaned over, "You have to talk more into it. They can't hear you."

I stepped closer. My voice came out in a thin line. "We're monitoring the volcano closely. There is no way to know if and when it will erupt, but we may be able to identify whether the lava will move slowly, or if we'd be talking an explosive eruption. It's hard to know, as this is quite a new development."

Beula pointed to another reporter.

"So are you saying that this is a new volcano?"

The mayor looked at me and tipped his head toward the microphone. This, too, apparently fell under the category of technical.

"We thought it might be at first, but no—there is no new volcano forming. This is Kohala herself showing us that even at sixty thousand years old, she's got some life left in her." Laughter.

"Why would a volcano be erupting?"

"Because it's there." More laughter.

I answered several questions, less nervous now that I'd warmed up the crowd. Beula, true to her word, was ignoring Pete until the mayor said, "This fellow's had his hand up for quite a while. You! You there!"

Pete stood, flipping his notepad over importantly. "A question for Ms. Baker-Kekuhi—I understand you were arrested on pornography charges. Given that, don't you think your being in charge of this effort poses a threat to citizens?"

For a moment, all I could hear was the hum of the generators. He was determined to get the last word. Then I remembered, not without a certain smug satisfaction: I had the microphone. I smiled. "Actually, the charges were erroneously reported in the *Bee*—but with any luck the rumors will prevent me from being sacrificed to Kohala as a virgin." Applause and laughter, much writing on note pads. Pete sat down, scowling.

"Let's stay focused here," Beula scolded the press. "You! Channel Two!"

"How will an evacuation be handled?"

I looked at the mayor. He'd been briefed on this one. He opened his mouth to answer when the stage started to shake violently. I braced myself to stay upright.

"It's the big one!" the mayor shouted. "Save the women!" With that, he tackled me to the ground. My head banged the floor of the stage, just as it collapsed beneath us. I could sense bulbs flashing and people shouting questions, but my head was throbbing so hard it was a blur.

As it turned out, it was barely a three-point tremor. Hardly enough to knock a picture off a wall, but in this case, enough to jiggle a leg on the stage that hadn't been tightened properly.

I had a group of people over to watch the evening news with Dante and me, including Regatta and Ted, my geologist buddies, and Bob and Lucy. I was glad to have them there because each time we saw a replay of the mayor shoving me to the ground, they'd say things like, "Nice lipstick," and "Your hair looks very bouncy as you're falling."

Of course, the drawback was that they kept glancing at the door for me to produce the husband I'd promised. Kam didn't show up until I was brushing my teeth for bed, at which time he tackled me to the bathroom floor, shouting "Save the women!" I would have been more amused if he hadn't been the hundredth person that day to do so.

AS A RESULT of my performance at the press conference, I'd become quite the media darling. TV stations might have picked up the scene with the mayor knocking me to the ground, but it was the virgin remark the reporters remembered. They'd call Beula, asking if they could talk to that virgin girl—they had a few questions about the volcano.

"You're like the Madonna of the geology world," John said after I'd managed to break away from my duties as an interviewee long enough to go over some maps with him in my cubicle.

The temp receptionist buzzed me. "You have a visitor. Someone representing a boat race? . . ."

I could hear a voice shouting through the phone. "It's me! Regatta!"

When I told the temp to send her back, she said, "I certainly will, Ms. Baker-Kekuhi"—the entire surname preceded by a courtesy title. That was the sort of respect I was commanding these days.

John left as Regatta sashayed up and gave me an air kiss. She was dressed in a suit, white gloves, a floppy straw hat, and big movie-star glasses.

"What's with the get-up? You look like Jackie O."

"Really? I was going for Joan Collins. At any rate, I have news." She took off her gloves, tugging on one finger at a time. "Remember the other day when we were talking? When I kept calling every ten seconds in a panic? Well, you said something that really got me thinking."

I knew it. I could tell I'd made an impact. I was like a regular elder, dispensing pearls of wisdom wherever I went. "Was it the part about marriage being more than the wedding? That you have to focus on the long-term commitment, not the I do's?" I'd impressed even myself with that one—didn't believe it for a minute, but delivered it with a convincing warmth.

"Actually, I was referring to the part where you said if you could predict the volcano erupting, you'd take off for Vegas."

"Excuse me?"

"Ted and I—we're getting married in Vegas! We're on our way to the airport right now!" She squealed and threw her arms around me in a hug, which forced me to jump up and down with her. "I couldn't take the pressure of worrying about the volcano erupting on my wedding. So I decided that I needed to keep perspective . . . that marriage was more important than the wedding, and—"

"A-ha! I *was* wise!"

She outlined her plan, all the while making the sort of gestures a person makes when they're wearing a hat and holding gloves. It can't be helped. They were going to honeymoon there, then come home to pack. She'd give Boston a year to grow warm.

Then she gave me a serious look. "How are things going with Kam?"

"Things with Kam . . . ," I said.

I thought about the night before. He was saying how much more often he took Dante to school than me, so could I for once quit my complaining.

I'd shot back, "You take him more of*ten*? More of*ten*? For Christ's sake, the *t* in often is silent."

"We have some kinks to work out," I told Regatta. "That's to be expected, especially with me being under so much pressure right now. It'll be fine." I reached out to adjust her hat. "You, girlfriend, have fun. Win big."

THE TREMORS KEPT up over the next few days. They stayed in three- to four-point magnitude—enough to cause concern, but not inflict damage. A cup might fall off a table here or there. People would pause, look up at the sky as though it had started there, and then go back to what they'd been doing.

The quaking could continue at that level for months, but I was reaching the breaking point. The hours were too much. I missed my kid. I had a marriage to salvage.

One morning I made a point of telling Kam to be home for dinner. I would be cooking. We were going to eat together like other families did. I made a similar announcement at work that evening. I had to go eat with my family. They gave me the same dull stare I'd gotten that morning. "So go," Wagner shrugged.

"Honey, I'm home!" I shouted, walking through the door and—ouch— banging into something. It was a desk in the foyer. Not just a desk. *The* desk.

Kam walked in, gnawing on a sub sandwich. I'd thought I'd told him I would be fixing dinner. I pressed my lips together—I'd made a vow to myself to quit picking so much. "What's with the desk?" I said, as though merely curious.

"It's from Suzanne. She was going to toss it."

"She brought it over herself?" I pictured her strapping it to her back, stomping along the streets like Quasimodo, dumping it on our floor.

"Nah, too heavy. I went over there."

"I didn't know you went to her house today."

"She said she was going to throw it away," he said, defensive. "Like it was trash or something." He opened and shut the drawers the same way he had the day he'd bought it. Knocked on the wood. "*Bullshit* she never liked it. This is a nice desk. She loved this desk."

I threw down my purse and knapsack, filled with work I'd need to do that evening. "Has Dante eaten?"

"Yeah, he ate," Kam said, sitting on the edge of the desk.

"What did he eat?"

"Shit, Keel, *food*. He ate food."

Later on, when Kam was napping in the hammock, I dragged the desk myself into the garage. While I was shifting things about to make space, without thinking I set the power drill on the desk's fragile surface, which left a nasty . . . hmm, nothing. I set the power drill harder on the desk so that . . . nope, still as shiny as ever. I picked up the drill, plugged it in, and drilled a pattern of holes in the surface of the desk in the shape of a heart. "Oops," I said to myself, setting the drill gingerly back on its roost on a shelf, "Now look what I've gone and done."

A few days after the desk debacle—Kam hadn't noticed as far as I knew, or at least never said anything—there was a tremor strong enough to topple the surfboards propped in the living room. It also managed to knock Suzanne's parents' house right out of escrow, so scared were the prospective buyers of what might happen. Kam thought Suzanne's plans might include moving anyway. "She's taking this hard," he told me when we crawled into bed that night.

"Help her move and die," I said, pulling the covers up over my head.

IT WAS THE earthquake that hit seven points on the Richter scale that forced the issue of evacuation. I'd done such an effective job of convincing the mayor he was the defender of the people, he'd page me after every tremor asking if it was time to save them yet. "Men, women, and children equally," he'd clarify, haven taken a bit of slack from feminist groups for the "Save the women!" line.

"We're not like California," the mayor told the few of us he'd gathered for a meeting after the seven-pointer had struck at 3 A.M.: Beula, my geologist friends, and me, and Wagner, who was snoozing in the corner of the conference room, shaking himself awake every few minutes as if suffering from his own personal aftershocks. "We *know* that more earthquakes are on their way. We don't have to be sitting ducks."

Beula clapped her hands together, startling Wagner awake again. "Yes! That's it!"

This time we made the official press announcement from the safety of the HUG offices, and I got the hard hat. We would start by clearing only a twenty-mile square area. It was the section of the island that, based on the angle of shifting rocks within the volcano, would most likely be annihilated with lava flow.

"Isn't this creating an unfair hardship for the families in that area?" Pete Peterson asked. I could see the mayor bristling. Was this another "save the women" fiasco?

"It includes my house," I said, "And I, for one, will feel better to know my son is off somewhere safe."

Beula unveiled her Don't Be a Sitting Duck campaign. She showed a poster of rubber ducks screaming as they were covered with lava. Another said, "Duck!" A rubber duck was crushed beneath a falling bottle of shampoo with the tag, "Watch for earth quacks!"

"It's voluntary at this point," Beula said, "But we're aiming for one hundred percent of the citizenry moved to safer ground."

"Men, women, and children," the mayor clarified, then added, "Dogs, cats, cows, all of God's creatures. In fact, not just God's creatures. For some of you, let me include Buddah's creatures, or followers of the great King Kamehameha, or friends of L. Ron Hubbard . . . heh, heh . . ." He wiped away beads of nervous sweat from his forehead while Beula frantically signaled *cut!* by running her finger across her neck. He blathered on like a train unable to stop itself, "But I suppose we don't have to worry about the Satan worshipers, because they'd probably like a lava bath . . . heh, heh . . ." Beula finally pulled the power line to his microphone.

Kam was home this time to watch my performance on TV, but I wasn't. He called me at the office afterwards. "Nice I had to hear about the evacuation on TV."

"I didn't tell you?"

"As long as your son is safe. That's what matters."

"What's that supposed to mean? Oh, hold on . . ." Beula was standing outside my cubicle, powder puff in hand, either giving me the peace sign or telling me she needed me for an interview with channel two. I told her to wait a minute and then went back to Kam. "I'm sorry, you were saying?"

"Nothing. Just that I thought it might matter that I lived here, too."

IT DIDN'T MAKE a difference that most of the times I'd seen Dante in the last month he'd had his eyes closed. It still felt like someone was lopping off one of my vital organs as I hugged him good-bye. There'd be no cuddling close to him in the middle of the night. Or waking him up when I got home, chatting, then laughing about it the next morning because he couldn't remember. He'd giggle, "I did not say I wanted spinach for breakfast," and I'd tickle him and say, *"Oh, yes, you did!"*

Ma was taking him to stay with the cousins in Naalehu. Kam would close up the house; then he'd join them. There wasn't much call for tours of the volcano since we'd barricaded it.

People had responded to Beula's campaign and had left in droves. We'd specifically mapped out an area that was mostly homes—not a lot of hotels or farms. For the most part, people packed bags and headed down the road to friends or relatives, except a few diehards who said, "I don't gotta leave—I got me a rowboat. Bring on the wrath of Kohala!"

I kneeled to bring myself to Dante's height, handed him a Pop-Tart. The sun was barely up. I was off to work, and he'd be gone when I came home. I had to brush his bangs apart to find his eyes.

"You be good for grandma, okay?"

"Yeah."

"Daddy's going to join you in a couple of days." I was already blubbering. So much for not crying.

"I want you to come."

"Mommy can't leave, sweetie. I'm in charge of the volcano. It's an important job, and I have to make sure everybody is safe. I hugged him again, dripping tears on him that he let lie on his neck without wiping away. "I'm going to miss you, but you'll have fun. And you'll be back home in no time. I promise."

"Mom?" he said, his voice muffled against me.

"Yeah, baby?"

"Don't be a sitting duck."

IT WASN'T UNTIL Kam called me to ask what he was supposed to do with the iguana that I thought, *Morna.* I'd never told her to cancel the divorce proceedings. Strangely, she hadn't contacted me in all that time, either.

I was manning the makeshift stations we'd set up near the main access road to the mountain—or, as the mayor kept correcting me, *personing* it. AGS had sent another team of volcanologists to help out. They were working with a crew to move rocks that would help direct lava flow away from houses and hotels.

I was ready to collapse in bed. It was seven o'clock. We were on twenty-four-hour watch—John was taking over supervising the night shift.

I called Morna on my cell phone. When she answered, I said, "You're not supposed to be there."

"Keeley! Long time no hear. It's so noisy where you are."

"We get a lot of honking."

The station house was yards from the town's main road. Every now and then, a car loaded with people and belongings would honk at our crews as they headed out of town. They'd shout things like, "Make it snappy! I can only stand my sister-in-law for so long!" The fact that the evacuation coincided with the holiday had many people treating it as such—except, obviously, Morna.

"You should have evacuated," I scolded her.

"Oh, yes, that. Well, my cow, Liz—you remember her, the spotted one? She refuses to budge. I figure she must know something we don't, so here we are!"

There was no point trying to convince Morna otherwise, I knew that. I moved on to the point of my call. "Kam and I aren't getting a divorce," I said.

"All right, then," she said cheerily. I'd expected more of a reaction. But I didn't have a chance to talk further. A worker ran into the station house shouting something or other in Hawaiian. I hurried off the phone.

"English, please," I said.

"We got a real *lolo* out here! A nut case," he said. "Me and my bud, we was about to wrestle him down, but he asked for you. Says he knows you."

I hurried after him the few yards to the entrance of Kohala's access road. Kam's Jeep was stopped in front of the barricade. A guard had his rifle drawn on it.

"What's going on? Put that gun down." The guard didn't move. "I said put that gun down, now."

He let it drop to his side. "I was only gonna shoot the tires. Asshole said he was going to break the barricade."

Kam was behind the wheel. He was wild-eyed, shaking. "Keel, you've got to help me out. It's an emergency. . . ."

"What are you doing?"

"Tell them to let me through. It's Suzanne. She . . ." He broke off to run his hands over his thighs in frustration. The guard saw him move and pulled the gun again.

"I said put that down."

"No way I'm letting him break that barricade," the guard said.

"Go ahead, shoot the tires," Kam said, his voice firm. "I'll go by foot, then. I'll fucking crawl up. I have to get up there." He pulled a piece of paper from beside him, unfolded it and handed it to me. "Suzanne taped it to our door. She'll do it, Keel. You have to let me through. I have to stop her before it's too late."

I read the note.

My darling Kam,
I can no longer go on in this world knowing you are with another. I am throwing myself in our pond. Don't try and stop me. Don't try and drive up the mountain to our pond and find me and stop me before I leap tragically to an untimely death over losing you. I have a secret way to get there, in case anyone mentions how I might have snuck past the barricade.

With eternal love,
Suzanne

"Oh, please . . . ," I said, disgusted.

"The water in that pond—it's boiling hot now, isn't it? You told me that."

"Kam, this is a fake. She's too chicken to really do anything."

He turned to me—terror had twisted his face so I hardly recognized him. "I'll get up there one way or another. I know you don't like her, but I can't believe you'd stand there and let her die."

Deflated, I motioned to the guard. "Move the barricade. Let him up."

"But lady, there's rocks falling up there. We're not liable—"

"Fine. I'll take full responsibility." I took my hard hat off, gave it to Kam. He didn't even thank me. He threw the Jeep in gear and hauled up the road until he was nothing but a cloud of dust.

I was heading toward the station house when I heard honking. I glanced down to the road, expecting to see the usual truck packed with a family and suitcases, but that's not the sight that greeted me. It was—and I didn't know whether to laugh or scream—Suzanne, cruising by in a convertible as if she were out on a Sunday afternoon drive.

The horn kept blaring until, at last, she pulled her hand from it. Then she used it to flip me off as she drove on.

WHAT TO DO, what to do. I looked up the mountain. Night was falling. I knew I'd only be able to get about halfway up the road before debris would block my path. I'd have to make the rest of the trek on foot. If I were going to get to Kam before he did anything desperate, time was of the essence.

I bummed a cigarette and a light from one of the workers, and then leaned against the Jeep's bumper. "You don't smoke, do you?" he said, confirming my suspicions that I still hadn't learned the smoker pose.

John looked up from a map he'd been reviewing with another one of the geologists. "What are you doing?"

"Thinking."

"You must be thinking hard. Your brain is emitting all sorts of smoke."

I sucked on the cigarette again. "That's because I'm out of practice."

"You used to smoke?"

"I used to think. Years ago. Considering taking it up again."

The thinking on the first cigarette was pretty much limited to pondering the act of smoking. All that breathing in, blowing out, suppressing coughs.

For years I'd been telling Dante that people who smoked were stupid, a statement I was going to have to retract. This was taking tremendous concentration. I had to bum a second cigarette before I could get to the real thoughts at hand.

"Lady, you're going to make yourself sick," my new friend said, but he handed it to me anyway. That's the sort of bond there is between us smokers.

Far from being nauseated, I had a head buzz that I found rather pleasant. It brought a clarity of mind that went something like this: Screw Kam. He's the one who had to go chasing after Suzanne. He's only getting what he deserved.

In the dusk of the evening, a woman leaned down to light her cigar off my cigarette; then she took a seat on a rock across from me. She wore a muumuu with the exact floral pattern of my couch, and—come to think of it—she was about the same size. She tried to cross her legs, but her girth was such that she could only balance a bare foot on her knee. "So dats how it's gonna be?"

"If you don't mind, I'm trying to think here."

"Fine wit me," she said, cigar balanced in her mouth. She brushed the sand off her foot, digging it from between her toes. "Just seems if you truly loved a man—"

"Oh, please, what would you know about how I feel?"

"I know that if you truly loved a man, you'd fight for him."

"Yes, I suppose that would happen, wouldn't it, if you truly loved a man," I said agreeably, and then proceeded to smoke the cigarette down to the filter.

I stepped on the woman's foot as I went to get into the Jeep. We both let out a howl—her from pain, and me from the shock that she was real. I'd been going on the notion that she was a nicotine-induced hallucination rather than what she was: a local who'd stopped by to see how things were going with the rock movers.

I'D HIKED KOHALA hundreds of times, but never at dark and with tremors rumbling beneath my path. I tried humming to alleviate my fears, but it only made things scarier. My thin voice floating in the nothingness made me all the more aware of how alone I was.

John had labeled me a fool for following Kam. But what could I do? Leaving him to wander the volcano, calling Suzanne's name until he was swallowed up in lava—it was tempting. But there'd go Dante's dad, and I'd have to spend the rest of my life securing male role models for my son so he wouldn't turn out to be a menace to society.

Oh, yeah, plus—it may be noted—this way I'd get to break the news to Kam that Suzanne had blown him off. And that would teach him not to say a simple thank-you for the hard hat I'd given him, now, wouldn't it?

My flashlight caught sight of something moving. I heard a twig snap and nearly experienced a flashback of my Davy Jones pants-wetting moment. Then Kam emerged from around the ledge of the mountain.

"She wasn't there," he said dully. "I thought for sure she'd be there, but . . ."

His arms were scratched from the brambles. There was a cut beneath his left eye. He seemed unimpressed by the sight of me there. This, I realized, was going to be more satisfying than I'd imagined.

"I just saw her drive out of town. She never intended to throw herself in the pond over you. It was a trick."

I'd been cheated out of watching him accept the divorce papers at the parade, but this time I got to see his pain. It flashed across his face like a waving hitting the shore, disappearing as quickly. It wasn't so much fun as I'd hoped, though, because it occurred to me that I was only the messenger.

"Let's go home, then," he said without emotion.

"Let's go home? Just like that?"

"If she's not up here, what's the point?"

It was as though the volcano had managed to contain itself, yet something had to blow. Who'd have known it was going to be me?

"The point," I screamed, my voice no longer a thin line in the darkness, but an energy that seemed to fill my head, to illuminate the very night, "the *point* is that I just had to endure watching you practically crawl over broken glass for this woman. The *point*, if I have to spell it out for you, is that I am all too aware that you never would have come after me like you did for her!"

He shrugged—*shrugged*! "You'd never do anything drastic."

"She didn't, either!"

"But she might."

With that he started down the path. The sight of his back made me furious, as if by receding it were, in fact, attacking. I was so tired of that back, of having to share my disappointment with his shoulder blades as he headed off to do whatever it was he wanted to do. It wasn't going to happen this time.

"Do me a favor," I snapped. "Hit me." Kam shook his head and continued on, but I grabbed his arm. "I mean it. Hit me."

"I am not going to hit you."

"C'mon! Lay one on me!" I threw my arms about to incite something in him—anger, passion, I didn't even care what it might be. The beam from my flashlight danced on the trees like a firefly.

"What the hell is wrong with you?"

"Fine, *I'll* hit *you*. Then you'll have to hit me back."

I went to slap him, but he jumped away before I could connect with skin. Then he smiled—*smiled*! That was worse than the shrug, the nervy bastard. He ran off.

"Don't you run!" I chased him, stumbling over rocks but managing to stay upright. He was teasing, turning back to taunt me. I kept after him, huffing from the effort, grumbling that if he hadn't left me, I'd have had more time to work out and be in better shape so I could kick his Hawaiian ass.

Then—I don't know, he must have shifted somehow—because he was chasing me. That was when I realized I wasn't flailing. My arms were pumping. It shocked me so much that I quit running. Kam skidded to a stop and had to grab my shoulders and whip me around to keep from crashing into me and knocking the two of us to the ground.

We were both bent over, hands on our thighs, trying to catch our breath.

"Why . . . ," Kam said between gasps, "do you want so bad . . . for me to . . . hit you?"

"Because then . . . I could really . . . hate you."

"You don't now?"

I straightened. How strange, I thought, that my heart could be pounding and breaking at the same time. "You have no idea how much easier this would be if I did."

"What would be easier?"

What, indeed? In a moment of supreme narcissism, I glanced upward, expecting Kohala to erupt just then, to speak for me. When she didn't, I tipped my head toward the path to indicate that we move on. There was no sound except the crunching of our feet on dirt, until I said, "If you won't have the decency to hit me, at least do this. Stand still."

He stopped, and I kept on until I was able to walk away from him—not far, just a few yards. Yet it was distance enough to give me the breathing room to do what I needed to do. I turned to him, my voice hushed. "The lady wearing my couch was right. I should be fighting harder for you. But the truth is, I can't. I won't. I don't want Suzanne's job. I'm not willing to nag endlessly to get you to do what I think you should be doing."

"Makes two of us." Kam stood in a pool of light, the beam from my flashlight connecting us.

"We made such a beautiful boy together. And I kept thinking, if we could do *that*, we could do anything. But I was wrong. I've been to hell and back trying to work up enough hatred toward you to justify ending a marriage that could produce something as wonderful as Dante." A rodent skidded across our path, and I let the light drop. "I can't hate you. But I finally understand," I said, "Maybe what we had was meant to be . . . but it isn't anymore."

In the darkness, I felt Kam coming toward me, his arms reaching around me. His cheek was wet against my forehead. "I don't get why we can't seem to make it work. I'm still the same guy you married," he said, his voice heavy.

"Yes," I sighed. "That's it exactly."

20

NOTHING CHANGED ON Kohala until days after Kam and I had walked along her curves and made the decision to split for good.

We'd talked the whole way down—about where we'd gone wrong, and what was going to happen from there. I finally got my apology, too. It's amazing what peace hearing the words *"I'm sorry I was such a lying cheat"* can bring to a woman. I may be paraphrasing, but that was the upshot.

The big blow-up actually happened three days later. Kam was off with Ma and Dante by then. Kohala gave a rumble, a 7.1 on the Richter scale. Then she let out a burst of sulfuric gas, releasing pressure from inside like steam from a teakettle. The boom shattered windows and pulled trees right from their roots. I swore I saw a woman riding a bike through the wind carrying a dog in her basket. Then it was over.

The entire island stank like a wet perm for days. There was surprisingly little damage other than a few downed trees and a caved-in shack or two.

The event became known as the belch heard round the world. I don't want to boast, but I coined that. The media had drifted away as soon as we found the temperatures receding and the earthquakes dying down. Beula was crushed, until I happened to give the belch-heard-round-the-world line at a press conference. It got national coverage. Our last hurrah.

Regatta called from Vegas to point out it had happened on Saturday. "My original wedding date," she said ominously. "I knew the gods were trying to tell me something. It was all about me."

BEFORE I'D LET Kam take so much as one of his socks from the house, I made him come over for dinner.

"Oh, no, not dinner," he said, "Can we order out?"

"Joke all you want. I'm not doing this alone."

We had to call Dante home from the Kus', where I'd let him play after at last feeling I could loosen the grip I'd had on him since he'd returned. He hurried through his food, eager to get back to playing.

"Sweetie, your dad and I have something we need to tell you," I said, and I saw Kam at that moment take a giant bite of sandwich, like I didn't know that trick. I shot him a look before continuing. "He and I love you very much. You know that, right?"

"Yeah," delivered as in, *Duh*.

"We'll always love you, no matter what."

"Forever," Kam said, food in his mouth.

"Baby, your daddy and I are going to stay friends, but we're not going to stay married. He's going to move back to the house he was living in before, with Suzanne. Do you understand what I'm saying?"

Dante nodded. "Can I go now?"

Luckily, Kam was still chewing, because he grunted "Yes," but I uttered the more clear, "Not yet. It's important that you understand that this is not your fault. It's nobody's fault. How do you feel about what I'm saying . . . what we're saying . . . your dad and I?"

Like mother like son, it took quite a bit of verbal probing to get Dante to open up. It wasn't until I said, "Would it help if your dad promised you could call him on the telephone anytime?" that the floodgates opened.

"You can," Kam said, pulling Dante onto his lap. "Day or night."

No wonder my mom always used this shit on us. I was going to have to tell her about this. Or maybe not.

We talked for a while, helping Dante think up other ways we could help ease the pain of separation. "Maybe a picture of me, you, and Dad," he suggested. As soon as he mentioned it, I grabbed a hammer and dragged Kam's and my wedding photo from beneath my bed to hang it on Dante's bedroom wall.

"You're in there," I assured Dante when he wrinkled his nose and said he wanted one with all of us. "You're going to have to trust me on that."

"You're the gleam in your mother's eye," Kam said.

"Or thereabouts," I added. "Anything else you need?"

"I was thinking," he said, the three of us staring at the photo of Kam and me smiling at the camera Ma had finally pointed my way, "Maybe a Game Boy."

"A Game Boy will ease your disappointment?" I said.

"Yeah, I think so."

"Then Game Boy it is," I said, and sent him off to the Kus' before the price of his emotional recovery went any higher.

Kam started lifting boxes as soon as we heard the back screen door slam. When I commented that he seemed awfully eager to clear out, he must have picked up the dejected note in my voice. "Don't take it personally. Suzanne said if I didn't get my stuff out of here by today, she was going to come take care of it herself." He balanced the box he had on his knee, "I may have to keep Suze away from you for a while. I said no to Fiji. She was pissed about losing out. She's ready for a cat fight."

I bit my lip to keep from visibly gloating—here I'd been thinking myself the loser.

After Kam hauled out the last truckload, the living room seemed so bare. I made him shift furniture around, trying to find a combination that would create a sense that people actually lived there. Then it hit me.

"Mind helping me hang something?" I dragged in the portrait from the garage and pulled the blanket off it.

"Awesome," Kam said, and he was right. It was every bit as stunning as I'd remembered it—although by comparison, my couch suddenly looked drab. I thought about Couch Lady in her muumuu, wondering if she'd go pale, too, if asked to stand next to my portrait.

Kam grunted as he lifted it onto the nail he'd driven into the wall. "The ass-grabber do this?"

"He has a name," I said. "It's Ian."

"Well, Ian the ass-grabber did a great job. You look amazing."

The next few days, with Dante in school and me taking a few days off work allowed plenty of opportunity to lie around looking at the portrait. I pretended I was held in the warm bosom of Couch Lady's arms, wondering what wisdom she might dispense if given voice. As it was, she was being very hush-hush. I tried to smoke a cigarette to see if I could recreate the moment we'd shared. Instead of the headrush, I got a stomachache.

I cracked a Diet Coke and positioned myself on my couch as if I was wallowing in a field of posies. I needed a song. Something to accompany the scenes I was editing together in my head—memories of Ian and me that seemed to leap from the portrait. Ian shouting "Hey, pitcha pitcha" before I dunked him in the booth. Him stealing booze from the first-class cart. The way his hair would flop in his eyes as he painted, his hand unknowingly keeping time with the beat of "Let's Hear It for the Boy."

Which was not going to be my song. I was thinking epic, like the theme to *Exodus*, if I could just think of how it went.

Or maybe an anthem. I tried humming "We Will Rock You," but it only made me think about that hilarious time at a baseball game when a pop fly came in our direction. Ian was so flustered he dropped the beer and hot dogs he was holding on the guy in front of us. The whole thing nearly broke into a fistfight. Oh, how we laughed and laughed the whole drive home.

Which, okay, never happened, but excuse me for wishing it could.

Forget the song. I didn't need a soundtrack. I needed to take action.

THE CRANE TOOK me an hour to fold. When I showed it to Bob, he said, "Hey, that's pretty good for a five-year-old. That boy of yours shows promise."

Close enough. I was willing to settle for a certain childlike charm. I dropped the crane in an envelope and tucked in the note I'd written to Ian. It had also taken quite a while, but at least for that I'd had the benefit of the couch.

"Ian," I'd written, snuggling down into the flowers for inspiration. "I love the portrait. Thank you again. I only hope that someday I can be the woman I see in it. I believe I've made steps in that direction. I'm sorry if some of them were all over the top of you. Love, Keeley."

I panicked, erased the *love*, then rewrote it because he'd be able to see the eraser marks. I had to crumple the note and write it again, signing it simply, "Keeley."

When I was done, I added, "P.S. This crane is for you. You probably know it symbolizes friendship. I've heard that folding a thousand of them brings luck, but I can tell you for a fact that 843 doesn't."

I made the drop on my way home from work. There wasn't much risk of being seen. Ian's mailbox was at the end of a long dirt driveway. Trees camouflaged the house and studio from the main road. I didn't even turn off my engine.

The second crane I folded was at least less lumpy. I tucked it in the mailbox, this time no envelope or note—just left it there on top of his *Architectural Digest*.

By the third crane I still hadn't heard from Ian. It occurred to me that he might despise me. I peeked in his mailbox each time, checking for a message telling me to stop stalking him. Or—I allowed a small part of me to fantasize—maybe a note saying hello. Nothing.

I wasn't going to stop. It was my penance.

Day four when I pulled up, there was a Japanese boy sitting next to the mailbox, bent over a task. He ran to greet me as I climbed from my vehicle.

"I'm supposed to give you these," he said, holding up a bucket. It was half-filled with folded cranes. The catch of the day. When I didn't pull it from his grasp right away, he shook it toward me. "Lady, take it! You're the redhead! The guy who lives here is paying me fifty cents a bird to make these for you."

"All right, then, thanks," I said, laughing, shoveling the contents of the bucket into the mailbox. It could hardly be construed as cheating if Ian himself were behind it.

The next few days, the number of schoolchildren at the mailbox increased, although still no sign of Ian. I continued to bring cranes I'd folded myself—until I spied a kid pocketing one as I turned to head back to the Jeep. "There's no way he'll pay us for this one," he whispered to a serious-faced girl. "Look how crappy it is."

It was a week of daily visits later that I arrived to find a paper bag skewered to the mailbox flag. The number 999 was written in neat child's handwriting on the outside. Dang—I'd been shamed into not folding any more cranes. Now I was one short.

I emptied the bag's contents into the mailbox. Although I could come back tomorrow with the final crane, I was dying to finish the job.

After rifling through my glove compartment, the only paper I could find was a proof of insurance form. I attempted to fold it using the Jeep's hood as a table. I brought the top edge of the insurance form down to form the beak, grumbling because that beak is, like, a tenth of an inch long, and I should have started with square paper because it was crumpling, and—

"It helps if you crease the edges," a familiar voice said. *Ian.* He was leaning against a tree trunk, hands jingling pocket change.

"I'll have you know that I'm perfectly capable," I replied. "I had fully intended to fold all of these myself."

Ian smiled but made no attempt to come closer. His camp shirt and slacks were as pressed and crisp as if the Japanese kids had folded him, too.

Sheepishly, I held up what appeared to be a wadded Kleenex. The last crane. "This is for you," I said.

"Quite interpretive."

When he didn't step forward for the crane, I walked it over to him. It was cooler in the shade and, frankly, the light more flattering, so all for the best, really, I told myself. He held out his hand to shake mine. "Ian," he said. "Ian Gardiner."

"Keeley . . . um, Baker."

"Miss Baker, pleasure to meet you." He looked at the origami I'd given him and, *oh*, how those crow's feet crinkled as he studied my handiwork. "Your technique is entirely new, I must say. Yet *you* . . . you seem vaguely familiar. As if we've met before."

"I don't believe so. I've been in a spin for months now. No man who met me recently would want to have anything to do with me."

"Hmm, then it's fortunate that we're only meeting now. Although"— and he busied himself with trying to straighten the crane's wings—"I should warn you that I only make a fool out of myself for someone once."

"Well, then, you're a smart man. That definitely puts you one up on me."

Over a very civilized cup of tea, he told me how he'd given up his work as an artists' rep to paint full time. "I have you to thank for that," he said. He dumped sugar cubes into my tea, looking up at me with alarm as I kept waving him on to indicate more since—I'd been right as a girl, I don't like tea. "Seems that while you were tearing my heart out and stomping on it with your bare feet, you also made me realize my capabilities."

"Ouch," I said, wincing.

"Well, I was inspired to take the risk at any rate. Even though my parents did respond as predicted."

"You're broke."

"Cut off entirely," he added happily. "Tossed out into the world to survive only on my wits, my abilities and," with a wink, "perhaps a wise investment or two."

I set my cup down, letting the hot water splash on my hand. "And you're squandering your pennies paying kids for origami?" I asked. It figured. No money and not a clue how to spend it appropriately—it worked better on me than pheromones.

He leaned back in his chair, put his feet up on mine, pushing my legs apart. "Did you know," he began, "that Davy Jones originally planned to be a jockey?"

"And you're sharing this with me because . . ."

"I spent days boning up on useless Monkees trivia in my effort to woo you. I'm going to impart all of it if it's the last thing I do."

And while I played with his socks to rumple them, I thought, *Crud*, I'd hoped those cranes would be my only penance.

OH, AND I called Morna during all this to let her know that the divorce was back on. She said, "It was off?"

Kam and I came up with the written agreement easily from there. The only surprise I found the day I pulled the final papers from the mailbox was that I'd been granted full custody of St. Ignatius.

There was no time for wallowing in what could have been. I had to stash the papers when I heard Dante run up to say those three little words only he could utter with such passion: "Mom, I'm *hungry*."

He and I sat on the porch, trying to eat Popsicles faster than the sun could melt them. My marriage was over, although it no longer felt like the ending I'd once thought it would be. Still, I'd just seen it there in black and white. An agreement of dissolution.

I felt as if I should be doing something significant to mark the occasion. Dante was concentrating fiercely on licking his Popsicle into a perfect point. I leaned over and gave him a very orange sticky kiss on the cheek.

Occasion marked.